LÍNGFÚ – SPIRITUAL AMULET

(OPIUM WARS AND EIGHT-NATION ALLIANCE)

靈 符

(鴉 片 戰 爭 與 八 國 聯 軍)

YÁNG, JWÌNG-MǏNG

ACKNOWLEDGEMENTS

I would like to express my deep appreciation to the following people: Ms. Nancy Hauser for her primary editing and Ms. Angela Laughingheart for her secondary editing.

Thank you to Mr. Olivier E. Pardo for his French translations.

Special Thanks go to Ms. Axie Breen for the cover design.

I would also like to thank Yáng, Měi-Líng, Colin Borsos and Susan Lau for proofreading this novel.

Finally, thank you to Mr. James Norman for proofreading and preparing this novel for publication.

HISTORICAL SITES, PERSONS, AND EVENTS

SITES

Yuánmíng Garden 圓明園

Yuánmíng Garden (圓明園), located in northeast Běijīng (北京), was a large royal garden built by the Qīng Emperor, Kāngxī (康熙帝), for his fourth son, Yìnzhēn (胤禛) in 1709 (康熙四十八年). Yuánmíng Garden was bordered with another big royal garden, Yíhé Garden (頤和園). The land covered by these gardens was 864.85 acres, nearly 50 acres of which were occupied with numerous buildings.

It was also called "the garden of myriad gardens" (Wàn Yuán Zhī Yuan, 萬園之園) and was the summer garden of Qīng emperors. This garden was also commonly used as an office for country policy making and military affairs during the summertime. Thus, it was also called "Summer Palace" (Xià Gōng, 夏宮).

When Yìnzhēn (胤禛) became Emperor Yōngzhèng (雍正帝) in 1722, he expanded the garden and built many new buildings, including Guāngmíng Palace (Guāngmíng Diàn, 光明殿), Qínzhèng Palace (Qínzhèng Diàn, 勤政殿), and many other smaller constructions.

Later when Emperor Qiánlóng (乾隆帝) inherited power (1736-1796), he reconstructed some buildings. He also added two more gardens, Chángchūn Garden (長春園), and Qǐchūn Garden (綺春園) (or Wànchūn Garden, 萬春園), next to the main garden. Since then, these two gardens together with the main one were called Yuánmíng Three Gardens (圓明三園). Other than these three major gardens, there were also many smaller gardens distributed on the east, west, and south of the main garden forming an arc shape.

Emperor Qiánlóng was in position for sixty years and then passed the throne down to his fifteenth son, Yóngyǎn (顒琰), who became Emperor Jiāqìng (嘉慶帝) in 1796. The new emperor again repaired and expanded Qǐchūn Garden (綺春園) (or Wànchūn Garden, 萬春園) into a larger garden for his summer residence.

On October 6, 1860, the British and French coalition army invaded China during The Second Opium War. When the invaders reached Běijīng (北京), soldiers entered the garden, looted, robbed, and set all the buildings on fire. After the war, Emperor Tóngzhì (同治帝) desired to repair the garden, but due to a lack of funding, the project was terminated.

Later, in the year of 1900, Běijīng was again taken over by the military coalition force of the Eight-Nation Alliance (八國聯軍) including Japan, Russia, Britain, France, the United States, Germany, Italy, and Austria-Hungary. Immediately after the war, the garden was again robbed by bandits and army deserters and was completely ruined.

Yuánmíng Garden-1 圓明園-1

Yuánmíng Garden-2 圓明園-2

YÍHÉ GARDEN 頤和園

Yíhé Garden (頤和園) (original name: Qīngyī Yuán, 清漪園) was another large-sized royal garden situated to the northwest of Hǎidiàn District (海淀區), Běijīng (北京), just next to Yuánmíng Garden (圓明園). It was built in 1750, Qiánlóng (乾隆帝) 15th year.

When Emperor Guāngxù (光緒帝) was 18 years old, Empress Dowager Cíxǐ (慈禧太后) handed over power to Emperor Guāngxù. To express his filial piety to Cíxǐ, and also hoping that Cíxǐ would not interfere in the country's policies again, he ordered the rebuilding of the Qīngyī Garden. To pay for the garden project, he reallocated the money that he had set aside to strengthen the Chinese navy. He also changed the name to Yíhé Garden. Unfortunately, this garden was destroyed by the Eight-Nation Alliance (八國聯軍) in 1900 and it took two years of repairs to recover its original condition.

Recognized as one of the World Cultural Heritage sites in 1998, Yíhé Garden occupies 716.59 acres of land with 17.3 acres of building sites. Yíhé Garden is considered to be the most complete royal garden today.

Yíhé Garden 頤和園

SHĀNDŌNG PROVINCE 山東省

Shāndōng Province is situated on the eastern edge of the North China Plain. The lower part reaches the shores of the Yellow River (Huánghé, 黃河) and extends out to sea as Shāndōng Peninsula (Shāndōng Bàndǎo, 山東半島). This province borders the Bó Sea (Bóhǎi, 渤海) to the north, Héběi Province (河北省) to the northwest, Hénán Province (河南省) to the west, Jiāngsū Province (江蘇省) to the south, and the Yellow Sea (Huánghǎi, 黃海) to the southeast. It shares a very short border with Ānhuī Province (安徽省), between Hénán and Jiāngsū Provinces. It also overlooks the Korean Peninsula (朝鮮半島) and the Japanese archipelago (日本群島) across a vast stretch of sea.

ZHÍLÌ PROVINCE 直隸省

A province during the Chinese Qīng Dynasty (清朝) (1644-1912), today Zhílì is known as Héběi Province (河北省). Héběi is a northern Chinese province where the capital city, Běijīng (北京,), is located. The well-known Chéngdé Mountain Resort (承德避暑山莊), the imperial summer residence of the Qīng Dynasty emperors, is also located there. Chéngdé contains 18th-century palaces, gardens and pagodas ringed by Buddhist temples. The Qīng emperors are buried to the south, in the monumental Eastern Qīng Tombs (清東陵) at Zūnhuà County (遵化縣) and Western Qīng Tombs (清西陵) in Yì County (易縣).

Shànghǎi 上海

Shànghǎi (also called Hù, 滬) is a renowned international metropolis. Situated on the estuary of the Yángzǐ River (揚子江、長江), it serves as the most influential economic, financial, international trade, and cultural center in Eastern China.

Tài Mountain 泰山

Tài Mountain is a mountain of historical and cultural significance located north of the city of Tàiān (泰安市), in Shāndōng Province (山東省), China. The tallest peak is the Jade Emperor Peak (Yùhuángdǐng, 玉皇頂), which is reported to be 1,545 meters tall.

Běijīng 北京

Běijīng, China's sprawling capital, has a history stretching back 3 millennia. This city is located in Héběi Province (河北省).

Éméi Mountain 峨嵋山

Éméi Mountain is located in Sìchuān Province (四川省), China, and is one of the Four Sacred Buddhist Mountains in China. Éméi Mountain sits at the western rim of the Sìchuān Basin (四川盆地).

PERSONS

Empress Dowager Cíxǐ (慈禧太后) (1835 –1908)

Empress Dowager Cíxǐ, of the Manchu Yè hè nà lā clan (葉赫那拉氏), name Xìngzhēn (杏貞), was a concubine of Emperor Xiánfēng (咸豐皇帝) in her adolescence. She gave birth to a son, Zàichún (愛新覺羅·載淳), in 1856. After Emperor Xiánfēng's death in 1861, the young boy became the Emperor Tóngzhì (同治皇帝), and she became the Empress Dowager (皇太后). In a short period of time, Cíxǐ ousted and killed eight regents appointed by the late emperor and assumed regency, which she shared with Empress Dowager Cíān (慈安太后). Cíxǐ consolidated control over the dynasty when she installed her four-year-old nephew as Emperor Guāngxù (光緒皇帝) after the death of Emperor Tóngzhì in 1875.

After Empress Dowager Cíān's death in 1881, Cíxǐ effectively controlled the Chinese government in the late Qīng Dynasty for 47 years from 1861 until her death in 1908.

Empress Dowager Cíxǐ (1835 –1908) 慈禧太后

EMPEROR GUĀNGXÙ (1871-1908) 光緒皇帝

At the age of 18 years old, Emperor Tóngzhì (同治皇帝) passed away on January 12th, 1875. At this time, his cousin Zàitián (載湉) was chosen as the succeeding emperor with the reigning title Guāngxù (光緒) by Empress Dowagers Cíxǐ and Cíān (慈禧、慈安太后), and Zàitián became the 11th Qīng emperor. He was only four years old. The actual power was controlled by both Empress Dowagers. Empress Dowager Cíān passed away in 1881. After which Empress Dowager Cíxǐ was alone in power. When Guāngxù was 18 years old, power was returned to Guāngxù in name only. Actually, Cíxǐ was still the one who controlled the entire country's policies. During the First Sino-Japanese War (1894-1895) (甲午戰爭), Emperor Guāngxù strongly advocated for the war and was opposed to a compromise with Japan. Unfortunately, due to the corruption of the Qīng court, the Chinese were defeated and the unfair Treaty of Mǎguān (馬關條約) was signed. After the war, Emperor Guāngxù strongly supported the Reform Party (Wéixīn Pài, 維新派) and implemented Wùxū Reform (戊戌變法) policies, but he was opposed by Empress Dowager Cíxǐ.

When he attempted to overthrow Cíxǐ's power, he failed and was put under house arrest in Xīyuàn Yíngtái (西苑瀛台). After Guāngxù's sudden death on November 14th, 1908 at the age of 38, Cíxǐ (慈禧) chose Guāngxù's nephew, three-year-old Pǔyí (溥儀), as the new emperor and honored herself as Grand Empress Dowager. She then died the very next day.

Emperor Guāngxù (1871–1908) 光緒皇帝

Qīng's Last Emperor, Pǔyí (溥儀)

SUN, YAT-SEN (1866-1925) 孫逸仙

Sun Yat-sen (Sūn, Yì-Xiān, 孫逸仙) was a Chinese philosopher, physician, and politician, who was the leader in overthrowing the Qīng (Manchu) Dynasty (清朝) and later served as the first president of the Republic of China (中華民國). He is also known as the father of modern China.

Sun, Yat-sen (1866-1925) (孫逸仙)

HISTORICAL EVENTS

FIRST OPIUM WAR (FIRST ANGLO-CHINESE WAR) (1839-1842) 第
一次鴉片戰爭

The war was caused by conflicts between British salesmen selling opium and the Qīng Coast Guard. The British were publicly selling opium from armed scissor sailboats, along the coast of Hong Kong (Xiānggǎng, 香港) and Canton (Guǎngdōng, 廣東). After many incidents, Emperor Dàoguāng (道光皇帝) ordered his Imperial Minister, Lín, Zé-Xú (林則徐) to capture, collect and burn all opium related contraband. Immediately after it was burned at Hǔmén (虎門), Emperor Dàoguāng broke off all commercial trade with the British. In order to re-open the market with China, Britain declared war on China. Qīng lost the war and the Treaty of Nanking (Nánjīng Tiáoyuē, 南京條約) was signed, thus opening the trade gate wide to all western countries.

Imperial Minister, Lín, Zé-Xú (林則徐)

First Opium War (First Anglo-Chinese War) (1839-1842) 第一次鴉片戰爭

SECOND OPIUM WAR (SECONDE GUERRE DE L'OPIUM) (1856-1860) 第二次鴉片戰爭

In order to widen the market and gain more commercial benefits, Britain and France used the excuse of The Arrow Incident (Yàluóhào Shìjiàn, 亞羅號事件) and the Auguste Chapdelaine Case (Xīlín Jiàoàn, 西林教案) to declare war against Qīng. China lost the war and signed the following unfair treaties, Treaty of Tiānjīn (天津條約), Treaty of Běijīng (北京條約), and Treaty of Àihún (瓊琿條約). This war was also called the Second Anglo-Chinese War.

Near the end of the war, the coalition army of British and French troops robbed and burned the royal garden, Yuánmíng Yuán (圓明園).

Second Opium War (Seconde guerre de l'opium) (1856-1860) 第二次鴉片戰爭

FIRST SINO-JAPANESE WAR (1894-1895) 甲午戰爭

Due to the Japanese invasion of Korea, the Sino-Japanese War was triggered between China and Japan. After China lost the war, the unfair Treaty of Mǎguān (馬關條約) was signed. Taiwan was ceded to Japan in 1895. It was not until the end of WWII that Taiwan was returned to China in 1945.

First Sino-Japanese War (1894–1895) 甲午戰爭

BROADSWORD SOCIETY (1894 – 1896) 大刀會

The Broadsword Society was a civilian martial arts society, also called "Golden Bell Cover" (Jīnzhōngzhào, 金鐘罩), during the Chinese Qīng Dynasty (清朝). This society was mainly active at Cáo County and Dān County in southwest Shāndōng Province (山東曹縣、單縣). It was called Broadsword Society because all of its members commonly carried broadswords for their martial arts practice. This society was a religious sect. They believed that with the power of a spiritual amulet (Língfú, 靈符), they were able to shield themselves against knives and guns.

At the beginning, this society took the responsibility to protect local civilians, especially farmers, against gangsters and thus received acquiescence from the local government. Later, it began to defend against Christian expansion and initiated numerous violent attacks against Christians. Due to protests by German and French ministers, Shāndōng Governor Lǐ, Bǐng-Héng (李秉衡), decided to repress its activity. Therefore, after the arrest and beheading of two leaders, Liú, Shì-Ruì and Cáo, Dé-Lǐ (劉士瑞、曹得禮), the public activities of the Broadsword Society were reduced significantly.

Cáozhōu Priest Case (1897) 曹州教士案

The Cáozhōu Priest Case was recognized as the proximate cause of the Yìhétuán's formation (義和團) (i.e., Boxer Rebellion). This case was initiated by a conflict between the general public and the Chinese Christian followers of a German Catholic Church in Jùyě County (鉅野縣) of Cáozhōu Prefecture (曹州府), Shāndōng Province (山東省). When Chinese gangsters, who were also church members, began to attack local farmers, the church took sides to protect the gangsters. This prompted the general public to lead a riot against the church, unfortunately killing two German priests. The priest incident led to an international diplomatic event resulting in the German navy invading and occupying Jiāozhōu Bay (膠州灣) of Shāndōng Province (山東省). This incident planted the seed of hate between the general public and Western churches.

Wùxū Reform (1898) 戊戌變法

With the support of "Wéixīn Party" (維新派) (Reform Party) led by Kāng, Yǒu-Wéi (康有為) and Liáng, Qǐ-Chāo (梁啟超), Emperor Guāngxù (光緒皇帝) announced a series of reform policies on June 11th of 1898. However, due to Empress Dowager Cíxī's (慈禧太后) opposition, the reform action failed on September 21st, having lasted only 103 days. This reform was also known as Wùxū Reform (戊戌變法). To avoid being executed by Empress Dowager Cíxī, Kāng, Yǒu-Wéi and Liáng, Qǐ-Chāo fled to Japan.

Kāng, Yǒu-Wéi (康有為)

Liáng, Qǐ-Chāo (梁啟超)

The Boxer Rebellion, Boxer Uprising, or Yìhétúan Movement (義和團
運動) was an anti-foreign, anti-colonial, and anti-Christian uprising
that took place in China between 1898 and 1901.

After the First Sino-Japanese War (Jiǎwǔ Zhànzhēng, 甲午戰爭),
powerful Western nations began to divide and occupy different territories of China. Many cases of farmers in conflict with churches, frequent natural disasters, and power struggles in Qīng palace initiated
armed riots in Shāndōng (山東省) and Zhílì (直隸省) (today's Héběi
Province) Provinces. During the spring season of 1900, thousands of
uprising farmers led by Plum Flower Fist (Méihuā Quán, 梅花拳) master, Zhào, Sān-Duō (趙三多), later called Yìhétúan (義和團) (Righteous
Gathering Group) (i.e., Boxer of Rebellion), launched an attack and
executed numerous Chinese Christians, Western missionaries, and
foreign citizens. They also burned their homes and churches. In June
of the same year, Qīng Government permitted Yìhétúan to enter
Běijīng (北京) to expand their rioting against Christians and Western-
ers. When mobs attacked Tiānjīn Rental Territories (天津租借) and
Qīng Government declared war against eleven foreign countries, the
army of The Eight-Nation Alliance (八國聯軍) entered China and
caused countless deaths and untold damage.

In 1902, Yìhétúan leader Zhào, Sān-Duō, after running and hiding
for two years, was finally arrested. He was put in prison at South Palace and, after seven days of hunger strike, died in prison. This ended
the activities of Yìhétúan.

Yìhétúan Movement (The Boxer Rebellion) (1898 – 1991) 義和團運動

THE EIGHT-NATION ALLIANCE (1990) 八國聯軍

The Eight-Nation Alliance (Bāguó Liánjūn, 八國聯軍) was a multi-national military coalition set up in response to the Yìhétúan (Boxer Rebellion) in China. The eight nations were Japan, Russia, Britain, France, the United States, Germany, Italy, and Austria-Hungary. In the summer of 1900, when the international legations in Běijīng were besieged by Boxer rebels supported by the Qīng Government, the coalition dispatched their armed forces, in the name of humanitarian intervention, to defend their respective nations' citizens, as well as a number of Chinese Christians who had taken shelter in the legations. The incident ended with a coalition victory and the signing of the Boxer Protocol (Xīnchǒu Héyuē, 辛丑和約) in 1901.

The Eight-Nation Alliance (1900)-1 八國聯軍-1

The Eight-Nation Alliance (1900)-2 八國聯軍-2

THE BOXER PROTOCOL (1901) 辛丑和約

On September 7th of 1901, The Boxer Protocol (Xīnchǒu Héyuē, 辛丑和

約) was signed between Qīng Empire and the Eight-Nation Alliance (Austria-Hungary, France, Germany, Italy, Japan, Russia, Britain, and the United States). This protocol provided military forces of the eight allied nations, plus Belgium, Spain, and the Netherlands after China's defeat in the intervention to put down Yìhétúan (Boxer Rebellion). It is often regarded as one of the most unequal treaties between China and foreign countries.

Signature of The Boxer Protocol (1901) 辛丑和約

RUSSO-JAPANESE WAR (1904-1905) 日俄戰爭

The war was fought between the Russian Empire and the Empire of Japan over rival imperial ambitions in Manchuria and Korea. The major battle fields were the Liáodōng Peninsula (遼東半島) and Mukden (Shèngjīng, 盛京) in Southern Manchuria and the seas around Korea, Japan and the Yellow Sea (黃海) near the Korean Peninsula (朝鮮半島).

Russo-Japanese War (1904-1905) 日俄戰爭

THE FOUNDING OF THE REPUBLIC OF CHINA (1912) 中華民國成立

After Wǔchāng Revolutionary Uprising (武昌起義), Qīng's last emperor, Pǔyí (溥儀), announced his abdication on February 12th and terminated China's sovereign system. The Republic of China was established on January 1st of 1912.

Precious Photo after Wǔchāng Revolutionary Uprising (武昌起義後)

Flag of The Republic of China 中華民國國旗

PRELUDE

All of Empress Dowager Cíxī's chancellors were gathered in a large meeting room of this royal summer garden, Yíhé Garden (頤和園), including Shìduó (世鐸), Rónglù (榮祿), Gāngyì (剛毅), Wáng, Wén-Sháo (王文韶), Qián, Yīng-Pǔ (錢應溥), Qǐxiù (啟秀), Liào, Shòu-Héng (廖壽恆), Xǔ, Jǐng-Chéng (許景澄), Zhào, Shū-Qiào (趙舒翹), and a few others. This meeting room in Yíhé Garden had often been used by Cíxī for secret meetings with high ranking officials. The expression on everyone's face was solemn and worrisome. Nobody knew what to expect when Empress Dowager Cíxī arrived.

After Emperor Guāngxù (光緒皇帝) and a few of his advisors launched the Wùxū Reform (戊戌變法) on June 11th of 1898, a coup to oust Empress Dowager Cíxī, which unfortunately failed, no one knew her temper anymore. She had had six of the emperor's advisors killed and put the emperor under house arrest at Yíngtái, Zhōngnánhǎi (中南海瀛台) on September 21st. She then re-seized power and now did not trust anyone.

They waited in the room patiently while a few eunuchs were busy serving them with tea. It had been more than one hour, and no one dared to complain but all were keeping quiet. Inside the meeting room, the ministers were divided into two groups - one team was made up of flattering villains, while the other team was really loyal to the country and concerned about its future.

Suddenly, "皇太后駕到！" ("Here comes Empress Dowager!") a eunuch announced with a loud voice.

Immediately, all of the chancellors positioned themselves and knelt down on the ground. Empress Dowager Cíxī entered with her trusted eunuch, Lǐ, Lián-Yīng (李蓮英), and sat on her imperial seat with a solemn expression on her face.

"皇太后萬歲，萬萬歲。" ("Long live Empress Dowager!") all the chancellors said loudly.

"平身。" ("You may stand up,") she said in an ice-cold voice.

"謝皇太后！" ("Thank Empress Dowager,") all the chancellors responded and stood.

"你們有那兩個叛逆，康有為和梁啟超的消息嗎？" ("Do you have any information about those two rebels, Kāng, Yǒu-Wéi and Liáng, Qǐ-Chāo?") She would never forget these two rebels who were the leaders of Wùxū Reform along with Emperor Guāngxù. She was still angry over what had happened. Unless she caught these two rebel leaders and killed them, she would never again feel peace in her heart.

"稟告皇太后！根據我們的諜報，他們兩人由於洋人的幫忙，已逃到日本了。" ("Report to Empress Dowager, according to the report from our spies, they have escaped to Japan through the assistance of foreigners,") her top minister, Shìduó (世鐸), reported.

"這些可恨的洋鬼子，總是跟我作對。" ("These detestable ocean ghosts (i.e., foreigners), have never ceased their attacks against me.")

"是啊！皇太后，自第一次與第二次鴉片戰爭後，我大清皇朝從沒有被這些洋人看得起過。我國主權已差不多被侵犯殆盡了呢！" ("Yes! It is true, Empress Dowager. After the first and second opium wars, our Great Qīng Dynasty has never been respected by foreigners. Our righteous authority has been invaded and torn apart completely.") Shìduó (世鐸) agitated Empress Dowager on purpose and tried to fire up her hatred against those foreigners.

"還不是嗎！尤其最近與日本的甲午戰爭所簽訂的馬關條約，更是使人痛心欲絕啊！我們的國土一塊塊的被列強所強佔了呢。" ("Isn't that true? The Treaty of Mǎguān signed with Japan after the Jiǎwǔ War especially makes everyone feel a great deal of pain. Our land has been forcibly divided and occupied by the strong foreign countries,") Gāngyì (剛毅), a conspirator of Shìduó, joined this escalation.

As expected, they had agitated Empress Dowager into an unbearable and uncontrollable temper.

"不用再提這些舊事了！這些事使我越想越生氣呢！" ("Don't mention these old painful incidents anymore! The more I think of these incidents, the more anger I have in my heart!") the Empress Dowager shouted with a loud voice and slammed her right hand on the chair arm. She could not forget the burning and looting of Yuánmíng Garden (圓明園) by British and French soldiers during the Second Opium

War. All officials kept quiet and were too afraid to say anything. After a while, she calmed down a little bit,

"你們倒告訴我曹州教案後山東省的情勢如何？" ("Now, tell me what the current situation in Shāndōng Province after Cáozhōu Priest Case is?")

"皇太后！您知道德國在兩名神父被暴民殺死後，出兵強佔了膠州灣及其沿海地區，他們以保護他們的僑民為理由，就不退兵了，我看這是要不回來了。" ("Empress Dowager! As you already know, after those two German priests were killed by rebelling civilians the German army used that incident as an excuse to occupy Jiāozhōu Bay and other nearby coastal territories. They said it was to protect their citizens, but they have no intention of withdrawing. I believe we will not be able to regain these territories,") Shìduó explained.

"皇太后，據報山東的情勢會越來越糟的。最近在山東和直隸兩個地區，很多民眾以'練拳'為名組織起來，攻打教堂，反洋教。您說朝廷為了避免像曹州教案的事件再發生，是否將這些拳民取締並逮捕呢？" ("Empress Dowager! According to the report, the situation in Shāndōng is becoming worse and worse. Recently, many civilians in Shāndōng and Zhílì Provinces used martial arts training as an excuse and organized the people to attack churches and Christians. What is Empress Dowager's opinion? To avoid having something similar to Cáozhōu Priest Case happen again, should we arrest these rebelling civilians?") Gāngyì (剛毅) reported.

"其實我大清老百姓對洋鬼子囂張的侵犯我國的主權也相當的悲憤啊！" ("But our Great Qīng civilians are also very angry with those ocean ghosts' (i.e., foreigners) arrogant invasion!") Empress Dowager expressed her opinion.

"可是皇太后！如果朝廷不加以制止，以後情況可能難以收拾啊，可能再重蹈曹州案件的覆轍呢！" ("But! Empress Dowager! If the government does not stop civilians from expanding their rebellion, the consequence can be disastrous. The Cáozhōu Priest Case may again repeat itself,") Administer Xǔ, Jǐng-Chéng (許景澄) expressed his opinion.

All the chancellors divided into two groups. One followed leader, Shìduó, and did not want to stop the riot but wanted to allow the mob to continue their revenge against foreigners. The other group, led by Xǔ, Jǐng-Chéng, was opposed to enlarging the riot in order to prevent further problems. After both sides argued their point of view for half an hour, finally,

"我看你們不用再爭了，我們就靜觀以待，看時勢的發展再說。" ("You don't have to argue against each other anymore. We will just wait calmly and see how the future develops,") Empress Dowager expressed her final decision.

CHAPTER 1
LEARNING MARTIAL ARTS
習 武

VISITORS 訪客

In the warm April weather, Dù, Zhèng-Háo (杜正豪), a 60-year-old man, along with his adopted son, Míng-Zhé (明哲), came to the South Village (南村) also known as Qīlǐbù (七里埠), located at the south of Tàiān Town (泰安鎮), Shāndōng Province (山東省). On the north end of the village one of the most well-known mountains, Tài Mountain (泰山), could be seen in the far distance. Beside the village, there was a creek where the crystal waters from Tài Mountain flowed constantly. Beside the creek, there were a few big fields growing various crops such as wheat, corn, sweet potatoes, soybeans, sorghum, millet, rice, and peanuts. It was the busy plowing time and many farmers were working in the fields.

When they saw a farmer pushing a small agricultural cart on the narrow road, Míng-Zhé asked politely,

"大伯！您好！請問前莊是否叫南村？" ("Dàbó (Big Uncle)! How are you? May I ask you if the village up ahead is 'South Village'?")

"是的！前面就是南村。也叫七里埠。您們找誰啊？" ("Yes, it is 'South Village' in front. It is also called Qīlǐbù. Whom are you looking for?")

"我們是找李浩軒，李爺。" ("We are looking for Lǐ, Hào-Xuān, Master Lǐ.)

"李浩軒大爺！有！有！就在莊上。您們一進莊，一問就知道了。" ("Master Lǐ, Hào-Xuān? Yes! Yes! He is in the village. After you enter the village, you can just ask anyone.")

"謝謝您！大伯。" ("Thank you, Dàbó.")

1

Both Zhèng-Háo and Míng-Zhé were very happy since they had been walking for one hour from Tàiān Town (泰安市). It was almost noon time and the sun was getting hotter and hotter.

"爹！我們就快到了。您累嗎？" ("Dīe (Dad)! We'll arrive soon. Are you tired?")

"沒事兒！我還興奮著呢！我與浩軒已十五年沒見了。我們曾是官場上的好朋友。那時兒，在官場勾心鬥角下，想找個知己還不容易呢！" ("No problem. I am excited. I have not seen Hào-Xuān for 15 years. We were good friends when we were government officers. At that time, it was not easy to find a real friend in officialdom, where everyone was involved in some intrigue or other against each other.")

"爹！您是如何認識他的？您曾提及您在北京當功夫教習與捕頭。他也在北京工作嗎？" ("Dīe! How did you know him? You mentioned that you were the police officer and also martial arts teacher in Běijīng. Did he also work in Běijīng?")

"不是！他是濟州剛上任的捕頭。有次，因為公幹他到北京。因為公事上的關係。我們時常碰面交換意見。最後成為好朋友呢！那時我已經是四十二歲了。他才二十四歲呢。" ("No! He was a newly hired police officer in Jìzhōu County. On one occasion, he came to Běijīng for government business. Due to that business, we often met and exchanged opinions. Finally, we became good friends. I was already 42 years old, but he was only 24.")

"爹！您們差了十八歲，怎麼會湊在一起呢。" (Dīe! Between you there were 18 years difference in age. How did you get along with him?")

"你不知道！他雖年輕，可是他的度量與見解都與人不同。因為我在北京功夫上的名譽與造詣，他虛心的向我請教一些武藝。認識後，一有空他就來北京與我切磋武術。有時公幹放假時，他來北京一住就是一個月呢！他認我是他的大哥，而我也把他看成自己的小兄弟。" ("This is what you don't know. Though he was young, his magnanimity and life viewpoints were very different from others. Because of my high-level of martial arts achievement, he humbly asked me to teach him some martial arts. Once we knew each other on a deeper level, whenever he had time, he would come to Běijīng and practice martial arts with me. Sometimes when he had vacation, he would come to Běijīng and stay for months. He considered me as his elder brother and I also treated him as my little brother.")

"可是您最後為什麼離開官場呢？" ("But why did you leave your government job at the end?")

"明哲！你知道因為練武，我到三十八歲還沒有結婚。我結婚後，到了四十二歲時我娘子才有孕。可悲的是次年她生產時遇到難產。她跟孩子都死了。

我在萬分的悲痛下，又見到清廷的腐敗，更受到旗人對漢人官場上的不平等待遇。我一氣之下，在四十五歲就辭掉了官職。最後決定到峨嵋山隱居，參修武功。" ("Míng-Zhé! As you already know, due to martial arts practice I did not get married until I was 38 years old. After my marriage, it was not until I was 42 years old that my wife became pregnant. Sadly, she encountered dystocia during delivery. Both she and the baby died. After that I lived in a condition of extreme emotional pain and depression. Furthermore, once I saw the corruptions of the Qīng Court and the unfair treatment to Hán officers by Manchurian's in officialdom, I resigned my job with anger and sadness. Later, I decided to seclude myself on Éméi Mountain and focus my efforts in martial arts training.")

"可是您那時又怎麼將我領養下來呢？" ("But how did you adopt me during that time?")

"我以前以為你還小，還不需要知道。既然你問起了，讓我告訴你。我四十五歲離開官場，想到峨嵋山隱居。我由北京一路遊山玩水，路過河南開封時，適逢大乾旱，一路看到成千上萬的飢民往南走，想找一個能夠活命的地方。到了開封我想藉機去包公廟看看。就在廟前，有善心人在施拾米粥。我看到一個老漢約六十歲，帶著你坐在廟前草地吃粥。你那時才三歲呢。" ("Before, I thought you were still so young and did not need to know. Now, since you ask me about this matter, let me tell you. When I was 45 years old and left officialdom, I was on the way to Éméi Mountain to live in seclusion. I traveled and enjoyed my sightseeing tour from Běijīng. When I passed Kāifēng County of Hénán, there was a severe drought in that province. I saw thousands of hungry people on the road heading south, trying to find a place that would give them a chance to survive. When I was in Kāifēng, I took the opportunity to visit Bāogōng Temple. Right in front of the temple there was some kindhearted person giving rice soup to hungry people. I saw an old man about 60 years old and you sitting on the lawn eating. You were only three years old at that time.")

"爹！那老漢是誰呢？" ("Dīe! Who was that old man?")

"我不知道。他只不過是一個逃難的飢民。他說兩天前在路上看見你在路旁哭。他問你你的爹娘呢？你說你不知道。你儘管在哭。他與你等了一陣子，可是一直沒人來找你。他就帶你一起過來了。" ("I didn't know him. He was only a hungry refugee. He told me that he saw you crying beside the road two days earlier. He asked you 'Where are your parents?' You replied that you did not know and kept crying. So, he stayed there with you and waited for a while, but when no one came to look for you, he brought you with him all the way to the Temple.") Looking at Míng-

Zhé, and remembering, he continued,

"在我跟他談話時，你一直看著我，對我笑，很可愛。那老漢對我說，他帶著你只是想能不能找到你的爹娘。他說他不可能繼續帶著你走，他已經老了，不能再照顧小孩尤其在這饑荒之時。他問我要不要？看到你，想到我的妻兒。如他們活著，我兒子應該是你那時的年齡。我考慮了一下，答應了。我給那老漢五兩銀子。謝謝他。我就將你帶到峨嵋山了。" ("When I was talking to him, you stared at me and smiled at me constantly, very lovely. That old man told me that he took you with him and was hoping to find your parents. Actually, it was impossible to bring you along with him since he was already old and could not look after you, especially during this difficult time of drought. Then he asked me if I wanted you. When I saw you, you reminded me of my lost wife and son. If my son had lived, he would be your age. After I thought for a while, I agreed. I gave him five taels of silver for taking care of you and thanked him. Then I took you to Éméi Mountain with me.")

This was the first time Míng-Zhé's adoptive father had told him about his background. Míng-Zhé experienced a deep feeling of loss, and at the same time appreciated his father's adoption and subsequent care of him. While they were talking, they had reached the entrance of the village. There they saw a few farmers who were preparing some plowing tools,

"對不起！請借問李爺，李浩軒住在那裡？" ("Excuse me! May I ask where Master Lǐ, Lǐ, Hào-Xuān lives?") Míng-Zhé asked.

One young fellow looked at them with curiosity.

"您找李師父啊！他在這條路的那一端。來！來！我帶你去。" ("You are looking for Shifu Lǐ! He lives at the end of this road. Come! Come! Let me take you there.")

"真麻煩您了！" ("We don't want to bother you,") Míng-Zhé thanked him.

"不用客氣。他是我的功夫師父呢。" ("Don't be so polite. He is my Gōngfū master.")

"你跟他學功夫？" ("You learn Gōngfū from him?") Zhèng-Háo asked.

"我們有七、八個小孩跟他學武呢。你大爺是。。。?" ("Total we have seven to eight students learning martial arts from him. You Dàyé (Big Uncle) are....?")

"我是他的舊知。我們已經十五年沒見面了。" ("I am his old friend. We have not seen each other for 15 years.")

"您是杜爺。杜正豪大爺？" ("You are Master Dù, Dù, Zhèng-Háo Dàyé?")

4

Both Zhèng-Háo and Míng-Zhé were shocked to hear this.

"你怎麼知道？" ("How do you know?") Míng-Zhé asked curiously.

"他老人家提起您不知多少次了呢？他說我們學的很多功夫還是您傳給他的呢。" ("I don't remember how many times he has mentioned about you! He said many of the Gōngfū we are learning were from you.")

"小兄弟！你叫什麼名字？我的名字是明哲。" ("Xiǎoxiōngdì (Little Brother)! What is your name? My name is Míng-Zhé.")

"人家都叫我小虎。因為我從小就很喜歡老虎。漂亮又威武。" ("People call me Xiǎohǔ (little tiger). This is because I have been like a tiger since I was small; beautiful and powerful.")

While they were chatting, they arrived at a house with a big front courtyard.

"請您們稍等一下，我去報告師父，他會很高興呢！" ("Please wait here for a few minutes. I will report to Shīfù. He will be very happy.")

Xiǎohǔ quickly ran into the house. He went straight to his master's meditation room as he knew that this was the time of day for his master's meditation. When he saw his master was meditating, he considered disturbing him even though he knew that he shouldn't. But Master Dù's visit was such a huge surprise.

While he was wondering and trying to decide if he should return to the front courtyard to tell Master Dù and Míng-Zhé about this,

"小虎！是你嗎？" ("Xiǎohǔ! Is it you?") a voice emerged from the room.

"哇！師父厲害！師父厲害！我沒出聲，您怎麼知道是我呢？" ("Wow! Shīfù is shrewd! Shīfù is shrewd! I didn't make any noise; how did you know it was me?")

"什麼事你這麼緊張？" ("What matter makes you so nervous?")

"師父！您的舊交，杜正豪大爺來了。他與他的兒子在前庭呢！" ("Shīfù! Your old friend, Dù, Zhèng-Háo Dàyé is here with his son. They are waiting for you in the front courtyard.")

"你說什麼？杜師父？他怎麼會有兒子呢？" ("What did you say? Shīfù Dù? How does he have a son?") Master Lǐ, was wondering about this since he knew that Master Dù's wife and unborn son died 18 years ago. However, he got up quickly upon hearing this exciting news.

He and Xiǎohǔ rushed to the front courtyard. When he saw his old friend, he was so happy! With a big smile, he said,

"大哥！真的是您。有點不太相信呢！十五年了。無時無刻都在惦記著您呢。" ("Dàgē (Big Brother)! It is really you. I cannot believe it. It has been 15 years. I have missed you all these years.") He stepped forward and could not help embracing his old friend. Then he looked at the young man with him and asked,

"這位是。。" ("This gentleman is...?")

"浩軒。他是我認養的兒子，叫明哲。有他陪著我，我十五年來才沒有寂寞過。來！來！明哲。叫大叔，我的好兄弟。" ("Hào-Xuān, meet my adopted son, named Míng-Zhé. With him as my companion, I did not feel lonely for the last 15 years. Come! Come, Míng-Zhé! Bow to your Dàshū (Great Uncle), my good brother.")

"大叔！您好？義父提及您不知多少次呢？" ("Dàshū! How are you? I don't know how many times Diē has mentioned you.") Míng-Zhé bowed deeply to Hào-Xuān.

While they were talking, a child, who was pushing a heavy farmer's cart with some tools in it, entered the gate.

"爹！我以為您在打坐呢？" ("Diē! I thought you were meditating?")

When Zhèng-Háo saw it, he was so surprised since this cart with tools must have weighed at least 800 kilograms, yet this tiny boy was able to handle it without too much effort. "好大的力氣！老弟，這小孩是。。。" ("Such a powerful strength! Lǎodì (My Old Brother), this child is ...")

"是小犬。我最小的一個，十二歲了。" ("My son. The youngest one, already 12 years old.") Then Hào-Xuān called to the boy,

"博武，快過來見見杜大伯。" ("Bó-Wǔ! Come quickly to meet Dù Dàbó (Big Uncle).")

"爹！他就是您常說的杜正豪大伯。" ("Diē! Is he the one you often talk about, Dù, Zhèng-Háo, Dàbó?")

"是的，還不趕快敬禮。" ("He is. Bow quickly.")

Bó-Wǔ was so happy. His father mentioned Master Dù so many times. He bowed to Zhèng-Háo deeply.

"爹！您說杜大伯的功夫好，能不能請他教我功夫？" ("Diē! You said Dù Dàbó's Gōngfū is excellent. Can you ask him to teach me Gōngfū?")

"那就要看你的造化了，先把大伯的東西搬進客房，告訴廚房我們有客人。" ("That depends if you have a good fortune. First, take Dàbó's luggage to the guestroom. Also, tell the cooks that we have guests.")

Bó-Wǔ took their two bags of belongings and entered the house.

"大哥！明哲！來，快裡面坐。" ("Dàgē! Míng-Zhé! Come, let's go inside the house.") Hào-Xuān said.

After they sat down in the living room, Hào-Xuān asked,

"大哥！您們這次來能待多久呢？" ("Dàgē! How long will you be able to stay this time?")

"我想如果你不介意的話，我們就打擾你一個月吧。" ("If you don't mind, we will disturb you for a month.")

6

"說什麼打擾。我還希望您們至少能住上一年呢！我們可以再切磋武術。我有很多問題還要向您請教呢！還有我那小犬特別喜歡練功，我希望您能指點他，教教他呢！" ("What do you mean disturb? I hope you are able to stay at least one year! We can practice martial arts together again. I have many questions to ask you. Also, my youngest son, he especially loves practicing Gōngfū. I hope you are able to correct and teach him.")

While they were talking, a servant came to serve them tea,

"老爺！午飯要一個小時。" ("Lǎoyé (Master)! Lunch will be ready in one hour.")

"知道了。誠賢，告訴廚房燒些熱水給客人洗塵。你去吧。" ("Understood. Chéng-Xián, tell the kitchen to prepare some hot bath water for our guests. Go!")

***

After lunch, Master Dù and Míng-Zhé took a bath, after which they felt much more comfortable since the long journey had left so much dust on their bodies.

"大哥！您們先歇伙兒，我先去把莊上的事物辦好，我們好敘舊。" ("Dàgē! Both of you take a rest now and let me take care of some farm duties, then we can talk about the good old times,") Hào-Xuān suggested.

"很好！我正想告訴你我需要休息一下，年紀大了，我正累著呢。" ("Very good! I was going to tell you that I needed rest. I am getting old and tired.")

Hào-Xuān took them to their room and left.

CHAT ABOUT THE OLD TIMES 敘舊

After dinner, Hào-Xuān and Master Dù went to the back yard and sat under a big tree. The sun was setting, and a soft breeze caressed their faces. It was so relaxing and comfortable.

"大哥！真還不相信能再見到您，已經十五年了。您還是精神好，身體朗健。" ("Dàgē! I still cannot believe that I can see you again. It's been 15 years. You still have a good spirit and a strong body,") Hào-Xuān said.

"甭說了！已經逾一甲子了，不像以前在官場上了。想起官場上的事，真痛心啊！清廷的官僚與貪污已經把我中華搞得不成樣子了。" ("Don't mention it. I have passed 60 years old. I am not the same as when I was in

officialdom. When I think about those incidents happening in officialdom, I still feel so much pain in my heart. Look what the Qīng
Court's bureaucracy and corruption have done to our country!")

"是啊！在您退出官場十年後，我也看破了。五年前我買了這塊地，現在
自己幹活，暇意多了呢。" ("Yes, it's true. I also resigned my official job
ten years after you. I bought this land and have become self-sufficient
with my work. Now, I feel so much more relaxed and comfortable.")

"還說呢！如果我不是在青島聽到我一個老鄉談及你，我還不知道如何找
你呢。" ("Now you talk about it! If I had not heard one of my old
hometown friends mention about you when I passed through Qīngdǎo
City, I still wouldn't have known how to find you this time.")

"大哥！您這位老鄉是誰？他這麼會知道我退出官場呢？" ("Dàgē! Who
is this old hometown friend you speak of? How did he know that I resigned from officialdom?")

"張德盛。他說他是你在濟南府的同事。" ("Zhāng, Dé-Shèng. He said
he was your officemate when he was working in Jǐnán County.")

"是的。他是在官場裡是比較正派的一個，我跟他很合得來，我們一起辦
過幾件案子。" ("Yes. He was one of the more honorable ones in officialdom. I got along with him very well. We had handled a few cases
together.")

"其實他也看不慣官場上滿洲的官僚與對漢人的歧視。幾天前我見到他時
，他給了我你的消息。他也說他已經近五十了，想退出那是非不清的官場呢。
我記得你還有一個兒子與女兒，這麼沒看到他們呢？" ("As a matter of fact,
he also did not like the Manchurian's corruption and discrimination
against Hàn people. When I passed Qīngdǎo City a few days ago, he
gave me the news about your resignation. He said he was already 50
and thought of quitting that discriminative officialdom. I remember
you have another son and a daughter, why have I not seen them?")

"您說博文與玉萍鄉！博文已二十三了。去年跟他討個小老婆，他堅持要
搬到北京去到北京衙門做捕頭公幹。我曾勸他留在家裡幫忙我農事，他說他想
憑他本事去北京幹一番事業。勸也不聽，就只好讓他去見見官場世面了。"
("You talk about Bó-Wén and Yù-Píng! Bó-Wén is 23 years old now.
He got married last year. After his marriage, he insisted on moving to
Běijīng and accepted a job as a police officer in the Běijīng Government office. I tried to persuade him to stay at home and help me farm.
But he said he would like to create his own future career in Běijīng. He
wouldn't listen to my advice, so I just let him go and let him experience a career in officialdom himself.")

"那你的女兒呢？" ("Then, how about your daughter?")

"她也十八了呢！她去看她姨媽，明天應該會回來。剛剛跟她做了門對，

8

年底就要出閣了。男家是曹州祝偉宸的大公子祝威宏。祝家是一個小地主，有二三十畝地。" ("She is 18 years old. She went to see her aunt and should be back tomorrow. I just matched her with a young man. She will get married near the end of this year. Her fiancé is the eldest son of Zhù, Wěi-Chén, Zhù, Wēi-Hóng, in Cáo County. The Zhù family is a small landlord and owns 20 to 30 acres of land.")

"那博武是在我到峨嵋山後出生的？" ("Then, Bó-Wǔ was born after I went to Éméi Mountain?")

"是的！是在您上峨嵋山後三年才生的，有點寵壞了，就是酷愛武術。還希望您能指點指點他呢！" ("Yes! He was born three years after you went to Éméi Mountain. He is a little bit spoiled and he loves martial arts very much. I hope you are able to correct him and teach him.") Hào-Xuǎn talked about Bó-Wǔ's deep love for Goōngfú again and urged Master Dù to teach him.

"好說！好說！先看看他的底子再說，我看他的力勁兒倒是很大。" ("Naturally! Naturally! But first, I need to see his foundation. However, I can see that he has tremendous strength and power,") Master Dù answered.

"他從四歲就跟我練功。我看他喜歡就把您教給我的大周天氣功叫他練習，沒想到倒把力氣練出來了。" ("He began his Gōngfú training with me when he was four years old. I saw he liked it very much, so I taught him the martial grand circulation that I learned from you. Surprisingly, he has developed such a tremendous power from it.")

"是沒錯！練武學大周天最受益的是力勁呢！這是練武最需要的根本，可惜大多數學武的都不知道這內家的秘傳呢！" ("There is no mistake! The most benefit one can receive with training martial grand circulation is the power. This is the most important and necessary foundation of martial arts training. It is a pity that most martial artists do not know this internal secret!")

"我退出後，就買了這十來畝的地，就做起農夫起來了。為了農作，我還顧了兩個長工，一個叫沈造哲另一個叫曹棟霖。他們的家境都不是很好。沈造哲有七個孩子，而曹棟霖卻有十個孩子。十年前，曹棟霖因為家境無法養這麼多小孩，他問我可以不可以領養他的六歲小兒。我看他很苦，就將他的小兒養下了，我叫他博威。兩年後，沈造哲也要求我領養他的小兒，那時小孩才五歲。我也答應了。我叫他博德。現在他們卻是我的好幫手呢！" ("After my resignation I bought this land, a little more than ten acres, and became a farmer. The farm has been so prosperous it created enough work that I also hired two long-term helpers. One is called Shén, Zào-Zhé and the other is called Cáo, Dòng-Lín. Both their family conditions are very poor. Shén, Zào-Zhé has seven children and Cáo, Dòng-

Lín has ten. Ten years ago, due to the difficulty of raising so many children, Cáo, Dòng-Lín asked me if I was able to adopt his six-year-old boy. I saw his family suffered so much, so I adopted his little boy. I called him Bó-Wēi. Two years later, Shén, Zào-Zhé also begged me to adopt his youngest boy. He was only five years old. I agreed to that also and called him Bó-Dé. Now, both of them are my best helpers.")

"他們也跟你學武嗎？" ("Do they also learn martial arts from you?")

"我教小犬時，他們也跟著學，可惜的是除了我的小犬，他們的資質不深，領悟不到要領。我還有五個莊裡的小孩也跟著我學。等會兒他們都會來練習，您可見見他們。" ("When I teach my little boy, they also follow and learn. However, unlike my little boy, they lack talent and can't comprehend the keys of training. I also have five more boys from the village learning from me. They will come later so you can meet them.")

"唉！想當初我們切磋武藝的時候，你還是年輕的小伙子，可惜的是你的功夫還算不到高手。你有那個天才，就差了一個名師的指點。" ("Alas! Think about the past when we were practicing together, and you were still a young fellow. Unfortunately, your Gōngfū could not develop to a high-level. You had talent; you were just missing the guidance of a high-level qualified teacher.")

"大哥！所以我認識您後我是多麼的高興，想跟您學學呢！" ("Dàgē! That was why I was so happy to know you. I had so much to learn from you.")

"其實啊！比起那些真正的高手，我還差了一節呢。" ("Truly, comparing with those real high-level martial artists, I am still quite a distance behind.")

"大哥！您見過真正的高手嗎？" ("Dàgē! Have you met real high-level martial artists?")

"當然見過，峨嵋山寺廟與道觀裡埋藏了不少的高手，真是真人不露相啊！" ("Naturally I did. There are many high-level martial artists hidden in the Éméi Buddhist and Daoist temples. Usually, those real high-level martial artists will not reveal their identity.")

Hào-Xuān was amazed that there were so many martial artists with a high-level of proficiency hidden in both Buddhist and Daoist monasteries of Éméi Mountain. He was going to ask Master Dù who those high-level martial artists were, but while they were talking, four young fellows came in, including Xiǎohǔ.

"師伯、師父好！" ("Shībó, Shīfù! How are you?") the young men said and bowed to both of them.

"你們今天來早了。" ("You came early today,") Hào-Xuān said. He was a little bit disappointed to have this conversation interrupted, since he was anxious to know who those high-level martial artists were.

"師父！我們聽小虎說師伯來訪，迫不及待的早來了。您提及他老人家不知道幾次呢？" ("Shīfù! We heard Xiǎohǔ say Shībó was here to visit. We just couldn't wait, so we came early. I can't remember how many times you have mentioned him,") one of the older students, Tóng-Jì (桐翼), replied.

"師伯！您老人家這次能待多久呢？我們真希望您能教教我們的武藝。" ("Shībó! How long will you be able to stay this time? We really hope you will be willing to teach us some martial arts,") another student, Mǐn-Xióng (敏雄) asked.

"我將待一個月。等下看看你們練習再說，你們先壓壓腿拔拔筋。" ("I will stay for one month. Wait till after I have seen your practice, then we can talk about it. First, you should stretch and warm up,") Master Dù answered with a smile.

Ten minutes later, Bó-Wǔ came in the back yard with Bó-Wēi, Bó-Dé, and two other boys. They bowed to Master Dù and Hào-Xuān.

"在你們壓腿、拔筋、暖身二十分鐘後先表演給師伯看看。" ("After you have stretched and warmed up for 20 minutes, perform some martial practice routines for Shībó,") Hào-Xuān said to the three of them.

All of the students were very excited, especially Bó-Wǔ. He knew from his father that Dù Shībó's skills were so high that his father could not even match him for more than 20 exchanges. After 20 minutes of warming up, all eight students lined up in front of Master Dù and Hào-Xuān. They saluted with a martial artists' hand posture and then stepped aside. Then one by one, from the eldest to the youngest Bó-Wǔ, they each performed what they thought was the best skill they had.

When Bó-Wǔ performed his routine with a battle saber that was specially designed to fight against a helmet and armor in battle, Master Dù could see the weapon was much heavier than other normal weapons. Yet Bó-Wǔ could handle it easily and swiftly without even being winded, as if it were a light weapon. He was very impressed.

"浩軒，這把刀有多重呢？" ("Hào-Xuān, how heavy is this saber?")

"大概有十來斤吧！從來沒秤過，這把刀是衙門朋友所用的，我退出官場時向他買的，這些小孩裡只有他舞的動呢。" ("I think it is more than ten catties. I have never scaled it. This saber belonged to a friend working in the government office. I bought it from him when I resigned my office work. Among all these boys, only Bó-Wǔ can handle it.")

"博武！把刀拿過來讓師伯瞧瞧。" ("Bó-Wǔ! Bring the saber here

and let Shībó take a look,") Hào-Xuān asked.

Bó-Wǔ brought the saber to Master Dù, who took it in his hand to feel the weight of it. Then he looked at the small 12-year-old Bó-Wǔ,

"真是一個練武的材料。" ("This boy really has talent and potential for martial arts training,") he said, looking at Hào-Xuān with a smile.

After two hours of practice, the training ended. Master Dù promised to offer some advice the next day. Then the students went home.

Master Dù and Hào-Xuān retired to the living room to continue their chatting.

"老弟！我可以看到你這些學徒練得很勤，可惜的是領悟力不夠。你也知道要訓練出一個出色的徒弟光靠練的勤是不夠的，必須要有智慧還要有品德呢！" ("Lǎodì (My Old Brother)! I can see that your students are practicing diligently. Unfortunately, their capacity for comprehension is still low. As you know, to produce an extraordinary disciple, diligent practice alone is not enough. The student must also have wisdom and discipline.")

"大哥！這個我知道，可是要找一個這樣的徒弟真是不簡單啊！我也知道我是熱愛武術，可是說到領悟力呢，我還差了一截。況且，要訓練出一個出人的弟子，更需要一個名師呢！" ("Dàgē! I know this. However, it is not easy to find such a disciple. I know I love martial arts. But talking about comprehension, I still have a long way to go. To produce an extraordinary disciple, a knowledgeable and qualified teacher is necessary.")

"唉！想十八年前你跟我學武的時候，你是練得很勤，可惜的是我們在三年內相聚的時間太短，否則您還可以更上一層樓呢。" ("Alas! You did train very hard when you practiced with me 18 years ago. Unfortunately, the three years of time that we were together was too short; otherwise, you would have been able to advance to the next higher level.")

"是啊！大哥！如果不是大哥看破紅塵與滿清的官僚而隱居峨嵋山，我還可以跟大哥練上幾年呢。" ("It is true, Dàgē! If you had not seen through the reality of this society and Manchurian bureaucracy and left for Éméi Mountain, I still could have practiced a few more years with you.")

"老弟！其實說起真功夫，我還差遠呢。真是人上有人，天上有天啊！" ("Lǎodì! As a matter of fact, if we talk about real Gōngfū, I am still far from it. It is true that 'above a talent, there is another talent and above the sky, there is another sky'!")

Hào-Xuān looked at Master Dù's face with curiosity and interest,

"您說過您在峨嵋山遇見了真正的高手，真的嗎？" ("You mentioned that you have met real high-level martial artists, is it true?")

"是的。我在峨嵋山十五年裡偶然認識了兩個人，功夫就遠超過我呢！" ("Yes! I have become acquainted with two persons in the last 15 years on Éméi Mountain by accident. Their martial arts levels are far beyond mine!")

"真難相信以大哥的身手，還有比您更高的。他們是誰呢？" ("It's hard to believe that with your high-level of skills, there are some others who are higher than you. Who are they?")

"一個是純陽觀的明道真人，另外一個是普賢寺的釋海法師，一道一僧。他們還是頂好的朋友呢！" ("One is Míngdào Daoist monk of Chúnyáng Temple, and the other is Shìhǎi Buddhist monk of Pǔxián Temple. One Daoist and one Buddhist, they are very good friends with each other.")

"大哥！這就奇怪了，一道一僧怎麼會湊在一起呢？" ("Dàgē! This is strange indeed! How can a Daoist monk and a Buddhist monk get together and become friends?")

"老弟，這你就不知道了。真正能體道知佛的修練者，僧道是一家的。雖然修練的路徑不同但體道的真理卻是一致的。" ("Lǎodì! This is what you don't know. Those who are sincere in comprehending the Dàoist and Buddhist ways understand there is no difference between Daoism or Buddhism. Though their paths of cultivation are different, their comprehension of the principle and truth of the Dào are consistent.")

"可是他們怎麼會認識上的？" ("But how did they get acquainted with each other?")

"釋海法師年已近七十了。他的俗名是董偉國，原是我二十幾年前的官場好友。他本是清朝大內高手清宮的一級護衛，可是他看到官場上的幾個清官被腐敗的清廷所殺，非常的痛心，毅然離家出走而到峨嵋山出家。剛開始，他是朝廷的逃犯，可是經過二十多年，此事就不了了之了。功夫底子非常的高。少年時，曾在少林寺學武到二十五歲，有鐵布衫功夫。可惜在腐敗清廷下，惜有大志。他的書法、書畫還首屈一指呢。" ("Shìhǎi monk is already nearly 70 years old. His original layman name was Dǒng, Wěi-Guó. He was my good friend in officialdom more than 20 years ago. He was the first-class royal palace bodyguard of Qīng Court. However, after he saw a few honest and upright officials killed by the Qīng Government, he was so broken-hearted he escaped from the palace to Éméi Mountain as a Buddhist monk. At the beginning, he was a fugitive of the Qīng Court. However, after 25 years, this incident has almost been forgotten. His Gōngfū level is very high. When he was young, he trained his martial arts in the Shàolín Temple till he was 25 years old. He has Iron Shirt Gōngfū. It is such a pity that though he had such a high will and enthusiasm to serve the country, this could not be fulfilled under the corrupt Qīng Court. His calligraphy and painting are second to none.")

"大哥！您們分開這麼久，又怎麼能再見面呢？" ("Dàgē! Both of you have been separated so long, how did you get together again?")

"我與明哲剛到峨嵋山時，我帶小明哲到處拜訪寺廟。我們很驚訝的就在普賢寺互相碰面了。真是天意啊！" ("When Míng-Zhé and I just arrived on Éméi Mountain, I took little Míng-Zhé to visit Buddhist temples. Surprisingly, we met each other in the Pǔxián Temple. This was a real destiny!") Master Dù said.

"那明道真人呢？" ("How about Míngdào Daoist monk?")

"明道真人啊？他也有六十來歲了，俗名陳宇正。他的師父是凌雲道人，本是武當道士。出道後，落腳嶗山明道觀當主持。陳宇正本是凌雲道人在嶗山時的俗家弟子，十歲從師父學武與道法。二十五歲時看破紅塵，經師父的介紹，到峨嵋山純陽觀當道士。內家功夫很高，尤其是金鐘罩內家功夫。" ("About Míngdào Daoist monk? He is also more than 60 years old. His original layman name was Chén, Yǔ-Zhèng. His Shīfù, Língyún Daoist, was originally a Wǔdāng Daoist monk. After his debut, he was sent to Míngdào Temple of Láo Mountain to preside. Chén, Yǔ-Zhèng was originally a layman disciple of Língyún Daoist in Láo Mountain. He began his learning, in both Daoism and martial arts, when he was ten years old. When he was 25 years old and had seen the reality of human society, after his Shīfù's introduction he went to Chúnyáng Temple and became a Daoist monk. His internal Gōngfū is very high, especially his Golden Bell Cover Gōngfū.)

"可是他們又怎麼會認識的呢？" ("But how did they get acquainted?")

"大約十年前，明道真人被邀請在峨嵋山腳下九寨溝鎮講道，釋海法師路過，停下來聽道。釋海法師覺得明道真人的道理很深，但還有些不明之處。聽道後，他向明道真人請教並談論佛法、道學、與武學。從此他們成為好友，每月必見面論道呢！" ("It was about ten years ago. Míngdào monk was invited to give a lecture about Dào in Jiǔzhàigōu Town at the foot of Éméi Mountain. Shìhǎi monk just happened to be passing by. He stopped and listened to Míngdào's lecture. Shìhǎi monk could feel Míngdào's lecture was very deep, but he was still unclear in a few places. So, after the lecture, he asked Míngdào a few questions about Buddhism, Daoism, and martial arts. Since then, they have become good friends and see each other to discuss Dào monthly.") Master Dù sipped some tea and continued,

"我到峨嵋山後，常帶明哲去拜訪釋海法師敘舊，並時常向他請教武藝。就在那時也跟明真道人認識了。" ("After I arrived on Éméi Mountain, I often took Míng-Zhé to visit Shìhǎi monk to renew our old friendship and also consult with him about martial arts. It was at that time I also came to know Míngdào monk.")

"噯！真可惜我從沒有機會看到鐵布衫與金鐘罩的功夫。我相信那不是三五年就可以練成的功夫。" ("Ai! It is such a pity that I have never had a chance to witness Iron Shirt and Golden Bell Gōngfū,") Hào-Xuān said.

They talked till almost midnight and then went to sleep.

TEACHING MARTIAL ARTS 教武

Master Dù woke up early the next day. After meditation, he sat planning how to set up a strict training schedule for Hào-Xuān's students. He deeply knew that the level a student could achieve was not just dependent on how talented the student was, but also on strict discipline. Next evening, when all the students had arrived, Master Dù gathered everyone.

"你們知道練武成功的要訣在那裡？" ("Do you know the secret of success in martial arts training?") Master Dù asked.

"要有領悟力。" ("You must have a comprehensive capability,") one of students answered.

"不錯！還有呢？" ("That's right! Any more?")

"那就是勤練了。" ("Then it is practicing diligently,") another student replied.

"對！一分學習九分練習。那麼告訴我你們多少人真正的把練習的精神放上去了？" ("That's correct. Success depends on 10% learning and 90% practicing. Then, tell me how many of you really place all your efforts and spirit in training?")

The group was quiet since they knew that most of them just practiced for fun.

"杜師伯！可是武術不能抵抗洋槍洋炮呢！我們為什麼還要拼命的去練習呢？" ("Dù Shībó, but martial arts training cannot defend against foreigners' guns and cannons. Why should we practice it so seriously?") one of the students asked.

"那你們將中國武術看得太淺薄了。你們誰說說看，我們練武的目的是什麼？" ("In this case, you have treated Chinese martial arts too lightly. Can anyone tell me what are the purposes of training martial arts?")

"那還不是為了防身嗎？" ("Isn't it for self-defense?") the same student argued.

"這只是其總之一。還有呢？你們想想看。" ("This is only one of the purposes. Any more? You think about it.")

"我知道！我知道！師伯。還有為的是強身，是嗎？" ("I know! I know, Shībó. It is also for the body's health and strength. Right?") Bó-Wǔ said.

"不錯！還有呢？" ("That's correct! Any more?")

Now, everyone looked at each other. They did not know if there were other purposes. When Master Dù saw the reaction, he knew they would not know.

"其實啊！真正練武的目的在修身養性呢！" ("As a matter of fact, the real purpose of training martial arts is for self-cultivation of temperament.")

All of the students looked at each other. Then the eldest one, Bó-Wēi asked,

"師伯！練武怎麼去修身養性呢？" ("Shībó! How can martial arts training be used for self-cultivation?")

"所以說你們把練武的宗旨看的太輕浮了，練武最總要的是調心養性去體驗做人的道理。" ("That is why I believe you have treated the purpose of martial arts training too lightly. The most important thing in martial arts training is to regulate the emotional mind and cultivate temperament. From this training, you experience your life and further your understanding of the meaning of life.")

"師伯！您是說師父常說的如何去克服自己，培養耐性，進而去瞭解人生？" ("Shībó! Isn't this what Shīfù often talks about? How to conquer yourself, cultivate your patience, and further understand the meaning of life?") Xiǎohǔ asked.

"是的！人生最難的是如何去克服自己，從克服自己漸漸的去體驗人生。你們要知道調心養性是看不到的，而強身防身的技巧是看得見的。一個是陰而另一個是陽。陰是陽根，如果一個練武的人，陰的理解不高，他的武技決定的不會高的。" ("Yes! The hardest challenge in life is conquering yourself. From conquering yourself, you will be able to experience your life. You should know that regulating the emotional mind and cultivating temperament are invisible while conditioning the body and the practice of skills are visible. One is Yīn while the other is Yáng. Yīn is the root of Yáng. If a martial artist cannot comprehend the Yīn side of cultivation, his external martial skills will not be able to reach high-levels.")

"師伯！您是說我們練武不應該只是練外面的架勢、身法、與應用。我們還需要練習內心的培養與感應，對嗎？" ("Shībó! What you said is that we should not just practice external postures, skills, and applications. We also need to practice inner cultivation and induction. Is that right?") Bó-Wǔ asked.

"對了！你想要練到高階次，你必須練到心到、意到、隨心所欲的境界。那也是說在潛意識上你能做到無為的境界。那時後，你的警覺性、警惕性就會達到很深的層次。"（"That is correct! If you wish to reach a high-level of achievement, you must practice until you reach the stage where your mind and your actions are corresponding to each other without thinking. What I mean is, you should reach a stage of effortlessness or 'doing of no doing' subconsciously. When this happens, your alertness and awareness will reach a very deep level."）

Now, everyone was confused and did not comprehend this deep meaning. Bó-Dé asked,

"師伯！什麼是無為？"（"Shībó! What do you mean 'doing of no doing'?"）

"那就是說當你練到一個層度後，你能隨心所欲的去反應而不用思考。這是一個潛意識的訓練呢。"（"That means when you practice up to a certain level, you are able to react and respond to situations with natural reflexes, without thinking. Actually, this is the training of your subconscious mind."）

Bó-Wǔ kept listening quietly. He had never paid attention to what his father said in the past. Now, from Master Dù's explanation, it seemed that he could begin to understand an important factor to achieving success in life.

"現在我要你們每天練習下列事項。我想在我離開前看看你們的能達到多高的境地。"（"Now, I want you to practice the following things every day and I will see how much progress you are able to reach before I leave."）

Master Dù gave Bó-Wēi a list on paper. When Bó-Wēi announced the items on the list to them, they were very disappointed since they had hoped to learn more fighting skills from Master Dù.

"師伯！這些基本功我們已經練好久了呢！師父說紮跟、平衡、調氣、練力、身法是最基本的，我們已經練習好久了呢。"（"Shībó! We have practiced these fundamental Gōng for a long time already. Shīfù always said, building the root, maintaining balance, regulating the Qì, training power, and building a correct body structure are the most fundamental. We have practiced these for a long time already."）

"你們應該知道，練武包括兩項，練功與練技。練功是根本而練技只是應用。基本功不高，技術也不會太高的，你們才練幾年基本功就以為夠了嗎？來！來！我站在這裡，我不動手，你們有誰能推動我，就算你的基本功底子深了。"（"You should understand that the two most important things in martial arts training are to train Gōng and to train skill. Train Gōng is to build a firm foundation while training skills is for applications. If the fundamental Gōng is not high, the skills manifested will not be high either. You just practiced only a few years of fundamental Gōng and believe it is already enough? Come! Come! I will stand here without any action. If anyone is able to push me and make me move, then your fundamental Gōng is deep.")

Master Dú stood at the center. One of the strongest older students, Cháo-Yuán (朝源), volunteered and stepped forward.

Hào-Xuān had been attending to his business while the students and Master Dù had their discussion. Now he had finished and was just stepping into the back yard when he saw Cháo-Yuán try with all his might to push Master Dù using all kinds of methods. But Master Dù did not move even slightly. Then another student jumped in to add his power on Master Dù, but still they failed. Finally, another joined them. Master Dù remained in his upright stance with a smile. Then, suddenly Master Dù took a deep inhalation and shouted "Há!," causing all three students to bounce away from him for a few yards. Everyone was so amazed to see Master Dù's rooting and power.

"你們現在知道這就是我曾經對你們說的千斤墜的紮根功夫，另外一個就是你們常聽說的鐵布衫內功呢。你們真的開了眼界了。" ("Now you know what I have told you about the Gōngfū of 'thousand catty drop.' Another is what you have often heard about the Gōngfū of 'Iron Shirt.' You really have had your eyes opened today,") Hào-Xuān said with a laugh. He was so glad that finally all the students could experience some of the deep training that he could not perform for them. He went on,

"大哥！謝謝您露這一手給他們看。" ("Dàgē! Thank you for showing these skills to them.")

"其實啊，你們都應該知道這都是基本功上練下來的。如我剛才所說，如果沒有這些深厚的基本功，你們學的武技是無法真正的顯現出來的。還有啊！這些基本功的深度是很難看出來的，你們必須去感覺、意識。感覺與意識的深度是無止盡的，所以你們練習基本功，不是用看的，而是去感覺與意識的，我希望你們能了解其中的奧妙。" ("As a matter of fact, all of you should know that all these performances are built upon the fundamental Gōng. As I said earlier, if you don't have a deep foundation in the principles of fundamental Gōng, the skills you have learned will not be manifested effectively. Furthermore, the depth of these fundamental Gōng cannot be seen visibly but can only be felt and sensed. I hope you are able to comprehend its marvelous keys.")

"我們知道了，師伯。我們會照您的指示去練習。" ("Now we understand, Shībó. We will practice following your instruction,") Bó-Wēi said. Since he was the eldest one among the group, all of the students treated him as the eldest martial brother.

After that, all of the students returned to basic training and tried to develop the feeling. They now understood that feeling was internal and was the root of all martial arts development. In just a couple of weeks, they had entered the new era of feeling.

***

Since it was the busy plowing season, other than taking care of farming business, Hào-Xuān tried to spend as much time as possible talking to Master Dù. However, when Hào-Xuān was busy, Master Dù and Míng-Zhé, borrowed horses from Hào-Xuān and visited various known scenic places around Tàiān Town (泰安市). They spent a few days visiting various Daoist monasteries on Tái Mountain (泰山), such as Dàimiào (岱廟) and Bìxiácí (碧霞祠), holy temples of Daoist Quán-zhēn Style (全真派). They also visited two of the most famous Buddhist temples, Pǔzhào Temple (普照寺) and Língyán Temple (靈岩寺).

One late afternoon when Master Dù and Míng-Zhé had returned home from a sight-seeing tour, Hào-Xuān noticed that Master Dù wore a solemn expression of sadness. Master Dù was very quiet during dinner. Hào-Xuān wondered if he was sick or if something was bothering him. After dinner, as they sat outside under the tree in the back yard, Hào-Xuān could not help asking Master Dù,

"大哥！您今天下午與明哲從外面回來，您臉色看起來不太對勁。您是不是有什麼不舒服或是不快意的事呢？" ("Dàgē! When you returned with Míng-Zhé this afternoon the expression on your face looked different. Are you feeling okay, or is there something that is bothering you?")

"噯！真是可悲啊！這事是越想越氣憤和傷心呢！今天我與明哲中午決定到泰安市吃中飯並想在市內逛逛。到了市內，我們看到到處年輕人一批一批都在吸食鴉片，身體衰弱，沈醉耽於在鴉片上，而不從事工作。這跟我在青島市所看到的一樣。我大中華看來再滿清統治下，是沒有希望的了。" ("Ai! It is so sad to talk about it. The more I think of it, the sadder and the angrier I am. Today Míng-Zhé and I decided to have lunch in Táiān City and after lunch had a tour in the city. But when we were in the city, we saw group after group of young people who were gathering and smoking opium, enjoying it. Their bodies were weak, and they were opium addicts without any jobs or thoughts of working. It was the same situation as we saw in Qīngdǎo City last month. As I have seen, our great

China is hopeless under the Manchurian rule.")

"是啊！大哥。我也知道這個可悲的事。可是我們能做些什麼事呢？這吸食鴉片的風氣已經遍佈在中國每一個角落了。" ("It is true, Dàgē! I have also known this sorrowful matter for a while. But what can we do? The people's addiction to smoking opium has spread to every corner of the country.")

"我看要救中國，只有推翻滿清。" ("As I see it, if we wish to save China, the only way we have is overthrowing the Manchurian government.")

"大哥！噤聲！隔牆有耳，被抓到，是要殺頭的。" ("Dàgē! Keep your voice down, if we are caught, we will be beheaded.")

"我躲到峨嵋山上去，雖然是不見為淨，可是我的底心裡是多麼的痛心啊！" ("Though I have lodged myself at Éméi Mountain and pretend to see nothing, I still feel so much pain deep in my heart!")

Since they could not do anything to change the situation, all they could do was sigh.

***

In the third week of training, Master Dù discovered that Bó-Wǔ really comprehended what he had said a couple of weeks ago and had advanced his foundation greatly. Bó-Wǔ had become the best student who had the strongest foundation. He was so amazed by this boy's wisdom and progress. One morning,

"老弟！你那小兒，天資真好。在短短的兩個星期他就進步了不少，是個難得的材料。我想在下兩個星期我走以前，多教他一點。可是我知道你們現在農耕很忙，你可能需要他。" ("Lǎodì! Your little boy has a splendid natural talent. He has made great progress in just a few weeks. He is the kind of person that is hard to find. I would like to teach him more in the next two weeks. However, I know you are in the busy farming season and you may need him,") Master Dù said.

"大哥！說什麼的話。您能抽空特別指點他，是他的福氣呢，農耕最忙的時候已過了，不欠他一個。您管教他，他會高興的不得了的。我還真希望您能多待一段時間呢！" ("Dàgē! What did you say? It is his great fortune that you are able to spend time to teach him. The busiest farming time is over. Without him, it will be okay. You teach him, and he will be so happy and excited. I am hoping that you are able to stay longer!")

"老弟！我也很想多待久一點。可是我跟釋海法師與明道真人約好六月十五日會武呢！我與明哲必須趕回去。除了這幾個月，我們十年來，從不失約。" ("Lǎodì! I also would like to stay longer. However, I have an appointment with Shìhǎi and Míngdào monks for martial arts study and discussion on June 15th. I must go back with Míng-Zhé. Except these few months, we have never missed an appointment in the last ten years.")

***

Since then, Master Dù gave Bó-Wǔ a very busy schedule and taught him how to apply the techniques to actual combat situations. To Bó-Wǔ, this was a new exciting challenge that he had never experienced before. He did not know that Master Dù actually gave him a lot of hard work at a high-level of training that normal kids of his age would have to work two or three times harder to reach. A couple of days before Master Dù's departure, Bó-Wǔ was almost able to match the sparring skills of Míng-Zhé, who had spent more than 15 years learning from and practicing with Master Dù.

After dinner, Master Dù and Hào-Xuān were in the living room chatting. They felt somewhat saddened since they knew they would be apart in a couple of days.

"老弟！我真的很喜歡你的小兒博武，我在想如果他能夠有名師的指點，他的武功造詣會很高的，我不知道你與夫人捨不捨得讓這孩子離開你們。我想帶他上峨嵋山去把功夫練上十年。除了我，還有釋海法師和明道真人可以教教他內家功夫呢。" ("Lǎodì! I really like your little boy, Bó-Wǔ. I believe that if he has a highly proficient master to teach him, his martial arts achievement will reach a very high-level. I don't know how you and your wife would feel if this boy parts from you, but I would like to take him to Éméi Mountain for ten years of training. Other than me, Shìhǎi and Míngdào monks can also teach him internal Gōngfū.")

"大哥！這是他的造化與福氣。可是我還是跟我夫人商討一下，到底博武是我們的么兒呢。" ("Dàgē! This is his fortune and blessing. However, I need to discuss it with my wife. After all, Bó-Wǔ is our last son.")

"明哲與我後天一大早必須上路，你們可以在明天晚上前作決定。" ("Míng-Zhé and I will take off the day after tomorrow. You may make your decision by tomorrow night.")

Apprentice Acceptance Ceremony 拜師

Hào-Xuān tried to convince his wife that it would be a very rare opportunity for Bó-Wǔ to be able to reach a proficient level of martial arts training under the discipline of three high-level masters. His wife,

Lǐ, Huáng-Huìlíng (李黃惠玲), after a long time of pondering and consideration, finally believed that it would be the best thing for Bó-Wǔ. If he stayed with the family, he might end up as a farmer or a government detective, like his brother. She finally agreed with her husband's decision. In the morning during breakfast,

"大哥！我與內人參討了一晚，我們最後認為博武能夠跟大哥學武是最好不過的了。我們今晚就讓他行拜師禮了。" ("Dàgē! My wife and I discussed it the whole night, and finally we decided it would be the best thing for Bó-Wǔ if he would be able to learn martial arts from you. We will have an apprentice acceptance ceremony tonight,") Hào-Xuān said.

When Master Dù heard of this, he was very happy. After all, to any master, finding a talented and committed student was one of the hardest tasks to accomplish in order to pass the true art down.

"老弟！請你跟弟夫人不要擔心，我會好好看顧他和教導他的。在他二十二歲生日時，我會要他回來與你們團聚。" ("Lǎodì! Please don't worry about him. I will take good care of him and teach him. Once his 22nd birthday arrives, I will send him back for a reunion.")

"大哥！這十年就要您費心了。" ("Dàgē! Then, he will bother you for the next ten years.")

***

All day, Hào-Xuān was busy in preparing for the apprentice acceptance ceremony. All the people in the village were invited to witness the ceremony. This was a very serious event. After the ceremony, Master Dù would not be just a teacher but also a father to Bó-Wǔ. It was estimated that nearly 200 guests would be there for this rare event. A lamb and a pig were ordered to be killed for the ceremony.

When Bó-Wǔ knew what was going to happen to him, in one way he was very happy since he was so committed to learning martial arts. But in another way, he was sad to depart from home, especially from his parents and grandma.

Before dusk, almost all of the guests were gathered in the large field in front of the house. This field was used to dry rice or other grains after harvest. However, tonight would be a larger, very different event. About 20 round tables were set up to serve dinner for all of the guests. There was a big square table in front of the house where the sacrificed lamb and pig were placed, and on it were also various fruits and cakes. There were also two big red candles burning on each side of the table.

When everything was ready, first there was a lion dance with drum, gong, and cymbals all played by Bó-Wǔ's classmates. Firecrackers were lit for the celebration. After the lion dance, many of Hào-Xuān's students performed martial arts. Half an hour later, after the performance, Hào-Xuān led Bó-Wǔ to the front of the table. They knelt down to face heaven in thanks for all that it gave. After they bowed and burned incense, they swore to heaven that they would be righteous and loyal to the country. After offering worship up to heaven, Hào-Xuān took Bó-Wǔ to stand in front of Master Dù, who was sitting on the right side of the table. Then, he returned to his seat on the other side of table and sat down next to his wife.

Bó-Wǔ knelt down to face Master Dù and then bowed his head down until it touched the ground. He repeated this motion two more times. Next, he stood up and stepped back for three steps. Again, he knelt down and bowed three times. Finally, he stood up and stepped forward for three steps and knelt down again to bow to Master Dù three times. He looked Master Dù in the eyes and begged to be accepted as his disciple. One of the students brought a cup of tea to Bó-Wǔ. Bó-Wǔ then offered the tea to Master Dù. Master Dù took the tea and drank it to show his willingness to accept this disciple. Then he stood up and stepped forward to raise his new disciple up from his knees.

Master Dù brought Bó-Wǔ to the other side of table where Bó-Wǔ's parents were sitting. Bó-Wǔ knelt down and bowed three times to his parents to thank them for raising him. He couldn't help that the tears rushed to his eyes. He knew he might not see his parents for ten years.

After the ceremony, dinner was offered to all the guests. When the sunlight had nearly disappeared, the entire celebration was completed. Now, officially, Bó-Wǔ was Master Dù's formal disciple. Though all the other students envied Bó-Wǔ, they were also happy for him.

Next morning, after saying good-bye, Bó-Wǔ, Míng-Zhé, and Master Dù left Hào-Xuān and his wife to make their way back to Éméi Mountain. On the way, they again visited many temples in these famous mountains. Bó-Wǔ had never left home and seen so many beautiful and magnificent mountains. They also went through many cities and towns and visited famous scenic places. Bó-Wǔ had never realized that the country was so big. It took them nearly one month of traveling before they finally arrived home on Éméi.

Bó-Wǔ Meets Two Uncle Masters 博武拜見兩位師伯

Master Dù purchased his five-acre parcel of land near the lower-section of Éméi Mountain, with savings that he earned while working for the government. He had also received a small inheritance from his father. There was a farmhouse on the north side of the land that could house three to four people comfortably. Next to the house, there was a storage shed for farming tools and firewood. Right in front of the house, there was a rice field and a small vegetable garden. There was a pond, just above the rice field, surrounded with willow trees. This pond was used to store water for farming, especially during the dry season. There was also a well not too far from the house. The well water was used for drinking and cooking. Around the area, there grew plenty of wild bamboo and mushrooms. Near the bottom edge of the land, there was a creek that was home to some fish, crabs, and fresh-water shrimps.

About two miles from the house, near the foot of the mountain, there was a town, Jiǔzhàigōu (九寨溝鎮) where they sold their wild bamboo shoots, mushrooms, some surplus rice and vegetables, and animal skins. Next to the pond, there was a flat field where they dried rice after the harvest. This field was also used for martial arts training. There were many specially designed constructions around the pond for martial arts conditioning.

They had two horses for farming and transportation. Master Dú and Míng-Zhé also used them for hunting. Various kinds of wild animals such as rabbits, pandas, tigers, snakes, antelopes, monkeys, deer, and all kinds of birds lived on the mountain. There was a plentiful meat supply. Whenever they had extra, either they preserved it or sold it in town.

Usually, during plowing and harvest seasons, in addition to themselves they had to hire two extra workers. However, it was not easy to find helpers since there usually was a shortage during the busiest farming seasons. When Master Dù and Míng-Zhé were gone, they hired two neighbor farmers to maintain the land and take care of the livestock, such as the horses and chickens.

***

Bó-Wǔ was very excited when they arrived home. It was so quiet and beautiful. It was not the same as his home in Shāndōng village where there were so many people around. This place was semi-remote and was the most desirable place for martial arts training, he thought.

On June 15th, two days after their return, Shìhǎi and Míngdào monks, as promised, would come to Master Dù's home for their monthly meeting. Normally, they met each other on the 15th of each month to discuss and practice martial arts. However, due to Master Dù and Míng-Zhé's travel over the last three months, they had not met during that period. That was the first time in the last ten years that they had missed their monthly meetings. It made this meeting especially precious and appreciated.

As usual, Míngdào arrived early since his Chúnyáng Temple (純陽觀) was only about one day's travel away, while travel from Shìhǎi's Pǔxián Temple (普賢寺) would take nearly two days since it was located in the deeper mountain area. For Míngdào, he just needed to get up early and would arrive by nightfall. However, for Shìhǎi, he would need to lodge half-way in a smaller Buddhist temple the first night.

Master Dù and Míng-Zhé were waiting anxiously, especially since they had not met for nearly three months. They knew Míngdào often arrived one day early and made it on time for dinner.

When Míng-Zhé saw Míngdào monk coming from a distance on the path, he was so excited.

"爹！博武！明道師伯來了。來！來！博武，我們去接他。" ("Dīe! Bó-Wǔ! Míngdào Shībó is here. Come! Come! Bó-Wǔ, let's go to welcome him.") He was very excited and asked Bó-Wǔ to go with him to receive Míngdào. They ran very quickly down the path toward Míngdào while Master Dù stood in front of the house laughing.

When Míng-Zhé and Bó-Wǔ approached Míngdào monk, Míng-Zhé said,

"二師伯！您好。" ("Èr Shībó! How are you?") While showing his martial greeting.

"二師伯！您好。" ("Èr Shībó! How are you?") Bó-Wǔ said and also showed his martial greeting.

Míngdào was very happy to see them, but he wondered who the boy was.

"明哲！這小孩是誰？" ("Míng-Zhé! Who is this boy?") he asked.

"二師伯！這是爹剛收的徒弟，他叫博武，才十二歲，是義父山東老朋友李浩軒師叔的小兒子。" ("Èr Shībó! He is the new disciple that dad just accepted. His name is Bó-Wǔ and he is the youngest son of dad's old friend, uncle Lǐ, Hào-Xuān, in Shāndōng.")

"噢！是李浩軒的兒子。你義父說起他好幾次呢！我還以為你義父不再收徒弟了呢？博武！你喜歡學武嗎？」("Oh! He is Lǐ, Hào-Xuān's son. Your dad has spoken about him many times. I thought your dad would not accept any more disciples? Bó-Wǔ! Do you like martial arts?")

"當然喜歡囉！否則師父不會收我的。" ("Of course! I love it, otherwise Shīfù would not have accepted me,") Bó-Wǔ replied with a smile.

While they were talking, they arrived at the house.

"正豪老弟！久違了。" ("Zhèng-Háo Lǎodì, it's been a long time,") Míngdào said.

"二哥！正想著您呢！一晃就三個月了。來！來！我們等著您吃晚飯呢。" ("Èrgē! I have missed you. It has already been three months. Come! Come! We are waiting for you to have dinner.")

They entered the house where dinner was ready on the table and sat down.

"正豪老弟，我年紀大了，走了一天倒是累了。恭喜你收了一個徒弟。" ("Zhèng-Háo Lǎodì, I am getting old. I feel tired after just one day of walking. Congratulations on your acceptance of this new disciple.") He used his right hand to slap Bó-Wǔ's shoulder gently to express his acceptance.

"不是嗎？真是歲月不饒人啊！博武的天質不壞，還希望您能夠多多指導他。來！來！我們先吃飯，吃完飯早點休息。" ("Yes, time waits for no one. We are getting old. Bó-Wǔ has a good talent. I hope you are able to teach him. Come! Come! Let's eat first, and after that, rest early.")

***

As usual, they got up early the next morning. Early morning is the best time for martial arts practice. They went to the practice field and warmed up. Then, while Master Dù was practicing his Tàijíquán and Bāguàzhǎng, Míngdào got Míng-Zhé and Bó-Wǔ together and explained the theory and some key points of internal martial arts. Though Bó-Wǔ had learned some of them from his father, by listening to Míngdào's explanation he was able to comprehend the deeper meaning. He listened carefully with interest.

"記住，練內功必須先築基，有了深厚的基礎，練出來的功力才高。" ("Remember! When you train internal Gōngfū you must first build your foundation. Only if you have a firm and deep foundation can your internal power reach a high-level!")

"二師伯！那如何去築基呢？我爹也說過築基的重要性，可是很多東西我還是不懂呢。" ("Èr Shībó! Then how can I build this foundation? My dad also mentioned about the importance of building the foundation.

But still I don't understand what some of it means,") Bó-Wǔ asked.

"博武！我也曾跟明哲解釋過了幾次，可是他還抓不到要領呢！築基包括兩個重要的練習，一個是怎麼去增強氣量，另一個就是怎麼有效的去操作與應用所培養出來的氣。氣量不夠，當然什麼都不用說了，那就跟常人一樣呢，甭談如何去高人一等與應用了。可是如果有了充沛的內氣，可是卻不懂的如何有效的去集中你的潛意識在應用上，那也達不到高深的境界。" ("Bó-Wǔ! I have also explained the meaning of these trainings a couple of times to Míng-Zhé, but he still can't grasp the key essence of the practices. Actually, building foundation includes two most important practices: knowing how to increase the quantity of Qí, and how to manipulate the Qí and apply it in applications effectively. If you don't have plenty of Qí, then there is nothing to talk about since you will be the same as other normal people. In that case, how can you talk about reaching a higher level of application? However, even if you have abundant internal Qí but do not know how to focus your subconscious mind in applications, then you also cannot reach a high-level.")

"二師伯！那如何去練氣量與應用呢？" ("Èr Shībó! Then, how do you increase your Qí quantity and apply it in applications?")

"那就要練丹田與意的集中了。要有更充沛的氣，你必須知道如何將食精轉換成氣。丹田是產丹之田，也叫丹爐。中醫叫氣海呢！這裡所說的丹就是氣，可以長生。靠著小腹呼吸的上下蠕動，這樣就可以將存在小腹的脂肪轉換成氣，這個呼吸叫煉精化氣也叫返童呼吸呢！" ("That will rely on the training of your Dāntián and the focus of your mind. If you want to have more abundant Qí, you must know how to convert the food essence into Qí. Dāntián means the elixir field and is also called the elixir furnace. In Chinese medicine it is called 'the sea of Qì.' What is called elixir here means Qí that is able to extend your life span. You must move your abdomen up and down in coordination with your abdominal breathing. In this case, you will be able to convert the fat stored at the abdominal area into Qí. This kind of abdominal breathing is called 'converting essence into Qí' and also called 'breathing of returning to childhood'!")

"這個我爹也曾跟我解釋過，可是當時覺得有點是是而非呢！雖然我當時不太了解，可是我就是拼命的練，我倒是把身體練壯了，而且力氣也比他人大了不少。" ("My dad also explained this to me before. However, I was confused at that time. Though I did not quite understand, I just practiced desperately. Surprisingly, it has made my body stronger and my power also stronger than others.")

"難怪我看你精神充沛的呢，你爹倒將你的根基打穩了。其實練習內功最重要的年紀在你現在這個年紀啊！" ("No wonder I have noticed that you have a high and abundant spirit of vitality. Your dad has helped you build this firm foundation. In fact, the best age for practicing internal Gōngfū is the age you are now!")

"二師伯！這是為什麼？" ("Èr Shībó! Why is this?") Bó-Wǔ asked again.

"因為你的身體現在正在成長、成熟的時期，如你練得得法，你的身體與氣量的成長可以加速並加倍於他人呢！如果你在十八九歲後身體已長成了再練內功，那成就就可就差多了。可惜的是大多數的小孩不懂這個道理和持恆，錯過了練內功的時間呢。" ("This is because you are in the period of growing and maturing. If you practice correctly now, your physical body and Qí quantity will grow rapidly with age; consequently, the achievement can be double that of others. However, if you practice internal Gōngfū after 18 or 19 years old when the body has already grown up, the result will be much less. Unfortunately, most children do not understand this theory and cannot maintain their patience in training. Consequently, they have missed the best time for training internal Gōngfū.")

"二師伯！我一定好好的練，有您跟師父的教導，我一定將內功練成。您說，有了氣量還需要集中力，那怎麼練集中力呢？" ("Èr Shībó! I will practice hard. With you and Shīfú's teaching, I will achieve the internal Gōng training. You also mentioned that other than Qí quantity, I still need focus. In this case, how do I practice this focus?")

"那就需要觀燭與打坐了。你先由觀燭開始，慢慢再練習武學上的打坐。你現在還小，先把丹田氣練好，再三五年後，我再告訴你武學上打坐的秘訣。" ("In this case, you must observe the flame of candles and practice meditation. You may begin with observing the flame of candles and gradually engage in martial meditation. You are still young. First you should train your Dāntían to build up Qí to an abundant level. After three to five years, I will teach you the secret of meditation.")

"那我怎麼去練觀燭呢？" ("How do I practice the observation of candles?") Bó-Wǔ asked again while Míng-Zhé listened and paid careful attention. Míngdào had explained these things to him before, but it had not caught his interest due to his lack of understanding.

"每天五分鐘，馬步站在蠟燭或油燈前，約兩步遠。兩步遠是平常對敵的距離。眼睛注視著火焰，觀看他的變化。注意不只是看，看到火焰的搖動，你的潛意識必須感應，這是第一步。如果你只看而潛意識沒有感應，那就白看了。" ("Five minutes a day Stand Horse Stance in front of a candle or an oil lamp flame with two steps' distance. Two steps is the normal distance when you match your opponent. Your eyes should stare at the flame and observe its actions. You should also know that this practice is not just observing. Your subconscious mind must have an attachment and response with the flame's action. This is the first step. If you just observe without your subconscious mind's response, then your observation will be in vain.")

"二師伯！這是為什麼？" ("Èr Shībó! Why is that?")

"因為你在對敵的時候，你的潛意識必須對敵人全身任何微動都要有所感應，有了這個感應，你才能有反應而產生對敵的措施。來！來！你就用最快的速度攻擊我，你就可以去體會什麼是反應了。" ("This is because when you are in a fighting situation against your opponent, your subconscious mind must have a quick response to any slight action your opponent initiates. Once you have this response, you will be able to establish a reflex against the opponent's action. Come! Come! Try to attack me with your fastest speed. This will help you comprehend the reflex reaction.")

When they were talking, Míng-Zhé hoped he could understand the meaning of this training this time.

Now, Bó-Wǔ got excited. These conversations had triggered his deep thinking. Now he was going to be able to experience it. He stood about two steps in front of Míngdáo and tried to use his right hand to touch Míngdáo's chest. But even before he initiated his action, Míngdáo looked at him and said,

"你想用你的右手打擊我的胸部。" ("You are thinking of using your right hand to strike my chest.")

Bó-Wǔ was so shocked to hear that Míngdáo knew his intention. Then, again he tried. This time he thought he would use his left leg to kick Míngdáo's left shin. Again, before he launched his kick, Míngdáo stopped him by pointing with his right index finger at Bó-Wǔ's left leg,

"你想用你的左腳踢打擊我的左小腿。" ("You are thinking of using your left foot to kick my left shin.")

Again, Bó-Wǔ was so amazed and wondered how Míngdáo knew his intentions? Finally, he decided to initiate a fake punch and then follow it with a speedy kick with his right leg. However, before his fake punch was launched, Míngdáo's right hand was already touching his right shoulder and pulling it down to prevent his right kick. All three times, it seemed that Míngdáo was a mind reader who could read his mind. Now he was so curious!

"二師伯！您怎麼會知道我想如何攻擊您呢？我的攻擊還沒出來，您就已經將我制止住了。" ("Èr Shībó! How did you know how I was going to attack you? Before my attacks were initiated, you have already

29

stopped me.")

"那是因為你已經告訴我你的意圖了。" ("That was because you told me your intention.")

"可是，二師伯，我沒有啊！" ("But, Èr Shībó, I did not tell you.")

"你知道，你每一個攻擊，必須先有身法，身法是在腿、手攻擊之前。你如果能夠先感應到敵人的身法，你就能在他攻擊你之前，知道他的意圖呢。" ("As you know, whenever you initiate an attack, you must first have body structure. The body's movements come before your hands' and legs' attack. If you are able to feel or sense your opponent's body actions, you will know his intention before his attack.")

"二師伯！我知道了，這是爹常說的，'敵不動，我不動。敵微動，我先動啊！'" ("Èr Shībó, I understand! Isn't this what my dad always said, 'when the opponent does not move, I do not move. When the opponent slightly moves, I move first!'")

"對了！要練習這個感應度，你就必須先練習觀燭。之後，你才能練習你的反應度呢！" ("Correct! If you wish to practice this reflex response, you must first observe the candle flame. Only after this will you be able to train your reflexes.")

"那我怎麼練習反應度呢？" ("In this case, how do I train my reflexes?") Bó-Wǔ looked at Míngdáo with curiosity.

"那就要找練伴並由真正敵對上去取得經驗了。" ("You must practice with partners and also experience it against an opponent in a real fight.")

Míng-Zhé knew that he had listened to this kind of conversation a couple of times in the past. However, he could not comprehend the deep meaning of the practice. Now, he deeply regretted that he was already 18 years old and had missed the most precious period of this crucial training.

***

Next day, before noon, Shìhǎi arrived while Master Dù and Míng-Zhé were preparing lunch and Míngdáo was teaching Bó-Wǔ how to read and write calligraphy in the living room. When Shìhǎi was about fifty yards away from the house,

"博武！你的大師伯，釋海法師到了。" ("Bó-Wǔ! Your Dà Shībó, Shìhǎi monk has arrived,") Master Dù shouted from the kitchen.

"真的嗎？我怎麼沒聽到什麼？" ("Really! How come I did not hear anything?") Bó-Wǔ said.

"那是你耳朵的敏感度，還有你的警覺性還不夠，多練習就會養成習慣了。來！我們出去歡迎他。" ("That is because your hearing sensitivity is not good and furthermore, your alertness is still low. After you practice a while, you will become accustomed to it. Come! Let's go to welcome him,") Míngdáo said.

When they stepped out, Shìhǎi was already standing outside the house.

"大哥！您好。這是博武，杜老弟最近收的小徒弟。" ("Dàgē! How are you? This is Bó-Wǔ, Dù Lǎodì's young disciple whom he accepted recently.")

Both Míngdáo and Bó-Wǔ greeted Shìhǎi with a martial hand greeting signal. Shìhǎi responded with this greeting as well.

"三個多月沒見了！你老弟還好嗎？他叫博武，對嗎？幾歲了？" ("It has been three months since I've seen you. How are you, my brother? His name is Bó-Wǔ, correct? How old are you?)

"大師伯！我已經十二歲了，我好高興見到您呢！" ("Dà Shībó! I am 12 years old. How happy am I to see you!")

When Master Dù and Míng-Zhé heard the talking, they stepped out of the kitchen.

"大哥！您好，我們一直在等著您呢！" ("Dàgē! How are you? We have been waiting for you,") Master Dù said with a martial greeting.

"大師伯！您好。" ("Dà Shībó! How are you?") Míng-Zhé said with excitement. He always respected Shìhǎi monk because of his deep understanding of Buddhist philosophy. He also liked to listen to Shìhǎi's stories of what he had experienced before he retired to Émeí Mountain. This was because Míng-Zhé had never left Émeí Mountain since he arrived when he was three years old. Other than visiting Jiǔzhàigōu Town (九寨溝鎮) occasionally, traveling with Master Dù three months ago was his first time visiting big cities.

"您們聊聊！午飯就快好了。大哥，吃完飯，您好好的休息。" ("You chat for a while! Lunch will be ready soon. Dàgē! After the meal, you should take a good rest.")

Since both Shìhǎi and Míngdáo monks were vegetarians, other than rice, there were vegetables, beans, bamboo shoots, and wild mushrooms. There was also some tofu that Míng-Zhé had made in the morning. After lunch, Shìhǎi, Míngdáo, and Master Dù went to take a nap while Bó-Wǔ and Míng-Zhé cleaned up the mess. When they were done cleaning, Míng-Zhé took Bó-Wǔ to the vegetable garden to work. It was the season for planting all the seeds for the garden.

***

Once all the masters woke up, everyone gathered in the practice field. Bó-Wǔ was very excited since he had learned so much just in a single day from Míngdáo yesterday. He believed he would learn more from Shìhǎi.

After the warm-up, the three masters practiced their internal routines such as Tàijíquán, Bāguàzhǎng, and Xíngyìquán while Bó-Wǔ and Míng-Zhé began to practice their routines, fundamental Gōng. These fundamental Gōng included running along the mountain trails with a fifty-pound bag, climbing ropes, grabbing jars, striking sandbags, walking/running on tree stumps, rooting on bricks, and tossing the stone lock. They had divided these fundamental conditioning trainings into three groups, and they repeated the same practice cycle every three days. After nearly two hours of fundamental training, they would practice sequences, matching drills, and sparring. They also practiced some matching drills on the raft floating on the pond. This training was important since a large area of southern China was covered by lakes and rivers. Very often, combat would occur on top of a boat. Therefore, practicing on rocking and unstable surfaces had become crucial to survival in southern China.

To start with, the raft was made with five logs tied together and was pretty stable. After they practiced for a while and had acquired better feeling and skill, then one of the logs would be removed. This training process continued until they were able to practice their routines on a single log. Naturally, the last stage was the most difficult since a single, rolling log was so difficult to control.

***

As usual, both monk masters stayed for four to five days. The day before their departure, Bó-Wǔ was so curious and enthusiastic in his heart. He wondered if he could ask Shìhǎi about training. He believed he could again acquire some crucial training keys like he received from Míngdáo.

From the last few days, he knew that Shìhǎi always woke up early and went to the willow tree area near the pond to meditate. So, this morning he woke up early and waited near the willow tree. The sky gradually turned bright and the roosters were calling. After he waited for about 20 minutes, he saw Shìhǎi leave the house and come to the area. He was so excited and walked toward him.

"大師伯！我有些問題，整晚睡不著，不知道您老人家能給我一點啟示嗎？" ("Dà Shībó! I have some questions and could not sleep the whole night. I don't know if you are able to help me with some inspiration?")

Shìhǎi was surprised to see Bó-Wǔ was alone there so early. However, over the last couple of days Bó-Wǔ had become a favorite of his, especially with his intelligence and enthusiasm in learning Gōngfū at such a young age. Together, they sat down on a log where Shìhǎi had meditated the last few mornings.

"你有什麼問題？你不是剛剛才來到峨嵋山的。" ("What are your questions? Haven't you just come to Éméi Mountain recently?") Shìhǎi was curious where the questions came from since Bó-Wǔ had just arrived at Master Dù's home only a week or so ago.

"四天前明道二師伯告訴我練習內功的訣竅。他說練內功必須練氣量和怎麼專注集中力將氣顯現出來。我可以明瞭怎樣練氣量因為我爹也曾經教過我，可是如何練集中力而將其有效的應用在發勁上，我爹卻不曾跟我提過。而明道二師伯卻只說這個需要靠打坐的練習才能有高階層的集中力。他只要我先練習觀燭。不知道您能不能再明確的指點我？" ("Èr Shībó taught me some crucial keys of practicing internal Gōng four days ago. He said to train internal Gōng, I must train my Qì quantity and how to manifest it effectively with a high-level of focus. I am able to understand how to train my Qì quantity since my dad had taught me. However, my dad never taught me how to train my focus so my power can be effectively applied in applications. Míngdáo Èr Shībó told me that I would need meditation to reach a high-level of focus. He only wanted me to begin with observing a candle flame. I wonder if you are able to instruct me and explain to me in more detail?")

"好說！好說！你年紀這麼小就想知道這深奧的練習，真是不簡單。可是就是你聽了也不見得會悟得其中的道理啊！" ("Okay! That's great! It is unusual that you are so young and already wish to know this deep and mysterious practice. However, even when you listen to my explanation, you still may not understand its theory.)

"大師伯！拜託拜託呢！我向您求情了。" ("Dà Shībó! Please! Please! Here I am pleading with you.") Bó-Wǔ came to Shìhǎi's front and knelt down with his head touching the ground. Shìhǎi could see how much he wished to learn. Though Bó-Wǔ might be too young to comprehend the deep theory behind the practice, Shìhǎi decided to teach him as much as possible.

"起來！我告訴你。首先你必須知道打坐中的意有兩種意，一個是平常所說發出大腦的意識，另一個卻是由泥丸宮發出的潛意識。大腦產生的意識是思考的，是比較操作和主宰的，是虛偽和製造假象的，而在泥丸宮的潛意識是靠直覺的，是比較真實的。"（"Get up! Let me tell you. You must first understand that there are two kinds of minds existing when you are meditating. One is the conscious mind generally known to be generated from your brain while the other is the subconscious mind initiated from the Mud-Pill-Palace. The conscious mind generated from your brain provides your everyday thinking, but it can also be manipulative and domineering. It can be hypocritical and false. However, the subconscious mind merging from the Mud-Pill-Palace is intuitive and more truthful."）

"大師伯！泥丸宮在什麼地方啊？為什麼它是這麼的重要呢？"（"Dà Shībó! Where is the Mud-Pill-Palace? Why is it so important?"）

"泥丸宮在頭的正中心，也是整個頭的氣場共振中心點，這個中心也叫做神室是我們精神的控制中心。練內功所謂意的專注是指這個潛意識而不是大腦發出的意識。如果妳能將潛意識提高到高階層的境界，那你的集中力，反應力，警覺力，與感應力都會跟著提高。不但如此，你的精神也可以達到一個較充沛的層次。"（"The Mud-Pill-Palace is located in the center of your head. It is the Qì resonance center of your head. This center is also called the spiritual residence that monitors our mental development and activities. The focus of the mind in internal Gōng training means the focus of your subconscious mind at this center, not the conscious mind generated from your brain. If you are able to promote your subconscious mind to a higher level, then your focus, reaction, alertness, and awareness will also increase to a higher level. Not only that, your spirit of vitality can also reach a stronger stage."）

"大師伯！您是說如果我要將氣量有效的發放出去，我必須要練習潛意識的培養嗎？"（"Dà Shībó! Is this what you mean? If I wish to manifest my Qì effectively, I must cultivate my subconscious mind?"）

"不錯！因為你在搏鬥時，你沒有時間去做思考再執行你的行動，一切都靠你的自然反應，而這個自然反應卻是由潛意識反射出來的。"（"Correct! This is because when you are in the middle of fighting, you do not have time to think and then execute your action. Every action relies on your natural reaction and this natural reaction is a reflex from your subconscious mind."）

"那我如何去練習潛意識的培養呢？"（"Then, how do I practice the cultivation of my subconscious mind?"）

"那你就要練習胎息靜坐了。胎息靜坐不是一天兩天就會懂的，必須要能悟出其中的道理與竅門。你還是先從你二師伯的建議，由練觀燭先，等你心能定了後，我再慢慢將你引進胎息的靜坐。"（"In this case, you have to learn Embryonic Breathing Meditation. Embryonic Breathing Meditation cannot be understood in a single day or two. You must first comprehend its theory and crucial training keys. I think you should accept your Èr Shībó's suggestion, and practice observing a candle flame first. Only after your mind is able to be calm and steady, I will lead you into Embryonic Breathing Meditation gradually.")

Bó-Wǔ felt that he generally understood, but also was not quite clear on many things. He believed he was not yet ready for further pursuit of this topic. He just had to wait patiently till one day when he would be ready.

ADVANCE MARTIAL STUDY 武藝的精進

Time passed very quickly. Other than learning Gōngfū from Master Dú, Bó-Wǔ also received much instruction from both Shìhǎi and Míngdào monks. Now, he had just turned 16 years old. Besides growing taller, his body was getting stronger each day, especially since he now knew how to apply the internal Gōng (內功) for his physical conditioning. Not only his strength but also his endurance increased significantly. He was more like a young man instead of a child.

Once he turned 16 years old, Master Dù started to teach him how to throw darts and also how to use a bow and arrow. Since then, when Master Dù went to hunt, he often took Bó-Wǔ with him. Since they had only two horses, whenever Bó-Wǔ went to hunt with Master Dù, Míng-Zhé would stay home to study his literature and practice the calligraphy and painting that he had learned from Shìhǎi. He enjoyed doing these things so much when he was alone. To Bó-Wǔ, hunting with Master Dù was the most joyful time. Since Bó-Wǔ was strong, his bow was also stronger than normal and was able to shoot a greater distance. The game animals they most frequently acquired were rabbits, deer, and fox.

With his older age, the number and the depth of his questions about training also increased. Now, he had more desire to acquire and comprehend the deeper aspects of Gōngfū than ever. His fighting skills had passed Míng-Zhé's already. One day, when he was training sandbag striking, he wished to ask Master Dù some questions that Míng-Zhé could not answer.

During the water break, after nearly two hours of training, Bó-Wǔ saw that Master Dù was not busy, so he went and greeted him with the martial hand symbol,

"師父！我有幾個問題，不知道您能不能告訴我與明哲師兄？" ("Shīfù! I have a few questions. I wonder if you are able to tell me and Míng-Zhé

Shīxiōng.")

"沒問題！你們有什麼問題呢？" ("No problem! What questions do you have?")

"以前聽我爹說過練習功夫有三種不同的發勁，但是我當時還小，不懂得什麼是發勁也不懂得如何發問。現在我跟您練了四年了，我還是對這個問題一直在打轉兒呢！" ("I heard my dad mention that there are three kinds of power manifestations called Fājìng in Gōngfū training. But I was still small and did not know what Fājìng was and also did not know how to ask about it at that time. Now I have practiced with you for four years. I am still wondering and confused about this question.")

"很好！你們聽我說，其實道理很簡單。如果你能有效的用意去引氣到手上或腳上，然後把力氣發揮到高層次的境界，這就是發勁了。所以勁力要猛，你必須要練氣量與集中力，這就是內功上的功夫。首先你們需要瞭解內家與外家功夫的不同。內家是由內往外練而外家是右外往內練。" ("Very good! Now you listen to me. In fact, the theory behind Fajing is very simple. If you are able to use your mind to lead the Qì to other parts of your body such as arms or legs and manifest them into a higher level of power, then, it is Fājìng. Therefore, to have a strong power, you must train your Qì quantity and your mind's focus. This is the Gōngfū of internal Gōng. You should first understand what the difference is between internal styles and external styles. The training of internal style is from internal to external, and external style is from external to internal.")

"師父！您說的是練武人常說的'外練筋骨皮，內練一口氣'嗎？這也是說外家拳練的是筋骨皮而內家拳練的是氣的培養嗎？" ("Shīfù! Is this what was meant when martial artists always said, 'external trains tendon, bone, and skin and internal trains a mouthful of Qì?' Does this mean external styles of martial arts only train tendon bone, and skin while internal styles train internal Qì's cultivation?") Bó-Wǔ asked.

"不是的！博武。其實不管是外家或內家的功夫，都練筋骨皮與內氣呢。所不同的是練習的途徑不同而已。外家，就以少林拳為例，先練身體、技法、與應用，之後，慢慢的進入意念與內氣的培養。內家，就以太極拳為例，先練氣量和以意引氣的功夫，之後，才進入技法與應用的練習。練力與練技是屬陽而練意與練氣是屬陰呢。不論那個門派都必須內外雙修，否則會出問題的。" ("No, it does not, Bó-Wǔ. In fact, it does not matter if the styles are external or internal. They all train tendon, bone, skin, and also internal Qì. The difference is that the paths of approaching the final goal are different. External style, Shàolínquán, for example, first trains the physical body, techniques, and applications. After that, you gradually enter the internal mind and Qì cultivation. Internal style, Tàijíquán, for example, first trains the Gōngfū of Qì quantity and how to use the mind to lead the Qì to the body. After that, then you enter into the practice of skills and applications. Training physical power and techniques belong to Yáng training while training the mind's focus and Qì's build up belongs to Yīn training. It does not matter which style, they all need to practice both internal and external, otherwise, there will be problems.")

"怎麼練武會出問題？" ("How can it be a problem in martial arts training?") Míng-Zhé asked curiously.

"如果你只加強練習筋骨皮的練習而忽略內氣的調養，你到老時，很容易得到散功。可是如果你只著重內氣的練習而忽略了筋骨皮的鍛鍊，那你即使有很強的內氣，你還是用不上去呢！" ("If you only emphasize the external tendon, bone, and skin practice and ignore the cultivation of inner Qì, when you get old you may experience energy dispersion. However, if you only focus on the internal Qì training and neglect the external tendon, bone, and skin training, even if you have cultivated a strong Qì, you still cannot apply it for external uses.")

"師父！什麼是散功呢？" ("Shīfù! What is energy dispersion?") Bó-Wǔ asked.

"那也就是身體練得太陽，練多了而不懂的內斂，導致氣一直往外擴散。到老了，氣收不回來，身體一直發熱，疲勞，結果可能導致高血壓和中風的。" ("That is when the physical body is so over-developed, it becomes too Yang. If you have not learned how to condense and conserve the internal Qì, then the Qì will continue to disperse externally. When you get old, the Qì's expansion cannot be reversed. Consequently, the body's temperature is higher than normal, gets tired easily and may cause hypertension and stroke.")

"師父！您是說要陰陽平衡，除了練外功外，您還需要練內功。對嗎？" ("Shīfù! What you said was Yīn and Yáng must be balanced. Other than training external Gōng, you still need to train internal Gōng. Right?") Bó-Wǔ asked again.

"不錯！就我來說，我年輕時專練外功而沒有機遇去學內功，所以現在我才專門練內功呢！很幸運的我能認識你兩位師伯，他們的內功造詣可真高呢。我跟他們近十四年來，學了不少啊！" ("Correct! Take me as an example. When I was young, I only focused on external Gōng training without an opportunity to learn internal Gōng. That's the reason I focus especially on internal Gōng training now. I am so fortunate that I was able to learn from both of your two Shībós. Both of them have reached extraordinarily high achievements. I have followed them for the last 14 years. I have learned so much from them.)

"義父！可是內家拳看起來軟軟的，很像不太重用呢？" ("Dīe! But internal martial arts look so soft, it seems that it is useless?") Míng-Zhé asked.

"那你就太小看內家功夫了。你們來！我們到沙包場去。" ("Then, you have underestimated the Gōngfū of internal martial arts. Come with me! Let's go to the sandbag field.")

Master Dù stood up and walked toward the sandbag field on the side of the practice yard. Once there, he chose one of the heaviest bags.

"你們看！這是外勁，也是硬勁。" ("You see! This is external power, also hard Jìng,") Master Dù said and then, with a firm stance and tightened right arm, he launched a punch to the bag. The bag was bounced away with explosive speed. Bó-Wǔ had never seen Master Dù's demonstration and was so impressed by his power, especially considering his age. If this power had landed on a human body, all the ribs would be broken. Master Dù continued,

"現在看！這是軟硬勁，先軟後硬。" ("Now you see! This is soft-hard Jìng, soft first and then hard.") Master Dù inhaled deeply with a relaxed torso and arms to initiate his punch. However, right before it landed on the bag, suddenly he tensed up his fist. When the bag received his punch, it corresponded with a jerking bounce. Though it was not impressive looking from the outside, compared with hard Jìng, it still showed the destructive power.

"義父！這軟硬勁好像沒有硬勁的威力呢？" ("Dīe! This soft-hard Jìng doesn't seem to have the same destructive power as hard Jìng,") Míng-Zhé said.

However, Bó-Wǔ did not agree. He could feel the penetration of the power into the bag. "師父！這拳打到身上，是會內傷的。是嗎？" ("Shīfù! When this fist lands on a body, it may cause inner injury. Right?")

"不錯！這是內外家的綜合勁，它的貫穿力較強。" ("Yes! This Jìng is a combination of both internal and external. Its penetration power is stronger.")

"再看！最後這個勁是軟勁。" ("Again, you see! This last one is soft Jìng.") Again, Master Dù launched a very soft and relaxed whipping punch; however, right before impact, he quickly bounced back his punch and the impact seemed so light that the bag only responded with a quick trembling. Now, Míng-Zhé was very confused. It seemed to him that this strike was not as powerful and impressive at all. However, again, Bó-Wǔ had a different view.

"師父！這軟勁的威力好大呢。這打到身上，內臟都要粉碎的呢！"

("Shīfù! This soft Jìng is so powerful! If it lands on a body, it would smash the internal organs.")

"義父！我還是不懂。我還是認為硬勁的威力是最大的呢。" ("Dīe! I still don't understand. I still believe the power of the hard Jìng is the strongest,") Míng-Zhé protested.

"這你就看不深了。來！去拿六塊磚頭過來。" ("That is because you could not see deeply. Come! Go and pick up six bricks.")

Míng-Zhé and Bó-Wǔ quickly went to pick up six bricks from next to the field.

"放三塊在這裡，三塊在那裡。" ("Place three over here and three there.") Master pointed to the places.

"你們現在看，這是硬勁。" ("Now, you see! This is hard Jìng.")

Master Dù, with all of his concentration, squatted down and used his right palm to strike the first pile of bricks on the ground. The top one suddenly broke down into pieces. Both Bó-Wǔ and Míng-Zhé had never seen this kind of destructive power.

"哇！師父真厲害！一塊硬轉將它打成碎片。" ("Wow! How ferocious is Shīfù's power! You have smashed a solid brick,") Bó-Wǔ said.

"再看這軟硬勁。" ("Now, see this soft-hard Jìng.")

Master Dù, moved to the next pile of bricks. Again, with deep breathing and high focus, he struck down at the brick. However, the amazing thing was the top two were perfect, while the bottom one was smashed into pieces.

"喔！真厲害。力勁透到最下面的一塊呢！" ("Oh! Very shrewd! The power penetrates to the lowest one.") Míng-Zhé was so excited to see this. He finally could see the difference between the two powers.

"對了！這是因為力勁透過上面兩層，加上地面的反抗力上彈，所以碎了。從這裡你可以瞭解軟硬勁的穿透力大於硬勁呢。" ("You are right! This is because the power has passed through the top two and manifested in the bottom one. With the bounced power from the ground, it is thus smashed.")

"師父！可是軟勁呢？師父可以示範嗎？" ("Shīfù! How about soft Jìng? Can Shīfù demonstrate for us?") Bó-Wǔ asked.

"那我就辦不到了！我的功力不夠深厚，這個功夫示範不出來。只有你兩位師伯才有這種功力呢，他們練內勁都有三四十年了。你們先把他們教你們的內家功夫練好，等他們下月來時，請他們表演給你們看。" ("That is something that I cannot do! My Gōngfū is not deep enough to demonstrate it for you. Only your two Shībós are able to perform this kind of Gōngfū. They have practiced for at least 30 to 40 years. You should practice those internal Gōngfū that they have taught you. Wait till they come again next month. Then we can ask them to perform it for you.")

***

More and more, Míng-Zhé felt that he was not as smart and talented as Bó-Wǔ. He felt so frustrated and sad. Though he knew he was not as enthusiastic about learning Gōngfū as Bó-Wǔ, he felt that with his age, being six years older than Bó-Wǔ, he should be better at it. He felt depressed and disappointed with himself. This affected his practice and it showed on his face. One day, when Bó-Wǔ went to search for wild mushrooms, Master Dù went to talk to Míng-Zhé.

「明哲！這幾天你好像有些心思，影響你的情緒與練習。」("Míng-Zhé! It seems that there is something bothering your thinking and that is affecting your mood and practice these last few days.")

「義父！我從小就跟著您練功，況且我還大了博武六歲，可是博武在功夫上的造詣，什麼都比我好。我覺得有點難過。」("Diē! I began my Gōngfū training from you when I was small. In addition, I am six years older than Bó-Wǔ. However, Bó-Wǔ's Gōngfū achievement is much better than me. I just feel sad.")

「明哲！你不要灰心，每個人的資質不同而興趣也不同。你雖然在功夫上比他差了點，可是你在文學上的造詣卻是他無法趕上你的。你比較屬於內向而他卻比較外向呢！我父親是個農夫，他跟我說一些話，我一直記在心裡頭。他說：『你想耕耘是因為你想耕耘而不是他人的影響，所以你耕耘。這樣的話，你為什麼要左顧右盼的看別人的耕耘怎麼樣？如果你比人超前，你就滿足，就惰了，而不繼續往前努力。如果你落在別人後面，你就懊喪而喪失你的鬥志與毅力。如果您真的想耕耘，你就低著頭，勤著鋤，不要左右觀看。有一天，你累了，想休息一下，你看了看，什麼人都不在你旁邊，因為你已經將他們遠遠的拋在後邊呢！』」("Míng-Zhé! You shouldn't be discouraged. Everyone has their own special talent and their interest are also different. Though your Gongfu is not as good as his, your literary skills are far above him. Your personality leans more towards the internal while his is more external. My father was a farmer and he told me an important lesson that I will always remember deeply in my heart. He said: 'if you wish to plow, it is because you want to plow, not because others have made you plow. In this case, why do you look around and compare yourself with others when you plow? If you are ahead, you are proud of yourself and satisfied, consequently, you become lazy and do not try hard again. If you are behind others, you are depressed and lose your will and perseverance. If you really want to plow, you should bow your head down and plow diligently. Don't look around. One day, when you are tired and take a rest, you will realize that there is nobody around you since you have dropped them far behind you.'")

"義父！謝謝您。這是一個很重要的做人道理。我對於自己想做的事，我應該埋頭苦幹，不要左顧右盼。" ("Dad, thank you! This is a very important principle about how to be a human. I should keep my head down and try diligently for whatever I like to do for myself.")

After talking with Master Dù, suddenly Míng-Zhé understood an important life philosophy: your thinking is more important than other people's thinking, as long as you have a strong will, you will achieve your goal. Since then, he practiced even harder, especially his literature and calligraphy, the things he was very interested in. Because his high-level of calligraphy skill had impressed Shìhǎi, Shìhǎi now also taught him how to use the brush to paint objects such as mountains, rivers, animals, and flowers.

***

One day after practice, Bó-Wǔ talked to Master Dù while Ming-Zhe was picking some vegetables from the garden for dinner.

"師父！我在想雖然我的年紀比明哲師兄小了不少，可是我覺得我對功夫的成就卻高於他不少呢。您看呢？" ("Shīfù! I am thinking even though my age is much younger than Míng-Zhé Xiōng, my Gōngfū achievement is much higher than his. What do you think?") Bó-Wǔ was so proud of himself that his martial arts achievement was higher than Míng-Zhé and was expecting Master Dù would give him some compliment and praise. However, Master Dù looked at his face. Instead of offering him any praise, he said,

"博武！你看到那些竹子嗎？他們長的越高就躬得越低。" ("Bó-Wǔ! Do you see those bamboo plants? The taller they grow, the lower they bow.") He used his finger to point to the bamboo growing beside the house.

Suddenly, Bó-Wǔ felt so ashamed and embarrassed. He had been carried away due to his achievement and had lost his humility. He bowed his head down with a flushed face. He felt so humble now and did not know what to say.

"博武，你知道中國有句諺語：'滿招損，謙受益'嗎？" ("Bó-Wǔ! Do you know there is a Chinese proverb: 'Satisfaction causes damage and humility receives benefit?'")

"師父！我爹跟我說過，今天師父一句話就像一支大木棍打在我的頭上。我會永遠記住師父的教訓。" ("Shīfù! My dad told me this before. Shīfù's one sentence today is just like a big staff hitting on my head. I will remember Shīfù's lesson forever.")

"所以說'天外有天，人上有人'呢。" ("That's why it is said: 'there is a sky above a sky and there is a talent above a talent.'")

This short conversation influenced Bó-Wǔ for the rest of his life. Whenever he had accomplished something and felt proud of himself, he thought of this conversation. Immediately, he bowed and became humble.

***

One night after dinner, they were sitting outside under the big tree in front of the house. The temperature had just cooled down after a refreshing summer rain. There were only a couple of mosquito repellent incense sticks burning around them. They usually had more mosquitoes during this time of summer. The breeze that touched their faces made them feel so comfortable. While they were enjoying all of it, suddenly Bó-Wǔ asked a question of Master Dù.

"師父！我一直在想為什麼武術界裡會有怎麼多的門派，而且每個門派裡又有好幾個分支的派別？這個倒使我產生的疑惑呢？我一直以為最古老的門派才是最傳統和最正確的。其他演變出來的分派，應該不是最正確的和最好的。譬如在螳螂拳裡就有許多不同的門派。到底那個門派才是最好的而且最有用的呢？" ("Shīfù! I keep thinking and wondering why there are so many styles in martial arts society. Furthermore, in each style, there are many branches derived from the original styles. I get confused about this. I always think that the most ancient styles were the most traditional and correct ones. All other derived styles should not be the most accurate and the best. For example, just in the praying mantis society, there are so many branch styles. Which one is the best and most effective in application?")

"博武！那你倒告訴我一加一等於多少？" ("Bó-Wǔ! Tell me first, how much does one plus one equal?")

When Bó-Wǔ heard the question, he was so surprised and wondered why Master Dù would ask him such a simple question.

"師父！一加一是等於二，這個誰都知道呢。" ("Shīfù! One plus one equals two. Everyone knows that.")

"那你就錯了。其實一加一不一定等於二的。" ("Then, you are mistaken. As a matter of fact, one plus one is not necessarily two.")

Now, Míng-Zhé also got confused and looked at Dù with a curious expression. When Master Dù saw their wondering expressions, he continued,

"你說說看，你父親等於一，而你母親也等於一，他們結合加在一齊之後，生了五個孩子，最後等於七。你倒說說看，一加一是不是一定等於二呢？" ("Tell me, your father is one and your mother is also one. Then they got together and gave birth to five children and they ended up with a total of seven. Now, you tell me, isn't it true that one plus one is not necessarily two?")

Now, both Bó-Wǔ and Míng-Zhé were surprised by this tricky question.

"義父！當然不是了，是等於七呢！" ("Diē! Of course not, it equals seven.")

"這就對了！如果你們將武藝的研習看成死的，那一加一是等於二。可是如果你認為它是活的，是啟發性的，是創作性的一種藝術，那麼它就能繼續的創作與發展呢！所以說，你們練習武術，不應該死板的練，要思考，要瞭解，要有啟發，要有創作。你們知道每個動作都有很多不同的應用，你們如果只會一個應用，那就死板了，那武藝所傳下去的是死的了。" ("Then this is right! If you treat martial arts as something that is dead, then one plus one equals two. However, if you believe it is alive, inspired, and creative, then martial arts can be created and developed continuously. Therefore, when you practice martial arts, you should not treat it as a dead art. You must ponder, comprehend, be inspired, and be creative. You should know in each martial arts movement, there are so many different applications. If you only know one application, then it is a dead art and naturally the art you pass down is also dead.")

"嗳！師父這些話真是開通了我阻塞的思慮呢！可是，師父！要達到能夠創作的程度，那可不簡單啊。" ("Ai! Shīfù! These talks have opened my mind. But, Shīfù! To reach such a high-level of creation, it won't be easy,") Bó-Wǔ said.

"沒有錯！那就要看你的程度如何了，你瞭解得深，悟得深，經驗深，你創出來的武藝就高深與實用，否則就是一些廢技啊！" ("Correct! This depends on the depth of your comprehension level. If you understand the art thoroughly, comprehend it intelligently, experience it profoundly, and feel it deeply, then the creation of your arts will be deep and applicable; otherwise, the art created is only rubbish.")

"師父！那麼如何去了解的深與悟得深呢？" ("Shīfù! How can I reach the deep level of comprehension and feeling?")

"那就要看你的悟性如何了！有了天質的悟性，還需要毅力，耐心，能刻苦，能下功夫呢！" ("That depends on your temperament for

43

comprehension. Other than the right temperament for comprehension, you still need perseverance, patience, endurance, and serious commitment.")

"師父！謝謝您的教導。我現在明瞭要成功，最重要的不是只有智慧與悟性，而是如何去建立自律的習慣再去培養高深的感覺呢。" ("Shīfù! Thank you for your teaching. Now I understand that if I want to be successful, the most important requirements are not just wisdom and the ability to comprehend, but also building a good self-discipline to cultivate a deep feeling of the art.")

This discussion had not just opened Bó-Wǔ's and Míng-Zhé's minds, but also provided them a key to their success.

***

Since their last discussion about Jìng and seeing Master Dù demonstrate his hard and soft-hard Jìngs, both Bó-Wǔ and Míng-Zhé were anxiously waiting for the next full moon when both Shībós would visit again. They both wanted to see how the soft Jìng was manifested. Finally, the day of the monthly reunion arrived. After both uncle masters had a whole day of recovery from traveling, they came to the training field in the afternoon.

"兩位師伯！兩星期前，我們請教師父關於發勁的道理與訣竅，師父解釋了道理並示範了硬勁跟軟硬勁。他說他還無法施展出軟勁的真功夫。他說只有兩位師伯才有這個能耐呢。您們兩位師伯，能否讓我們開開眼界呢？" ("Both Shībó! Two weeks ago, we asked Shīfù about the theory and crucial secrets of emitting Jìng. Shīfù explained the theory and also demonstrated hard Jìng and soft-hard Jìng. He said he could not demonstrate the real Gōngfū of soft Jìng. He told us that only both of you, Shībó, are able to do so. Can you both Shībó demonstrate this soft Jìng to us and help us to open our eyes?") Bó-Wǔ asked.

Shìhǎi looked at Míngdào with a smile. They seldom demonstrated these high skills of martial arts to anyone. They seemed to be hesitating,

"大哥，二哥，這裡沒有外人，您們就教教他們，幫他們理解吧！" ("Dàgē Èrgē, there are no outside people here. Please teach them and help them to understand,") Master Dù encouraged both uncle masters to demonstrate for them.

Shìhǎi looked at everyone, then said,

"好吧！你們誰先來。我就示範軟勁裡面的拿勁吧，這個勁裡包括了纏、黏、聽、隨四種勁。" ("Okay, then. Who will come first? I will demonstrate how to control Jìng in the soft Jìngs. This Jìng includes coiling, adhering, listening, and following - four Jìngs.")

Míng-Zhé was so curious, he stepped forward.

"我就用我兩手的食指與中指沾黏在你的雙腕，看你能夠脫開我的纏黏嗎？來！伸出你的兩手。" ("I will just use my index and middle fingers of both hands to attach to both your wrists. See if you are able to get out of my coiling and adhering. Now, extend your hands.")

When Míng-Zhé extended his two hands, Shìhǎi used just the index and middle fingers of each of his hands to attach to Míng-Zhé's wrists.

"試試看你能脫離我的拿勁嗎？" ("See if you are able to get away from my controlling Jìng.")

Míng-Zhé was so curious and thought this should be pretty easy. All he needed to do was move his hands away from Shìhǎi's attachment. However, when he tried to pull back, Shìhǎi's fingers followed him and continued to adhere to his wrists. He then tried to rotate or coil Shìhǎi's hands, but again failed. Finally, he quickly stepped backward and tried to separate from Shìhǎi's adhering. Shìhǎi just followed his stepping and kept the same distance between them while his fingers were still adhering to Míng-Zhé's wrists. After he tried for a couple of minutes,

"真奇怪！我的手腕好像被蒼蠅紙給黏上了一樣，脫也脫不掉，想翻轉到上面也不行，被封死住了。我的上身一直暴露在大師伯的攻擊下，如果大師伯真的想打我那真是輕而易舉的呢。" ("It is so strange! I just felt both my wrists had been stuck with fly paper and I could not get out of it. Even when I tried to turn and coil my hands to the top, I failed completely and was sealed. My upper body was exposed to Dà Shībó's attack all the time. If Dà Shībó really wanted to attack me, it would be so easy for him.")

"這就是軟勁的沾黏聽隨的功夫，你會了這個技巧，你就可以將敵人控制在你的手下，讓你隨所欲為。" ("This is the Gōngfū of attaching, adhering, listening, and following using the soft Jìng. If you know this skill, you will be able to control your opponent and it will allow you to do whatever you wish to do.")

When Bó-Wǔ saw the demonstration, he refused to believe that he could not detach from Shìhǎi's adhering and sealing.

"大師伯！我能不能試試看？" ("Dà Shībó! May I try?")

"沒問題！要知道最重要的是親身的體驗。來！來！" ("No problem! The most important key of learning is to experience it. Come! Come!")

Bó-Wǔ held his hands out and once Shìhǎi Shībó had attached, he tried the fastest speed he could to step backward, forward, and to the side. He also tried to withdraw his hands quickly or climb over Shìhǎi's attaching fingers. But after a few minutes, he failed. Shìhǎi's fingers were still adhering to his wrists and controlling his arms softly. Finally, he was amazed with this demonstration. He had never seen or experienced this kind of skill before. However, this demonstration had provided him with a new understanding of soft styles. Then he looked at Míngdào,

"二師伯！您可不可以也露一手給我們瞧瞧呢？" ("Èr Shībó! Can you please also demonstrate some skills for us?")

"好吧！你去拿一大把草紙來。" ("All right! Go pick up a pile of raw toilet paper.")

Both Bó-Wǔ and Míng-Zhé were even more curious this time! Why would Míngdào need a pile of raw toilet paper?! Immediately, Bó-Wǔ ran to the house and brought back a pile of raw toilet paper. Everyone was wondering what this toilet paper was for.

"將草紙數一百張放在桌上。" ("Count 100 sheets of raw toilet paper and place them on the table,") Míngdào said and Bó-Wǔ immediately counted 100 papers and placed them on the table.

"現在你們誰告訴我我的力勁該打在第幾張？如果沒錯，我大概可以將手印印在近五張的誤差。" ("Now, which one of you wants to give me the sheet number on which I should leave my Jìng imprint. Roughly I am able to put a print on the sheet within a five-sheet margin of error.")

This announcement shocked everyone including Master Dù and Shìhǎi monk. This was because it was extremely difficult to deliver the power through such soft material and reach the right depth accurately. Everyone was quiet till Master Dù said,

"二哥，就第六十張吧。" ("Èrgē! How about the 60th?") From his experience, he knew that controlling the penetrating power through to the sheets on the top one-third and the bottom one-third of the pile would be easier.

Without saying a word, Míngdào took a deep soft breath and, when he exhaled, he slapped his right palm on the top of the pile and immediately bounced it back right after his palm touched the top sheet of paper.

"你們誰來數數看，手印在第幾張？" ("Which one of you will check it and see which number of papers have my handprint on it?")

Everyone was wondering and curious about how such a light, bouncing touch could generate a handprint on a specific sheet in a pile of papers. Master Dù said,

"我來數。" ("Let me count it.") He just could not believe that it was possible. He began to count the papers from the top and at the same time checked for the handprint. When he counted to 62, everyone was so amazed that there was a clear palm print on the paper. It was only off by two.

"老弟！我真的是服了，您的功力是高深莫測啊！用這個特技來打穴，真是輕而易舉啊！" ("Lǎodì! I am really impressed and convinced. Your Gōngfū is so high beyond what people can imagine. Using this power to strike cavities, it would be so effective and easy,") Shìhǎi monk said.

"其實您們也太客氣了，我從十歲跟師父凌雲道人練武，練了近五十年才練出這內家的精髓呢。" ("In fact, you are too polite. I have practiced martial arts since I was ten years old under my Shīfù Língyún, and it has taken me nearly 50 years to reach the essence of internal arts.")

This demonstration inspired Bó-Wǔ's and Míng-Zhé's practice significantly. They both profoundly realized that the complexity and expanse of martial arts could be deep beyond any general layman's imagination. Since then, they strengthened their confidence and practiced harder than ever. Their skills of both internal and external arts advanced rapidly, and this made Master Dù very happy. He knew both of them were very lucky to have such a rare chance to learn from two senior masters.

***

BROTHER'S VISIT 長兄來訪

One day in May, when Bó-Wǔ was 18 years old, he was practicing his rooting on the rafts by jumping from one to the other with a long spear. Ahēi (阿黑), the black dog they had adopted two years ago when they went to Jiǔzhàigōu Town to trade some goods, began to bark. This dog always liked to follow Bó-Wǔ wherever he went, even to practice.

Bó-Wǔ was curious why Ahēi was barking at something down the hill. He jumped from the raft to the shore to take a look. In the far distance, he saw a person coming along the hill. They seldom had any visitors. As the person came closer, he was surprised to notice something familiar about the way this person was walking.

"奇怪！這人走路的型態就像大哥博文。" ("Strange! This person walks like my elder brother, Bó-Wén,") he thought. While he was wondering about this, the person began to run towards him and was waving to him.

"真是我的長兄博文。他怎麼會到這裡來呢？" ("It really is my elder brother, Bó-Wén! Why is he here?") This was definitely a surprise!

"是不是家裡發生了什麼事？不知奶奶、爹、娘安好？" ("Is there something happening at home? Are grandma, dad, and mom okay?") Bó-Wǔ wondered.

He ran toward Bó-Wén with eyes that were red. He had not seen his brother for more than six years and he had not expected such a sudden visit either. When he left home six years ago with Master Dù, his brother had already been in Běijīng for his work as a government detective. He hadn't even had a chance to say good-bye. While he was happy to see him, he was also worried something might have happened at home.

"大哥！是您,您好。奶奶、爹、娘都好嗎？" ("Dàgē! It is really you. How are you? How are grandma, dad, and mom?") he asked with a worried look.

"博武,你長高了,十八歲了吧,都差點認不出來了。奶奶、爹、娘都很好,只是奶奶有點風濕,走路較不方便,他們都很惦記著你呢！" ("Bó-Wǔ, you have grown taller! You must be 18 years old now. I almost could not recognize you. Grandma, dad, and mom are all good. Just grandma has some arthritis, so it's harder for her to walk. They all miss you very much!")

After Bó-Wǔ heard this his mind was more relieved and relaxed. He looked at his brother,

"那您怎麼會到這裡來的？" ("How and why did you come here?")

"只是有件公幹,被派到四川成都查案。辦案完後,我想既然成都離峨嵋山不遠,就順道來看你了。" ("It's because I had government business to take care of. I was sent to Chéngdū, Sìchuān to investigate a case. After I finished, I thought Chéngdū was not too far from Éméi Mountain, so I came to see you.")

"大哥,您知道我好高興見到您,我藏在這深山已經六年了,很想家呢！特別是奶奶。" ("Dàgē! Do you know how happy I am to see you? I have been in hiding on this deep mountain for six years. I miss home very much, especially grandma.")

"我知道,奶奶一向就是最疼你了,你在這裡好嗎？" ("I know. You were always grandma's most favorite. Are you okay here?")

"很好,師父待我像自己的兒子,就是太嚴了。" ("Very good. Shīfù treats me as his own son. But he is just too strict.")

"博武,你聽著,師父對你嚴就是要你好。你嫂子欣怡已有孕了,我想如

48

果我愛我的孩子，我會對他很嚴的。你聽過嗎？ 老一輩的說'嚴師出高徒'這可不是假的。" ("Bó-Wǔ! Listen to me. The main reason Shīfù treats you strictly is because he wants you to be good. Your sister-in-law, Xīn-Yí (欣怡), is pregnant. I believe if I really love my child, I will also be very strict with him. Haven't you heard of this? Those old generations always said: 'strict teacher produce high-level student.' This is not false.")

While they were talking, they arrived at the house. As they entered the house, they saw Míng-Zhé was preparing lunch.

"師哥！這是我的長兄。大哥，這位是明哲，我的師兄。" ("Shīgē! This is my eldest brother. Dàgē! This is Míng-Zhé, my elder classmate.")

"哇！這真是個驚喜。來，快請坐。" ("Wow! This is a real surprise. Come! Have a seat.") Míng-Zhé showed his martial greeting.

"師哥！師父呢？" ("Shīgē! Where is Shīfù?") Bó-Wǔ asked.

"他到後山採藥，大概也快回來了。你們坐，聊聊。" ("He went behind the mountain to pick up some herbs. He should be back soon. You sit and chat.") Míng-Zhé returned to the kitchen to prepare more food since they now also had a guest to feed.

Bó-Wén just asked Bó-Wǔ about his training, while Bó-Wǔ was more interested to know about their family and what was going on in the outside world. While they were talking,

"明哲！有客人來訪嗎？" ("Míng-Zhé! Is there any guest visiting?") Master Dù shouted before he entered the house.

When Bó-Wǔ heard of this, he ran out of the house,

"師父怎麼會知道呢？我的長兄在這裡。" ("How does Shīfù know? My elder brother is here for a visit.")

"怎麼會不知道？你一看阿黑怎麼興奮，就知道了。" ("How could I not know? When I saw how excited Āhēi was, I knew,") Master Dù laughed.

"大哥，這是我的師父。師父，這是我的長兄，博文。" ("Dàgē! This is my Shīfù. Shīfù, this is my eldest brother, Bó-Wén.")

Bó-Wén knelt down in front of Master Dù and touched his head to the ground for respect,

"晚輩參見杜師伯。" ("My respect to Dù Shībó.")

"好說！好說！請坐好說話。你小時候我見過你的，時間真快啊！" ("Good! Good! Please sit and let's talk. I met you when you were small. The time has passed so quickly,") Master Dù said as he raised him up from his knees.

"你有幾天假期啊？好好陪陪博武，他在這裡有點悶慌了呢！" ("How many days of vacation do you have? Be a good companion to Bó-Wǔ.

He is quite bored staying in this remote place!") he went on.

Bó-Wǔ was surprised that his master understood him so well.

"我請了五天假期，之後，我必須趕回北京。北京亂的一蹋糊塗呢！" ("I have five days' vacation. After that, I need to rush back to Běijīng. Běijīng is in a state of chaos and confusion.")

"六年前我回山東時就已經很亂了。真痛心啊，我大中華給滿清弄的這樣的地步，更可恨的是那些洋鬼子趁著這個機會正在瓜分我中國呢。" ("When I returned to Shāndōng six years ago, the condition was already very disordered. It is so heart breaking. Our great China has been poorly managed by the Manchurians. Especially hateful are those foreign ghosts who have taken this opportunity to divide the country into pieces.")

"師伯！這慈禧太后可是我中華的大罪人啊！如果沒有慈禧干政，光緒皇帝還是有些作為的。" ("Shībó! Empress Dowager Cíxǐ is the biggest sinner in China. If only Cíxǐ would stop interfering and controlling all of the government policies, Emperor Guāngxù would still be able to accomplish something.")

"你既然知道，怎麼還在那渾水裡呢？" ("Well, since you already know this, why are you still staying in that muddy water?").

"師伯！我現在是身在江湖身不由己了。還要看時機呢！我一直在想，如果我不下地獄，誰下地獄，如果每人都逃離而不管，那國家會更不可收拾的。" ("Shībó, I don't have a choice! I am waiting for an opportunity, but I am unable to escape right now. I keep thinking that if I don't go down to hell, who will go down. If everyone escapes and does not take responsibility for the country, then this country will end up with even more disaster.)

"可是在這個時代裡，自身難保，明哲保身啊！" ("However, it is not easy even protecting yourself in this era! You need to be wise to protect yourself,") Bó-Wén went on.

Upon hearing this news, Master Dù sighed deeply.

While they were talking, Míng-Zhé stepped in,

"義父！午餐準備好了。" ("Diē! Lunch is ready.")

"來！來！先用餐，以後再說。" ("Come! Come! Let's eat first and talk later.")

***

After lunch, Master Dù would take a nap and leave the three young men to talk to each other. Before he left,

"你們多談談。你在這裡這幾天與博武和明哲多多切磋武藝，雖然博武在武功上進步不少，可惜的是他與明哲都缺少實戰的經驗呢！" ("You talk with each other more. Bó-Wén, while you are here these few days, you should practice more martial arts with Bó-Wǔ and Míng-Zhé. Pitifully, though Bó-Wǔ's martial arts training has advanced much, both he and Míng-Zhé still have a lack of real battle experience.") Said Master Dù.

"師伯！我會跟他較量幾下，家父叮嚀著要知道他進步了多少，怕他偷懶不聽您師伯的話呢？" ("Shībó! I will fight with him a few times. My father asked me to test him and see his progress. He was afraid that he was too lazy and did not listen to Shībó.")

"沒有的事，博武很聽話，就是容易動感情，想家想得厲害呢。其實再熬過最後的四年，他就可以下山了。這四年是最重要的應用練習，如果所學的不能應用，那也只是空架子而已。我有點累！想休息一下。你們也去休息，兩個時辰後我們練武場見面。" ("There is no such thing. Bó-Wǔ is a very good boy. However, he is more emotional. He misses home a lot. As a matter of fact, all he needs is four more years of practicing, then he can go home. These next four years are the most important for his application practice. If he cannot apply what he has learned in a real situation, then all he has learned is useless. I am tired, I need to take a rest. You should also rest for a while. We will meet each other at the training field in three hours.") Master Dù laughed and left.

Bó-Wǔ took his brother to his room so he could rest.

"大哥！您這幾天就在這裡休息，柴房裡有個空間，我可以在那裡搭個睡鋪。" ("Dàgē! You will rest here for the next few days. There is a space in the firewood room where I can build a simple bed and sleep there.")

"那很委屈你了。博武！" ("Then you will suffer, Bó-Wǔ.")

"那裡的話，您來我好高興呢！當釋海與明道師伯來時，我與明哲都睡在柴房裡呢！" ("What are you talking about? I am so happy to have you here! Actually, when Shìhǎi and Míngdào Shībó are here, both Míng-Zhé and I sleep in the firewood room.")

***

MARTIAL MEETING 會武

Three hours later when the sun was softer, they met each other in the training field. First, Master Dù asked Bó-Wǔ and Míng-Zhé to demonstrate some techniques for Bó-Wén.

From the demonstration, Bó-Wén was happy to see that Bó-Wǔ's skills had actually surpassed Míng-Zhé's. He could see how much effort Bó-Wǔ had put into his training. After the demonstration,

"你們就切磋切磋！我練我自己的了。" ("You practice with each other and I will practice my own routines by myself,") Master Dù said and went to the other side of the field. Actually, he was still paying attention from a distance to how things were going with the young men.

"博武！來！我們過幾招看看。" ("Bó-Wǔ! Come! Let's spar for a few rounds,") Bó-Wén asked.

Actually, Bó-Wǔ was very excited since he had always practiced with Míng-Zhé. This was a rare chance to test his skills with a different opponent. After he greeted his brother, he stood in a defensive position. First, Bó-Wén tried some simple techniques to attack him; however, in just a few minutes, he realized that his younger brother's skills had already reached a stage that might have surpassed his own. Bó-Wǔ's techniques were not just manifested powerfully but also accurately. Then Bó-Wén tried the best special expertise techniques that he had, but it seemed that he could just match his brother equally. In one way, he was happy for his brother, in another way, he felt some awkwardness and embarrassment that he could not handle a person who had not had very much combat experience. After a few more minutes, he realized that his endurance was not able to match Bó-Wǔ's.

"明哲！來！來！你來替我。" ("Míng-Zhé! Come! Come! Come to replace me.")

"可以！可是師哥，我們常玩著呢。在這裡，除了義父，他就只有跟我對招了。" ("No problem. But, Shīgē, we have always been practicing together. Here, other than dad, I am the only one that he can practice with.")

"沒問題！我只是想看看他的耐力呢！" ("No problem! I just want to check his endurance.")

After Míng-Zhé heard this, he stepped in to exchange martial techniques with Bó-Wǔ. However, it seemed that Míng-Zhé could match Bó-Wǔ easier than Bó-Wén could. As Bó-Wén was wondering about this, suddenly he realized that since they had been practicing for many years, they actually already knew all of each other's techniques. After ten minutes of matching, Míng-Zhé was already panting while Bó-Wǔ still felt comfortable and natural.

"師哥！他的耐力一向都比我好呢。招式上，我們相當，可是耐力上，他可就高於我了。" ("Shīgē! His endurance has always been better than mine. Though we know each other's techniques well, his endurance is far above mine.")

"我們先歇會兒，再來。" ("Let's rest for a while, then spar again.")
They drank some water and rested for five minutes,

"來！明哲，我們過幾招看看。" ("Míng-Zhé! Let's match each other for a few techniques,") Bó-Wén said. He positioned himself and prepared for combat.

Míng-Zhé stepped onto the field, greeted his opponent, then initiated an attack. After five minutes of exchanging techniques, Bó-Wén felt that Míng-Zhé was not as powerful and skillful as Bó-Wǔ. He began to realize that Bó-Wǔ's talent was actually much higher than Míng-Zhé's. He believed that he could help his younger brother acquire more combat experience over the next five days. He also knew that, from sparring with his brother, he would actually be training himself to a higher level.

***

The next day they met each other on the training field again. After doing some stretching and warming up, they practiced some martial arts routines. Only in the last hour would they spar against each other. After checking three of their practice sessions, Master Dù would again go to the other side of the field to practice his Tàijíquán, Bāguàzhǎng, and Eighteen Luóhàn Hands himself. After he had practiced for 15 years, he could see the differences between internal and external martial arts and had started to realize why internal arts were considered to be on a higher level in Chinese martial arts society. If he had not been a good friend of Míngdào and Shìhǎi, he would probably never have had a chance to learn these internal arts.

Other than teaching Bó-Wǔ and Míng-Zhé the external praying mantis style Master Dù had mastered throughout his life, he also taught them some basic internal martial Qìgōng learned from his two good friends. Today, while they took a break for some tea, Bó-Wén asked,

"杜師伯！我看您練的功夫是內家拳，外面比較難見到呢，我聽家父說起，您是螳螂拳的高手，這些內家功夫不是螳螂拳吧？" ("Dù Shībó! I think the Gōngfū you were practicing is internal styles. It is hard to see these in the outside world. I heard my dad say that you are proficient in praying mantis. Aren't these internal Gōngfū praying mantis?")

"當然不是！我練的是太極拳，八卦掌，和十八羅漢手。這些內家拳是在到了峨嵋山後才學的。我的太極拳與八卦掌是跟明道真人學的，而十八羅漢手卻是跟釋海法師學的。這些內家拳比較鬆軟，適合我這個年紀呢。" ("Of couse not! What I was practicing were Tàijíquán, Bāguàzhǎng, and Eighteen Luóhàn Hands. I learned these internal fists after I came to Éméi Mountain. I learned my Tàijíquán and Bāguàzhǎng from Míng-dào monk while Eighteen Luóhàn Hands was from Shìhǎi monk. These fists are soft and more suitable for my age.")

"可是這些拳看起來軟軟的，在實戰中管用嗎？" ("But from looking, it seems they are very soft. Are they effective in real combat?")

"這你就小看內家拳了。你知道內家拳練拳時為什麼要軟、要鬆？這是因為內家拳專練內氣的運轉。內氣強，不但對身體好，他發出的功力軟硬兼施，威力可大呢。氣要運得順行的強，身體就必須要軟，身體繃緊了，氣得運行就滯了。" ("In this case, you have looked down on the internal styles. Do you know why it is soft and relaxed in internal style training? This is because in internal style training, the focus is on Qì's circulation. When internal Qì's circulation is strong, not only is it healthy for the body, but also when it is applied to the power's manifestation, it can be both soft and hard. Its power is tremendously strong. If you want the Qì's circulation to be strong and smooth, the body must be soft. If the body is tensed, the Qi's circulation will be stagnant.")

"可是氣是如何去運呢？" ("But, how do you circulate the Qì?")

"那你們就不知道了。其實啊，這內家功夫功夫起於達摩的易筋經呢。易筋經練習的基本訣竅是以意引氣，由氣而動。意專則氣沛，氣沛則勁強。" ("Then you really don't know. In fact, these internal styles Gōngfū were originated from Buddhi Dámó's Muscle/Tendon Changing Qìgōng. The fundamental secret of muscle/tendon changing is using the mind to lead the Qì, and from the Qì actions are initiated. When the mind is highly focused, the Qi's circulation is abundant, and when the Qi's circulation is abundant, the power manifested will be strong.")

While they were talking, both Bó-Wǔ and Míng-Zhé also paid attention to Master Dù's explanation. This was a great chance to hear Master Dù's explanation about the basic concept of internal martial arts.

"來！來！博文，我把我的手臂抬起來，放在我的胸前。你推推看，看你能否推得動？" ("Come! Come, Bó-Wén! I will lift my right arm and place it in front of me. You may push it and see and see if are you able to move it?")

Bó-Wén was so curious and wondered about this test. To him, to push an old man's arm would be just too easy. He stepped closer while Master Dù used his mind to lead the Qì to his right arm in coordination with his breathing. His body was very relaxed and without tension.

First Bó-Wén used some minor strength to push Master Dù's arm with two hands. Suddenly, he felt like he was pushing against a solid wall or tree. He was so surprised and when he looked at Master Dù, Master Dù was still relaxed, without tension. He could not believe or understand why this was, but he increased his pushing power to his maximum. However, Master Dù remained in his relaxed position without the slightest movement. Finally, Bó-Wén stopped.

"杜師伯！這就很奇怪了，為什麼您這麼鬆軟，而我卻推不動您？" ("Dù Shībó, this is very strange! How could you be so soft and relaxed, but I could not move you with a push?")

"這就是內家的功夫。當氣運的強，所發的勁力就強。當氣運的弱，勁力就難以發揮了。" ("This is the Gōngfū of internal styles. When the Qì's circulation is abundant, the power manifested will be strong. However, when the Qì's circulation is weak, then the power will be difficult to manifest.")

"師伯！可是這麼把這些運氣用到實戰上呢？" ("Shībó! But how can you apply this Qì's circulation and manifestation into a real battle?")

"那就要看你練習的功夫了。你必須練到意到氣到的境界。而這個意卻是潛意識的意而不是平常的意。因為你在實戰中，一切技能都是靠潛意識去反射發揮的。" ("That depends on how much Gōngfū you have practiced. You must train your mind to the point that when the mind arrives, the Qì also arrives automatically. This mind we talk about is the subconscious mind instead of the conscious mind. This is because when you are in a battle situation, all skills are manifested by reflex subconsciously.")

Both Bó-Wǔ and Míng-Zhé had already heard this theory a couple of times. But this was the first time that they saw it demonstrated by Master Dù.

"來！來！試試內家拳的實戰訣竅，你就試試用你的武技攻擊我吧。" ("Come! Come! You may experience the secret of internal styles. Try to use your best skills to attack me.")

Master Dù stood there and got ready to accept Bó-Wén's attack. Again, to be polite, Bó-Wén did not use his special skills and power to attack Master Dù at first. However, he was so shocked that whenever he initiated an attack, Master Dù was able to use his hands to attach to his attacking hands and stick with them. Immediately, Bó-Wén's hands were trapped and sealed. He could not separate from Master Dù's sticking and adhering, and his upper body was completely exposed for Master Dù's attack. This reminded both Bó-Wǔ and Míng-Zhé of what they had experienced with Shìhǎi monk a few years ago.

Master Dù released him,

"再來！再試試！" ("Again! Try again!") Master Dù urged him.

Bó-Wén then increased his speed and power and tried to escape from Master Dù's attachment and adherence. However, he failed again. Both his arms were trapped under Master Dù's control and his upper body was again completely exposed for attack. When he tried to use his legs to kick, all Master Dù did was pull his arms down to immobilize the kick. Finally, he gave up trying.

"以前聽過人家說內家拳的厲害，到今天才真正體驗到內家拳的武技。師伯，您真了不起。" ("I have heard people speak about how ferocious and effective the internal martial arts were in the past. It was not until today that I really experienced these skills. Shībó, you are fantastic,") Bó-Wén said.

"你太高攀我了！比起明道真人與釋海法師法師，我這是小巫見大巫了。" ("You have looked too high in my capability! Comparing with Míngdào and Shìhǎi monks, my skills are just too awkward.")

"師伯！真可惜的是我沒緣見見這兩位高人呢？" ("Shībó! It is a real pity that I don't have the fortune to meet them.")

"其實，你要見他們也不難，只是你不可能多待一天。" ("As a matter of fact, it is not difficult if you wish to meet them. Unfortunately, you are not able to stay one more day.")

"師伯！為什麼？" ("Shībó! Why is that?")

"因為明道真人的純陽觀與釋海法師的普賢寺離這裡都有一兩天的路程，我們約好每月十五日在這裡見面敘舊會武呢！我們一次聚會都要四五天呢。這個月十五日恰好是你要離開的那一天，如果你能多待一天，你就有機會跟他們認識了呢！" ("This is because the traveling distance from the monasteries of Míngdào and Shìhǎi is a couple of days. We have an appointment to meet each other monthly on the 15th. They always stay for four to five days. Unfortunately, the 15th of this month is also the day of your departure. If you could stay one extra day, you would be able to meet them.")

"那麼我就多待一天，能見到他們，也是一個緣份。就是我回去的時間會比較趕呢！" ("In this case, I will stay one more day. It will be such a great opportunity to meet them. However, my return trip will then need to be more rushed.")

BÓ-WÉN MEETS TWO UNCLE MASTERS 博文拜見兩位師伯

Míng-Zhé and Bó-Wǔ had been busy preparing some vegetarian dishes for lunch. Today, on the 15th of the month, was a very special day for them. This was not just because they would be able to learn more from Míngdào and Shìhǎi monks, but they would also get to see Master Dù's excitement. Master Dù was always excited for each month's meeting.

***

Before noon, Míngdào monk arrived. When Bó-Wǔ saw him,

"二師伯！您好。師父去挖些竹筍並找些草菇，應該很快的回來。" ("Èr Shībó! How are you? Shīfù went to find some bamboo shoots and wild mushrooms. He should be back soon,") he said while showing his martial greeting. While Míngdào was wondering who this person was that was standing next to Bó-Wǔ,

"二師伯！這是家兄，博文。因為公幹到四川順道來看我。" ("Èr Shībó! This is my eldest brother, Bó-Wén. He had some government business in Sìchuān, so he took this opportunity to come to see me.") Bó-Wǔ said.

"二師伯！您好。承蒙您教導和照顧小弟。他能跟您老人家學習功夫和做人的道理，是很幸運的。" ("Èr Shībó! How are you? Thank you for teaching and looking after my younger brother. He is so lucky that he is able to learn Gōngfū from you, and about becoming a good man,") Bó-Wén said. He already knew that Míngdào was younger than Shìhǎi from his brother.

"好說！好說！以他的根底，再勤練幾年，他的造詣會很高的。" ("No problem! No problem! With his firm foundation, he will be able to reach a very high-level if he practices diligently for a few more years.")

While they were talking, they saw Master Dù coming back with Shìhǎi. They had met each other in the bamboo field next to the path.

"老弟！您已經到了。我還以為這次我會比您早呢！" ("My old brother! You have already arrived. I thought I was earlier than you this time!") Shìhǎi looked at Míngdào with a laugh.

"釋海兄，這位是博武的長兄，他借四川公幹，順道來訪。來！我們先進去坐再談。" ("Shìhǎi brother! This is Bó-Wǔ's eldest brother. He came to Sìchuān for government business and took this opportunity to see his brother. Come! Let's go inside the house and talk,") Master Dù said.

When they entered the house, Míng-Zhé came out of the kitchen and greeted the two uncle masters. He been learning how to cook from Master Dù since he was small.

57

"各位前輩！中飯很快就可以準備好了。" ("All masters and brothers! The lunch will be ready soon,") Míng-Zhé said and returned to the kitchen.

"博文！既然你是從外面來，告訴我們外面的近況如何？" ("Bó-Wén! Since you came from outside, please tell us what the situation is out there?") Shìhǎi could not help asking Bó-Wén this question. Even though he ran away from his government job a long time ago, he was still concerned about the country and the Chinese people.

"大師伯！談起來可傷心透了呢。一個大好江山，落在滿清手裡，竟然給搞得如此破爛不堪難以收拾啊！" ("Dà Shībó! It is so sad to talk about. Such a great country, after falling into Manchurians' hand, has been mismanaged into a condition of total disorder!")

When Bó-Wén said this, his eyes turned red and he became emotional.

"阿彌陀佛！你不要激動，慢慢說給我聽。" ("Amitabha! Don't be too agitated. Tell me slowly.")

"您知道在道光皇帝時，第一次鴉片戰爭後 (1839-1842)，中國的大門被迫打開，在南京條約下，我大中華失去了自主權，任由洋人進出貿易，將中國的財富盡力剝削。接著，在咸豐皇帝時，洋人又借亞羅號事件與西林教案又發起了第二次鴉片戰爭(1856-1860)。清朝戰敗後，簽了三個不平等條約，天津條約，北京條約，和瓊璃條約。從那時候開始，鴉片就氾濫我整個中國。最可恨的是在第二次鴉片戰爭時，英國與法國借機洗劫圓明園，大火燒了三天三夜。整個圓明園是被毀了。" ("As you know, after The First Opium War between 1839 and 1842 during Emperor Dàoguāng period, China's gates were opened wide. Under the Treaty of Nánjīng, our great country lost its autonomy and has had to give foreigners authorization to have free trade in China. This has greatly drained the Chinese treasury. A short time later, foreigners again used The Arrow Incident and The Auguste Chapdelaine Case to initiate The Second Opium War between 1856 and 1860 during Emperor Xiánfēng's period. After the Qīng government lost the war, three unequal treaties, Treaty of Tiānjīn, Treaty of Běijīng, and Treaty of Àihún were signed. Since then, opium has flooded into all of China. The most painful and hateful event was during The Second Opium War, when British and French armies took the opportunity to burn and loot Yuánmíng Garden. The entire Yuánmíng Garden was completely destroyed, after it burned for three days and nights.")

Shìhǎi responded,

"這些我都知道。我年輕二十五歲時，剛從少林寺學藝返鄉，看到中國在第一次鴉片戰爭打敗後所受到的侮辱。我在憤怒下，毅然從軍想報國。兩年後，因為我的武藝高超被選為大內護衛。一直到二次鴉片戰爭後，我已經是四十二歲了。可是我看到清廷的腐敗與漢人被滿人的歧視，毅然逃出宮廷。之後就一直隱居在峨嵋山普賢寺。真痛心啊！這一切都是清廷的腐敗、脆弱所召來的啊！" ("I knew all of this. When I was young, only 25 years old, I just finished my martial arts training from Shàolín Temple. After I saw the foreigners' insults due to the loss of The First Opium War, I was so angry that I joined the army and hoped to regain the dignity of our country. Two years later, due to my high-level of martial arts skills, I was chosen to be the bodyguard of Qīng Court till The Second Opium War. I was already 42 years old at that time. However, after I saw the Qīng Court's serious corruption and also the unequal treatment of the Hàn people by Manchurians, I escaped from the court resolutely. After that, I have lived in seclusion at Pǔxián Temple. It is really heart-breaking. All of these problems were caused from Qīng Court's corruption, weakness, and vulnerability.")

"咸豐皇帝死後，他與慈禧的兒子，載淳，繼位為同治皇帝，他才六歲呢。從此大全落在慈禧手裡。可惜的是同治皇帝在位十二年就死了，年紀才十八歲呢。之後，慈禧太后就立咸豐帝之弟奕譞的兒子載湉入嗣大宗，繼承皇位，改年號為光緒。繼位時，他才四歲呢，當然大權還是落在慈禧手上。尤其在光緒七年時，孝貞賢皇后暴崩，慈禧更是為所欲為了。" ("After Emperor Xiánfēng passed away, the son he had with Cíxǐ, Zài-Chún, became Emperor Tóngzhì. He was only six years old. Since that time, all political power has fallen into the hands of Cíxǐ. Unfortunately, Emperor Tóngzhì was in position only 12 years and died when he was only 18 years old. After that, Cíxǐ chose Zài-Tián, the son of Xiánfēng's younger brother, Yì-Xuān, to succeed the emperor position, named as Guāngxù. When Zài-Tián took the position, he was only four years old. Naturally, the power was still controlled by Cíxǐ. The situation was worsened after Empress Dowager Xiàozhēn's sudden death in the seventh year of Guāngxù. Since then, Cíxǐ can do whatever she wishes,") Bó-Wén continued.

"之後呢？" ("What happened after that?") Shìhǎi asked anxiously. He did not know all of these events since these had happened after his escape.

"最近的兩件大事是光緒十一年的中法戰爭和光緒十四年的大婚。中法戰爭是因為清朝為保護越南而與法國發生的戰爭，最後簽訂了中法新約，承認法國對越南的保護權。光緒在大婚後，慈禧表面上是歸政給光緒，並成立北洋水師，這帶給了中國一個新氣象與希望。光緒是個賢君，就是希望慈禧不再干政呢！" ("The two most important and big events happening recently were the war between China and France, and also Emperor Guāngxù's wedding in Guāngxù's 14th year. The war between China and France was caused due to Chinese protection of Vietnam against France. After the war, the Treaty of China-France was signed, and China admitted that France has the whole authority in controlling Vietnam. As to Emperor Guāngxù's wedding, immediately after his wedding, it was disclosed to the people that Cíxǐ had returned power to Guāngxù and also desired to establish a Chinese Navy. This has given Chinese people a new attitude of hope. Guāngxù is a good emperor. Everyone just hopes that Cíxǐ does not interfere with governmental policies anymore.")

"根據我個人的看法，慈禧是不可能不干政的。這個女人高高在上，自私無知，自以為是，我想不干政是做給人看的，我認為這個局勢不會撐太久呢。" ("According to my personal opinion, it is not possible that Cíxǐ will stop interfering in governmental policies. This woman treats herself above anyone, she is selfish and dominating. I believe that her claim of not interfering with policies is only a show. This condition will not last long,") Shìhǎi expressed his opinions.

"大師伯！您的看法是沒錯，其實歸政於光緒，只是個幌子，大權仍然握在慈禧手裡呢！光緒想做什麼事，都還得奏請慈禧的批准啊。如果中國要強，除非慈禧死了。" ("Dà Shībó! There is no mistake with your viewpoint. In fact, returning the power to Guāngxù is only a guise. The real power is still in Cíxǐ's hands. Whenever Guāngxù wants to do anything, he still needs to acquire Cíxǐ's approval. Only if Cíxǐ dies, will China get strong again.")

"那麼老百姓的情況呢？" ("How about the conditions of the Chinese people?")

"師伯！那就更痛心了。由於幾個不平等的條約，洋人可以大量進口鴉片，現在百姓吸食鴉片的惡習已遍佈整個中國了，官場上吸食鴉片更是普遍。因為購買鴉片，不但人民愈來愈窮，而整個民生的健康是每況愈下啊！更由於滿清的腐敗，列強將我江山一塊塊吞食過去。現在日本對朝鮮野心勃勃的，我想為了保護朝鮮，中日近期內可能會有戰爭呢。" ("Shībó! It's even more painful to talk about that. Due to so many unfair treaties, foreigners are allowed to import large amounts of opium. Now, the people's opium addiction has spread to all over the country, and it is even worse with government officers. Because of purchasing opium, people are poorer and poorer, and their health has gotten worse and worse! Furthermore, due to the Manchurian's corruption and weakness, all strong foreigners have divided our land and taken it piece by piece. Now Japan has become ambitious in invading Korea. I believe that in order to protect Korea, we may have a war soon between China and Japan.")

In everyone's heart, sadness and anger poured out.

"噯！我已經出家了，其實不應該再對塵世如此關懷、留念。可是我心裡的深處卻無法完全出世，到底我還是中國人啊！" ("Alas! Because I have separated myself from laymen society and become a monk, I should not worry and concern myself with all of these problems seriously anymore. However, deep in my heart, I cannot help it. After all, I am a Chinese.")

"釋海兄，我從來沒看到您如此的激動。" ("Shìhǎi Brother! I have never seen you so agitated,") Míngdào said.

"明道道友，這很難啊，我曾經在圓明園做大內護衛近八年呢。圓明園被燒毀時，我還在宮內呢。" ("Míngdào, my friend, this is very difficult for me. I had worked as a palace bodyguard in Yuánmíng Garden for nearly eight years. When Yuánmíng Garden was on fire, I was still in the palace.")

"釋海兄，這些事是愈談愈傷心呢，清廷這樣的腐敗，即使我們我愛國的心，也無可奈何啊。來！來！我們喝茶。" ("Shìhǎi Brother! All these things, the more we talk, the sadder we will be. Qīng court is in such a corrupted situation, even if we have a patriotic heart, it is still helpless. Come! Come! Let's drink tea,") Master Dù said.

While they were talking, Bó-Wǔ was just listening. Since he came to the mountain when he was only 12 years old, he did not know much about the outside world. However, a hate of foreigners surged from his deepest heart. He also felt so sorry that the Manchurian government was so corrupt and made the country so weak. While they were talking, Míng-Zhé came in from the kitchen,

"各位前輩，中飯已經好了。博武，你能夠幫我端出來嗎？" ("All Masters and brothers! The lunch is ready. Bó-Wǔ, can you help me to bring it out?")

Bó-Wǔ nodded his head and stood up, following Míng-Zhé to the kitchen. Everyone put the table at the center of the room and arranged the chairs.

"我還真餓著呢！明哲煮的菜，不是說的，尤其近幾年，他烹飪的手藝是更高一層樓了。" ("I am really hungry! There is no question about Míng-Zhé's cooking. This is especially true for the last few years. His cooking skills have reached to another high-level,") Míngdào said to the laughter of everyone.

After lunch, Shìhǎi, Míngdào, and Master Dù took a nap while the other three young fellows talked. The practice time would be about two hours later when the sun was not as strong.

AFTERNOON PRACTICE 下午的練習

Bó-Wén, Bó-Wǔ, and Míng-Zhé were in the training field warming up. An hour later, three masters came to the field. Immediately, all three youngsters went to greet them. Míng-Zhé rushed to the kitchen to bring some hot water. Three chairs and a tea table with tea, tea pot, and cups were already set up next to the field. Beside the table, there was a big pot of water and a few bowls. Three masters sat down.

"你們三個先練習些拳套給兩位師伯看看，之後他們可以給你們一些矯正與建議。" ("The three of you perform some training routines for two Shībós first. After that, they can offer you some corrections and suggestions,") Master Dù said.

All three youngsters practiced one by one while the three masters watched and drank tea. During the practice, Míng-Zhé occasionally again went to the kitchen to bring more hot water for tea. After about two hours, Master Dù said,

"你們可以休息一下，喝點水。" ("You may rest for a while and drink some water.")

Everyone came to the table and used the bowls to drink water. It could be seen that after two hours of practice, Bó-Wǔ had the best endurance, Míng-Zhé the second, and Bó-Wén the last. Bó-Wén felt some embarrassment at his shortness of breath.

"博文！你可以感覺到你的耐力比較他們兩個要差點嗎？這原因可能是你在官場上比較少時間練習。你們三人，博武的內力最強，所以他能撐得久。" ("Bó-Wén! Can you feel that your endurance is less than theirs? Because you are working in a government office, perhaps you have less time to practice. Among the three of you, Bó-Wǔ's internal strength is strongest. That's why he could last longest,") Shìhǎi said.

"大師伯！這我在真幾天與他的對練中，已經感覺到了。我現在才知道當我父親告訴我杜師伯教他的武學大周天而要我練習時，我才九歲。可惜我當時對內氣的培養不瞭解也沒有很大的興趣。如今看來，我已失去了練氣的最好時機了。博武自六歲就跟家父勤練大周天氣功，這內家氣功倒是給他領悟和練出來了。" ("Dà Shībó! Actually, I have felt the same thing when I sparred with him these past few days. Now I realize that when my dad asked me to practice martial grand circulation that he learned from Dù Shībó, I was only nine years old then. Unfortunately, I was not able to comprehend the concept of internal Qì's cultivation and did not have too much of an interest. As I know today, I have lost my best time for this Qì training. Bó-Wǔ has learned this martial grand circulation from my dad since he was six years old. Surprisingly, he has comprehended this internal Qìgōng and is also able to accomplish it.")

"其實你也不必灰心，你還年輕。雖然你已超過了最佳練習的時候，只要你勤練，還是會有些成果的。" ("In fact, you shouldn't be discouraged. You are still young. Though you have passed the best time for practicing, as long as you train diligently from now on you will still achieve a middle level.")

"二師伯！您還有什麼指點嗎？" ("Èr Shībó! Do you have any corrections and suggestions?") Bó-Wén asked, since he was very curious about Míngdào's opinion and advice.

"您們應該知道，練拳在應用上，最重要的是什麼？" ("You should know when you train martial arts, what are the most important requirements?")

"速度，力勁，和技術。對嗎？二師伯。" ("Speed, power, and skills. Right, Èr Shībó?") Bó-Wǔ answered.

"不錯，這些是很重要，可是不是最重要的。你所說的三樣都可單獨練，可是還是不能達到最有效的實戰應用呢。" ("Correct! Though these three are important, they are not the most important things. What you said about those three practices can be achieved by yourself. However, they still will not lead you to the most effective applications in a real battle.")

Everyone was wondering what could be more important than speed, power, and techniques.

"其實啊，最重要的是你的警惕性與警覺性呢！沒有高深的警惕性與警覺性，即使你有速度、力勁、與高超的技術，還不見得用得上呢！高度的警惕性與警覺性可以促進你高度的反射性。有了這些條件，你就可以達到'敵不動，我不動。敵微動，我先動'的境界。" ("As a matter of fact, the most important requirements are your alertness and awareness. If you don't have a high-level of alertness and awareness, even if you have a good speed, power, and highly skillful techniques, they still cannot be applied efficiently. When you have a high-level of alertness and awareness, your reflex level will be increased. Once you have reached this level, you will achieve the stage of 'when the opponent does not move, I do not move. When the opponent slightly moves, I move first.'")

"二師伯！師父和大師伯也跟我談過這些道理。可是要怎樣才能練出這樣的境界呢？他們說要練出高程度的警惕性與警覺性，我必須要培養修煉潛意識。您在四年前也告訴我在等幾年，您就可以教我。不知道您跟大師伯認為我現在可以學了嗎？" ("Èr Shībó! Shīfù and Dà Shībó have also told me this theory. However, how can I train to reach this level? They told me that in order to establish a high-level of alertness and awareness, I must train and cultivate my subconscious mind. You also told me four years ago that you would teach me after a few more years. I don't know if you and Dà Shībó think if I am ready to learn it?") Bó-Wǔ asked.

"這就看你能懂多少了！其實說起來簡單，做起來倒不是這麼容易呢！" ("Well! This will depend on how much you will be able to comprehend. As a matter of fact, talking about it is simple, but to do it is not so easy,") Míngdào said and looked at everyone, then continued,

"首先你要了解在我們的身體裡具有兩儀。這兩儀是我們氣場的共振點。你能夠悟出這兩儀的重要性並能夠去感受並意守著這個兩氣場中心，那你就能抓到控制你身體氣場的訣竅。" ("First, you must understand that there are two poles in our body. These two poles are the resonant points of our body's Qì field. If you are able to comprehend the importance of these two poles and are able to feel them, and keep your mind at these Qì field centers, then you will be able to grasp the secret key of controlling your body's Qì field.")

"二師伯！那麼這兩儀在身體的什麼地方呢？" ("Èr Shībó! Then where are these two poles in the body?")

"那就是道家所謂的上丹田與下真丹田了。上丹田在頭的中心而下真丹田卻是在你的物理中心。這兩個中心由衝脈連接著。衝脈是身體氣場運轉上最沒有阻力的，所以叫衝脈，因為氣可以一衝而過。所以說嗎，在物理上我們有兩儀，可是在做用上，可是同一個系統因為它們的感應可以同步呢！" ("They are what the Daoist called the 'Upper Dāntían' and the 'Lower Real Dāntían.' 'Upper Dāntían' is located at the center of the head while 'Lower Real Dāntían' is situated at the center of your physical body. These two centers are connected with the 'Thrusting Vessel' (spinal cord). Resistance to Qì's circulation is the most minimal in the 'Thrusting Vessel', thus it is called 'Thrusting Vessel' because the Qì is able to thrust through it. Therefore, even if we have two poles physically, in function, there is only one since they are able to correspond with each other simultaneously.)

"二師伯！您所說的上丹田在頭的中心，這不是大師伯所說的泥丸宮嗎？" ("Èr Shībó! Isn't what you said about the center of the head the same as what Eldest Shībó called 'Mud-Pill-Palace'?") Bó-Wǔ asked while Míng-Zhé was listening carefully. Naturally, this was also a great opportunity for Master Dù to review all these theories.

"不錯！頭是圓的，頭的正中心正是頭的震盪中心，控制整個頭的氣場。這個中心也叫'神室'，是你精神的所在。你的意能守住這個地方，你的神就能內斂。如果你能夠做到這個地步，你的精神旺盛，你的集中力強，警惕性高，警覺性靈敏。這是練功最重要的，也是最高層的境界。" ("No mistake! The head is round, and its center is the resonant center of the head that controls the Qì field of the entire head. This center is also called the 'Spirit Residence' and it is where the spirit resides. If your mind is able to locate and remain at this center, you will be able to condense your spirit there. If you are able to do so, your spirit of vitality will be vigorous, your focus strong, alertness high, and awareness sensitive. These are the most important requirements in training Gōngfū and also the highest level to be reached.")

"大師伯跟我說過，這頭中心也是我們潛意識的所在呢！" ("Dà Shībó told me that the center of the head is also where our subconscious mind is generated!") Bó-Wǔ got excited. Now, he could begin to comprehend the deeper theory of focusing.

"哈哈！不錯！不錯！你懂的真快。你要知道，在我們的身體裡其實有兩個生命同時存在。一個是物理上的生命而另外一個卻是靈神的生命。我們在生時，兩個生命同時存在我們的身體裡，可是我們一旦死亡了，物體進入大自然回到塵土，而我們的靈神脫離了物理身體，再尋覓新生而步入迴輪。這個泥丸宮就是你靈神的住處。如果你能夠將你的靈神修煉到能夠再打開你的天目，那你就有達到了神通的境界。" ("Ha, ha! No mistake! No mistake! Your comprehension is very fast. You should know that there are two lives in our body. One is physical life and the other is spiritual life. When we are alive, these two lives coexist in our body; however, once we are dead, the physical life will return to the dust while the spiritual life will separate from the physical life and look for a new body to repeat the birth-death cycle of reincarnation. This 'Mud-Pill-Palace' is where your spirit resides. If you are able to cultivate your spirit to a stage so that you can re-open your sky eye, then you will reach the stage of spiritual enlightenment.")

This discussion also amazed Master Dù, since Míngdào's talk had reached a very high-level of spiritual cultivation, of enlightenment.

"二師伯！這樣的話，既然上面上丹田是我們靈神生命的中心點，那麼下真丹田是不是我們物理生命的中心呢？" ("Èr Shībó! In this case, if the top Dāntían is the center of our spiritual life, then the Lower Real Dāntían must be the center of our physical life, isn't it?") Bó-Wǔ asked with shining eyes.

"真不壞！可教！可教！這個下真丹田可是我們身體產氣與存氣之所，叫做'氣舍'。在這個地方，如果氣產的沛存的旺，那你的物理身體就會很強。所以說上丹田練性而下真丹田練命。這也是道家所說的'性命雙修'啊！" ("Really not bad! You are teachable! You are teachable! This Lower Real Dāntían is where the Qì is produced and stored and is called 'Qì Dwelling.' If you are able to produce abundant Qì and store it there, then your physical body will be very strong. Therefore, it is said 'the Upper Dāntían is for temperament cultivation while the Lower Real Dāntían is for physical life.' This is what the Daoist society says: 'the dual cultivations of physical life and spiritual life.'")

"老弟！你倒是將者性命雙修的道理說的清清楚楚啊！了不起！了不起！" ("My Old Brother! You have explained so clearly the theory of 'dual cultivation of physical life and spiritual life.' Splendid! Splendid!") Shìhǎi was so happy that Míngdào was able to explain these theories so clearly.

"可是二師伯！為什麼物理中心叫下真丹田呢？那那個地方是假丹田啊？" ("But Èr Shìbó! Why is the physical center called Lower Real Dāntían? Where is the False Dāntían?") Míng-Zhé asked.

"假丹田在肚臍下一寸半的地方。醫家叫它'氣海'，而道家也叫它作'丹爐'因為他是產丹之所。醫家叫它'氣海'因為這裡可以產氣無窮盡就像大海一樣。假丹田接近皮膚表面而真丹田卻在腹部的中心點，也就是大小腸的中心點。" ("The False Dāntían is located about one and one-half inches under your navel. Medical society calls it 'Qì Ocean' and Daoist society also calls it 'Elixir Furnace.' Medical society calls it 'Qì Ocean' because this place is able to produce unlimited Qì just like a big sea. The 'False Dāntían' is closer to the skin surface at the abdominal area while the 'Lower Real Dāntían' is deeper inside at the center of the body. This is where the center of your large and small intestines is located,") Míngdào explained.

"二師伯！我還是有點不懂。為什麼既然這丹爐可以產無窮的氣，還叫它是假丹田？" ("Èr Shìbó! I still don't understand. Since this Qì furnace is able to produce unlimited Qì, why is it still called 'False Dāntían'?") Míng-Zhé asked again.

"這是因為這假丹田雖然可以產氣，可是氣卻不能儲存到很高的地步。這是因為這假丹田是在任脈上，所以當氣產到一個階段，氣就順著任脈傳送到身體各處去了。所以這假丹田可以拿來練習達摩所說的'易筋經'，可是拿來練'洗髓經'，那就不可能了。" ("This is because though this 'False Dāntían' is able to produce Qì, it cannot store it to a very high-level. That's because this 'False Dāntían' is located on the Conception Vessel. When Qì storage reaches a certain level, it will leave the False Dāntían, enter and follow the Conception Vessel and distribute it to the entire body. Therefore, this 'False Dāntían' can be used to train Dámó's Muscle/Tendon Changing but cannot be used for Brain/Marrow Washing Qìgōng.")

Míngdào's lecture had attracted Shìhǎi's interest very much. This was because though many monks understood Muscle/Tendon Changing Qìgōng, only a few really understood Brain/Marrow Washing Qìgōng.

"老弟！我到要請教你，為什麼須要練真丹田才可以拿來洗腦髓？" ("My

Old Brother! Why do we have to train Lower Real Dāntían for Brain Washing?") Shìhǎi asked.

"大哥！因為要打開天目，你必須要練返精補腦、練氣昇華呢！如氣量存的不夠，補腦或洗腦都有問題呢？所以我以前跟您談過，練下真丹田，是胎息的一個重要階段呢。" ("Big Brother! Because if you wish to re-open the sky eye, you must train 'returning the essence to nourish the brain' and also 'train Qì for sublimation.' If the storage of Qì is not enough, then you will have a problem for both nourishing the brain and washing the brain. That's why I told you before that training Lower Real Dāntían is an important process in Embryonic Breathing Meditation.")

"二師伯！如果我想練，應該先從哪裡著手？" ("Èr Shībó! If I want to practice this, how do I begin?") Bó-Wǔ asked again. It was getting late and both Shībós would leave the next morning. He was anxious to know how he could start. Furthermore, it seemed Brain/Marrow Washing was too deep for him. He realized that even Shìhǎi Shībó did not know it very well.

"第一步，你先要練習去感覺你的泥丸宮。如果你不能感覺到這個中心，那你又如何能將你的靈神守住在這裡？你就先練習看看。你需要知道，這個不是很簡單。你必須先懂得這麼去降伏你的情魔，也就是說你的七情六慾。" ("The first step is to practice feeling your Mud-Pill-Palace. If you are not able to feel this center, how will you be able to keep your spirit there? You should practice this first and see. Also, you should know it is not easy since you must first know how to drop your emotional devil. That means your seven emotions and six desires.")

"那我就試試看！如有問題，我再請教您！" ("In this case, I will try first. If I have questions, I will ask you again.")

"明道兄！真是聽君一席話，勝讀十年書啊！希望你們三人能好好去思考裡面的深意。" ("Míngdào Brother! Listening to your few wise words is superior to studying ten years of books! Hopefully these three young men are able to ponder the deep meaning within,") Master Dù said.

"杜老弟！其實這只是道家練習胎息中的第一步，要真正的瞭解一切，還是要研習老子的道德經呢！一切胎息的竅門都在裡面呢！" ("My Dù Brother! As a matter of fact, this is only the first step of Daoist's Embryonic Breathing Meditation. If you really like to comprehend the entire theory, you must study Lǎozǐ's Dào Dé Jīng. It contains all the crucial secrets of Embryonic Breathing.")

"對道家來講，為什麼胎息是這麼的重要呢？" ("Why is Embryonic Breathing Meditation so important for Daoist practice?") Master Dù asked again.

"那時因為胎息是道家練習內丹的根基，由胎息而產聖胎，進而神通，而到最後的成仙或成佛的地步。這些修煉是俗家所沒有興趣的，而且也不是俗家在塵世裡所能做到的。所以很多道德經後的胎息文獻都藏在道觀裡而不外傳呢。" ("This is because Embryonic Breathing Meditation is the foundation of internal elixir practice in Daoist society. From Embryonic Breathing, the holy embryo is produced and further allows you to open the heaven eye (i.e., The Third Eye), and finally reach the stage of spiritual immortality or Buddhahood. These cultivations are not of any interest to outside laymen and thus cannot be seen in lay society. That's why many of the Embryonic Breathing documents developed from the Dào Dé Jīng are hidden in monasteries without ever being revealed to the outside world.")

"佛學跟道學真是高深啊！以後我們有機會再談這些。來！來！你們再練習散打給兩位師伯看看。" ("How deep of both Buddhism and Daoism! We will talk more when we have the opportunity. Come! Come! You young men practice some sparring with each other to show both Shībós,") Master Dù sighed.

Bó-Wǔ and Míng-Zhé stepped into the field and fought for about ten minutes. However, since both uncle masters had observed these two fighting each month many times now, they did not have too many new corrections or suggestions. After their fight, Bó-Wén stepped in to fight Bó-Wǔ. During the last four days of sparring with Bó-Wǔ, he had gained more experience of how to handle the situation. After he showed his greeting to the masters and then Bó-Wǔ, he initiated a fake attack. To Bó-Wǔ's surprise, he was tricked a few times by a fake attack and the punches fell into his body.

Bó-Wǔ was a little bit upset and began to attack by using his whole strength. However, Bó-Wén remained calm and either blocked or dodged every attack Bó-Wǔ initiated. After ten minutes, they stopped. It seemed that Bó-Wǔ could not defeat Bó-Wén. He also had run out of energy this time. When they came to the masters,

"我不知道為什麼我今天會敗給家兄？" ("I don't understand why I was defeated by my elder brother today,") Bó-Wǔ looked at the masters and said.

"這就要博文跟你解釋了。他今天打的很穩、沈著，還有策略。" ("Then, you need Bó-Wén to explain it to you. He fought steadily, calmly, and also had strategies today,") Master Dù said.

Bó-Wén felt great with Master Dù's compliment. He said,

"博武！這是因為在這四天我們練習中，我看清了你常用的技術，加以揣摩思考對付你的辦法。我避重就輕，這樣而已。" ("Bó-Wǔ! This is because after the last four days of practice, I have seen clearly the techniques that you commonly use. After I pondered about how to handle your techniques, I just avoided and dodged your high-level skillful attacks and focused on your weak points. That's all.")

"這真是要拳打兩不知啊！如果對方知道了你的技巧，那什麼也用不出來了。" ("How truthful it is that when two persons are matching, they should not know each other's techniques! If your opponent knows your techniques, then your applications will be useless,") Shìhǎi said with a smile.

"其實是因為博文在江湖闖盪了有些時候，他的經驗比你多呢！" ("This is because Bó-Wén has been in martial arts society for a longer period of time, so he has had more experiences than you,") Master Dù said to Bó-Wǔ.

"兩位師伯！我一直想體驗一下鐵布衫與金鐘罩功夫的不同點。不知道兩位師伯您為我開導嗎？" ("Both Shībós! I am always curious and would like to experience the difference between Iron Shirt and Golden Bell Cover Gōngfū. I wonder if both Shībós are able to show me and enlighten me?") Bó-Wén asked since he had always been so curious about these high-levels of martial skills.

"沒問題！博文。來！你打我幾拳試試看，不用客氣盡力地打。" ("No problem! Bó-Wén, come! You just strike me a few times. Don't be polite and try your best,") Shìhǎi said. He stood up and smiled as he got into horse stance. Bó-Wén stood in front of him and first showed his greeting of respect. He then firmed his root with Bow and Arrow Stance to initiate his first punch to Shìhǎi's stomach area. To his surprise, when his punch landed, he felt a sharp pain in his fist. He felt like he had hit a tree or a wall. However, Shìhǎi maintained his smile and acted as if he had felt nothing. Bó-Wén could not believe that, since his punch had at least a few hundred kilograms of impact behind it. He initiated another punch but aimed this time for Shìhǎi's chest where there were more vital areas. However, he encountered the same fate.

"大師伯！您真厲害，這每一拳都有幾百斤呢。" ("Dà Shībó! You are really awesome! Every strike that landed on your body had at least a few hundred kilograms of force.")

"其實鐵布衫功夫是根據達摩的易筋經的道理演化出來的，知道他的道理後，其實也沒有什麼大學問呢。只是道理簡單，要練成卻是不簡單。" ("As a matter of fact, Iron Shirt Gōngfū was developed and derived from Buddhi Dámó's Muscle/Tendon Changing Qìgōng. There is nothing to it after you have comprehended its theory. However, understanding theory is easy, but to practice it successfully is not simple.")

"博武有沒有跟您學這個功夫呢？" ("Does Bó-Wǔ practice this Gōngfū with you?")

"博文！我沒有教他。因為外家鐵布衫功夫的練習很陽，練到一個層次，必須練陰的洗髓經來平衡陰陽。否則，到老了，會散功的。練易筋筋鐵布衫只需要幾年，可是練洗髓經可要一二十年呢。" ("Bó-Wén! I have not taught him. This is because training external Iron Shirt Gōngfū can make the body very Yáng. After you train to a certain stage, you will need to practice Marrow/Brain Washing Qìgōng - that is the Yīn side to balance the body's Yīn and Yáng. Otherwise, once you get older, the energy can be dispersed. It may take only a few years to achieve Iron Shirt training, but it will take more than ten or even 20 years for Marrow/Brain washing training.")

"您是說易筋經的練習屬陽而洗髓經的練習屬陰，他們必須兩方都要練，才不會有散功的危險？" ("What you just said is Muscle/Tendon Changing belongs to Yáng while Marrow/Brain Washing belongs to Yīn. They must be practiced together so there is no danger of energy dispersion?") Bó-Wén asked, confirming what he heard.

"是的。可是我這鐵布衫功夫是我年紀大了才練的，不像明道的金鐘罩，他是從小就練的。所以比起明道的金鐘罩，我還差一層呢！" ("Yes. I began my Iron Shirt Gōngfū training when I was older. It is not like Míngdào's Golden Bell Cover. He started his training when he was a child. Therefore, compare to his Golden Bell Cover, I am far behind him.")

Bó-Wén was very anxious to understand and turned to Míngdào,

"二師伯！您能為我們開開眼界嗎？" ("Ér Shībó! Can you help us open our vision?")

"沒問題！來！你也打我兩拳試試看。" ("No problem! Come! You may also strike me a couple of times.") He stood up and then smiled as he assumed the Horse Stance.

Again, Bó-Wén stood with his firm stance and punched Míngdào's stomach and then chest. He felt like he was punching an air ball or a strong balloon. Though he did not feel any pain in his fist, he was bounced back a few steps both times.

"二師伯！這就奇了，我打在大師伯身上，是硬邦邦的，可是打在您身上卻是軟軟的並將我的力勁反彈了回來。" ("Ér Shībó! This is very strange! When I struck Dà Shībó's body, it was very hard. But when I struck your body, it was very soft and bounced me back powerfully.")

"博文！這就是內氣的培養了。當內氣培養到高階層，可將氣充滿身體的筋膜而將身體轉換成像氣球一樣，把對方的力勁反彈回去。" ("Bó-Wén! This is because of the cultivation of internal Qì. When internal Qì has been cultivated to a high-level, you are able to fill up Qì in body's tendons and fasciae to energize them, which will make the body respond to a strike like a balloon and bounce the coming power back.")

"我相信這比鐵布衫更難練了！當然博武也沒有練這個功夫了。" ("I believe that this training is even harder than Iron Shirt. Naturally, Bó-Wǔ may not have learned this either.")

"其實只要懂得練氣和運氣的原理，經過時間的練習，他還是可以練出來的。就只是怕沒有師父的教導，可能會'走火入魔'的呢！" ("In fact, as long as he is able to understand the training theory and method of circulating Qì, after practicing for a period of time, he can still achieve this goal. The only concern is if he does not have a qualified and experienced master's teaching, he may 'walk into the fire and enter the devil.'")

"我聽過一些練氣功的師父說過'走火入魔'。可是什麼又是'走火入魔'呢？" ("I have heard about 'walk into the fire and enter the devil' from a few Qìgōng masters in the past. But what does it mean to 'walk into the fire and enter the devil'?")

"其實很簡單，走火是氣走叉了而入魔是思慮進入了幻想魔界。初學氣功的人，練內丹氣功最怕的就是'走火入魔'呢！來！你們再練練，我跟你師父與大師伯去走走。" ("As a matter of fact, it is very easy to understand. Walk into the fire means the Qì has been led into the wrong path, and enter the devil means your thought has entered the false imagination or fantasy. To an internal Qìgōng beginner, 'walk into the fire and enter the devil' are the deviations of which they are most afraid. Come! You continue your practice. I will take a walk with your Shīfù and Dà Shībó.")

Míng-Zhé returned to the house to prepare some dinner while Bó-Wén and Bó-Wǔ started to discuss the techniques and fighting strategies.

About dusk, everyone returned to the house where Míng-Zhé had already prepared the dinner. Usually, Bó-Wǔ also helped to prepare meals, however, since his time with his brother was so limited, Míng-Zhé had told him to spend more time with his brother.

EVENING'S QUESTIONS AND ANSWERS 晚上的問答

Bó-Wén still had many questions for which he hoped he could acquire answers from both Shībós. After dinner they sat outside of the cabin, drinking tea and watching the sky gradually fading into darkness. The shining moon slowly climbed up from the edge of the mountain. It was so glowing and round. With a nice breeze on their faces, they all felt and enjoyed the soothing power of nature. This was the best time for relaxation especially after a long day of hard training.

"兩位師伯！我明天必須趕回北京，否則我會被處罰的，真希望我有更長的時間能受教於您們。" ("Both Shībós! I must rush back to Běijīng tomorrow, otherwise, I could be punished severely. I wish I could stay longer to learn from you.")

"我們佛家說的是隨緣！也許我們會再相聚的。" ("Buddhist society says, 'follow destiny!' We may have a chance to see each other again,") Shìhǎi said.

"可是我現在還有些問題想請教您們，我對這些事一直非常的迷惑呢！" ("But I still have some questions to ask you. I am still very confused about these things.")

"什麼事情讓你這麼迷惑？" ("What has made you so confused?") Míngdào asked.

"現在山東盛傳梅花拳有鐵布衫、金鐘罩的功夫，再加上道教靈符的威力，他們可以抵擋洋人的槍砲呢！很多人都跟著盲從相信呢！您們說，這是真的還是假的呢？" ("Currently, the news is widespread that martial artists of Méihuā Style have the Gōngfū of Iron Shirt and Golden Bell Cover. They claim that with additional power of Daoist Língfú (i.e., spiritual amulet), they are able to withstand being fired upon by guns and cannons. There are so many people that blindly believe it. What is your opinion? Is it true or fake?")

Míngdào could not help but laugh after he heard this question.

"這當然是假的！那有鐵布衫、金鐘罩的功夫能夠這麼簡單就練出來的？那只不過是一種欺人的伎倆。" ("Of course it is fake. How can Iron Shirt and Golden Bell Cover Gōngfū be trained so easily? It is only a trick to fool people.")

"可是二師伯，我還真真看到一些梅花拳的信徒，在貼上靈符，念上咒語後，還真的能夠挨上砍打而不疼痛呢！" ("But, Ér Shībó! I did see some disciples of Méihuā Style who, after spiritual amulet was attached to their body and with execration, could be stuck and chopped by a knife without feeling pain!")

Before Míngdào replied, Shìhǎi expressed his opinion,

"阿彌陀佛！善哉！善哉！博文，這只不過是一種心理上的催眠作用而已啊！念咒本身就是一種吹眠作用，從念咒裡潛意識得到催眠鼓舞，身體的疼痛都不會感覺到的。可是真正的拿肉體去抵抗武器槍砲，那還是不可能的。那只是一種意識上的洗腦，卻仍不能改變身體的結構的。" ("Amitabha! Good blessing! Good blessing, Bó-Wén! This is only a psychological hypnosis. Execration itself has the function of hypnosis. From execration, your subconscious mind will be invigorated, and this can trigger the body to have a dull feeling against the pain. If this is used for the fresh physical body to resist against the guns and cannons, it is still impossible. It is only a trick of the mind's being brainwashed, but it cannot change the body's real structure.") Shìhǎi looked at Bó-Wén and continued,

"博文！你知道有幾種的方法能夠洗腦改變人的思想呢？" ("Bó-Wén! Do you know how many methods can brainwash and change people's thinking?") Shìhǎi asked.

"您是說除了念咒，還有其他的方法？" ("Did you imply that other than execration, there are some other methods?")

"當然了！除了念咒、祈禱外，還有用藥物的，譬如鴉片甚至香煙呢。譬如吸食鴉片就能忘掉身體上的疼痛與心理上的悲苦。" ("Naturally! Other than execration and prayer, drugs are also commonly used such as opium or even burning incenses. For example, when you smoke opium, you may forget the pain both physically and mentally,") Míngdào said.

"二師伯！您是說燒香拜佛的香煙也是一種吹眠？" ("Ér Shībó! Did you imply that burning incense is also a kind of hypnosis?") Bó-Wǔ asked. He could not believe what he heard.

"是的！為了改變你心裡的困惱，你在佛祖面前誠心的祈禱、念咒、再加上香煙的作用，你的思想就會被改變的。問題就在你信不信，如果你相信，就靈，如果你不相信，那就不靈了。" ("Yes! In order to change your troublesome mind, you would pray and chant in front of Buddha. With the help of burning incenses, your thought will be changed. The question is, do you really believe? If you believe, it is effective, and if you don't believe, it will not work as effectively,") Míngdào continued his explanation.

"所以說嘛！任何事成功不成功否，就要看你如何去建立你的思想與信心了。其實就是因為這些問題，我才會跟明道認識的。我們常為這些問題，以道家、佛家不同的觀點去探討啊！" ("That's why the success of any task depends on how you establish your thinking and confidence. It was also because of these questions, I got acquainted with Míngdào. We often discussed these topics from different viewpoints, Daoist's and Buddhist's,") Shìhǎi added.

"你也知道，要控制一個人，最重要的是控制他的思想。思想控制住了，你要他死，他都會情願的，這就是一種洗腦的功用啊！" ("As you also know, in order to control a person, the most important thing is to control his thinking. Once his thinking is controlled, even if you want him to die, he will do it willingly. This is the function of brainwashing,") Míngdào said.

"那麼說洗腦都是壞的？" ("Does that mean all brainwashes are bad?")

"那也不見得，那要看洗腦的目的是什麼？如果洗腦是用來控制或愚弄他人，那是邪惡的。可是如果洗腦念咒去幫忙自己建立信心，去解脫心裡上的困惱，那是正派的。" ("No, not necessarily! It all depends on what is the purpose of the brainwashing. If you use brainwashing to control and abuse other people, then it is evil. However, if you use chanting to brainwash yourself to establish your confidence, or to dissolve the psychologically disturbing thought, then it is righteous.")

"二師伯！您是說如果我用唸咒，我就可以改變我潛意識的概念與感應。譬如說，我常念佛，經過一段時間後，我就信佛的存在與佛的神力。從這個信念我的想法就不一樣了。" ("Ér Shībó! Are you saying if I use chanting, I can change my subconscious thinking and feeling? For example, if I chant the name of Buddha, after a period of time I will believe the Buddha's existence and his power. From this thought, my deep thinking will be different.")

"沒錯！博文。" ("That is correct, Bó-Wén!")

"謝謝兩位師伯！現在我才知道梅花拳怎麼用念咒、貼靈符去洗腦並左右他們的隨從者。我這一趟來峨嵋山這是不虛此行了。" ("Thank you, both Shībós! Now I understand how Méihuā Style martial artists were able to use execration and the amulet to brainwash their followers. I really did not waste my time making this trip to Éméi Mountain.")

FAREWELL 辭行

Early the next morning after breakfast, Míng-Zhé gave Bó-Wén some dried food he had prepared for him. Bó-Wén was ready to leave.

"大哥！謝謝您來看我，您保重。請代我向奶奶、爹、娘請安。" ("Dàgē! Thank you for coming to see me. Please take care of yourself. Please give grandma, dad, and mom my respect and greeting for me.") When Bó-Wǔ said it, his eyes were red and shining with tears.

"博武！你也要自己保重。好好練習，更上一層樓。我會告訴奶奶、爹、娘你很好。" ("Bó-Wǔ! You too take care of yourself. Practice harder and advance to the next level. I will tell grandma, dad, and mom that you are great!")

Then, he turned to Master Dù,

"杜師伯！謝謝您的教導。更謝謝您照顧教導博武，我替我爹、娘跟您拜謝了。" ("Dù Shībó! Thank you for your teaching. Thank you more for looking after and teaching Bó-Wǔ. I thank you deeply for my parents as well.") He knelt down to the ground in the martial gesture of respect. Master Dù picked him up from ground,

"博文！代我向你奶奶、爹、娘問安。告訴他們博武會在四年後回來。"
("Bó-Wén! Please give my greeting to your grandma, dad, and mom. Tell them that Bó-Wǔ will return after four more years.")

Finally, Bó-Wén faced Shìhǎi and Míngdào,

"兩位師伯！謝謝您們的教導。您們保重，希望後會有期。雖然我們只相處了一天，可是我的受惠卻是一生的。" ("Both Shībós! Thank you very much for your teaching. Please take care of yourselves. I hope we are able to meet again. Though we were only together for one day, the benefits I received from you will last my whole life.") Again, he knelt down to the ground in a final, respectful farewell.

"大哥！我送您一程到九寨溝鎮。" ("Dàgē! Allow me to keep you company till Jiǔzhàigōu Town,") Bó-Wǔ said.

They talked and walked. After two hours, they arrived at Jiǔzhàigōu Town.

"博武！你留步吧，好好保重。" ("Bó-Wǔ! You may stop here. Take care of yourself.")

Bó-Wǔ was sad to see his brother's departure. After the visit from his brother, his feeling of homesickness got worse. It was all he could do to concentrate his mind on his training. He still had trouble calming his emotional mind and leading the Qì to Mud-Pill-Palace. This was the first step to stabilizing his mind so his spirit could stay at the residence.

SAY GOOD-BYE TO MASTER DU 拜別杜師父

A couple of days before Bó-Wǔ's 22nd birthday, Master Dù told him,

"博武！我跟你爹約定的十年再兩天就到了，你可以開始準備你的行程了。" ("Bó-Wǔ! The ten-year's time that I promised to your father will arrive in two days. You may begin to pack and get ready for your journey home.")

"'師父！以前我很想家，可是現在時間快到了，我真是依依不捨啊！師父，您的教導，我畢生難忘，我會永遠記住師父的教導。師父！我有個請求。我能不能多待三天，在這月十五日後再離開，我想跟兩位師伯告別呢！" ("Shīfù! I missed home very much in the past. But now when time gets closer, I am really reluctant to leave you. Shīfù! I will forever remember your teaching. Shīfù! I have a request. Can I stay three more days and leave after the 15th of this month? I would like to say goodbye to two Shībós.")

"我相信你的爹、娘不會為了多幾天而惦記你的。你就待到師伯們來後再走吧！" ("I believe your dad and mom will not mind a few more days. You may stay till your Shībós' arrival.")

"謝謝師父！這幾天裡，我還要多謝謝明哲兄這十年內他對我的照顧。他一直當我是他的小弟看待我呢。" ("Thank you, Shīfù! I would also like to thank brother Míng-Zhé for taking care of me the last ten years. He has always treated me as his younger brother.")

"博武！你走後，我不會太寂寞的。我已經與沈媒婆說好一門明哲的親事，我想他在近期內，會結婚的呢。女方是九寨溝菜市場，張彤新的女兒。她時常幫他爹、娘在市場賣菜，跟明哲照面了幾次，我知道他們互相是挺喜歡的。" ("Bó-Wǔ! I will not be too lonely after you are gone. I have already arranged a match for Míng-Zhé through matchmaker, Mrs. Shěn. I think he will get married soon. The lady is the daughter of Zhāng, Tóng-Xīn, working in the Jiǔzhàigōu vegetable market. She often helped her parents sell vegetables and has met Míng-Zhé a few times. I know they like each other very much.")

"那明哲兄，他知道嗎？" ("Does brother Míng-Zhé know this?")

"我昨晚跟他說了，他還挺高興的呢！" ("I told him last night and he was very happy about it.")

***

Five days later, as usual, Shìhǎi and Míngdào came to visit. Bó-Wǔ was very emotional since he had been treated by them more like a grandson and Bó-Wǔ treated them like his grandpas.

"兩位師伯！請您們保重，希望我們後會有期。" ("Both Shībós! Please take care of yourselves. I hope we are able to meet again.")

"博武！你自己保重，你已經不是小孩子了，你師父，明道，和我年紀都大了，還不知道以後我們能再見面嗎？" ("Bó-Wǔ! You take care of yourself. You are not a child anymore. Your Shīfù, Míngdào, and I are old now. We still don't know if we will meet again,") Shìhǎi said.

"博武！你好好繼續練習。這是我隨身攜帶的道德經手抄本，就送給你作留念。好好的研習它。" ("Bó-Wǔ! Continue your hard practice. This is the handwritten manuscript of Dào Dé Jīng that I carry with me all the time. I give you this manuscript as a souvenir. Study it diligently,") Míngdào said.

Bó-Wǔ knelt down to the ground and gave the three masters three bows to thank them.

***

The night before Bó-Wǔ's departure,

"博武！你回去時，由重慶先搭船到上海，再由上海轉海輪到青島市，由青島市轉陸路回到泰安市。你這樣走法有兩個原因。一是由四川到青島市走水路比較快。二是我有兩件事想麻煩你。" ("Bó-Wǔ! When you return to your home, you should take a river ship from Chóngqìng to Shànghǎi, then sea ship from Shànghǎi to Qīngdǎo City. After that, travel on land from Qīngdǎo City to Tàiān City. There are two reasons for traveling this way. First, it is faster to Qīngdǎo City across the water. Second, I have two things to request of you.") said Master Dù.

"師父！您有什麼事，請儘管吩咐。" ("Shīfù! What things do you want me to do? Please tell me.")

"你到青島市時，第一到我老家傳個信，告訴我家人，我一切安好。第二，我有一位在青島市的好友，陳進隆。在我十年前回山東去拜訪他時，提起釋海師伯的書法與畫畫，他希望釋海師伯能為他寫些字與畫個畫給他呢。這裡是釋海師伯的字畫，請你也幫我送給他，了了我一個心願。" ("When you arrive in Qīngdǎo City, first, go to my home and tell my family that I am all okay. Second, I have a good friend, Chén, Jìn-Lóng, in Qīngdǎo City. When I returned to Shāndōng ten years ago, I went to visit him and mentioned about Shìhǎi Shībó's calligraphy and painting. He hoped that Shìhǎi Shībó would be able to write some calligraphy and paint a painting for him. Here are Shìhǎi Shībó's calligraphy and painting. Please give them to him so my promise to him is completed.")

"師父放心！這兩件事我一定做到。" ("Shīfù! You have my assurance. I will complete these two things.")

The next morning, Bó-Wǔ said good-bye to everyone and left with tears and also excitement. He was going home.

CHAPTER 2
AMBITION OF POWERFUL
COUNTRIES
列 強 的 野 心

HONG KONG BRITISH HIGH-LEVEL CABINET MEETING 香港英國內閣 高階層會議

On Monday, June 14th of 1897, the British Governor, Sir William Robinson, was sitting in front of a large oval meeting table in the conference room of the British Hong Kong Governor's Building. He had spent almost the whole afternoon the day before thinking about how to handle this cabinet meeting and make it more successful. The British held these high-level meetings quarterly to review how well past policies were carried out, and to discuss current problems and solutions. Naturally, they also needed to set up the development of future strategies.

Behind him on the wall was a large portrait of Queen Alexandrina Victoria. From the windows of the meeting room, you could see a number of small Chinese barge boats and a few large foreign ships in the port of Hong Kong. The temperature was extremely hot today. It was only 9 o'clock in the morning, but the thermometer had already risen to 35 degrees Centigrade.

There was a total of 12 persons at this meeting, including four high-ranking British officials and one Royal British envoy who had just arrived in Hong Kong from London a week earlier. On Governor Robinson's right was Sir Henry Arthur Blake who would take over the position of the British Hong Kong Governor next year. Another high-ranking British officer, Sir George William Des Voeux, was sitting on the left side of Governor Robinson. Sir Des Voeux was the governor's right-hand man. He had been in China for more than 20 years and knew almost all the developments and inter-relationships between the Chinese Government and all the powerful nations that had business in China. He was an 'Old China Hand' and spoke fluent Cantonese and Mandarin.

First, Governor Robinson stood up. "Gentlemen, first I would like to welcome you all to this meeting, especially those five gentlemen who just arrived last week. Second, I want to remind you that all that the contents of this meeting should be kept to ourselves. Please don't discuss anything with outside people." He paused for a moment to see if everyone was paying attention. Then he continued,

"As usual, Sir Des Voeux will give you a briefing. To help those who just arrived, he will first summarize the history of China's past since the First Opium War in 1839 until the present. After his brief summary, as usual, we will review and verify if the policies we made in the past were effectively carried out. Then, we will discuss the current situation in China and decide whether or not the new policies are able to handle these changes." He sat down and Sir Des Voeux stood up.

"Good morning! For those of you who do not know me, I am Sir Des Voeux. I have been in China for more than 20 years. I am aware of almost all of the past history of China and the conflicts between the Qīng Government and other powerful foreign nations. This historical summary will be brief. After that, I will update you on the current problems and developments." He looked at the faces of everyone sitting around the meeting table. Then, he continued,

"As you probably know, after the Qīng lost The First Opium War with Britain, from 1839 to 1842, the Treaty of Nánjīng (南京條) was signed. When the Treaty of Nánjīng was signed, it forced the Qīng Government to open its gates, allowing Britain to have free commercial trading rights in China.

"In addition, the Qīng Government ceded to the British Empire in perpetuity. Since then, Hong Kong has become our colony.

"Two years later, after seeing the commercial benefits Britain received from China, the United States also forced the Qīng Government to sign the Treaty of Wàngxià (望廈條約) and demanded the same treatment and conditions that Britain had received from China. Three months after, following this action by the United States, the French Government also demanded the same treatments as Britain and the United States, and thus the Treaty of Huángpǔ (黃浦條約) was signed. Since then, many European countries compete with each other to do business in the Chinese market.

"Then, in 1856, Britain, France, Russia, and Japan combined forces to initiate The Second Opium War. This war lasted till 1860. During this period, China was forced to sign the Treaty of Tiānjīn (天津條約) which allowed all four nations to establish individual territories and embassies in Běijīng. It also gave permission to missionaries to preach religion in China without restrictions. Our government also forced the Qīng Government to cede Kowloon (九龍) to us. The most important benefit we received, however, was that from this war we acquired the legal right to sell opium in China. Since then, the sale of opium in China increased from 40,000 chests annually in 1842 to 60,000 chests in 1860. The number of opium imports has continued to grow until now. This has benefitted the British economy significantly.

"The Russian Government also used this opportunity to occupy a huge portion of northern China. However, that treaty did not satisfy the Russian's aggressive ambition so under their demand, the Treaty of Àihún (瓊琿條約) between Russia and China was signed. That treaty allowed Russia to take control of 60,000 square miles of land between the north of Hēilóng River (黑龍江) and the south of Xìng'ān Mountain (興安嶺).

"Next, Britain and China signed another treaty in 1876, Yāntái Treaty (煙台條約). This treaty opened the gate that allowed Britain to expand their right to enter the Chinese west and south areas. Seeing the additional benefit Britain had received, again, Russia demanded yet another treaty, the Treaty of Yīlí (伊犁條約) in 1881, that allowed Russia to expand their northern Chinese territory further south.

"Later, in 1885, the war between France and China (中法戰爭) took place over Chinese protection of Vietnam against the French occupancy. After China lost the war, a Peace Treaty between China and France (中法和約) was signed that allowed the French Government to control Vietnam.

"The most recent event was from 1894 to 1895 between Japan and China. In order to protect Korea from Japanese invasion, the war between China and Japan was initiated. After China lost the war, the Treaty of Mǎguān (馬關條約) was signed between China and Japan. In this treaty, besides receiving a large compensation from China, Japan also took complete control over Korea, Táiwān and Okinawa." After his long briefing, Sir Des Voeux took a mouthful of the tea in front of him.

"Do you have any questions about this brief summary of past history in China?" he asked.

One of new officials asked,

"Sir Des Voeux, since China was so weak and corrupt, I wonder why our government did not have a policy for turning China, like India, into our colony? In that case, we would have the entire control of China, instead of sharing it with other countries."

"Honestly, yes. We did think about it and also wanted to do so. That was why, right after The First Opium War in 1842, we tried to control China exclusively and did not want to coordinate or cooperate with any other nations. Later, our government realized that the Chinese political condition was not the same as in India. The Chinese central government had a high-level of authority. Under Emperor Dàoguāng's authority, China's central government was able to effectively control the entire country at that time. It was not like India, where the whole country was divided into many different parties. There, it was much easier for us to use one party to subdue another and finally bring all of them under our control. Furthermore, France, Russia, the United States, and some other countries would not have been happy if China had become a British colony at that time. That was the reason we changed our policy."

"Then what was the new policy that our government adopted?" the royal special envoy asked. He had to be clear on the past history of governmental policies so that he would be able to report to the Queen and offer any advice for the future.

"When other powerful nations realized the advantages to be gained in China, then they all wanted to have a part of it. Therefore, these other countries were searching for excuses to start a war with China. That triggered The Second Opium War, and after the war in 1860, different treaties were signed, and more rights and advantages were received from the Qīng Government. As I said earlier, Russia used that opportunity to occupy a big portion of northern China. Since then till now, we have had to share this remaining Chinese land and huge market with other nations."

"If I may ask, other than France, Russia, and the Japanese, how many other powerful countries are also competing with us for this market?" the envoy inquired.

"There are seven, the United States, Germany, Italy, the Netherlands, Spain, Belgium, and Austria-Hungary."

"Among these countries, which ones are our allies? Do they cooperate with us or do they choose their own policies independently?"

another new official asked.

"Well! Among these countries, other than France, the ones we have the most concern about are Russia, Japan, Germany, and the United States. These four countries are aggressively competing with us. The other five, Italy, Netherlands, Spain, Belgium, and Austria-Hungary are not a threat to our market at all. However, we have to watch Russian, Japanese, and German ambitions closely. In order to cooperate and coordinate with each other, we also hold meetings with the other countries twice a year and discuss our coordination and co-operation. By the way, let me just remind you that our next European Alliance Coordination Meeting will be held on October 15th this year."

"What is the current situation of our market in China?" asked one of the officials who was more interested in that topic.

"Well! In the occupancy of territory in China, Russia is the most aggressive and has occupied the most land. As to the commercial market, we are still the major import and export country in China."

"Can you please tell us the marketing history from the past to the present in China? This will help me ponder the new strategy today. Thank you," the economic advisor asked.

"As you already know, China was our main supplier of tea, silk, and porcelain to Britain. Roughly speaking, just for tea we consumed nearly 30,000,000 pounds annually in Britain in 1830. Importing tea from China was a crucial source of tax revenue for our government. While at the same time, China only imported clocks, watches, music boxes and small quantities of these kinds of items. Because of this trade imbalance, China earned a lot of money from British exports. Later, around 1839, many British businessmen had access to opium produced in India and began to smuggle opium to China. These opium exports had become a means for the British Government to raise taxes. Therefore, more and more opium was imported into China and the Chinese population rapidly became increasingly addicted to the drug. This upset the Qīng Emperor, Dàoguāng. He gave an order to confiscate more than 20,000 chests of opium in Hong Kong and burn them. This triggered The First Opium War and The Second Opium War. The main reason for the wars was to liberalize the opium trade with China. After China was defeated, the opium market was wide open for our business and Hong Kong became the 'free trade' nexus of the East. This also encouraged United States opium traders and merchant bankers to open business in China."

"How about other import businesses? Are they still active?" one official asked.

"Yes, we imported cotton from India and other non-essential European goods such as watches and clocks. The major trade now is opium. And as I said, the United States is our strongest competitor currently. Somehow, they have found sources for opium supplies from Turkey and India. The problem now is that, due to their addiction to opium, the Chinese general public does not have the money to buy any other goods from us except opium."

Everyone was quiet for a while. They knew that Britain had successfully expanded their territories and colonized many parts of the world. It seemed that now China would be the next victim, not to become a colony, but an opium slavery country.

"What other matters should we be aware of right now?" the envoy asked.

"Well!" Sir Des Voeux answered, "There is some new development, especially in the Shāndōng Province area. Since the Qīng Court has been so afraid of the powerful foreign nations, especially under so many treaties, they haven't dared to interfere with any of the activities of those nations. There are three main groups of Christians preaching and spreading around China. These three groups are Protestants, Russkaja Pravoslavnaja Tserkov (Russian Orthodox Church), and also Catholics. Among them, Catholicism is the biggest and has spread over almost all of south-east China. As you already know, the missionaries of the Catholic Church come from a range of European countries. These three groups are also competing with each other. In their preaching, they discriminate against traditional Chinese Buddhism and Daoism. However, in order to absorb more believers, almost all of the churches accept new members without considering what kind of people they are. This means that new members include many Chinese gangsters who, under the protection of the churches, cause disturbances and even take lands from farmers illegally and forcibly. Since the Qīng Government was afraid to upset the foreign churches, they did nothing to resolve the problem. Because of that, in 1894 a large number of martial artists formed an organization called the Broadsword Society (大刀會). Their mission was to protect farmers from gangsters and to help their local governments maintain peace. In the beginning, their activities were endorsed by the local governor. Later they began to attack churches to retaliate against the aggressive attacks of Christian gangsters. Finally, under the protests of both German and French ministers, the Shāngdōng Governor decided to suppress the Broadsword Society's activities. After he arrested their two leaders and executed them, the public activities of this society ceased. This suppression of the Broadsword Society encouraged more Chinese Christian gangsters' aggression against the local farmers. The situation has continued to worsen every day. Actually, it is estimated that there have been more than 400 cases of conflicts between farmers and churches in the last three years."

"May I ask, which churches have encountered the most conflict?"

"German and French churches in Shāndōng Province. Unfortunately, the conflicts between churches and farmers has also spread to other provinces. The hostility of the farming communities against all of the churches has spread to all of China now, including the capital of Běijīng."

"What are the possible developments in the future? Sir Des Voeux, do you think we and other countries need to send troops to Běijīng to protect our diplomatic officers and their families?"

"Yes, if the situation continues to get worse, and I believe it will. I personally believe that the German Government's failure to stop their churches' aggression was intentional. As I see it, they were always waiting and searching for excuses to start a war against China so they could use it as a reason to occupy some Chinese territories. We have to wait and see how it develops."

"What is the updated situation in the Qīng Government?" the envoy asked again.

"When Emperor Guāngxù turned 18 years old, officially he took over power from Empress Dowager Cíxǐ. In reality, according to our intelligence agent's report, Cíxǐ was still in charge. Last year, Emperor Guāngxù planned to build a strong naval force to defend his country. However, it seemed that Empress Dowager Cíxǐ wanted to use the money to repair her damaged garden instead."

"Is Emperor Guāngxù a good and wise emperor?"

"Yes! But his hands are tied up. He does not have any real power in his hands while Empress Dowager Cixi is still alive."

"What is our current policy, Sir Des Voeux?" one member asked.

"As far as I know, we wait and watch further developments closely. The opium trade market is still to our advantage, so we should maintain our favorable situation."

Governor Robinson stood up,

"Gentlemen! Now you know the past and understand the current situation. Just a reminder to you that we will have a meeting with the other nations on October 15th. We will want to find out what their decisions are."

EUROPEAN ALLIANCE COORDINATION MEETING 歐盟協調會

Members of this alliance, Britain, France, Germany, Spain, the Netherlands, Italy, Belgium, and Austria-Hungary were all assembled in a Hong Kong Government's conference room. Occasionally, members from the United States, Japan, and Russia were also invited to discuss problems if there were some matters related to them. However, unless it was necessary, usually only United States diplomats participated in these meetings. In addition to all these officials and diplomatic officers, a representative of the British East India Company (EIC) (英國東印度公司) was also invited. This company had received permission from Queen Elizabeth I on December 31st of 1600 to have special trading privileges in India. Now it was the biggest importer and exporter of goods in and out of China. Another special person who was invited was a local Bishop and representative of the Vatican. He was invited for this presentation because the number of conflicts between Chinese people and churches had increased significantly in just the last couple of years.

In this meeting, other than British Governor Robinson, his two right-hand men, Sir Henry Arthur Blake and Sir George William Des Voeux, and a few selected officials represented Britain. Since all of the diplomats spoke English, no translation was necessary.

On the day of the meeting, October 15th of 1897, the weather was gloomy and it seemed that rain would come soon. The atmosphere in the conference room, just like the weather, was somber as well. All the diplomats from every country had their own country's interests in mind. Glory and dignity were their first concerns.

First, Governor Robinson stood up at one end of the large oval conference table. It was maybe a little bit crowded today, but still comfortable.

"First, I would like to welcome all of you to this meeting. As usual, I hope this meeting can provide us with a productive future and benefits. I would like my right-hand man, Sir George William Des Voeux, to preside over this meeting. He will first explain the current situations in China, and then we will discuss possible solutions. After that, if you have any other questions that need to be discussed, please don't hesitate to bring them up." After he sat down, Sir Des Voeux stood up.

"Basically, there are a few issues that we need to discuss. First, how do we restrain ourselves from occupying more of China's land? Second, what policy can we take regarding Russian and Japanese aggressive occupancy of Chinese territories? Third, how do we handle the farmers' riots against the churches, especially in Shāndōng Province? Last, how do we protect our diplomats and their families working in China, and also those Christian missionaries in China," Sir Des Voeux said.

"Why do we have to restrain ourselves from taking over Chinese land? Britain has long been colonizing the world. Now, Russia and Japan have also taken Chinese land piece by piece. Why don't we divide China and share it?" one of the German diplomats replied. This placed the British officials in an awkward situation, since it was true that Britain had more than 100 colonies around the world.

"The problem is that if all of the world powers intend to take over Chinese land, it will trigger conflicts among us and wars will be inevitable. If we maintain Chinese authority, we will have unlimited economic profits and sharing in this land," Sir Des Voeux replied.

"I don't believe Russia and Japan will agree to this restriction. As you have seen, Russia has already occupied nearly one-fifth of China's northern lands, and Japan, after the First Sino-Japanese War two years ago, also aggressively demanded the Qīng Government cede Táiwān, Okinawa, and Korea to them. I believe this problem will remain unless we are able to convince Russia and Japan to agree. And as we know, Russia and Japan have been competing to acquire land in Chinese Manchurian territory. I think a conflict between Russia and Japan is inevitable in the near future," a French diplomat said.

The discussion continued. Some countries, such as Belgium, the Netherlands, and Austria-Hungary, agreed, since they did not have the same amount of power as some other strong countries in this competition. However, France and Germany did not agree to this proposal since they were searching for excuses to invade China again. Spain and America remained neutral. After an hour of argument, there was no final decision made. Finally, they agreed to restrain themselves as much as possible and at the same time sent a memorandum to both the Russian and Japanese embassies regarding their discussion. They hoped through this effort, Russian and Japanese aggression toward China could be eased.

"Now," Sir Des Voeux brought up the next issue on the agenda, "let's talk about strategies and policies of how to handle the increasing riots and violence against our missionaries and their followers. As I understand it, due to the competition between the three Christian groups, **Protestants**, Russkaja Pravoslavnaja Tserkov (Russian Orthodox Church), and also Catholics, all of the churches have accepted their followers with no restrictions. Consequently, many Chinese gangsters have joined these churches in order to gain their protection while they conduct illegal and improper acts against farmers. Under the support of local martial artists, the Broadsword Society, farmers formed a resistance group to repel the Chinese Christian gangsters' aggression. Though under French and German demands the Broadsword Society was suppressed, due to the fact that aggressions by the Chinese Christian gangsters are getting more serious, this may trigger a bigger problem in the near future. Actually, the number of attacks against foreign missionaries, and hostility against foreign civilians and diplomats, has increased rapidly over the last couple of years."

"Well! It seems that this issue has to be solved by those countries who have missionaries here in China. If the churches belonged to the Vatican, then it has to be decided by the Vatican," an American diplomat said.

"Yes, that is the reason that you are here and also that the Vatican's local representative was invited here," Sir Des Voeux replied.

"I believe that this matter must be dealt with by both sides, the Qīng Court and the churches. We should warn the Qīng Court about the possible consequences if they do not find a way to solve the problem. Not only that, we have to urge all of the churches to reject those troublesome Chinese Christian gangsters," the Belgium diplomat suggested.

"We can notify the Qīng Court, but the churches and all relevant countries must set policies together about this. After this meeting, we will send a notification to the Qīng Government and see what their reaction is," Sir Des Voeux said. He paused for a while, then continued,

"We still have the last issue that we need to discuss. That is, if the riot enlarges and this situation gets worse, how do we protect our citizens, diplomats, and missionaries?"

"If the Qīng Court does not have a good solution or just does nothing, this will give us a reasonable excuse to send our troops to China. However, we must first wait for their response. In addition, we must receive their permission to send our troops into Běijīng to protect our diplomats. After all, Běijīng is their capital. If we enter without permission, war will be inevitable," the German diplomat said.

Since no one had a better suggestion, they agreed to take no further action until hearing the Qīng Court's response.

CHAPTER 3
AN UNKNOWN DESTINY
一個未知的命運

MISSIONARY - PIERRE GIGOT 傳教士 - 披爾。冀冀

On a sunny morning, aboard the deck of the cargo vessel El Dorado owned by Jardine, Matheson & Co., stood Father Pierre Gigot. Pierre was a 22-year-old recently ordained priest, who felt so very lucky that he was chosen to serve God in the Catholic Church in China. He had heard a lot about this mysterious oriental country but did not know much about this new culture. However, in his adventurous mind, he was pretty confident that he would be happy there and would serve God well. He did not have any idea what to expect when he arrived at Jìnán County, Shāndōng Province, China (中國山東濟南府). There was only one thing that made him a little bit worried. It was that his Chinese Mandarin was still poor, as he had had only eight months to train for this mission before his departure.

Father Pierre Gigot's traveling companion, Father Benjamin Jessen, was still very sick after last night's storm and was in bed. Father Jessen was not as happy as Pierre, since he did not like to travel long distances at his age. He was nearly 55 years old and he did not care too much for adventure. He had been in China four years ago and this was his second trip there.

It would be another week or so before they reached India, Jawaharlal Nehru Port. The vessel would dock there for five days to unload and load goods. After that, this vessel would sail for Hong Kong.

Once Pierre felt peaceful and calm, a few memories emerged from within his mind.

LEFT HOME FOR VATICAN 離家到梵蒂岡

"Pierre, mon enfant. Ton père et moi avons pris la décision de t'envoyer au Vatican pour devenir un prêtre. Tu sais que nous avons huit enfants dans la famille et il est devenu de plus en plus difficile pour ton père de supporter l'ensemble de la famille. Puisque tu es le plus jeune garçon, nous pensons que tu es le meilleur choix." ("Pierre, my child. Your father and I have made a decision to send you to the Vatican to be a priest. You know, we have eight kids in the family and it has become harder and harder for your father to support the entire family. Since you are the youngest boy, we think you are the best choice.") Pierre's mom, Diane, looked at him with some sadness and solemnity.

"Mais maman! J'ai seulement 10 ans et je ne veux pas vous quitter." ("But Mom! I am only ten years old and I don't want to leave you.") Pierre looked at his mom with tearful eyes. He couldn't believe that his parents were giving him away to the church to become a priest.

"Pierre! Mon pauvre enfant. Tu es toujours celui qui nous écoute, ton père et moi. Je suis si réticente de te laisser partir. Mais tu le sais, la condition de la famille n'est pas très bonne, surtout du fait de la maladie de ton père. Tu dois aider la famille. Je crois que ta vie comme missionnaire sera paisible, calme et plus heureuse. C'est mieux que de souffrir ici de la pauvreté de la famille." ("Pierre! My poor child. You are always the one who listens to your father and me. I am so reluctant to let you go. But you know, the condition of the family is not great, especially with your father's sickness. You need to help the family. I believe life as a missionary will be peaceful, calm, and happier for you. It is better than suffering here from the family's poverty.") Diane extended both her hands to hold Pierre's and looked at him with red eyes.

"Maman, j'ai peur! Je ne suis jamais parti de la maison, je ne suis jamais allé loin. Le Vatican est à Rome, en Italie. C'est très loin d'ici. Je ne veux pas partir maman. Maman, je t'en prie. S'il te plaît, ne m'envoie pas," ("Mom, I am scared! I have never been away from home or gone to faraway places. The Vatican is in Rome, Italy. It is very far away. I don't want to go, Mom. Please, Mom! Please don't send me away,") Pierre continued to beg.

"Tu sais Pierre, servir Dieu est un honneur qui t'apportera de la gloire. Il y a tant d'enfants sur la liste d'attente. De plus, nous recevrons de l'église une compensation financière généreuse. J'ai parlé hier au Père Nocolas Thomas. Il t'a bien aimé et a dit qu'il serait très heureux de te recommander comme candidat pour le Vatican. C'est une opportunité rare, Pierre! Si tu fais cela, tu n'apporteras pas seulement un grand honneur à la famille, mais aussi l'argent que nous recevrons nous permettra de payer un médecin. Tu sais, la maladie de ton père..." ("You know, Pierre, serving God is an honor and will bring you glory. There are so many children on the waiting list. Furthermore, we will receive a handsome financial compensation from the church. I talked to Father Nocolas Thomas yesterday. He really liked you and said he would be very happy to recommend you as a candidate for the Vatican. This opportunity is rare, Pierre! If you do this, you will not just bring great honor to the family, but also the money we receive will allow us to be able to afford a doctor. You know, your father's sickness ...") She could not help but cry out loud.

Pierre stepped forward and hugged his mom tightly. He felt this hug was particularly precious since he did not know how many more times he was going to be able to hug his mother.

"Maman! Je t'en prie, ne pleure pas. J'irais maman ! Je t'en prie, ne pleure pas," ("Mom! Please don't cry. I will go, Mom! Please don't cry,") Pierre cried out.

On June 2nd of 1878, Pierre left the Port of Le Havre, Cedex, with Father Thomas. There were two other boys with them. It took them three days of sailing to arrive in Naples, Italy.

After their arrival at the Vatican, though all of the priests treated the newcomers very well and there was always plenty of food, the life of training in the Vatican made Pierre feel like a puppet. They had to follow the daily routines and disciplines strictly. It was not like the way of life as a farmer in France. However, he knew he was supposedly training to be a missionary when he graduated. He tried very hard to rise above his childish thinking and restrain his behavior.

Other than routine worship to God, Jesus Christ, and other holy divinities, he had to learn all the lessons required to be a priest including languages such as Latin, English, Spanish, and German. He also needed to learn about different cultures and the history of various countries. Life was busy and soon he had been at the Vatican for six years.

FATHER'S PASSING 父親的死亡

One day in the fall, after the routine morning worship service, Pierre was called in to see Bishop Bruno, who was also his English teacher. Pierre did not know if he had been summoned because of something he had done wrong. Still wondering, he knocked on the Bishop's office door. The Bishop asked him to enter.

"Pierre, my child! I have bad news for you. We just received a telegraph that your father passed away yesterday."

Pierre was frozen for a moment by this shocking news, and then tears rushed out from his eyes. Though his father had always been solemn and not as close to him as his mother, this was still a shock to him.

"Father Bruno, how did it happen? He was still young," Pierre asked.

"According to the telegraph, he caught a cold and then it turned into pneumonia. He died of a lung infection."

Now Pierre began to worry about his mother, and he didn't know how the family would be able to deal with this new situation. From a few letters he had received in the past, he knew that his elder brother had begun to work for a land holder. So financially there was no problem for the family's survival.

"You mother wishes for you to return home for a week or so. She misses you and wants to see you," Father Bruno continued.

"I miss her very much too, Father Bruno. But am I allowed to go home for a short visit?"

"I spoke with Archdeacon Colombo this morning; he has granted you a short leave of absence. He said there was a Bishop, Father Martin, who would be traveling to France in the next couple of days and you may go with him. But you have to come back by yourself."

***

This was Pierre's first home visit in his entire six-year stay. In one way he was excited, but in another way, he was sad and felt somewhat lost. When he was on the homeward vessel that carried him and Father Martin, he was attracted by some beautiful young ladies wearing elegant dresses. He felt like talking to them and getting to know them. He was 16 years old and did not know why he was so attracted and interested in beautiful young ladies. One morning on the deck, he felt somewhat embarrassed when he was staring at one young girl about his age, and Father Martin came to the deck and noticed the scene. When Pierre noticed that Father Martin was looking at him, his face turned flushed. He felt so shy and embarrassed.

"Father Martin! Is it a sin to look at beautiful ladies?" Pierre asked.

"Of course not, my child! It is normal for your age. You are becoming a young adult. However, since we have committed ourselves to serve our Lord, we should not be tempted or allured by this type of imagination."

"But I feel depressed sometimes when I think of it. I also feel so sinful every time. How do I deal with this problem, Father Martin?"

"You should pray to God to give you strength to control your desire."

"But I don't know why, the more I pray, the more I become confused."

"Yes, I know. This is the first huge obstacle to becoming a priest." Father Martin looked at this innocent child with merciful eyes since he also went through the same questions and emotional confusion. Now he was nearly 60 years old, and though he could control his emotional desire, he also felt like he was a machine without too much self-inner-feeling or freedom. However, he could not tell that to this young teen. He knew this poor young man would struggle with these thoughts for a long time.

"When time passes, you will get used to it and it will become easier for you to control," he tried to comfort this future priest.

***

The next morning, Pierre woke up early. He had not been able to sleep the whole night. He was so confused by the differences between what the church doctrines taught, and his own deep, inner feelings. He still did not know which was the right way that he should follow. While Father Martin was still sleeping, he went up onto the deck. He had always been attracted to the big seas and oceans, so wide and often so peaceful. When he was standing on the deck and watching the sun rising in the east, he felt moved that it was so beautiful and relaxing. While he was watching,

"Good morning, Father. It is so beautiful, isn't it?" a voice behind him said.

When Pierre turned his head, he saw a beautiful young lady wearing a nice elegant dress was smiling at him.

"Oh! Good morning, Madam. I am not a Father yet. I am still a student at the Vatican," Pierre smiled back at her and said.

"And I am not an adult woman yet. I am still a teen, only 16 years old," the girl responded with a laugh. Pierre felt a little bit embarrassed.

"Do you enjoy looking at nature? Where are your parents?" he asked her.

"They are still sleeping. I like to see the sunrise, so I got up early. What is your name, future Father? My name is Elsie."

"My name is Pierre! I am on the way back to see my family."

"Oh! You are French. But your English is so perfect."

"Yes, we have to learn many languages, especially Latin and English, in the Vatican."

"Well! My father had a business meeting in Naples last week. After business, we went to Rome, that amazing city, so classic and ancient. Now we are going to Paris. My father still has to take care of some business in Paris. After that, we will go back home to London. I don't want to go home. I feel so free and happy to see the world."

"Me too! I like nature, I like adventure, and I love to travel. I have been a student in the Vatican for the past six years and felt so bored there. Every day, the same routines, like being a puppet."

After a few minutes of talking with her, Pierre felt more comfortable. When he took in all the details of this girl, he found out she was not just beautiful, but also innocent, genuine, and truthful. He could not help saying to her,

"You are very beautiful, Elsie." He looked at her smiling.

In Elsie's mind, she thought,

"He is very good looking, but unfortunately, he will be a priest, otherwise, we could be very good friends." But she believed it might not be appropriate to say it, since Pierre was a priest and she was a girl. Instead, she smiled back and said,

"I need to go back. My parents may be looking for me. Anyway, the best part of the sunrise is over. I hope to see you again."

She ran back to her lodging.

***

After Elsie left, Pierre had some mixed feelings of loss, and sweetness at the same time. He knew that his emotions should not be aroused by a beautiful lady. But in his deep heart, the more he did not want to think about it, the more his mind was on it. He went back to his room and took out his Bible to read. He hoped that, by reading the Bible, he could keep his mind from imagining Elsie. In his deep heart, he hoped he could see her and talk to her again. He had had such a good time chatting with her that morning. They would arrive at the Port of Le Havre, Cedex tomorrow. After that, he might not ever see her again.

It became obvious that reading the Bible could not help him much. His mind kept hanging on Elsie, the beautiful and innocent girl he just met. While Father Martin was still sleeping, he lay down on his bed quietly. In just a few minutes, he began to fantasize about Elsie. When he noticed his penis had risen to a hardened state, he felt ashamed and uneasy. Finally, he took his towel and went to the bathroom down the hallway to take a shower. He hoped that a shower could somehow ease his temptation.

Once he took his clothes off and entered the shower, he felt his mature and muscular body as he put the soap on it. The more he washed his body, the more the illusions and fantasies emerged. In just a minute, his penis hardened again. His eyes were red, and the physical sensations of his body caused an emotional disturbance. Finally, he used his hands to touch and massage his penis. Instead of easing his anxiety away, the more he stroked his groin area, the more excitement and anxiety it aroused. In just a few minutes, he reached orgasm and ejaculated. This was the first time he experienced masturbation. Afterwards, though he felt good physically, emotionally he experienced a serious feeling of guilt.

He went back to his room and knelt down next to his bed.

"Oh God! Please forgive me. Please help release me from this emotional bondage."

***

When the vessel arrived at the Port of Le Havre, Cedex, he was very excited even though he was also disappointed that he didn't see Elsie again. However, this port reminded him of his departure when he was only ten years old.

Pierre separated with Father Martin since Father Martin would go on to Paris, while he would go to his village in the town of Avallon near Dijon. He took a train from the Port of Le Havre to Dijon. After that, he hired a carriage to take him to Avallon. When he arrived home, it was already seven days since his father's death.

His younger sister, Emma, was outside of the house sweeping

fallen leaves. When she saw him, she was so excited since she had been only eight when Pierre left home for the Vatican. She had not been sure that Pierre would be able to come back.

"Pierre!" ("Pierre!") She looked at him with a curious expression for a moment.

"C'est toi, Pierre. Enfin! C'est toi." ("It is you, Pierre. Alas! It is you.") Emma could not keep herself from stepping forward to give him a big hug. She knew that Pierre had sacrificed himself for their family six years ago. She had missed Pierre a lot since they were the two youngest children in the family, and they had played together often.

"Maman! Pierre est à la maison. Maman! Pierre est à la maison." ("Mom! Pierre is home. Mom! Pierre is home.")

Diane rushed out from the kitchen. She had been hoping that Pierre would be able to come home. She missed him very much especially after his father's passing. Her eyes were all red,

"Mon pauvre enfant! Comment vas-tu?" ("My poor child! How are you?")

Before Pierre could answer, she went on,

"Laisse-moi te regarder. Tu as grandi." ("Let me take a look at you. You have grown up.")

She pulled Pierre toward her and hugged him tightly. Pierre felt warm but a little bit uneasy since he had not been hugged for six years.

"Maman! Tu... Tu m'as manqué." ("Mom! I, ... I missed you.") Tears rushed out of his eyes. It seemed that a lot of emotions that had accumulated and hidden in his heart suddenly burst out. He felt like an abandoned child finding his sweet home again. Life in the Vatican was peaceful and calm but missing one important thing, a mother's love. He tried to control all of his emotions since he should be solemn as a priest. But he could not.

His other brothers and sisters were working at a nearby farm. This was the harvest time and every worker was needed. They had to take this opportunity to earn more money for the family. His mom and sister took him to his father's tomb, only one hundred meters from the house.

"Ton père est mort paisiblement, Pierre. Tu lui manquais. Il était toujours désolé et se sentait coupable que nous t'ayons envoyé au Vatican." ("Your father died peacefully, Pierre. He missed you. He always felt sorry and guilty that we sent you to the Vatican.")

"Maman, tout va bien! Je suis tranquile là bas," Pierre tried to comfort his mother." ("Mom, I am fine! I feel at peace there,") Pierre tried to comfort his mother.

Pierre had a good time with his family. His elder brother had gotten married and now had a little boy. Though he felt at home, in his deep heart Pierre felt he really did not belong to the family. He knew that it was because he now belonged to God. He was God's servant. After seven days, he would need to return to the Vatican. He had a mixture of many confusing feelings,

"What is life? What is the meaning of it? Do I want to be a priest? Is it the destiny of my life to become a priest?"

An Unexpected Experience 一個意想不到的經歷

After Pierre returned to the Vatican, he took the advice of Father Martin. Whenever he had a deep conflict in his mind, especially about sexual desire or temptation, he prayed to God.

"My Lord! Please forgive me for being without the strength to resist the desire that is like the devil in my heart. Please direct me to the right path that can offer me a clear understanding and guideline to serve you," he prayed sincerely almost every day. However, it seemed that the devil in his mind did not even fade a little, instead it grew stronger every day as he continued to grow up.

Now, at 18 years old, he was so curious about how the ancient documents might describe and explain his emotional thinking and behavior. He decided to go to the basement of the library where the oldest documents were stored. He hoped to find the answer to his prayers for guidance. Today was Sunday and no one would be in the library. It would be a good chance to find available documents and study them.

It was semi-dark in the basement, with only a bit of light coming in from small windows. He felt somewhat uncomfortable about researching this topic. But he needed to know. He stepped quietly into the basement. Suddenly, he heard someone talking at the far end of the room. He could not believe that someone else was in the basement talking to someone.

"Maybe someone is praying to God," he thought.

He did not want to disturb this person, so he quietly approached the last aisle of bookshelves where the oldest documents were. Suddenly, he saw two priests were in the corner kissing each other. He was frozen for a moment. One of the priests noticed his presence and opened his eyes. Pierre recognized him since they were classmates.

It was Franco Colombo, who was from Spain, but he could not see the other person's face. Pierre's face turned red and he walked away from the scene quickly and quietly.

He wondered how they felt. Did they feel sinful? Were their minds as conflicted and confused as his?

He decided not to report this incident since he was not sure if it was really sinful. Furthermore, as he also had his fantasies about girls, he was no longer sure what was right and what was wrong.

***

After breakfast the next morning, Pierre went to the garden to meditate. He needed to be alone and quiet. There were too many knots tangling his mind. While he was sitting on the lawn, he was surprised to find that Franco had followed him to the garden. When they saw each other, Pierre did not know what to say.

"Thank you, Pierre, for not reporting me about what you saw in the basement library."

"Don't worry, Franco. I have also been confused about this matter for a while." Now, he took a closer look at this young priest's face. He had never before paid any real attention to his looks.

Franco had kept his body in good shape. With his good looks, definitely, he would be one of the highest candidates for a woman's happiness. When Pierre thought of this, he could not help smiling.

"May I sit down and talk to you before class begins?" Franco asked.

"Sure! Even though we have known each other in class, we have never really talked together. What's in your mind? Did you feel guilty or sinful for what you did?"

"I did at the beginning, for a long time. Later, I kept questioning myself, we are human and why should we be celibate? Isn't sex our natural desire?"

"Then, why did you commit yourself to serve God? Isn't it your choice?"

"No, Pierre, I did not volunteer. I was sent here by my parents when I was ten."

"That is just like me," Pierre thought. However,

"To serve God is an honor and brings glory to you and your family, don't you think? I was also sent here by my parents. Don't you think we should honor our parents' decision?"

"I thought so at the beginning. However, I began to question it when I was 16. Now I am not sure, and I don't feel as much guilt as I used to."

"Do you still want to serve God, Franco?"

"Yes, since I have been following this path. However, I also have a need to find the freedom of my inner feelings. I don't want to feel that I am trapped in a cage."

Even though Pierre had a similar feeling, he was still loyal to his belief. "Engaging in sexual activity is a sin and goes against the doctrines for being a priest," he argued.

"As a matter of fact, I know there are many priests doing the same thing in the darkness."

"Do you mean homosexuality? Is that normal and natural?" Pierre argued.

"As a matter of fact, since there are no women around, your passion will definitely alter and lead you toward the same sex. Honestly, I receive the same excitement and satisfaction."

The more they talked, the more Pierre felt uncomfortable and his guilty feelings grew stronger each minute.

"Let's go! It is almost time for class." Pierre did not feel like continuing the conversation.

In the following few weeks, Franco kept looking for a chance to talk to Pierre. However, Pierre tried to avoid him. The sinful feeling from their first talk still stuck in Pierre's mind. In one way, he tried to keep a distance from Franco while in another way, he wanted to be close with him. He felt Franco was open-minded and without a thick mask on his face when they talked, while Pierre's mind was in conflict and confused. All he could do was keep asking God's forgiveness whenever he prayed.

First Encounter 第一次的遭遇

After Sunday morning Mass, Pierre returned to his dormitory. He did not notice that Franco was following him. Since Pierre had intentionally kept a distance from him, Franco had decided to act more aggressively.

Fortunately, Pierre's roommate, Jose Cabello, was not in their room. After Pierre entered, Franco also immediately entered the room. While Pierre was shocked for this intrusion, before he could say anything Franco stepped forward to hug him and kiss him. While Pierre was overcome with confusion, their mouths were already together. He tried to push Franco away, but he also felt excitement from this rough and passionate action. This was because he was always curious about what it might feel like to kiss. After a bit, Pierre just allowed it to happen and relaxed.

He was both stimulated and physically excited. When he realized that his penis was straightened out, his face flushed red and he gently pushed Franco away.

"Please don't do it again, Franco. People may see us."

"Pierre! You know I have liked you a lot since we were 16 years old. I have been fantasizing about this moment, to kiss you, and would like to have a deeper relationship with you."

"Please don't, Franco. It is a sin to behave that way. Jose may come back anytime."

"Let's talk more, Pierre. Let's go to the garden. I know where there is a hidden place in the far corner of the garden. Very few people go there."

"But I don't feel comfortable talking about this subject. It is sinful." Though he said so, Pierre still allowed Franco to take his right hand and lead him to the door. He was curious and had a lot of questions. He needed to know so he could untie a number of tight knots in his mind. These mental knots continued to torment him day and night.

After they left the room, Pierre followed Franco to the garden. Fortunately, there were not too many people around. Though the sun began to emerge from behind a thick cloud, the morning weather was still chilly. Finally, they came to the corner of the garden.

Since there were a few people in the garden, they just chose a bench near the corner of the garden. After they sat down, when Franco found out there was nobody around, he extended his hands and tried to hold Pierre's. But Pierre felt so uncomfortable in this public place. His heartbeat got faster and faster. Though he felt very touched, he quickly withdrew his hands. He did not know what to do next. All he was hoping for was to find some answers for his conflicted mind. Talking to Franco might just clear up his questions, since Franco was so open-minded on this subject.

"Franco! Please just let us talk without any physical action. Other priests may see us."

"My innocent Pierre! Why do you care about what others are thinking? They are just like you, very confused about this thing. They are just too afraid to talk about it."

"No! No, Franco! We have to keep our minds firm. We are God's servants. Doing these things is sinful. Just tell me, how did you untie the emotional knot in your mind?"

"After I had confused feelings for a long time, one day I just decided to let it go and set my emotional feeling free. Since that day, I have felt good and like a human again. Don't you want to feel this way, Pierre?"

"Have you even kissed a girl before?"

"You must be kidding, Pierre. There is no girl in this monastery. Only guys."

"Franco! Isn't this abnormal? With guys?"

"I don't think or feel so. To me, it is normal. Actually, homosexuality has been in existence throughout human history. In fact, there have been many priests who were homosexuals in the past." While Franco was speaking, he also extended his hand to touch Pierre's groin area.

Pierre was shocked by Franco's action. He jumped up and ran. He went into the church and knelt down in front of God and asked for forgiveness. Though he enjoyed kissing with Franco, his feeling of pleasure also made him feel more guilty. He sat in the church for nearly an hour. His mind was deeply confused and struggling.

SECOND ENCOUNTER 第二次衝突

Pierre had tried to avoid Franco for a while now. He thought Franco was a messenger from the devil who was sent to test his will. However, in his deep heart he knew the devil was inside of him, not outside.

Somehow, he missed the feeling from the kiss he had had with Franco. His sexual desire was heightened. He was hoping to get together again with Franco, but at the same time, he was afraid the demon in his mind was going to dominate his entire being.

It was a full moon and the weather was warm. One Sunday night, after he tried to get to sleep for half an hour, he decided to take a walk to the garden. He hoped that after a walk, he could calm down his disturbed mind. It was late, nearly midnight, and everyone was sleeping.

After he walked for a few minutes, he came to a bench where there were some flowers and some heavy brush nearby. After he sat down, he heard Franco's voice talking to someone. First, he thought that it was the ghost voice of Franco that was ringing in his ears. Soon, he realized that the voice was not his imagination. He was curious and looking through the moonlight, he saw that Franco and another student, Roberto Russo, were both naked and were hugging each other on the lawn under the bush. Roberto was from an Italian family. He was sexy and charming. The type that all girls would dream of.

He was startled by the scene. Before he could run away, Franco quickly stood up and pulled him into the bush. Both Franco and Roberto pulled him down to the ground. Franco kissed him and used his tongue to play with his tongue skillfully. Pierre felt some high-level of sensation that he had never experienced before. His penis grew large and stiff in just a few seconds. While at the same time, Roberto used his hands to stroke his groin area.

These feelings were so amazing that he could not help but release some moaning sounds. His eyes turned red and his heartbeat got very fast. He felt excited in one way, and yet he was also in shock and ashamed. He had an orgasm in just a few minutes. Although he had privately touched himself, and masturbated his testicles and penis before, he had never before experienced such an exciting orgasm. He did not know what he should do next.

When Roberto began to take his pants off, his guilt-filled mind woke up suddenly.

"I am sorry! I can't." Pierre stood up quickly and ran away from them.

He rushed to the church and knelt down in front of the cross.

"My Lord! Please forgive me. I am unfaithful and have betrayed your trust. My Lord! Please forgive me." This was one of many times he knelt down to the cross and confessed.

He did not know how other students handled their sexual desires when their hormones were high. He tried to find a way to forgive and comfort himself. He was searching for an excuse to ease his guilty feeling. He felt he was a sinful person that had betrayed God and the church.

Over the next eight months, he kept away from and avoided coming close to both Franco and Roberto unless it was necessary. However, both Franco and Roberto pretended that nothing had happened. Naturally, they could not show any sign of their true feelings in public.

CONFESSION TO MENTOR 對主教的懺悔

When Pierre was 19 years old, finally, he decided to confess to the church. He made an appointment with his Diocese's Bishop, Father Wilson. After lunch, when everyone was resting, he came to Father Wilson's office. After he took a deep breath, he knocked on the door. He heard Father Wilson's voice,

"Come in!"

When he entered the office, he saw Father Wilson was sitting in a chair waiting for him. He knelt down in front of Father and kept his head down. Father Wilson picked him up and said,

"Sit down, my son! How can I help you?"

Pierre stood up and sat on a chair in front of Father Wilson. His eyes were red, and he felt shameful inside his heart. He looked at Father Wilson,

"Father, forgive me! I have been unfaithful to the church and to God. Since I was 16 years old, I have been allured by a sexual fantasy. I know I am chosen to serve God; I should not be allured by this fantasy. However, the more I tried to stop it, the worse it has become. I am deeply in pain. I have felt I am so sinful. What can I do? Father! Please help me." When he said it, his tears rushed out. Father Wilson could see the emotional conflict he was in.

Father Wilson looked at him with a smile,

"My son! The fantasy you have is very normal for your age. It is a natural development of a human. You feel sinful because you feel you have betrayed the trust of the Church and of God. In fact, this problem has always existed since the Church Doctrine set up a rule of sexual abstinence. This was because once you are married and have children, you would not have time to serve God. Not only that, you would not be concentrating on the job that God gives you. Once you have committed yourself to your service to God, you should sacrifice your regular human life."

"I know that, Father. But I don't know how to stop my fantasy of sexual allure. The more I want to stop, the worse it has become. I believe that even with just a thought of sex, I have already betrayed God's trust. May I ask if you had this kind of fantasy when you were young, Father?"

"Honestly, I had, just like you. However, my will was so strong to serve God that, gradually, I conquered it," Father Wilson replied.

"But, how did you do it, Father?"

"My son! Everyone is different. It depends on, deeply in your heart, which is more important, serving God or having a normal human life. Serving God is a holy commitment. To me, living a normal human life cannot compare with sacrificing for God and becoming his servant."

"But, Father, how did you control your emotional mind and prevent the evil thoughts emerging from inside you?"

"Well! I did the same as you did. I prayed to God to give me strength to conquer this devil inside me. I also kept myself busy in studying the Bible and serving people."

"But do you know that there are some priests in the Vatican who have the same problem and they have surrendered to the devil?"

"Yes, we know. However, that is God's will. They have to learn how to conquer themselves. This conquering is the way of spiritual growth. Even though we know, we just keep our silence and don't ask. Now, you have to make up your mind, to conquer yourself or let the devil conquer you. From my experience, it seems that after you graduate from here and begin to serve God in the outside world, you will be busier, and this will make your self-conquering easier."

"Yes, I will graduate next year. I hope the change of environment will improve my situation. Thank you, Father. This conversation has helped me greatly."

"Go now, my son. God blesses you."

When Pierre left Father Wilson's office, he had much fewer feelings of guilt. Now, he knew all that had happened was God's test to see if he was committed to this vocation.

***

One year passed quickly. Pierre tried to avoid physically or emotionally engaging with Franco or Roberto. He focused all his mind on studying the Bible and in prayer. Whenever there was a thought of sexual allure, he immediately went to church and began to pray.

After his graduation, when he was 20 years old, he was assigned to work at a church in Marseille, France. Now he was busy with church business. Gradually, his sexual desire was reduced though he sometimes missed the encounter that he had had with Franco and Roberto. But he was able to conquer himself and pull himself back from his fantasy.

Since Marseille was not too far from Dijon, he was able to visit his family more often. Now, his second brother also got married and then his eldest sister. It seemed his mom was happier with four grandkids to take care of.

After one year and four months of service in the Marseille church, he received a notification from the Vatican that he would be sent to China to serve God there. He was excited by this news since he had always wanted to see the world and have some adventures. In preparation for his future trip, he began to study Mandarin, the formal language of China. This language could be used in most areas in China.

Finally, the date of departing from France to go to China arrived. Pierre was so excited. As he had been told, he would have Father Benjamin Jessen to travel with him. Father Jessen was 55 years old and had once before been to China.

Two days before their departure, Father Jessen came to his church, Église Saint-Laurent de Marseille, to meet him. They did not have enough time to get well acquainted with each other since both of them were busy packing and participating in a few final meetings with the local bishop.

On July 18th of 1897, they were on the cargo ship from Marseille Fos Port to Hong Kong. This cargo ship belonged to the biggest import/export company, British East India Company (EIC) (英國東印度公司). Though the main purpose of this ship was transporting cargo, it also carried passengers who were traveling to South Africa, India, and China. Therefore, this ship would first sail to the Port of Durban near the Cape of Good Hope for a few days. Then, it would sail to Mumbai Port in India. Finally, it would arrive at Hong Kong, the final destination.

After the ship took off, finally, Pierre had a better chance to get to know Father Jessen. However, Pierre couldn't get into a deeper relationship with Father Jessen. Father Jessen was quiet and always prayed and read the Bible. From a short conversation with Father Jessen, Pierre learned that he didn't like to travel, especially on a ship as he got seasick easily. He also learned Father Jessen had been to China before. Since he knew that Father Jessen had been in China before, he hoped to be able to receive answers to some of his questions about the Orient.

On just the second day after departing from the Port of Durban, they encountered a big storm and the ship was heaved from side to side. Pierre got a little bit sick since he seldom traveled by boat. But it was much worse for Father Jessen. His face turned pale and he threw up many times. After he got sick, he laid down on his bed and hoped for the storm to end soon.

***

While Pierre was on deck thinking about the past, Father Jessen came to stand next to him. It seemed that his seasickness was much better with today's calm ocean. Pierre could see that Father Jessen was in a better mood this morning.

"Father Jessen! It looks like you feel better this morning?"

"Yes, Pierre. I felt terrible yesterday with the stormy weather. I feel much better now. Now I am even hungry. Let's get something to eat."

They went to the cafeteria and saw there were a few passengers who had just woken up and were now eating. It was already nearly 10 o'clock in the morning. It seemed that there were several other passengers who were also sick from yesterday's storm.

After they ate, they returned to the deck and found two chairs to sit down on. With Father Jessen's better mood today, Pierre was anxious to ask him some questions about China since he had been there once before.

"Father Jessen! I know you were in China four years ago for a period of one year. I wonder if you can tell me anything about China, the Chinese people and their culture. More importantly, what are the missionary goals of the Church's service there?"

"Well! As you know, China is very different from European countries. Its culture is deep, conservative, and unique. You may probably never understand the Chinese unless you live there for more than ten years. And I can tell you, it is not a good time now for foreigners to travel to China, especially missionaries."

When Pierre heard of this, he wondered about it. He believed that helping and persuading people to believe in God was a good deed. Why was this not a good time to go to China?

"Why, Father Jessen?" Pierre asked.

"Let me explain to you, my son. There are three main Christian churches in China. The biggest one, of course, is the Catholic Church (天主教) backed by the Vatican, the second one is Protestant (新教), backed by Germany, and the third is Russia's pravoslavnaja tserkov' (東正教). Since the First Opium War in 1839, China was forced to open its gates to our western culture, and these three main Christian groups were given the right to spread their doctrines to Chinese society. Since then, these three church groups have been competing with each other. After that, a series of treaties were signed between China and various powerful countries such as France, Russia, Japan, and of course Britain, so that now all Christian churches have special rights and are under the protection of the Chinese government."

"Father Jessen! Among the three Christian churches, which one has the widest influence?"

"Of course! It is the Catholic church since it is the biggest organization of all the Christian churches. Catholic churches have already spread almost everywhere in the south-east of China. However, in the north-east territory such as the Manchurian or Shāngōng territories, most are Protestant or Russia's pravoslavnaja tserkov'."

"Father Jessen! If Christian churches are under the protection of the Chinese government, then that's a good thing and should be an advantage to us. Don't you think so?" Pierre asked with curiosity.

"Unfortunately, due to competition among the different churches, all of the churches accept their new members without discernment. This has resulted in many Chinese gangsters joining the churches in order to use the churches for protection from being punished for their crimes. They are violent against local laymen, disturb the peace of society, and even worse they have begun to violently take land away from farmers. This has agitated the Chinese people to rebel against Western Churches. By now, it is estimated that more than 400 conflicts have already occurred since the First Opium War."

"Why don't the churches change their policies to reject the gangsters?"

"There are two reasons. All of the missionaries in Christian churches believe they are able to convert these gangsters into good people and save their souls. The second, as I mentioned earlier, is that due to the competition to gain new members, they just accept everyone. As far as I know, the worst situation is in the Shāndōng Province of China."

"Isn't the church in Jìnán City (濟南市) that we are going to in Shāndōng Province, Father Jessen?"

"Yes, that is why I am being sent there, to see about the new situation. After my investigation, I will go back and report to the Vatican. I learned in the last meeting before I left the Vatican that the farmers are united and have organized and gained the support of local martial artists to resist the Chinese Christian gangsters. I was also told that the most frequent conflicts were centered around Catholic churches on the East territory of Jìnán City."

"I can see now, Father Jessen, that the Chinese hatred for Christian churches will also involve us."

"And there is another serious problem that you should be aware of. After the First and Second Opium Wars, all Western countries, especially Britain, have had the authority to import opium and sell it in China. Now, due to a great deal of opium addiction amongst the general Chinese public, this country is not simply more impoverished each day, the people's health has also declined very rapidly. This has triggered and enhanced the Chinese people's hatred toward all foreigners including diplomats, their families, and also missionaries. I believe a new storm is forming, and sooner or later it will cause a huge catastrophic conflict between the foreign countries and the Chinese government."

"Father Jessen, don't you think it is immoral and unrighteous for foreign countries to do these things?"

"Of course! However, since the Chinese government is so corrupt and weak, to the foreign countries the Chinese marketplace is like a delicious piece of meat on a cutting board just waiting to be cut and consumed. Alas! There is no justice or morality in politics, just reality."

"What should we do in this situation, Father Jessen?"

"There are plenty of nice, kind, and good Chinese people around. We just have to show our good hearts and do our good deeds. Through our own efforts, they will understand that we are not all bad either."

"Thank you, Father Jessen. You have helped me a lot to prepare for this trip psychologically."

***

The next stop would be Mumbai Port, India. Again, Pierre was very curious about this old culture and its customs. Unfortunately, they were stopped in India for only two days and that did not give Pierre much of a chance to get to know this culture. Since India had become a colony of Britain, gradually India's own culture had been neglected and destroyed. Learning the English language and Western style of life was now the fashion. Britain used this colony to grow opium and cotton and then ship them to China for gold and silver.

When Pierre was on board waiting for their departure to Hong Kong, he saw tons and tons of opium being loaded onto the ship. He also saw a lot of cotton. When he saw so much opium on board the ship, he thought,

"I feel so sorry for the innocent Chinese people. Due to the corruption and weakness of their government, powerful and controlling foreign countries can do whatever they want to do to their country. The Chinese people are only victims in this situation." He sighed with a deep compassion toward the Chinese people.

Yáng, Jwìng-Mǐng

ARRIVING IN HONG KONG 抵達香港

As scheduled, the ship arrived at Hong Kong Port on August 10th of
1897. Father Jessen and Pierre would stay at a local Catholic church,
Holy Trinity Cathedral, for two days. After that, they would take another smaller ship from Hong Kong to Shànghǎi, and then on to Qīngdǎo Port.

After they arrived at Qīngdǎo City on August 15th, they would hire a
carriage to take them to Jìnán City, which was about 350 kilometers
away. It would take less than two days of travel by muddy road. If everything went smoothly, they should arrive at Hóngjiālóu Catholic
Church (洪家樓天主教堂) in the morning of the next day.

After they had settled down in Holy Trinity Cathedral, Father
Jessen favored the idea of taking a long rest. He was so tired after
nearly a month of traveling already. Pierre took the opportunity to
look around Hong Kong and tried to practice his Mandarin. Unfortunately, he realized that except for a few people, almost all Chinese in
Hong Kong did not speak Mandarin but instead spoke the Cantonese
dialect. He also noticed that some Chinese people were very friendly
to foreigners while some others had a hateful hostility. A couple of
Chinese, after they saw him, even spit at his back. He was a little bit
perturbed. After he thought about what Father Jessen had told him, he
could understand their situation. He realized that his task in serving
God in China might be harder than he thought.

***

When Pierre and Father Jessen had still been on the ship from
Hong Kong to Qīngdǎo City, he had wanted to know more about the
situation at the church where they would stay. Though Father Jessen
would only be there for a short period of time, Pierre would have to be
there for the next few years. One night in their lodging room,

"Father Jessen! I wonder if you know the area, the people, and the
church where we will be staying?"

"The church where we will stay is Hóngjiālóu Catholic Church (洪
家樓天主教堂). The land for this church was purchased by Bishop Eligio
Pietro Cosi, O.F.M (顧立爵神父) about 30 years ago. After 30 years of
development, though the church is not big, it is the oldest Catholic
church in Jìnán City, and it has served God very well."

"How about the people around there? Are they hostile to foreign
missionaries?"

"Usually, people in the big city are more friendly to foreigners. Furthermore, all foreigners are under the Qìng Government's protection. The problems are in the south of Shāndõng Province, Cáo County (曹州) where the German Protestant (新教) churches are. As far as I know, the conflicts between farmers and the local Chinese Christian gangsters are getting more frequent and serious."

"Why hasn't the German government tried to stop these incidents from happening, Father Jessen?"

"I don't have any idea. Maybe the German government has different viewpoints and policies."

"How long will you be in Jìnán City?" Pierre asked.

"Well! I will be there for only three months. After that I will be in Běijīng. It seems that hostility there against foreigners has elevated in the last few years. The Vatican needs to know about the current situation."

"Father Jessen! Do you have any advice for me?"

"My son! Just use your kind heart and compassion to serve God well. There is no personal glory or benefit. Just contribute yourself to God."

"Thank you, Father Jessen."

***

After they arrived in Qīngdǎo Port on August 15th, since there was no Catholic church in Qīngdǎo City they stayed in a local hotel. Most of the Qīngdǎo City area was controlled by Germany. Although there was no train available from Qīngdǎo to Jìnán they were able, through the hotel services, to arrange for a small carriage to take them to Jìnán City the next morning. Pierre could hear that almost everyone in Northern China was speaking Mandarin.

The carriage came to pick them up the next morning. They were on their way to Jìnán City.

CHAPTER 4
UNEXPECTED ENCOUNTER
意 外 的 遭 遇

UNEXPECTED ACQUAINTANCE 偶然的邂逅

On August 15ᵗʰ of 1897, after visiting Master Dù's family Bó-Wǔ went to see Master Dù's old friend, Mr. Chén, Jì-Lóng (陳進隆), to give him Shìhǎi monk's calligraphy and painting. Mr. Chén was so happy and surprised. He had thought his old friend, Master Dù, might have forgotten his request of ten years ago. Mr. Chén insisted Bó-Wǔ stay at his home for a night to rest before Bó-Wǔ continued his journey home. The next morning, Bó-Wǔ set out once again on his way to his hometown, Tàiān Town (泰安鎮). In order to conserve money, instead of hiring an expensive carriage he chose to walk. It would take him at least three or four days to arrive home.

In the late afternoon of the second day, Bó-Wǔ was thinking about the re-union with his family while he was walking. As he thought about seeing them again, he couldn't help to reveal his smile on his face. He was so happy and excited that finally he could go home. About an hour later, heavy clouds moved in quickly. When he was still two miles from Zhāngjiāpō Town (張家坡鎮), suddenly a thunderstorm approached. In just another hour or so, rain poured down like a waterfall and the small dirt road became messy and muddy. Immediately, he found a big tree to shelter himself under to avoid getting wet. There was no one else on the road, especially in this stormy raining weather.

While Bó-Wǔ was wondering how long the rain would last, he saw a carriage coming from a distance at a fast speed. As he wondered who might be in the carriage and in such a hurry in the storm, suddenly he saw one of the carriage's wheels hit a rock and separate from the carriage. The wheel broke and the driver was thrown twenty feet in front. The horse and the carriage collapsed onto the road. Without hesitating, Bó-Wǔ ran to the carriage to see if he could help. When he took a closer look, he saw two passengers that had also been thrown and were lying not too far from the carriage. The luggage that had been tied up on the roof of the carriage was scattered on the ground.

First, he rushed to see if the driver was okay and discovered that the driver had passed out. Immediately, he carried him on his shoulder and moved him to a place under the tree. Then he went to see if those passengers that had been thrown out of the carriage were okay. When he got a closer look at these passengers, he was surprised to see that they were not Chinese but were two foreign Christian missionaries, one older and one younger. Though he did not like foreigners, Bó-Wǔ still demonstrated his compassion and helped them get out of the mud.

"謝謝您！先生。" ("Thank you, Mister,") the young priest said.

"不用客氣！" ("Don't be so polite!") Bó-Wǔ smiled back, realizing that this young priest had spoken some Chinese Mandarin.

Bó-Wǔ helped the missionaries walk over to stand under the tree where he had been sheltering. Then he went back to the carriage to move their luggage to the tree. After that, he took a look at the driver who was just waking up from his blackout. It seemed that he was okay and without serious injury.

"您們好幸運！幸好沒有人受太大的傷，這是不幸中的大幸呢。" ("You are very lucky! Fortunately, no one got seriously injured. This is a good fortune within misfortune,") Bó-Wǔ said.

"您先生貴姓？謝謝您幫忙我們。" ("What is your surname, sir? Thank you very much for your help,") the driver asked.

"我姓李，叫博武。您呢？" ("My surname is Lǐ, and I am called Bó-Wǔ. What is yours?")

"人家都叫我小陳，我的名字是大鵬。" ("People call me 'Little Chén', my name is Dàpéng.")

"我們現在該怎麼辦呢？" ("What can we do now?") the young priest asked with a worried expression on his face. The old priest was quiet but for moaning with pain and shock.

"前面約兩公里是張家坡鎮。如果我們能在天黑前趕到那裡，我們就可以在那裡先歇歇了。" ("There is a town called Zhāngjiāpō Town two miles in front of us. If we are able to arrive there by dark, we can rest there,") Dàpéng said.

"希望這場雨不要下得太久，天黑了下雨天不好走路。我可以幫忙你把車子推到鎮裡，到了那裡一切就方便多了。這位傳教士，您的大名是。。？" ("I hope this rain does not last long. After dark, it will be hard to walk on this muddy road. I can help you move the carriage into town. Once we get there, it will be easier and more convenient. This missionary, your name is ...?") Bó-Wǔ asked.

"我叫披爾。我的漢語不很好，可是您們說慢一點，我大概可以聽得懂的。" ("My name is Pierre. My Mandarin is not very good. However, if you speak slower, I can roughly understand what you say.")

"那您的同伴呢？" ("How about your companion?") Bó-Wǔ asked.

"他是我們梵蒂岡教會的神父，耶森師父，他不會講漢語。" ("He is a Father of the Vatican church, Father Jessen. He does not speak Mandarin.")

"這裡到鎮裡有兩公里，您說他可以走得動嗎？" ("It is about two miles from here to town. Do you think he is able to walk there?")

"我問他看看！我看這也只有這個辦法了，天氣黑了後，會冷得很快呢。何況我們的衣服都濕了。" ("I will ask him. I believe this is the only option. After dark, the weather will get colder very quickly and so will we, especially since all our clothes are wet.")

Pierre turned his head to face Father Jessen and asked him his opinion. Then he turned back to Bó-Wǔ,

"他說這也沒有其他辦法了，只有這樣做。" ("He said since there is no other solution, he will do what he has to do.")

"您們計畫到哪裡去呢？" ("What was your plan and where are you going?") Bó-Wǔ asked.

"本來計畫明天可到濟南市的，我看是到不了了。" ("Originally, we planned to arrive in Jǐnán City tomorrow. As I see it now, we will not be able to get there on time.")

"我們先到鎮上再說吧！這馬車修理也要幾天呢。如果運氣好，您們可以另外雇一輛馬車載您們到濟南市。" ("Let's go to the town first. It will take a few days to repair this carriage. If you are lucky, you may be able to hire another carriage to take you to Jǐnán City,") Bó-Wǔ said and then turned his head toward Dàpéng.

"小陳！那您打算怎麼辦呢？" ("Little Chen! What do you plan to do?") Bó-Wǔ asked.

"到了鎮上，我的大舅子住在那裡，他可以幫我找到鐵工修理我這個爛車子，可是我沒有錢退給他們。" ("My brother-in-law's family are living in the town. After we arrive there, I can ask him to help me find a blacksmith to repair this broken carriage. But I don't have any money to refund the missionaries.")

The small group waited under the tree and hoped the rain would subside. After half an hour,

"現在雨較小了，我們走吧！再過兩個時辰，天就要黑了。" ("Now, the rain is smaller. We better get going. Just two more hours and the sky will be dark,") Bó-Wǔ suggested.

"可是我的馬車的一個輪子壞了，怎麼弄到鎮上呢？" ("But one of my carriage's wheels is broken. How can we move this carriage to the town?") Dàpéng wondered with worry.

"來！我們試試看，我可以抬一邊跟著走。" ("Come! Let's try it. I can carry the side with the broken wheel and follow you,) Bó-Wǔ replied.

"先生！這馬車可重著呢，不容易吧？" (But, sir! This carriage is very heavy. It will not be easy,") Dàpéng said.

"先試試看！不行，只有推到路邊，明天您在請人來拖了。" ("Let me try first. If it does not work, all we can do is push it to the side of the road. You can then hire someone to help you move this carriage to town tomorrow.")

The driver took a look at the horse and it seemed to be okay. Bó-Wǔ picked up the side with the missing wheel to test its weight and felt it was manageable. He placed the broken wheel and luggage on the carriage. When everyone saw his strength, they were so surprised.

"先生！您好大的力氣啊！" ("Sir! How strong you are!") Dàpéng said.

"沒事兒！可是我們可能需停休息幾次呢。" ("No problem! But we may need to take a few breaks,") Bó-Wǔ replied.

"您需要休息時，請告訴我。" ("When you need a break, please tell me,") Dàpéng said.

While they were talking, Pierre and Father Jessen stood by, amazed at Bó-Wǔ's strength. They had never met someone with such power. They did not know Bó-Wǔ was a martial artist.

The small group began to walk toward the town. There was nobody else traveling the muddy road, especially with nightfall coming. They had to stop three times for Bó-Wǔ to catch his breath. Occasionally, Pierre went to help. Though they were strangers to each other, through this incident they came to feel a closer connection with each other. Before they reached the town, they already felt like friends.

After they arrived in town, Dàpéng said,

"謝謝您！李先生，如果沒有您，我真不知道該怎麼辦呢！車子可以放在那棵樹下，我去找我的大舅子來幫忙。他們兩位，請您繼續幫忙他們一下。鎮裡，迎來客棧就在前面，您們可以試試看。" ("Thank you, Mr. Lǐ. If there had been no help from you, I just don't know what we would have done. The carriage can be placed under that tree. I will go to find my brother-in-law to get his help. About these two missionaries, can you please continue to help them? There is a hotel called 'Yínglái Inn' in town just ahead of us. You may try there.")

Dàpéng bowed to Bó-Wǔ and the two missionaries, then left. The rain had almost stopped. Bó-Wǔ looked at Pierre and Father Jessen,

"我們先到客棧再說。" ("Let's go to the inn first.")

He helped Pierre carry some of the luggage and walked toward the center of the town.

FRIENDSHIP 友情

Eventually they saw an inn, Yínglái, ahead. Once they went in. " 老闆！你們有兩間客房嗎？" ("Boss! Do you have two rooms?) Bó-Wǔ asked the man at the counter.

"有！有！我們有。最後兩間，因為大雨，客人較多，只是小了一點，每間都只有一個床呢。" (Yes! Yes, we do. The last two. Because of the heavy rain, we have more guests. But these two rooms are smaller and there is only one bed in each room.") The innkeeper saw that there were three of them and did not know how to arrange them.

"沒問題！您能夠在一個房中搭個地鋪嗎？" ("No problem! But can you set up a floor bed for us in one of them?") Bó-Wǔ replied.

"搭地鋪是沒問題，可是不太舒服呢！" ("There is no problem to set up a floor bed, but it will not be too comfortable.")

"沒問題！先燒些洗澡水，再準備一些餐點給我們。" ("No problem. Please prepare some hot bath water, then prepare some food for us.")

The clerk took them to their rooms. While Pierre was wondering about the sleeping arrangements, Bó-Wǔ said.

"披爾！您告訴耶森師父那是他的房間，您我可以共用一個房間。您可以睡床上，我可以睡地鋪。" ("Pierre! Please tell Father Jessen that this is his room. You and I can share this other one. You may sleep on the bed and I can sleep on the floor.")

"博武！這樣是不行的，是很不好意思的。" ("Bó-Wǔ! You cannot do this. I feel embarrassed that I am taking advantage of you,") Pierre replied.

"披爾！沒問題，不要太客套了，對我中國人來講，您是客人，而我卻是主人呢。" ("Pierre! There is no problem. Don't be so polite. To me as a Chinese, you are the guest and I am the host.")

After everyone took a bath and had a nice simple dinner, Father Jessen went immediately to bed. He was so tired he fell asleep within a few minutes. Bó-Wǔ and Pierre, however, felt like getting to know each other better.

"博武！真謝謝您。今天如果沒有您，我們不知該怎麼辦呢？"("Bó-Wǔ, really, thank you! If you had not been there today, we would not have known what to do!") Again, Pierre mentioned his appreciation of Bó-Wǔ's help.

"披爾！不用太客氣了。我很高興認識您。以前我一直以為所有的外國人都很壞，欺負中國人。現在很高興的知道有些外國人還是挺客氣的。"("Pierre! You don't have to be so polite. I am very happy to get acquainted with you. I always thought all foreigners were bad and just took advantage of Chinese people. Now, I am very happy to know that there are many foreigners who are kind and polite,") Bó-Wǔ said with a big smile.

"我今天看到您的力氣，非常的驚訝。那不是平常人能夠有的。"("When I saw your strength today, I was so surprised. This is not the strength that normal people have.")

"喔！我是練武的。我在峨嵋山跟我三個師父練十年，剛剛才下山呢！"("Oh! Well I am a martial artist! I have trained for ten years in martial arts on Éméi Mountain with my three Shīfùs. In fact, I have only just come down from the mountain.")

"難怪！難怪！可是您這麼年輕，怎麼可能跟您師父們練了十年？"("No wonder! No wonder! But you are still so young, how could you have practiced for ten years with your Shīfùs?")

"其實在我十二歲時，經過我爹娘的允許，我就跟著師父上山了。"("Actually, when I was 12 years old, with my parents' permission, I followed my Shīfù to the mountain.")

"那您現在是二十二歲了？我也是二十二歲呢！"("Does that mean you are 22 years old now? I am also 22 years old!")

"您也是很年輕。怎麼就當起傳教士了呢？"("You are also very young. How could you be already a missionary?") Bó-Wǔ asked with a big smile.

"我在十歲時就被我父母送到梵蒂岡去學習神學當傳教士。"("When I was ten years old, I was sent by my parents to the Vatican to learn theology and to become a missionary.")

"喔！那不是就像我們中國人的父母？當他們發現他們的孩子對陰靈有特別的感應時，他們就認為他們有佛緣或道緣。很多父母就送他們到寺廟或道觀去學習修煉神靈上的東西。就像我，我對武術有興趣與才能，我父母才送我到山上去修煉呢。披爾！您對神學有興趣嗎？"("Oh! That is just like Chinese parents! When they discover that their child has a special connection with Yīn spirit, they believe their child has a special affinity with Buddhism or Daoism. Many of them will send their children to Buddhist or Daoist temples to study and cultivate those things related to spirit. Like me, for example. I am very interested and also have talents in Chinese martial arts. That's why my parents sent me to the mountain for training. Pierre! Are you interested in theology?")

"我不知道呢！我還在揣摩學習呢。其實，我對自己都還不了解呢？" ("I don't know. I am still trying to figure it out. Truly, I don't even know myself yet.")

"我師父說，人生就是這樣，一直在揣摩與學習呢。" ("My Shīfùs told me that this is life, always looking for answers and learning.")

They talked about Chinese customs since Pierre wanted to know more about them, while Bó-Wǔ was more curious about foreign cultures and people. They talked almost till midnight in their room. Somehow, though Pierre's Mandarin was still poor, they found a way to communicate with each other without a problem. By the next morning, they had become good friends.

***

After breakfast, Bó-Wǔ talked to the clerk of the Yínglái Inn and returned to his room.

"披爾！店裡小二說鎮的東邊有一家雇用馬車的店。我們可以去問問看他們可有空的馬車？您們到濟南市，如果雇用馬車只要一天的路程，如果是走路，可能要兩三天呢。" ("Pierre! The clerk of the inn said there was a store where you can hire a carriage. We can go there to ask them if there is any carriage available for hire. If you want to go to Jǐnán City, it will take only one day to get there by carriage. However, if you walk, it will be two or three days.")

"不行走路啊！耶森師父會受不了的，我們去看看有沒有馬車可以雇用？" ("No! We can't walk. Father Jessen won't be able to stand it. Let's go to see if there is a carriage for hire.")

They walked to the east side of town and found the store where they could hire a carriage. After they talked to the owner, they discovered that there was one carriage available, but it had just returned from Qīngdǎo City and the driver was very tired. They told the driver about the address of the church the missionaries were going to and started to negotiate. Finally, Pierre agreed to pay double the usual cost to the driver and also allow him to rest for one day. They would take off the next day early in the morning.

On the way back to Yínglái Inn,

"披爾！我們必須告訴客棧老闆您們還須要住一天。" ("Pierre! We have to tell the boss of the inn that you will be staying one more day.")

"博武！那您今天就要離開我們了？" ("Bó-Wǔ! Does that mean you are going to leave us today?") Pierre asked with regret and a sad expression on his face. He had really treated Bó-Wǔ as his best friend. Bó-Wǔ did not mask his emotions from his face but was honest, simple, nice, and very easy to get along with. He was not like Pierre's classmates at the Vatican that always wore heavy masks on their faces, acting in ways that weren't true to their nature.

When Bó-Wǔ saw the expression on Pierre's face, he realized how deep their relationship had become in just one day. After he thought it over, he believed staying with a good new friend for another day was probably worth more than arriving home one day earlier.

"披爾！其實我可以待到明天的。可是我也不想跟您們添麻煩。事情已經辦妥了，您們應該會沒有問題的。" ("Pierre! Actually, I can stay till tomorrow. However, I don't want to give you more trouble. Everything is settled now. You shouldn't have any more problems.")

"可是博武，我還想更進一步認識您。這個機會一過，我不知道我麼什麼時候才可以再見面呢？" ("But, Bó-Wǔ! I still wish to get to know you better. Once this chance is over, I don't know when we might be able to meet again.")

Actually, Bó-Wǔ was also very anxious to know Pierre better. They had had such a cheerful and truthful talk last night. Truly, Pierre could be the best friend in Bó-Wǔ's life.

"如果不麻煩您們，我就多待一天了。" ("If it is no trouble for you, I will stay one more day.")

"說什麼的話！我高興還來不及呢。其實我還有很多問題要請教您呢！" ("What did you say?! I am happier than you could ever know. Truly, I still have so many questions that I would like to ask you.") Pierre was very happy that Bó-Wǔ was able to stay one more day till their departure the next morning.

After they returned to the inn, they asked the Yínglái innkeeper if they could stay one more night.

"客官！今晚我們會有多的房間，如果您們要換一間較大的，我可以幫您們安排。" ("Respectable guests, yes! And we will have more rooms available tonight. If you wish to change your room to a bigger one, I can help you to arrange it.")

"不用了，老闆。我也習慣了，反正只有一晚。" ("There is no need, boss. I am already accustomed to it. Anyway, it is only one more night.") Actually, their talk last night had had a deep meaning to Bó-

Wǔ. He would miss their conversations when Pierre was gone.

After they told Father Jessen about the plan, they asked him if he wanted to go out to do some sight-seeing. But Father Jessen said he preferred to stay at the inn and study. He was still tired from the day before. Bó-Wǔ made arrangements for his lunch. Pierre and Bó-Wǔ would return to the inn before sunset and have dinner with Father Jessen.

They walked in Zhāngjiāpō Town and some nearby scenic areas. They ate lunch in a small restaurant in town. They just enjoyed talking to each other. They had a very good time.

"博武！您有時間，歡迎您來濟南市看我。" ("Bó-Wǔ! When you have time, you are welcome to visit me in Jǐnán City,") Pierre said emotionally at the end of their tour.

After dinner, they went right to sleep since they had to get up early to continue their journey.

The next morning, they said good-bye, then Pierre and Father Jessen left for Jǐnán City in the carriage while Bó-Wǔ continued walking toward his hometown.

REUNION WITH FAMILY 與家人團圓

After two more days of walking, the closer Bó-Wǔ got to his village the more excited he became. It had been ten years since he had been there. He barely remembered the path to get to the village. Some of the farmers who passed him could not even recognize him. It made him feel like he was a stranger. But when he entered his home village, South Village, it looked just the same as it had ten years ago. Bó-Wǔ rushed home and saw his third brother, Bó-Dé, in the front yard collecting dried grains on the ground.

"三哥！是您。大家都好嗎？" ("Sāngē (Third Brother)! It is you. How is everyone?")

When Bó-Dé took a closer look and recognized Bó-Wǔ, he was so surprised and happy.

"大家都不知道你什麼時候會回來呢？我差一點認不出你來了，你現在是長得又高、又帥，又壯呢！奶奶自你的生日起就一直唸著你，不知道你什麼時候會到家呢。" ("Nobody knew when you would be back home! I almost cannot recognize you. You have grown so tall, handsome, and strong. Grandma has kept talking about you since your birthday and did not know when you would arrive home.")

Bó-Dé stepped forward and extended his hands to hold Bó-Wǔ's.

Bó-Wǔ remembered how close they had always been, since their ages were the closest together. Bó-Dé was emotional, kind, funny, and talkative. Whenever they had been together ten years ago, they could talk and laugh and have a good time. Not like with Bó-Wēi, who was older, and also quiet, serious, and more thoughtful. Ten years had passed already! It seemed that the time passed faster and faster as you got older.

When they entered the house, Bó-Wǔ saw his grandma sitting in the living room, chanting Buddhism.

"奶奶！是我，博武。我回來了。" ("Nǎinai (Grandma)! It is me, Bó-Wǔ. I am back.") Bó-Wǔ moved in front of her, knelt down, and held her legs.

"博武！真的是你，你想壞我了，十年了，不認得你了。" ("Bó-Wǔ! It is really you. I have missed you badly. Ten years. I cannot recognize you.") Her eyes turned red and tears rushed out.

"奶奶！您好嗎？我也真想您呢？" ("Nǎinai! How are you? I have also really missed you!")

"還可以！就是風濕，有點走不動。" ("I am alright! Only I have arthritis and cannot walk comfortably.")

"娘呢？還有爹呢？" ("Where is Níang? Also, Diē?")

"你娘在後廚房，你爹也快回來了。" ("Your Níang is in the kitchen and your Diē should be home soon.")

Bó-Wǔ gave his grandma a big hug and ran to the kitchen. There he saw his mom was cooking with a maid.

"娘！我回來了。" ("Níang! I am back.")

"博武，是你。我們從你生日那一天就一直等著你呢。來！來！讓我看看你！" ("Bó-Wǔ! It is you. We have been waiting for you since your birthday. Come! Come! Let me take a look at you.")

His mom's eyes were red from excitement. After she hugged Bó-Wǔ for a long while, she looked at him carefully.

"你已經是大人了，在我印象中，你還是小孩子呢。" ("You are already a man. In my mind you are still a child.")

"娘！我已經二十二歲了，十年不見了，我好想您。" ("Níang! I am already 22 years old. I have not seen you for ten years. How much I have missed you!")

After he greeted all of the other three house helpers - two that he still remembered, but also the younger one whom he had never met before - Bó-Wǔ went to the living room again to chat with his grandma. He could see how happy his grandma was. While they were talking, he saw his father and Bó-Wēi coming in from the front yard.

He stood up and bowed to his father.

"爹！我回來了。"("Diē! I am back.")

"安全回來就好了，大家不知道為什麼你從四川到山東需要這麼久的時間。尤其你奶奶，真是一直掛在心頭上呢！"("It is alright that you have returned safely. We were wondering why it took you so long to travel from Sìchūan to Shāndōng? Especially your Nǎinai, she kept worrying about you,") his father said.

"爹！那是因為師父要我順道到青島市一趟，看看他的老家，並拜訪他的一位好朋友。"("Diē! That was because Shīfù wanted me to visit his old home and also his good friend in Qīngdǎo City on the way back here.")

Bó-Wǔ did not want to tell them about the incident and encounter with the two foreign missionaries since he did not know how his family felt about foreign people. All he knew was of the hate the Chinese had against foreigners beginning from the First Opium War in 1839 and getting worse after the Second Opium War in 1856.

Later Bó-Wǔ was told that his sister, Lǐ, Yù-Píng (李玉萍) had gotten married a few months after he left home ten years ago. She was married to a farmer, Zhù, Wēi-Hóng (祝威宏). Wēi-Hóng's father, Zhù, Wěi-Chén (祝偉宸) was an old friend of Bó-Wǔ's father. He lived in Cáozhōu (曹州) as a farmer who owned more than 20 acres of farmland. When Bó-Wǔ's father was in Cáozhōu as a government official about 17 years ago, he met Wěi-Chén and they became good friends. Now, Bó-Wǔ 's sister already had three children, two girls and one boy. Bó-Wǔ also learned that his second brother, Bó-Wēi, had already gotten married and had two children, one boy and one girl.

***

During dinner the night of Bó-Wǔ's arrival, Bó-Dé said,

"爹！我上個月去看玉萍姊時，知道姊夫家附近的農民與當地的土霸有衝突。這些土霸靠著基督教會的勢力，漸漸將曹州的農民土地，一塊塊的霸佔了。因為教會受清廷的保護，農民也無可奈何。這些土霸嚐到了甜頭後，得寸進尺的快要擴到姊夫的耕地了。真是無法無天，我們怎麼辦呢？"("Diē! When I went to see Yù-Píng last month I learned that there were some conflicts between neighboring farmers and local gangsters. These gangsters used the protection of Christian churches to gradually and forcibly occupy famers' lands in Cáozhōu. Because all churches are under the protection of Qīng Court, those farmers could not do anything. Now that gangsters have taken over some lands successfully, they will soon expand their aggression to brother-in-law's land. There is no law and no justice. What can we do?")

"可恨的是清廷這麼腐敗，才會招致洋人如此對我們的侵略剝奪啊！更可恨的是洋人教會不分好壞，保護他們的教民，有些壞教民借機剝奪老百姓的土地。清廷怕洋人怕得這麼屬害，報上去也是沒用啊。" ("It is so detestable that due to Qīng Court's corruption and weakness, it has caused these foreigners' invasions and the people are deprived of their land. More hateful is that those foreign churches accept all people without checking and protect them whether they are good or bad. Consequently, those Chinese Christian gangsters took the opportunity to deprive civilians of their lands. Qīng Court is so badly afraid of foreigners, even if we report it, it is useless,") Hào-Xūan replied with a sigh.

"那我麼就拿這些土霸沒辦法了？" ("Then, we cannot do anything to defend against these gangsters?") Bó-Dé asked.

"博德！我也不知道怎麼辦呢？何況有些教民不但靠教會清廷的保護，他們還有洋槍呢？" ("Bó-Dé! I also don't know what to do. These Chinese Christian gangsters are not only protected by the churches, but also they have foreign guns!")

As Bó-Wǔ listened to them talking, his anger against the foreign churches again emerged. He decided to make a trip to Cáozhōu to visit his sister.

"爹！我也十年沒見到姊姊了，我想這兩天去曹州看看她並瞭解一下詳細的情形。" ("Diē! I have not seen my sister for ten years. I am thinking of going to Cáozhōu to visit her and also to understand the situation there.")

"好！我也跟你去，我知道路，我可以帶你去。" ("Good! I can also go with you. I know the way. I can take you there,") Bó-Dé said.

"你去看看你大姊也好，只是遇到什麼事，不要衝動。" ("Maybe it is good to see your sister. However, if you encounter any incident, do not lose your temper impulsively,") Hào-Xūan cautioned.

Two days later, they were on their way to Cáozhōu.

CHAPTER 5
FORMATION OF THE YÌHÉTUÁN

義 和 團 的 形 成 與 運 動

During the period from 1894 to 1896, the chaos and confusion in Cáo and Dān Counties (山東曹縣、單縣) of Shāndōng Province provided an opportunity for many gangster groups to begin invading farmers' properties. Since the Qīng Government did not have either the capability or the willingness to stop the gangsters' aggressions, in 1894 two martial artists, Liú, Shì-Ruì (劉士瑞), and Cáo, Dé-Lǐ (曹得禮) founded a society called the Broadsword Society (大刀會) to protect farmers. The main areas they protected were southwest of Shāndōng Province. The group was named Broadsword Society because its members often carried and practiced with broadswords. Members also claimed that they had the Golden Bell Cover (金鐘罩) Gōngfū. With the additional protection of Língfú (靈符) (i.e., spiritual amulet), they were said to be able to defend themselves against knives and guns.

Due to the stated mission of the Broadsword Society is to protect farmers from the gangsters' aggression and to help local governments maintain peace, the Society was accepted and tolerated by the local governor, Lǐ, Bǐng-Héng (李秉衡). Later, many gangsters joined churches and became Christians, recognizing that under the churches' protection the Qīng Government would not dare to arrest them. When more and more gangsters joined the churches and increased their aggression against local farmers, the number of conflicts between Christian gangsters and the Broadsword Society members multiplied rapidly.

Since then, members of the Broadsword Society turned their anger toward the Christian churches. They began to attack innocent Chinese

Christians, plundering their properties, and burning their houses. Finally, under the protests of both German and French ministers, Governor Lǐ, Bǐng-Héng decided to suppress the Broadsword Society's activities. He arrested their two leaders and executed them, after which the public activities of the Society ceased. This suppression encouraged the Christian gangsters to become even more aggressive against local farmers. The situation got worse and worse every day.

REUNION WITH SISTER 與姉姉的團圓

Bó-Wǔ and Bó-Dé were on horseback on their way to Cáozhōu County to see their sister, Yù-Píng (玉萍). It took them nearly six hours to get to Cáozhōu. When they arrived in the late afternoon, they were surprised to see a group of farmers gathering in the front yard of Yù-Píng's home.

"不知道發生了什麼事？" ("I wonder what has happened?") Bó-Dé said.

After they dismounted their horses, they saw some people's faces were covered with blood and a couple of others' arms were broken. Yù-Píng's father-in-law, Zhù, Wěi-Chén (祝偉宸), was standing in front of his door and listening to the farmers' complaints.

"祝員外，請你幫我們做主，我們受的委屈與欺負，沒地方投訴啊。" ("Zhù Landlord! For justice, please help us. There is no other place that we can appeal for help from the bullies that fell upon us.")

Since Mr. Zhù had been known and recognized as a main leader in these few local villages, and he was also a friend of Jùyě magistrate, Xǔ, Tíng-Ruì (許廷瑞), all the farmers had come to ask for his help.

"我知道，你們都很受委屈，可是你們知道，自從幾年前甲午戰爭，我們被日本打敗了，簽了馬關條約後，台灣給割讓了，清廷是怕列強怕得不得了呢！我想即使我們告上衙門，我想也是沒有用的呢。" ("I know your grievance deeply. But as you already know, since China was defeated in Jiǎwǔ War against Japan a few years ago, resulting in signing of Treaty of Mǎguān and Taiwan being ceded to Japan, the Qīng Court has been terribly afraid of those powerful countries. I think even if we pursue this case to the court asking for justice, it is still useless,") Mr. Zhù explained. Actually, he also did not know what to do. It seemed the situation was getting worse every day.

"那我們就只有忍氣吞聲了嗎？" ("Does that mean all we can do is endure our pain and keep silent?") one of the young farmers shouted with anger. When Mr. Zhù saw Bó-Wǔ and Bó-Dé, he said to the crowd,

"你們先回去養傷，讓我冷靜下來想個辦法。" ("First, go home and take care of your wounds. Allow me to calm down and find a solution.")

Since they did not have any better solution, all of the farmers went home and took care of their injuries. Some of them had already lost their lands to local gangsters. Some others were afraid to be attacked and had no choice but to stay with their relatives or friends.

**

After the crowd had dispersed, Bó-Wǔ and Bó-Dé stepped forward to greet Mr. Zhù.

"親家翁，您好。" ("Dear in-law, how are you?") Bó-Dé greeted Mr. Zhù. Mr. Zhù knew Bó-Dé very well since they had already met each other a few times.

"這位是。。" ("This gentleman is ...") Mr. Zhù looked at Bó-Wǔ and asked.

"這是博武，我爹的小兒子。" ("He is Bó-Wǔ, my Diē's youngest son.")

"喔！你就是那個十年前上峨嵋山學武，玉萍的小弟？" ("Oh! You are Yù-Píng's little brother who went to Éméi Mountain for martial arts training ten years ago?")

"是的！親家翁，我拜見您了。" ("Yes, dear in-law. Here I bow to you.") Bó-Wǔ greeted him with a deep bow.

"來！來！我們進去談，玉萍提過你幾次呢！看到你，她一定會非常的驚喜呢！你也還沒有見過我的幾個小孫子呢？" ("Come! Come! Let's go in and talk. Yù-Píng has talked about you a few times. When she sees you, she will be very surprised and happy! You have not met my few little grandkids yet?") When he mentioned his grandson and granddaughters, Mr. Zhù revealed a big smile.

They entered the house and saw the whole family were gathered together talking about the conflict between the local Christian gangsters and the farmers. When Bó-Wǔ saw his sister talking to her mother-in-law, he yelled out,

"大姊！您還認得我嗎？十年了，我離家時，我才十二歲呢。" ("Dàjiě (Elder Sister)! Can you still recognize me? It's been ten years. When I left home, I was only 12 years old.")

"哎呀！你是博武啊，真長得又高、又帥，真有點認不得你了。爹、娘、奶奶都好嗎？" ("Ah! You are Bó-Wǔ. You have grown up tall and handsome. I almost cannot recognize you. How are Dīe, Niáng, and Năinai?")

"他們都很好，只是爹有點惦記著您們這邊的耕農與當地土霸的衝突呢！" ("They are all well! It is just that Dīe is somewhat worried about the conflicts of farmers and local gangsters in this area!")

"這是親家母。娘！這是我的小弟，博武。" ("This is my mother-in-law. Niáng! This is my little brother, Bó-Wǔ,") Yù-Píng introduced him. After Bó-Wǔ bowed deeply to the mother-in-law, Yù-Píng said,

"這是你的小外甥！明珠八歲了，志雄六歲，最小的淑珍才三歲呢。來！來！你們叫舅舅。他是你們從沒見過的小舅舅。" ("And these are your nieces and nephew! Míng-Zhū, eight years old; Zhì-Xióng, six years old; and the smallest one, Shū-Zhēn, only three years old. Come! Come, meet your uncle! He is the little uncle whom you have never met.")

The three kids were shy and hid behind their mother.

"您們談談，我去幫忙準備晚餐。" ("You talk! I will go help prepare dinner.") Yù-Píng left to go to the kitchen while her kids went to their grandma.

***

They all went into the living room and sat down. Yù-Píng brought out a pot of tea and a few teacups. While they were chatting, a man came in and stood there, wondering who this stranger in the room was.

"威宏！這是你的小舅子，博武。" ("Wēi-Hóng! This is your brother-in-law, Bó-Wǔ,") Mr. Zhù said.

"哇！你就是博武，玉萍提起你好幾次呢！" ("Wow! You are Bó-Wǔ? Yù-Píng has mentioned you a few times.")

When Bó-Wǔ heard this, he realized that the person who had just stepped in was his brother-in-law whom he had never met.

"姊夫！您好，我博武在這裡跟您請安。" ("Jiěfū (Sister's Husband)! How are you? I, Bó-Wǔ, bow to you and greet you here.")

"姊夫！您好。我們今天下午才到的。博武自峨嵋山回來，一直念著要來看大姊和跟姊夫認識呢！" ("Jiěfū! We just arrived this afternoon. Since Bó-Wǔ returned home from Éméi Mountain, he kept saying that he wanted to come to see our sister and meet you,") Bó-Dé said to Wēi-Hóng.

Wēi-Hóng had just returned from Jùyě City, where he had gone that morning to purchase some seeds for farming.

125

"不用客套，我們都是一家人，歡迎你們來。" ("Don't be like strangers, we are all in the same family. Welcome! We are happy for your visit,") he said.

"親家翁，上次我來時，您們這裡的農民跟一些土霸教民衝突的事情，從今天下午農民來找您的情況看來，很像繼續惡化呢。" ("In-law! When I came last time, I already saw some conflicts between farmers and Christian gangsters. From this afternoon's situation, it seems that the conflicts have been getting worse,") Bó-Dé said.

"我今天早上在巨野城時，在縣府前擠滿了一大堆民眾向縣長伸冤呢！" ("When I was in Jùyě City this morning, I saw a big crowd gathering in front of the county government building to bring their grievance to Jùyě magistrate,") Wēi-Hóng said.

"看來情況不只是在這裡，這個土霸霸佔農民土地的事，已經遍佈整個巨野縣了。為什麼這些教會要保護這些暴徒教民呢？" ("It seems that these incidents are not just happening here. The problems of gangsters who forcibly occupy farmers' land have spread to the entire Jùyě County. Why do those Christian churches protect these Christian gangsters?") Bó-Wǔ asked.

"其實基督教的基本教義是仁慈、友善的。很可惜的是為了吸收更多的教民，他們不但惡意的批評與攻擊佛教與道教，他們更沒有原則的，不論好壞的招納教民。現在在中國有三派基督教，天主教、新教、與東正教。他們彼此三教其實也互相的競爭與攻擊呢。其中以天主教與德國的新教在巨野區比較具有挑戰性。" ("Actually, the fundamental teachings of Christianity are kind and friendly. It is pitiful that in order to absorb more Chinese people and convert them into Christians, they are not just criticizing Chinese Buddhism and Daoism maliciously, but they are also, without principle, accepting new members without discriminating between good or bad. Now there are three major Christian groups in China, Catholic (天主教), Germany's Protestant (新教) and Russia's pravoslavnaja tserkov' (東正教). In fact, due to competition with each other, they also criticize each other. Among the three, Catholic and Germany's Protestant are the most aggressive in Jùyě area,") Mr. Zhù said with a deep sigh.

"親家翁，我十年來一直在峨嵋山上，不知道外面的這些事情，您們能不能幫我多瞭解一下目前的情況？" ("In-law! I have been on Éméi Mountain for the last ten years. I don't know too much of these outside matters. Can you please help me understand the current situation?") Bó-Wǔ asked.

"因為教會利用他們的特權去保護他們的教徒，近幾年間，已經發生了四百多件教案呢！最可恨的是因為清廷的貪污、腐敗，又被洋人打怕了，不敢為老百姓出頭呢。老百姓積在心裡的怨恨越來愈深啊，我怕早晚這天下要搞得天翻地覆呢。"（"Because Christian churches use their special privileges to protect their followers, there have already been more than 400 incidents in the last few years. The most hateful thing is, because of the Qīng Court's corruption and weakness, in addition to their fear of acting against foreigners, the Qīng Government is also afraid to appeal to foreigners for justice. The resentment accumulating in the people's hearts grows deeper and deeper. I am afraid that this whole world will be turned upside down sooner or later."）

"爹！您知道因為清廷對百姓痛苦申冤的忽視，為了保護農民，今年春天有一位梅花拳的拳師叫趙三多的聚集了兩千多人，向教會勢力與官府示威，'亮拳'三天。從今年三月到現在已經幾次當教會勢力前來尋釁時，趙三多率領群眾與他們對抗並攻打教堂，聽說還殺死了兩位教民呢。他們稱他們的組織為'義和拳'。現在拳眾都集合在沙柳寨一帶，大規模的起義可能一觸即發啊！"（"Die! Do you know, due to the Qīng Court's neglecting to care for people's grievances, in order to protect farmers a martial artist of Méihuā style named Zhào, Sān-Duō has gathered more than 2,000 people and demonstrated their power and willingness to go against churches and the Qīng Government. They protested their willingness with martial arts demonstrations for three days. Actually, there have been a few times when those Christian gangsters came to challenge them. Zhào, Sān-Duō led his group to resist the gangsters and attack the churches. I have heard that they killed two Christians. They call themselves 'Yìhéquán' (Righteous Harmonious Fist). Now, all members are gathering in Shāliǔzhài area. A large-scale uprising can be initiated at any moment,"）Wēi-Hóng said.

"這個我也略有所聞，可是詳情我卻不知道。這麼看來，這表示民眾對教會的武裝鬥爭已經開始了。他們為什麼叫'義和拳'呢？趙三多不是梅花拳的拳師嗎？"（"I have also heard of this, but I don't know details. This means the armed confrontation has already begun. Why did they call the group Yìhéquán? Isn't Zhào, Sān-Duō a martial artist of Méihuā style?"）Mr. Zhù asked with another sigh and shook his head.

"爹！這是他因不得以武犯禁与滋事的門規，以及為避免連累累師門之故，改稱'梅花拳'為'義和拳'他們打著口號'掃清滅洋'與'官逼民反'為口號呢。"（"Die! This is because he had to avoid the rules of the Méihuā style that forbid their members to use martial arts to cause trouble. In order to prevent the involvement of what he did with his teacher and classmates, he changed Méihuāquán to Yìhéquán. They have two slogans: 'get rid of Qīng and annihilate the foreigners,' and also 'misgovernment drives the people to revolt.'"）

"這下他們不但與教會作對，還與清廷舉著反幟呀！可憐的農民百姓啊！記得兩年前山東按察使毓賢與巡撫李秉衡曾下令大量逮捕處決曹縣與單縣的大刀會會員嗎？這就是他們打著反清的旗幟啊！" ("In this case, they are not only against the churches, but also raise their flags against the Qīng Court. Poor farmers and civilians! Remember two years ago, Shāndōng Chief Prosecutor, Yù-Xián and Governor, Lǐ, Bǐng-Héng gave orders to arrest and execute a huge number of Broadsword Society members in Cáo and Dān Counties? That was because they were raising the flag against the Qīng Court.")

"可是，爹！義和拳的拳民可是義民啊！他們只是對滿清政府太失望了呢！" ("But, Dīe! These members of Yìhéquán are righteous people. They are just very disappointed with the Qīng Government.")

"威宏！你陪我明天到縣裡去見知縣許廷瑞，我看他的意見如何？到底我跟他還有些交情。" ("Wēi-Hóng! You accompany me to see the Jùyě magistrate, Xǔ, Tíng-Ruì tomorrow. I would like to ask his opinion. After all, I still have some old friendship with him.")

"親家翁！我跟博德也可以跟去嗎？" ("In-law! Can I and Bó-Dé come with you?") Bó-Wǔ asked.

"最好不要，因為太多人不太適合，這到底是我跟他私人的計議，何況你們跟他不熟，他不能也不敢坦白的表示他的意見。威宏是我的兒子，應該是比較沒問題。" ("It's better if you don't. This is not the right occasion to have many people. After all, this is only a private discussion between him and me. Furthermore, you don't know each other well. If you go, he will hesitate to express his real opinion. Wēi-Hóng is my son and shouldn't be a problem.")

Since Mr. Zhù said so, both Bó-Wǔ and Bó-Dé did not persist. While they were talking, Yù-Píng came in.

"爹！你們大夥，晚飯好了。" ("Dīe, everyone, dinner is ready.")

They all stopped talking and went to dinner. Bó-Wǔ and Bó-Dé were very curious about what the county magistrate, Xǔ, Tíng-Ruì, would say. Mr. Zhù and Wēi-Hóng left to go see him the next morning. Bó-Wǔ and Bó-Dé stayed behind, chatted with their sister and practiced martial arts. Since Bó-Wǔ had returned home, Bó-Dé was very anxious to learn from him what he had learned on Éméi Mountain. Bó-Dé was amazed by the stories that Bó-Wǔ told him, especially about Shìhǎi and Míngdào monks.

Meeting with Jùyě County Magistrate 與巨野縣長面談

Mr. Zhù and Wēi-Hóng came to the front door of the county

government building. There they saw some farmers who were assembling to request a meeting with Magistrate Xǔ. They knew that in a few more hours, the size of the group would swell to a huge amount. Mr. Zhù gave his card to the door guard and told him his intention to see Magistrate Xǔ.

"可是府台大人這幾天都不想見人呢！" (But Magistrate Xǔ does not want to see anyone these few days,) the door guard said.

"還是請麻煩傳遞這名帖給府台大人，告訴他故友來訪。" ("I understand, however please deliver this card to the magistrate and tell him that his old friend is here to visit him,") Mr. Zhù insisted and offered the guard a small bribe.

"我試試看，你們等著。" ("Let me try, you wait here.")

After ten minutes or so, the guard returned,

"你們跟我來，輕聲，不要驚擾其他的人。" ("You follow me. Keep quiet. Do not disturb other people.")

Then, he led Mr. Zhù and Wēi-Hóng into the building and took them to a study room.

"請等在這裡，我轉告府台大人。" ("Please wait here. Let me notify the magistrate.")

While they were waiting, a servant came with a tea pot and teacups, poured the tea into the cups and handed them to Mr. Zhù and Wēi-Hóng. While they were drinking tea, Magistrate Xǔ came in.

"府台大人！您好。有幾年不見了吧！這是小犬，威宏。" ("Magistrate! How are you? It must be a few years already since we saw each other. This is my son, Wēi-Hóng,") Mr. Zhù introduced his son to Magistrate Xǔ. Wēi-Hóng gave Magistrate Xǔ a deep bow.

"偉宸！不要跟我這麼客氣，我們是小時候的好朋友呢！" ("Wěi-Chén! Don't be so polite with me. We have been good friends since we were small.")

"可是現在不同了，您是我們的父母官呢！" ("But it is different now. You are our government official.")

"甭提了！現在做官並不比老百姓安穩，時機不同了。你來見我有什麼事嗎？" ("Don't mention it. Today's officials are not much more comfortable than general people. The time is different. What has brought you here to see me?")

"沒什麼大事，只是看到教案重重，百姓農民受到無限的委屈，只想知道朝廷的策略如何？我想如果朝廷不阻止暴徒教民對百姓農民的侵犯，事態會變成很不可收拾的呢！我們祝家莊可能是暴徒教民的下一個目標呢！" ("There is nothing too serious. I just see the number of conflicts between farmers and Christian gangsters multiplying rapidly, and civilians and farmers are suffering tremendously. I am wondering what the government's policy is? If the government does not stop the aggression of those Christian gangsters against civilians and farmers, the situation will become unmanageable soon. My Zhù village may be the next target for these Christian gangsters.")

"偉宸！你也看到每天有多少受委屈的農民來縣衙申冤，可是我卻做不得主啊！私底下講，朝廷怕那些洋人怕得不得了，就像一隻縮頭烏龜呢！我也呈上幾次奏摺，但一直都沒有回訊呢！" ("Wěi-Chén! As you have already seen outside, there are so many farmers who come here every day to speak their grievance and appeal for relief. But I cannot do anything for them. Privately speaking, Qīng Court is so afraid of those foreigners, they are just like a shrunk-head turtle. I have also submitted my memos about the situation to the top authorities a few times but have never received their response.")

"可是您知道，有個梅花拳師從今春一直在召集民眾，組織起來，以武力向教會抗衡！因為朝廷不能採取措施去阻止暴徒教民對農民的侵犯，他們已經有近兩千人了呢！" ("But do you know that there is a martial artist of Méihuā style who has begun to assemble people since this spring? He has organized them, and they have used force to resist the churches' aggression. Because the Qīng Court does not have an effective policy to stop those Christian gangsters from invading farmers, this group has already gathered nearly 2,000 people.")

"偉宸！這個我也知道。他們稱他們的組織叫'義和拳'，領導人物是叫趙三多的。清廷也都知道。可是清廷對洋人的痛恨，無法採取任何措施，他們也只有讓'義和拳'繼續發展下去。就可惜的是他們不應該打著口號'掃清滅洋'與'官逼民反'呢！清廷現在只有任其發展，觀時而動啊！這也就是山東按察使毓賢為什麼不再積極的阻止'義和拳'的擴展而逮捕這些義民呢！" ("Wěi-Chén! I also know this already. They call their organization Yìhéquán and the leader is Zhào, Sān-Duō. Actually, the Qīng Court also knows about this. However, due to the Qīng Court's hate of the foreigners, and since they cannot find an effective solution to the foreigners' incursions, they just allow the development of Yìhéquán to continue. Unfortunately, they should not use the slogans: 'get rid of Qīng and annihilate the foreigners' and also 'misgovernment drives the people to revolt.' But the policy of the Qīng Court is to allow them to continue to develop and wait to see what happens. This is why Shāndōng Chief Prosecutor, Yù-Xián does not stop Yìhéquán's aggressive expansion and arrest those righteous people.")

"那您的態度呢？" ("Then, what is your attitude?") Mr. Zhù asked.

"只要上面不施壓下來，我們只有睜一隻眼，閉一隻眼呢。" ("As long as

there is no pressure from the top, what we can do is open one eye and close the other.")

"我看您在這個時機，必定很忙，我們就此告辭了。" ("I believe you must be very busy during this urgent period. We will just say good-bye.")

"好說！好說！我們等這個危機完後，再敍敍舊往。記住我們所談論的這些不要對外面提起，如出事你我可要殺頭的。" ("Good! Good! We will wait till this crisis is over, and then we can sit comfortably and talk about the past. Remember, do not mention to outside people what we have talked about today. If anything bad happens, we could be beheaded.")

Mr. Zhù and Wēi-Hóng left with deeply pained hearts. They hated the Qīng Government's corruption and weakness that allowed those foreign powers to destroy their country. After they went home, they just told Bó-Wǔ and Bó-Dé the meeting had not been very hopeful. They did not want to talk much about it since it might trigger various problems. A few days later, Bó-Wǔ and Bó-Dé left to return home since the busy harvest season was approaching.

INEVITABLE RIOT 不可避免的暴動

After harvest season was over, both Bó-Wǔ and Bó-Dé kept worrying about the development of the conflict between farmers and Chinese Christian gangsters. They knew that, sooner or later, the aggression would fall upon their sister's family. Therefore, one evening during dinner,

"爹！上個月初，我跟三哥到大姊家時，暴徒教民與農民的鬥爭已經很緊張了。我一直在擔心大姊家目前的情況。現在今年農事已了，我可以跟三哥再去看看大姊那邊的情況嗎？" ("Dīe! At the beginning of last month when Sāngē and I went to see Dàjiě, the tension between Christian gangsters and farmers was already high. I keep worrying about Dàjiě family's current situation. Now that harvest time is over, may I again visit Dàjiě with Sāngē and see the situation?") Bó-Wǔ asked.

"博武！其實我也一直掛在心上呢！最好博威也跟你們一起去，他比較老成，不會太衝動。這事你們必須要小心。還有不要太露眼，記得你的大哥是北京衙門教頭，不要牽連了他。" ("Bó-Wǔ! Actually, this has also been hanging in my mind. It is better if Bó-Wéi also goes with you. He is more mature and not so impulsive in temperament. You must be very careful about this matter. Do not reveal too much of your identity and receive too much attention. Remember, your Dàgē (eldest brother) is a government detective in Běijīng. Do not pull him in to get him involved in this trouble.")

"爹！有二哥跟我們一起去是最好的了，有事可以跟他商量。" ("Dīe! It is best if Èrgē is able to go with us. We can consult with him whenever needed.")

***

They left riding three horses early the next morning to go to Cáozhōu. By nightfall, they had arrived. When they entered the Zhù family's village, everything seemed quiet and peaceful. However, to the three brothers, it had an unusual feeling that left them uneasy. It was too quiet.

They went into Zhù's house and were shocked to see that the whole family was gathered in the living room. When Yù-Píng realized her brothers had arrived, she couldn't help running toward them and released her sadness with tears.

"大姊！發生了什麼事？" ("Dàjiě! What has happened?") Bó-Wéi asked her.

When they got close enough to take a look, they saw Wēi-Hóng was seriously injured and lying unconscious on a comforter on the ground. A doctor was there examining his injury.

"今天下午與土霸教民的械鬥，威宏他。。。" ("There was armed fighting against Christian gangsters this afternoon. Wēi-Hóng, he ...") Yù-Píng started to say but couldn't continue and began to cry out loud. Mr. Zhù saw her break down and explained,

"我們與土霸教民已經打鬥幾天了。隔村是曹家莊，莊長曹作勝與巨野縣張家莊裡天主教堂的德國人主持薛田資神父以前有過口角，近幾天土霸教民就拿曹家莊開刀了。因為我們就在隔壁，知道土霸教民的下一個目標可能就是我們了，因此我們接受了曹家莊的邀請幫忙他們跟教民抵抗。所以我就聚集莊裡二十來個不平的莊民去幫忙他們，幾天來各有傷亡，不想今天威宏受了重傷回來。雖然他們人不比我們多，可是他們有幾隻洋槍，是最難對付的。" ("We have been fighting with Christian gangsters for a few days already. Our neighboring village is the Cáo Family Village. The leader of the village, Cáo, Zuò-Shèng had a serious quarrel in the past with the German Father Stenz, priest of the Catholic church located in the Zhāng Family Village of Jùyě County. Therefore, those Christian gangsters decided to invade the Cáo Family Village a few days ago. Because we are next to it and know that the next Christian gangsters' target is probably us, we accepted Cáo Family's plea for help to resist against Christian gangsters. I gathered more than 20 malcontent young people in the village, and they went to help them. There have been a few injuries and casualties in the last couple of days, but I did not expect that Wēi-Hóng would come back with such a serious injury today. Though the number the gangsters had was not as many as ours, they had a few foreign guns and that was the hardest to deal with.")

While they were talking, the doctor stood up and everyone paid attention to him.

"他腿上的刀傷，只要不要發炎，應該是沒問題。可是他左邊的排骨斷了一根，這比較危險。你們幫我小心的將他抬到臥室床上，待我將他矯正後，不要去移動他。他需要先躺二十來天，最好少移動，不要讓他太激動，你們知道他甚至連呼吸都會痛的。最近二十天內是最重要的，如果不惡化，他就可以完全恢復的。" ("The wound on his leg, as long as there is no serious infection, should be okay. However, there is a broken rib on his left side. This is more dangerous. Help me carry him to his bed. After I correct the rib and put it back, do not move him. He needs to stay in bed for more than 20 days. The less he moves the better. Do not excite him. You know, he will be in pain even just breathing. The next 20 days are the most important. If he does not get worse, he will recover completely.")

Bó-Wǔ stepped forward,

"讓我來，他上身最好不要動得太厲害，二哥，您幫我抬腳。大姊，您帶我到您們的臥室去。" ("Allow me! It is better if I can lift him without too much moving of his upper body. Érgē! Help carry his legs. Dàjiě, take us to your bedroom,") Bó-Wǔ said to Bó-Wéi, since Bó-Wéi was stronger and more careful than Bó-Dé.

The doctor was worried that if there were too many people carrying Wēi-Hóng, without perfect coordination, it could make the rib's separation worse. However, everyone also worried that Bó-Wǔ might not be able to handle Wēi-Hóng's heavy body. But when they saw Bó-Wǔ was able to pick up Wēi-Hóng so easily and stably, they were shocked by Bó-Wǔ's strength. With Yù-Píng's guidance, they came to the bedroom. Bó-Wǔ and Bó-Wēi placed Wēi-Hóng on the bed carefully. After they put him down, Wēi-Hóng woke up and moaned painfully.

"不要動，也不要激動。你的排骨斷了一根，你亂動會惡化你的情況。" ("Don't move and also don't be excited. One of your ribs is broken. Too much random movement will worsen your condition,") the doctor reminded him quickly. Then, the doctor used his professional skill to correct and align the broken rib. After he took care of the rib injury, he took a needle out to stitch closed the open wound that was a couple inches long on Wēi-Hóng's front right thigh. Finally, he put some herbs on the wound to prevent infection.

"幸好沒傷到動脈，否則就不堪設想了。腿傷要保持乾淨，避免用水去洗他，需要保持乾淨，知道嗎？否則會造成發炎的。如果需要清潔傷口，就用高粱酒。我隔兩天再來看他。" ("It is fortunate that the wound did not reach an artery. If it had, the disaster would be unimaginable. The wound area must be kept clean. Avoid using water to wash it. Do you understand? Unsanitary water may cause an infection. If you wish to clean the wound area, use sorghum liquor. I will come to see him again in two days.")

"大夫，天晚了，您就留著吃過飯再走吧？" ("Doctor, it is late. Why don't you have dinner first with us and then go?") Mr. Zhù asked politely. He deeply appreciated the doctor's treatment of his son. He also gave the doctor two taels of silver for his help.

"不行啊！我必須趕回曹州市，最近由於農民與教民的械鬥，很多人受傷，我必須趕回去。" ("Oh, thank you but I can't! I need to rush back to Cáozhōu City. Because of the armed fighting between farmers and Christian gangsters, there are many wounded people. I need to get back quickly.")

"博德！麻煩你送他一程，你來過幾次，對這裡的路面比較熟悉。" ("Bó-Dé, can I trouble you to accompany him for a distance? You have been here a few times before and are more familiar with this area.")

"沒問題，親家翁。來！博武，你跟我一起去。二哥，您就留在這裡看還有什麼需要幫忙的。" ("No problem, in-law! Come, Bó-Wǔ, you come with me. Èrge! Please stay here and see if there is anything that you can help with.")

Bó-Dé and Bó-Wǔ went outside and mounted their horses. They accompanied the doctor for five miles.

"你們回去吧，從這裡我可以自己走，記得兩天後我會再來。" ("You may go back. I can find my way from here. I will be back in two days,") the doctor said.

"謝謝您，大夫。" ("Thank you, Doctor,") Bó-Dé replied.

On the way back, Bó-Wǔ and Bó-Dé talked about the incident. They were angry and decided to help the farmers fight against the Chinese Christian gangsters.

***

ARMED CONFLICT 械鬥

Since the three brothers were guests, Mr. Zhù did not ask them to help the next morning. Yù-Píng also worried that if they joined the fight that day, her brothers might be wounded or even killed. However, when Bó-Wēi, Bó-Wǔ, and Bó-Dé got up early in the morning, they saw some villagers were gathering again with some weapons such as sabers, swords, bows and arrows. Since most of the farmers did not have any actual weapons, they brought some farm tools to fight with. Actually, nearly 90% of the villagers were farmers. Only a few had trained in martial arts in the past.

"二哥！博武昨天跟我決定今天插手幫忙他們。您也參加我們嗎？" ("Èrge! Bó-Wǔ and I decided yesterday to join them to fight against gangsters today. Will you join us?") Bó-Dé asked Bó-Wēi.

"我也跟去看看，可是千萬要小心啊！" ("I will also go to see the situation. However, we have to be very careful.")

When Mr. Zhù knew that they intended to join the fight, in one way he was touched that they wanted to help, but he also worried about their safety. By 8:00 in the morning, there were already nearly 20 people assembled. The group went to Cáo Family Village. In half an hour, they had arrived and saw at least 100 Cáo villagers had gathered, prepared for another day of confrontation.

By 9:30 in the morning a group of gangsters, at least 60, marched to the entrance of the village and built a temporary defensive wall in the distance. Almost one-third of the village people, such as women, children, and seniors, had already been evacuated to other towns or cities. If the confrontations continued for another month, without better weapons the villagers would not have a chance. The pressure of giving up the village got stronger and stronger.

Half an hour later, those gangsters started to move their wall closer and closer to the village gate. When they were within shooting range, the villagers began to shoot some arrows. Unfortunately, it seemed it was useless. The arrows just stopped the gangsters for about ten minutes or so and then they started their advance again. When Bó-Wǔ saw that, he left the shelter of a temporary shield built with old tables and farm vehicles and shouted at the gangster group,

"你們講不講道理？那裡有人這麼野蠻的？" ("Why are you so unreasonable? How can you be so barbaric?")

Suddenly, a gunshot, Peng! A bullet went by his left ear. He was not aware that he was exposed within the shooting range of their guns since he had never seen guns. Immediately, he hid himself behind the defensive obstacles.

"博武！不要再出去了。危險啊！" ("Bó-Wǔ! Don't go out again. It is dangerous,") Bó-Wēi said with a worried face.

The Christian gangsters again moved their defensive wall closer to the village gate, getting even closer than they had yesterday. Seeing that, the leader of Cáo's village, Cáo, Zuò-Shèng, gave an order to charge and nearly 100 people ran toward the gangsters. When Bó-Wǔ and Bó-Dé saw it, they also joined the assault. But about 30 meters from the gangsters' offensive line, the villagers were forced to retreat in a hail of arrows and gun shots. Immediately, a few farmers fell, injured. The rest of them tried to help the wounded ones and ran back to their defensive line very quickly.

It was very similar to yesterday. The villagers realized that they could not stop the gangsters' advance till a certain distance that their arrows could reach. However, the gangsters had guns, at least five, and the guns could shoot much farther than arrows. This was the fifth day of confrontation, and more and more villagers were getting injured. Both sides maintained their positions till dusk. Before nightfall, the gangsters began to cease their aggression and left. All the villagers also returned to their homes except some night guards who were assigned to keep watch on conditions during the night.

When the three brothers returned to Zhù village with the other helpers, they knew two more villagers had gotten injured today. Though the injuries were not life threatening, they still needed to be treated.

After dinner,

"這樣僵持下去，也不是辦法。從今天看來，似乎他們的人越來越多。而我們受傷的人也越來越多。唉！這不是長久之計啊。這樣拖下去，早晚曹家莊會被霸佔的。" ("If both sides continue to resist like this, it will not end well. From what we saw today, it seemed that the gangsters had more people than yesterday while our side had more injuries. Ai! This is not a long-term solution. If the situation like this continues, Cáo's village will be occupied by them sooner or later,") Mr. Zhù looked at everyone and said.

"親家！您們有沒有考慮到請義和拳來幫忙抵抗他們呢？" ("In-law! Have you considered inviting Yìhéquán to help us resist them?") Bó-Wēi asked.

"我想到過。可是義和拳在沙柳寨一帶，離這邊有一段距離呢。何況我們並沒有門路跟他們聯絡。還有的是他們願意來幫忙我們嗎？" ("I thought of it. But Yìhéquán is at Shāliǔzhài area, and that is some distance from here. Furthermore, we don't have any connection to reach out to them. Again, we also don't know if they will come to help us,") Mr. Zhù replied.

While they were talking, one of the servants, Zūn-Xián (尊賢), said,

"老爺！我知道祝忠義的大兒子，永年，是義和拳團員。他是趙三多的門徒。" ("Lǎoyé (Master)! I know the eldest son of Zhù, Zhōng-Yì, Yǒng-Nián, is a Yìhéquán member. He is a disciple of Zhào, Sān-Duō.")

"這樣的話，尊賢，麻煩你一趟，去請祝忠義來這裡商談一下。" ("In this case, Zūn-Xián, can I trouble you to find Zhù, Zhōng-Yì and ask him to come here to discuss this?")

***

Twenty minutes later, a 52-year-old villager Zhù, Zhōng-Yì, was in the living room with them. He had been getting things ready so that, if the situation got worse, he would move to Shāliǔzhài to live with his son. His son, Yǒng-Nián, had gone to Shāliǔzhài to work when he was 18 years old. A year later, through his friend's introduction, he began to learn martial arts from Zhào, Sān-Duō.

"祝老！您也知道我們這邊與教徒暴民衝突的事。現在唯一能夠保全我們祝家莊的希望就是請義和拳來幫忙我們。忠義說您的大兒子，永年，是義和拳領導，趙三多的門徒。您想我們能不能透過您的兒子跟趙三多聯絡，請他們來幫忙我們對抗教民暴徒？" ("Old Zhù! You already know about the conflicts we have had with those Chinese Christian gangsters. Now, the only way to protect our villages is to ask Yìhéquán's help. Zhōng-Yì told us that your eldest son, Yǒng-Nián, is the disciple of Yìhéquán leader, Zhào, Sān-Duō. Would you be able to help us establish a connection with Zhào, Sān-Duō through your son and ask them to help us to resist Christian gangsters?")

"祝鄉長！這是義不容辭的事啊！我也為我們祝家莊擔心呢。" ("Chief Zhù! This is also my duty. I also worry about our Zhù village.")

"尊賢！你幫忙準備兩匹快馬，明天一早你陪祝老到沙柳寨。" ("Zūn-Xián! Can you prepare two fast horses and accompany Old Zhù to Shāliǔzhài tomorrow?")

"我也可以跟他們去。" ("I can also go with them,") Bó-Wǔ said.

"你的功夫好！我希望你明天還可以幫忙我們對抗教民暴徒。我看博威比較老成點，我看還是博威跟去好照顧一切。" ("Your Gōngfū is great! We need you to stay to help us against Christian gangsters tomorrow. Bó-

Wēi is more mature and has more experience. I think it is better that Bó-Wēi go with them and take care of them.")

Since Mr. Zhù said so, Bó-Wǔ did not resist. Actually, he also worried about the next day's conflict. In the morning, Bó-Wēi escorted Zhù, Zhōng-Yì and Zūn-Xián on their journey to Shāliǔzhài. Traveling on horseback, they should arrive there by late afternoon.

***

Both sides resisted against each other for three more days. Then, before dusk, a huge group of Yìhéquán members arrived. Altogether they numbered at least 600. The Yìhéquán leader, Zhào, Sān-Duō had sent one of his assistants, Chén, Shàng-Zhōng (陳尚忠), to lead the group. In one way, Mr. Zhù was happy that they were able to come to help, in another way, he did not know how to take care of this big group of people in such a small village. There were only about 120 farming families still in the village. Each family would have to provide food and lodging for an average of five Yìhéquán members. Even if Zhù Village shared the responsibility with Cáo Village, it was still a big burden, especially if the Yìhéquán stayed for a long time. Having their protection was not a long-term solution either.

Their captain, Mr. Chén, and three of his top assistants were invited to have dinner with Mr. Zhù so they could discuss strategies for handling the problem. Naturally, Cáo Village leader, Cáo, Wén-Xìng (曹文信) was also invited. After Mr. Zhù and Mr. Cáo explained the situation to Captain Chén,

"我們最重要的不是製造更多的問題。最重要的是讓教民暴徒知道我們的勢力，希望他們能知難而退。用暴力解決問題，是最後的辦法。" ("The most important thing is we should not create more problems. The most important thing is making those Christian gangsters acknowledge our power and that we are able to stop their aggression. Using violence to solve the problem is the last solution,") Captain Chén said.

"我們也希望不要將這件事擴大。只要他們不再來干擾我們，我們就滿足了。" ("We also hope not to enlarge this conflict. As long as they don't bother us, we are satisfied,") Mr. Zhù replied.

"明天我們就在曹家莊亮拳示威。如他們還不懂的進退，那只有付之武力了。" ("We will demonstrate our power at Cáo's village tomorrow. If they still don't know their limit, then we will have to use violence,") Captain Chén said.

They agreed on the strategy. Cáo took about 250 Yìhétuán members with him to Cáo Village to share the burden of feeding and housing them that evening. Cáo Village had only 62 farming families now. All others had left before the conflict got worse.

***

Early the next morning, the entire group from Zhù Village including 80 villagers and more than 350 Yìhéquán members, went to Cáo Village. With the Yìhéquán members' help, they made the defensive wall stronger and safer. They waited till 9:30 in the morning, then they saw the gangsters' group of at least 65 people again approaching the Cáo Village entrance.

When the gangsters arrived, they were surprised to see there were so many people ready to defend Cáo Village. This made them worried and scared. From the uniforms, they recognized that their new enemies were Yìhéquán members. As the gangsters knew, at least half of Yìhéquán members were martial artists. Furthermore, they knew the Yìhéquán would not hesitate to use violence and to kill if necessary. They were not like farmers who could be scared easily. They all knew that the Yìhéquán had already killed two Christian gangsters in another village during conflicts in the past.

In just a few minutes, the gangsters heard the loud sounds of drum, gong, and cymbals being played by the villagers' side. After a few more minutes, a group of Yìhéquán members came out onto the road between both sides and performed martial arts. They simply wanted to demonstrate their power to the gangsters.

Bó-Wǔ and his two brothers also performed some martial arts. Bó-Wǔ demonstrated his extraordinary strength by lifting a heavy farmer's vehicle above his head. Everyone knew that this farm vehicle had a weight of at least 300 kilograms. Both sides could not believe his power.

This big group and also its demonstration of its martial capability made the gangster group hesitant to carry out any aggression. They knew if they attacked, it would be their ruin on that day. After the demonstration, the gangster group retreated very quickly and disappeared from sight.

All the villagers and Yìhéquán members were shouting cheerfully. They laughed and were happy. This was the first time that the gangsters had been scared away. Everyone remained to defend the village till afternoon, but those gangsters never returned.

***

That evening during dinner, everyone was talking about the day's victory. After dinner, the villages' leaders and the captain of the Yìhéquán, Mr. Chén, had a meeting to discuss a long-term solution.

"陳領隊！先謝謝您們今天的幫忙。可是我在擔心一旦您們回去以後，他們還會再來找麻煩呢。" ("Captain Chén! First, I would like to thank you and your team members for their help today. However, I am worried that once you leave, they will return again to make trouble,") Mr. Zhù said.

"祝鄉長！曹鄉長！最好的辦法是我將五十位義和拳團員留在這裡一段時間。如果他們再來找麻煩，他們可以幫忙你們。如果情況不佳，他們可以馬上關照我們，我們可以馬上趕來支持。" ("Village Chief Zhù! Village Chief Cáo! The best solution is keeping 50 Yìhéquán members here for a period of time. If those gangsters come to look for trouble again, they can help you. In addition, if the situation gets worse, they can notify us and we will come to support you immediately,") Captain Chén suggested.

"謝謝您！陳領隊。他們可以待多久呢？" ("Thank you very much, Captain Chén! How long will they be able to stay?") Mr. Cáo asked.

"他們可以待到一切平息下去後再離開。" ("They can stay till the conflict ceases.")

They all agreed on this arrangement. It would be easier for the villagers to take care of 50 helpers instead of 600. Furthermore, these 50 helpers were all martial artists.

After the meeting, Captain Chén found a chance to talk to Bó-Wǔ, Bó-Wēi, and Bó-Dé. He looked at Bó-Wǔ,

"從今天的亮拳，我知道你的功力很高。我們義和拳正需要向你們這樣的人才。希望你們三位能加入義和拳，為我大中華伸展正義。" ("From today's martial arts demonstration, I know your martial skills are very high. Yìhéquán group needs a talent like you. I hope the three of you are able to join Yìhéquán and help us achieve justice for our great China.")

"沒問題我們可以加入你們的陣營。" ("There is no problem. We can all join your organization,") without further consideration Bó-Dé replied with excitement. He was so happy that they had defeated the gangster group that day.

"我想我們還是先回去後跟我們父母商量後再做決定。" ("I think it is better for us to consult with our parents first before we make any decision,") Bó-Wēi said more calmly and thoughtfully. He believed that they should not jump in and make a decision without considering it first. He remembered his Dīe mentioned that their eldest brother, Bó-Wén, was a government detective. If Yìhéquán was not recognized and accepted by the government, it could mean trouble for them in the future.

"這樣的話，在你們決定後再來找我。" ("In this case, come to see me when you have made your decision,") Mr. Chén replied.

Two days later, Bó-Wēi, Bó-Dé, and Bó-Wǔ went home.

Due to his family's cautious nursing care, Wēi-Hóng recovered very quickly within a month. He could now walk by himself without being helped. However, he still could not use his arm to do any heavy work. The doctor had said it would take at least three months for a complete recovery. A smile returned to Yù-Píng's face.

After one month when they saw that the Christian gangsters had not come back to make trouble, the Yìhéquán members left the village and returned to Shāliǔzhài.

CÁOZHŌU PRIEST CASE (ALSO CALLED THE JÙYĚ INCIDENT) (GERMAN: JÙYĚ VORFALL) 曹州教士案/鉅野教案

The weather was cloudy, and a cold wind blew hard in the late evening of November 1st of 1897. It was quiet except for the sound of the wind's blowing. The streets were empty since all the people in the Zhāng Village (張家莊) were sleeping on this dark cold night. Suddenly, there was a group of more than ten people sneaking swiftly in the darkness toward a church in the village. In their hands, daggers or small knives could be seen. Finally, they arrived at an empty stable 50 yards beside the church. This was their final check before executing their plot. From what they knew, the priest they were looking for should be in the dwelling behind the church.

"我希望薛田資這小子在裡面，我想幹掉這個德國洋神父有好久了。" ("I hope this villain, Stenz, is inside. I have wanted to kill this German missionary for a long time,") one of the plotters said.

"噤聲！不要打草驚蛇。" ("Xū! Keep quiet. Don't act rashly and alert the enemy!")

"可是就是因為這個老鬼對教民的庇護，我們才落到今天這個地步啊。我們有多少兄弟因為這個老鬼而喪失了生命呢。" ("But it is because of this buster's protection of Christian gangsters that we have ended up at this stage. How many of our brothers have died because of him?")

"這個我們都知道，不用再說了。我們從四面包抄，不怕他逃掉。小心！不要驚動鄰家的狗。"("We all know this. Don't say any more. Let's surround this dwelling and don't let him escape. Be careful, do not disturb any dogs in this neighborhood.")

Immediately, they divided into four groups to surround the priest's dwelling and went in through the front and rear doors. In this dwelling, there was a living room, a small kitchen, and a large bedroom. The plotters quietly snuck in and went to the bedroom. However once there, they discovered not one but two foreign priests sleeping inside. They did not know which one was Father George M. Stenz (薛田資神父), the head priest stationed in Zhāng's Village. Without hesitating, they stabbed and killed both of the priests. Then one of the plotters used a match to light the candle on the desk. In the light they found out that neither of the persons they had just killed was the Father Stenz they were targeting. They didn't know that they had just killed Father Henle (能方濟) and Father Nies (韓理迦略) from Yánggǔ (陽谷) and Yùnchéng (鄆城) who had come to visit Father Stenz the day before.

"我們殺錯人了！這兩位洋傳教士不是薛田資。"("We have killed the wrong persons. These two missionaries are not Stenz.")

"不管怎樣，所有的洋傳教士，都是壞蛋，都該殺。"("It does not matter. All foreign missionaries are bad and deserve to die.")

"可是薛田資這小子躲到那裡去了？"("But where is this buster, Stenz, hiding?")

Suddenly, a dog near the church sensed some activity and began to bark. Soon its barking triggered all of the dogs in the village to bark.

"我們必須趕快離開這裡，被抓到了就不妙了。"("We better get out of here quick. If we are caught, it will be a disaster.")

"走！開溜。盡快離開這裡，我們明天劉良寺廟口見面。"("Go! Let's separate and leave here as soon as possible. We will meet each other at Liúliáng Temple tomorrow.")

Father Stenz was awakened by the dogs' barking. Soon, he heard noises from people gathering in the church dwelling. Since he had given the two most comfortable beds to his guest priests, he was sleeping in a small resting room in the church this night. He did not know what was going on and did not realize that he had just escaped an assassination targeting him. He went out the back door of the church and saw a few Chinese Christians with lanterns. When they saw Father Stenz, they were so surprised.

"薛神父，您沒事。那房子裡面被殺死的兩位傳教士是誰？"("Father

Stenz, you are alright! Then, who are those two missionaries who were killed in the room?") one of the Chinese Christians asked.

"他們是我的朋友，是陽谷與鄆城的神父，能方濟與韓理迦略。他們昨天來拜訪我，我將我的臥房與客房給他們睡，而我睡在教堂裡的小房間，沒想到出了這個意外。" ("They are my friends. They are Fathers from Yánggǔ (陽谷) and Yùnchéng (鄆城), Father Henle and Father Nies. They came to visit me yesterday. I let them sleep in my room and I was sleeping in the small room in the church. I did not expect this to happen.")

"張莊長，明天一早請您幫我處理能方濟與韓理迦略的屍體。我明天必須趕到濟寧電告德國駐華大使將這事轉給德國政府。" ("Chief Zhāng, please help me take care of Father Henle and Father Nies' bodies tomorrow morning. I must rush to Jìníng City to report this incident to the German Embassy and ask them to pass this news on to the German government,") Father Stenz said.

The next day, with two Chinese Christians' escort, Father George M. Stenz rushed to Jìníng (濟寧城). After he sent a telegram to the German Embassy, since he was afraid there might be a follow-up attack against him, he stayed in a Catholic Church in Jìníng City and waited for further instruction from the German government.

The Chinese government investigated and came to the conclusion that the murders were most likely conducted by surviving members of the Broadsword Society (大刀會).

CONSEQUENCES OF JÙYĚ INCIDENT 曹州教案之後果

When the message reached the German government, an emergency meeting was called. All the top advisers of Emperor Wihelm II assembled in a large meeting room. While everyone's face was solemn and serious, Emperor Wihelm II could not help letting a small smile cross his face.

Emperor Wihelm II always regretted that Germany did not find opportunities to invade other countries and turn them into German colonies like Britain, Spain, France, and the Netherlands did. To him, it seemed the great opportunity to expand German territories into other countries had been missed. There was less and less land still available that could be colonized. Therefore, since he took power, he had aggressively enlarged the size of the German Navy and enhanced its power, waiting for an opportunity to expand Germany's territories. The Jùyě Incident had just given him the excuse he needed to invade China. Without this excuse, it would be hard to explain his actions to other countries such as Russia, Britain, France, and Japan.

By the time the meeting was over, the decision was made. On November 14th, 1897, the German Empire used the murders of their missionaries as a pretext, under the command of Admiral Diederichs, to attack and seize Jiāozhōu Bay (膠州灣) and neighboring territories on Shāndōng's east coast.

Under German threats, the Qīng Government was also forced to remove many Shāndōng officials including Shāndōng Governor Lǐ, Bǐng-Héng (李秉衡), Cáozhōu Mayor Wàn, Dé-Lì (萬德力), and Jùyě County Magistrate, Xǔ, Tíng-Ruì (許廷瑞) from their posts. The German government also demanded that the Qīng Government build three Catholic churches in Jìníng (濟寧), Cháozhōu (曹州), and Jùyě (巨野) at the Qīng Government's expense.

The families of the two priests that had been attacked also received 3,000 taels of silver in compensation. Churches also received the right to construct seven fortified residences in the area at the Qīng Government's expense. This settlement strengthened missionary work in southern Shāndōng Province. In addition, the Qīng Government had to pay 220,000 taels as a final settlement. The Qīng Government lost any power it had to control the powerful foreign countries' expansions. Finally, on March 6th 1898, the Chinese Imperial Court leased the area of Jiāozhōu to Germany for 99 years, the entire province was declared a German sphere of influence, and Germany was given the right to construct two railways from Jiāozhōu to the province capital of Jìnán. On April 27th, 1898, Germany officially declared Jiāozhōu as her colony (Schutzgebiet).

Imitating Germany, other powers (Russia, Britain, France, and Japan) began "a scramble for concessions" to secure their own spheres of influence in China. In fact, the Jùyě Incident was the main cause leading to the Yìhétúan's (Boxer's) uprising (1899–1900 A.D.), a movement against the Christian and foreign presence in northern China.

Historian Paul Cohen has called the Jùyě Incident "the opening wedge in a process of greatly intensified imperialist activity in China" and Joseph W. Esherick comments that the Jùyě killings "set off a chain of events which radically altered the course of Chinese history." Japanese "Diplomatic Times" (外交時報), described this settlement, saying "[e]very Qīng Government's movement or action was governed by German Government just like the actual power of controlling Manchuria was by Russia. Now, the real controlling power of

Shāndōng has fallen into Germany's hands." ("華政府于山東一舉一動，皆受德人指使，似滿洲之實權歸俄人掌握。彼山東之實權，亦將歸諸德人矣。")

CHINESE RESENTMENT 中國人的怨恨

In this Chinese New Year of 1898, Hào-Xuān's whole family was together. Cheerful feelings and laughter filled the whole family. All the women were preparing various kinds of delicious foods and desserts, while all the men got together to chat. Eventually the conversation moved on to the topic of the Jùyě Incident and Germany's recent invasion.

"嘿！你們想是誰去巨野殺那些德國傳教士的？" ("Hey! Who do you think killed those German missionaries in Jùyě?") Bó-Dé first mentioned this topic.

"我想應該不是義和拳幹的。因為義和拳的組織剛剛成形，到目前為止他們一直採取防禦的態度，根本很少去攻擊教會，何況是外國神父。依我看來，最可能的是大刀會的餘黨。他們幹這件事是為了替他們的領導報仇。" ("I believe that was not done by Yìhéquán. This is because the Yìhéquán organization has just been established. So far, their attitude and policies are defensive, and they seldom attack churches, not to mention they were foreign missionaries. According to my opinion, the killing was committed by Broadsword Society. I think they did this as a revenge for their two leaders,") Hào-Xuān expressed his opinion.

"可是他們想殺的卻沒殺到，而殺死二位無辜的德國神父。他們只是死的很冤枉。" ("But they didn't kill the one they wished to kill, instead killing two innocent German missionaries. They had died in vain,") Bó-Wǔ said.

"可恨的是德國政府卻因為這個教案找到了藉口。我聽說他們已經出兵將膠州灣與沿海一帶全佔領了。" ("It is so hateful that due to this incident, the German government has found an excuse to invade China. I heard their soldiers have occupied Jiāozhōu and neighboring territories,") Bó-Dé said, his anger reflected on his face.

"我相信這次德國政府會再獅子大開口，提出很多條件呢。" ("I believe that the German government will use this opportunity to demand many concessions from the Qīng Court,") Hào-Xuān said.

"不知道大姊那邊情況怎麼樣了？" ("Do you know what the situation at Dàjiě's place is?") Bó-Wǔ asked with concern.

"對了！忘了告訴你們。昨天我們村里，正榮，從曹州回來。他說自從上次義和拳到曹州去幫忙祝家莊和曹家莊後，他們就不敢再去找麻煩了。"

("Yes! I forgot to tell you. Our villager, Zhèng-Róng just returned from Cáozhōu yesterday. He said, since Yìhéqúan helped the Zhù and Cáo villages last time, those gangsters have not dared to cause more trouble there,") Bó-Wēi said.

"唉！義和拳還是有用的。只要我們團結，相信那些教民暴徒不敢輕舉妄動呢。可是如果義和拳像大刀會一樣的亂攻擊洋人，我相信早晚會引起不堪設想的後果。而且如果洋人像大刀會一樣的對清廷抱怨與威脅，清廷怕洋人，可能會對義和拳大開殺戒呢。" ("Ai! Yìhéqúan is still useful. If we unite, those Christian gangsters will not dare to initiate more aggressions. However, if Yìhéqúan members begin to attack foreigners randomly without consideration, I believe the negative consequences will be unimaginable sooner or later. If foreigners complain and threaten the Qīng Court, due to their fear of foreigners the Qīng Court may begin to slaughter Yìhéqúan members like they did with the Broadsword Society,") Hào-Xūan expressed his opinion.

"爹！上次我跟二哥、三哥去幫忙大姊時，義和拳領隊邀請我們參加義和拳。您看呢？" ("Dīe! When Érgē, Sāngē, and I went to help Dàjiě last time, the captain of Yìhéqúan invited us to join their organization. What is your opinion?") Bó-Wǔ asked.

"博武！我的看法是不要輕舉妄動。如果清廷那天決定對義和拳開刀，那你們就糟糕了。而且如出事，你們可能會給你大哥博文帶來很大的麻煩。" ("Bó-Wǔ! My viewpoint is, do not act rashly. If the Qīng Court decides to eliminate Yìhéqúan one day, then you will be in a terrible situation. Not only that, if this happens you may bring huge trouble to your Dàgē.")

"爹！可是保家衛國是我們每個人的責任與義務啊。" ("But Dīe! Protecting the family and guarding the country is the duty and obligation of every one of us.")

"沒有錯！可是你們要考慮到後果啊。何況並不是所有的洋人都是壞的。有些傳教士是很善良、仁慈的。可恨的是因為傳教士裡有些壞傳教士，在他們政府的支持下，去煽動鼓舞那些壞教民做這些事。其實罪魁禍首是列強政府。由於他們對我中華的侵掠與無理的要脅，才會成為這個情況呢。" ("You are correct! But you must consider the consequences. Furthermore, not all foreign missionaries are bad. Many of them are kind and benevolent. The most hateful problem is that some of those bad missionaries, under their government's support, agitate and encourage those Christian gangsters to do bad things. Traced back to its root, the culprit of this situation is the foreign governments. Their invasion and unreasonable threats to China have resulted in this situation.")

They did not think of any good solutions during their discussion.

They would just have to wait and see. Due to Hào-Xūan's disagreement about Bó-Wǔ and his brothers joining the Yìhéqúan, the brothers kept quiet.

***

WÙXŪ REFORM 戊戌變法

After Germany declared that Jiāozhōu was their new colony and demanded so many conditions and compensation from the Qīng Court, many Chinese saw the hopelessness of the future of China under the Qīng Government. Their only hope was with Emperor Guāngxù (光緒皇帝). They knew Guāngxù was a wise emperor. Unfortunately, the power was in Empress Dowager Cíxǐ's hands. When Guāngxù turned 18 years old in 1889, he got married and Empress Dowager Cíxǐ (慈禧太后) announced that she would return power to Emperor Guāngxù. Unfortunately, whenever Emperor Guāngxù intended to carry out any policy, he still needed to receive approval from Cíxǐ. Therefore, actual power was still in Cíxǐ hands and the country's conditions were getting worse and worse every day.

After a year, a reform party called "Wéixīn Party" (維新派) was founded and led by Kāng, Yǒu-Wéi (康有為) and Liáng, Qǐ-Chāo (梁啟超). They hoped that with Emperor Guāngxù's support, through this party China would be able to find a new hope and establish a strong new China. Therefore, Emperor Guāngxù announced a series of reform policies on June 11th of 1898. However, due to Empress Dowager Cíxǐ's opposition the reform action failed on September 21st and lasted only 103 days. Afterward, Cíxǐ killed the emperor's six advisors and put the emperor under house arrest at Yíngtái, Zhōngnánhǎi (中南海瀛台). She re-seized power completely and did not trust anyone. To avoid being executed by Empress Dowager Cíxǐ, with the assistance of some foreign countries, Kāng, Yǒu-Wéi and Liáng, Qǐ-Chāo fled to Japan. This reform was also known as Wùxū Reform (戊戌變法).

THE FORMATION OF YÌHÉTUÁN 義和團的形成

Germany's invasion of Shāndōng Province caused much anger and sadness among the Chinese general public. In one way, they were angry at Germany's invasion, in another, they felt hopeless for their future under Qīng's corrupt and weak government.

Originally, the Chinese people had a big hope for their country under Emperor Guāngxù's leadership when he turned 18 years old. However, after the failure of the Wùxū Reform and Emperor Guāngxù's house arrest, people were extremely disappointed. More and more Chinese people realized that since they could not trust the Qīng government anymore, China might have a chance only if all the people united together against the foreigners.

China's situation worsened when the Shāndōng and Zhílì (today's Héběi) Provinces suffered a big flood in 1898. Immediately after the flood, a severe drought followed. Furthermore, an additional disaster fell on the area in the form of a serious locust infestation. Words were spread out among innocent and general blind believers that all these disasters were caused by the Christian expansion. In order to save the situation, they believed they must get rid of the Christians and foreigners. The number of Yìhéquán continued to increase rapidly.

When Shāndōng Governor (巡撫), Yù-Xián (毓賢) saw such a huge force of Yìhéquán, since the Qīng Court was afraid to do anything, he permitted their activities. When he passed the message to Empress Dowager Cíxǐ, he received Cíxǐ's silent approval.

Then when, after demanding many unfair conditions, the German government declared that Jiāozhōu was their colony, this made many Chinese angry. More and more people joined Yìhéquán. As their numbers swelled, the Yìhéquán members became aggressive. Now they were not just defending farmers but also attacking churches and foreigners. In addition, due to Yìhéquán's effective protection of the farmers, more and more farmers joined Yìhéquán. Their members had increased from a few thousands to more than 20,000.

***

After the busy harvest season was over, Hào-Xuān's entire family again were gathered and chatting.

"爹！外面都在說義和拳的運動已經收到山東巡撫毓賢的安撫與鼓勵。他們還說慈禧太后也不反對義和拳的運動呢。" ("Dīe! People from outside said the Yìhéquán's activities have already received Shāndōng governor, Yù-Xián's support and encouragement. They also said even Empress Dowager Cíxǐ was not against Yìhéquán's activities,") Bó-Dé said.

"真的嗎？看來清廷是已經對洋人沒辦法了。清廷支持義和拳可以得到民眾的支持，同時，他們也可以出一口怨氣。" ("Really! It seems that the

Qīng Court has exhausted their strategy against foreigners. The Qīng Court's support of Yìhéquán cannot only acquire people's support, but also can get rid of their resentment,") Hào-Xūan said.

"爹！如果清廷不反對義和拳運動的話，我可以去參加他們嗎？" ("Dīe! If the Qīng Court is not against Yìhéquán activities, can I join them?") Bó-Wǔ asked.

"最好不要，博武。如果那天清廷受洋人的壓力又反悔，義和拳可能就要遭殃了。" ("You better not, Bó-Wǔ. If the Qīng Court changes again one day after receiving foreigners' threat and regrets, all Yìhéquán members will be ruined.")

"可是我們應該保家衛國啊！爹！" ("But we should protect our family and guard the country, Dīe.")

"不用再說了！我還是反對你們涉入義和拳，況且我這農莊還需要你的幫忙呢。" ("Don't say anymore! I am still against your involvement in Yìhéquán. Furthermore, I need your help for this farm.")

***

Two days later, Bó-Wǔ was talking to Bó-Dé,

"三哥！我真想去參加義和拳。我白練了一身的功夫，現在應該是可以拿來應用的時候。" ("Sāngē! I really want to join Yìhéquán. I have trained my Gōngfū to such a proficient level, it is time that I use it to help.")

"可是爹不准我們去呢。" ("But Dìe will not allow us to go.")

"我想明天一早我就偷偷的離家去參加義和拳。我認為這是我們所有的中國人都應該做的事。" ("I am thinking of running away from home early tomorrow morning and going to join Yìhéquán. I believe this is what all Chinese should do.")

"那我跟你一起走，打洋鬼子去。" ("Then I will go with you. Let's go to fight against those foreign ghosts.")

Early the next morning, Bó-Wǔ and Bó-Dé snuck out of the house and ran away. Since the family horses were needed for farming, Bó-Wǔ and Bó-Dé left on foot and walked from Tàiān Town to Gùan County. From what they had heard, the ceremony before the first big scale uprising would be on October 26th. It would take them only two days of walking to reach Gùan County. They would be able to catch this meaningful and righteous assembly on time. They were excited and had big hopes for the future.

After 8:30 in the morning, Bó-Wēi could not find either Bó-Wǔ or Bó-Dé for work. He went to Bó-Wǔ's room and discovered a letter on his bed. He took it to Hào-Xūan right away.

"爹！我一直找不到博武與博德。我在博武的床上找到這張信。"（"Dīe! I cannot find both Bó-Wǔ and Bó-Dé. I have found this letter on Bó-Wǔ's bed."）

"爹！娘！奶奶！對不起。我跟三哥去參加義和拳了。他們準備近期內在冠縣起義，我跟三哥決定去參加這個救國的義舉。我們會很小心，請勿念。博武、博德百拜。"（"Dīe! Níang! Nǎinai! I am sorry. Sāngē and I have gone to join Yìhéqúan. They are preparing their first grand uprising at Gùan County that will happen soon. Sāngē and I have decided to join this righteous activity to save our country. We will be very careful. Please don't worry about us. Bó-Wǔ and Bó-Dé bow repeatedly."）

When Bó-Wǔ's grandma heard of this, she almost fainted. She couldn't help crying aloud,

"軒兒！博武住在山上十年，一直沒有接觸過大世面，還是像個小孩子啊！而博德也一直沒長大，還很天真無知呢！怎麼辦呢？軒兒！怎麼辦呢？"（"My son, Xūan! Bó-Wǔ grew up in the mountains for ten years. He has never seen the world or encountered big events in this society. He is still like a child. In addition, Bó-Dé is still innocent and naïve. What can we do? Xūan! What can we do? Xūan!"）

After Hào-Xūan thought for a while,

"博威！你比較老成，在社會有經驗，做事比較穩重。現在農事剛忙過。你就趕去冠縣勸他們回來。萬一他們堅持留下，你也留下來照顧他們。可是在明年三月前要趕回來，我們這裡會又開始忙碌了。"（"Bó-Wēi! You are more mature and have had more experience. When you do things, you are calmer and more serious. The busy farming season is just over. Go to Gùan County to persuade them to return. If they resist, you may stay to help them. But you have to be back by next March when plowing season begins."）

Since Hào-Xūan said so, Bó-Wēi left home for Gùan County (冠縣) to look for his two brothers.

YÌHÉTÚAN 義和團

Once Bó-Wǔ and Bó-Dé arrived in the late afternoon, they saw a huge crowd including young and old, men and women, in the camp.

"怎麼這麼多人？很像他們也是剛加入義和拳的。"（"How come there are so many people here? Looks like they have just joined Yìhéqúan,"）Bó-Dé said.

"三哥！他們看起來是難民。可能是黃河氾濫與最近乾旱的難民。"（"Sāngē, they all look like refugees! Maybe they are refugees of the recent Yellow River's flood and drought."）

"我們怎麼找陳領隊呢？天快黑了，我們必須趕快想辦法。" ("How can we find Captain Chén? It is getting dark soon. We must think of a solution quick.")

Captain Chén, Shàng-Zhōng (陳尚忠) was the Yìhéquán leader they had met a year ago in their sister's Zhù Family Village.

"我們先到處走走，先看看情形。" ("Let's walk and look around first to see the environment,") Bó-Wǔ replied.

When they walked around, they realized that the majority of these newcomers were farmers, many of whom had lost their homes in the Yellow River's flood. Many others had lost their farms to Chinese Christian gangsters. There were also some industrial workers, transportation laborers, and monks, as well as rogues, gangsters, and vagrants. There were only a very small number of intellectuals. Both Bó-Wǔ and Bó-Dé were disappointed to see such a disorder and chaos in the huge crowd. While they were looking around, they also saw a few people were passing out some propaganda flyers to new arrivals. Bó-Wǔ saw one of the flyers on the ground. He picked it up and read,

"天災人禍都是洋人與傳教士引起的。驅逐洋人侵略者與傳教士可以救國救自己。" ("All these natural and human disasters were caused by foreigners and their missionaries. By driving out these foreign invaders and missionaries we will be able to save our country and ourselves.") He went on,

"利用持符念咒、請神附身，我們可以抵抗洋人的槍砲。" ("With the help of the amulet and execration, the divine spirit will adhere to us. This will allow us to stand against foreigners' guns and cannons.")

"助清滅洋。" ("Support Qīng and eliminate foreigners.")

There were also written on the flyer a few poems and songs that had the same ideas for people to chant and sing. They urged people to chant these poems and sing the songs repeatedly. The reason that poems and songs were created was because the majority of the crowd was illiterate. It was easier to teach them or brainwash them with poems and songs.

"這些民眾也真可憐！這傳單上所寫的怎麼會是真的？" ("All these people are really pitiful. How can any of what the flyer says be true?") Bó-Wǔ said with a deep sigh.

"博武！可是如果能將這個大團體組織起來，這是一股很大的力量啊！" ("Bó-Wǔ! But if Yìhéquán are able to organize this huge group and unite them together, it would be a tremendous power.")

"是沒有錯，可是這是迷信啊！三哥。" ("No mistake! But what this flyer says is superstition, Sāngē!")

While they were talking and walking, they saw a man wearing a Yìhéquán uniform trying to organize a group. Bó-Wǔ asked him,

"這位大哥！請問我們怎麼能夠找到陳尚忠領隊？" ("Dàgē! May I ask where we can find Captain Chén, Shàng-Zhōng?")

"陳尚忠？他在後面。從這裡往這個方向一直走，你們會看到一個大帳篷。他在那裡處理一些難民。" ("Chén, Shàng-Zhōng? He is to the rear. Walk straight in this direction, you will see a big tent. He is there to take care of some refugees.")

"謝謝您！大哥！" ("Thank you, Dàgē.")

They followed the direction, walking and asking if they were going the right way whenever they saw a Yìhéquán member. Finally, they found Captain Chén outside of a big tent organizing a huge group of refugees and vagrants that had just arrived.

"陳領隊！您還記得我們嗎？" ("Captain Chén! Do you still remember us?") Bó-Wǔ asked and bowed to him.

It took a moment for Captain Chén to remember. Then,

"喔！是不是去年祝家莊見過面的？你叫博武。對嗎？" ("Oh! Didn't we meet each other in the Zhù Family Village last year? You are called Bó-Wǔ. Right?") He then looked at Bó-Dé and appeared to not remember his name. When Bó-Wǔ saw it, he said,

"是的。我叫博武，他是我的三哥，博德。" ("Yes, I am called Bó-Wǔ. And this is my Sāngē, Bó-Dé.")

"歡迎你們來參加我們。剛來一批水災後的遊民，大約有六七百人，我們正在為他們安排一切。你們先去後面篷帳裡，吃點東西，我們等一下再談。" ("Welcome! Glad you have come to join us. There is a group of flood refugees that just arrived, about six to seven hundred. We are trying to help them settle down. Why don't you go inside the tent and eat something? We can talk later.")

Bó-Wǔ and Bó-Dé walked to the back of this small temporary headquarters. They entered the tent and inside had some food. They picked up bowls and started to eat. Even though all they had was some buns and jam, they felt better since they had not eaten since morning.

"三哥！看起來這些民眾都是沒有受過教育的。至少你跟我還懂得一些字。你想利用這些民眾可以對抗了洋人嗎？" ("Sāngē! From the looks of it, these people are not educated. At least you and I know some words. What do you think? Is it possible to use these people to fight against foreigners?")

"這就是要靠廣大的民眾，如果人數大於洋人幾十倍，這力量可就大了。" ("This will depend on if we have a big crowd of people. If our number is dozens of times more than the foreigners, then the power can be big.")

"可是如果這麼多的人不能團結，那也等於一盤散沙啊！起不了什麼作用的。" ("However, even if we have so many people, if they cannot be united together it will still be like a pile of loose sand. The accomplishment can still be nothing,") Bó-Wǔ expressed his opinion.

"不知道上面的負責人怎麼將這麼大的團體組織起來？就是養著這一大群的人也是個問題呢。" ("I don't know how the top responsible persons are able to organize such a huge group. It will be a problem even just to feed them.")

"等一下我們可以問陳領隊，看看他們的組織結構。" ("We can ask Captain Chén later and see how their organization works,") Bó-Wǔ said.

Bó-Wǔ and Bó-Dé just waited and chatted in the tent. When it was getting dark, Captain Chén came into the tent to get some drink and food. Both Bó-Wǔ and Bó-Dé stood up and bowed to him again.

"歡迎你們來參加義和團這個義舉和救國的行動。我只有十分鐘休息。這一批剛到的有六七百人。看來我今晚是沒辦法休息的了。" ("Again, you are welcome here to participate in this righteous saving-country action. I only have ten minutes of break. This group that just arrived has several hundred people. It seems that I won't be able to rest tonight.")

"陳領隊！我們可以問您幾個問題嗎？" ("Captain Chén! Can we ask you a few questions?") Bó-Wǔ asked.

"你們不要再叫我陳領隊了。我們這裡都稱老輩的團員大師兄或二師兄等。你們有什麼問題呢？" ("Don't call me Captain Chén anymore. Here, we commonly call senior members, Dà Shīxiōng (Big Brother) or Èr Shīxiōng Second Brother) and such. What questions do you have?")

"我們知道您很忙，可是您能不能簡單的告訴我們義和拳內部的組織與結構？" ("We know you are very busy. But can you please tell us briefly about the internal structure of the Yìhéquán organization?")

"這個嘛！義和拳全團根據八卦分八門，分乾、坎、艮、震、巽、離、坤、兌。其中以乾字號身上以黃布為標記和坎字號以紅布為標記的權利最大。其他六門比較沒有統一的組織和集中領導。每門的基本組織是壇。也就是說由門再分不同的壇口。比如我來說，我本來是坎字號的門人，現在被派任到艮字號當大師兄。我現在要做的是如何將這些新的難民編入不同的壇口呢！" ("Well! About this! The entire Yìhéquán is divided into eight divisions that use the eight doors of trigram, Qián, Kǎn, Gěn, Zhèn, Xùn, Lí, Kūn, and Duì. Those who belong to the Qián division have a yellow cloth band on their clothes while those who belong to the Kǎn division have a red cloth band on their clothes. These two divisions are considered to have the greatest power and authority. The other six divisions are not as organized and there is no absolute authority of leadership. Every division is again divided into numerous fundamental altars. What I mean is, from each division numerous altars can be established. For example, I was originally a member of Kǎn division. Then I was sent to become the Big Brother (leader) of the Gèn division. Now, what I am doing is assigning all these refugees to different altar groups.")

"我們剛到！不知道怎麼安排呢？"("We just arrived and don't know, what division do we belong to?") Bó-Dé asked.

"那你們就在我艮字號的管下。今晚你們先找個地方休息。我明天早上有空再跟你們安排。"("In this case, you will be in my Gèn group. Why don't you find a place to rest first tonight? I will help you settle in tomorrow morning.")

"陳大師兄！我還有個問題。義和拳現在有多少人？"("Chén Dà Shīxiōng! I still have questions. How many members does Yìhéquán have now?") Bó-Wǔ asked again.

"我想至少有兩萬人。這個數目還會增加。現在每天都有好幾百人來參加呢！"("I believe there are at least 20,000. This number is still increasing. Currently, there are many hundreds of people coming to join us each day.")

"可是義和拳怎麼去處理這麼大群眾的民生問題呢？"("But how can Yìhéquán handle all living necessities of such a huge crowd?")

"其實義和拳八門分得很廣。每門都有他們自己的管轄區並負責他們自己門人的民生問題。八門之間的來往並不多。只有在有運動的時候，所有不同門的團員才聚集起來。因為在每個門的轄區的廣大農民在門人的保護下來對抗教民的侵略，所有的糧食都是有農民自動供給的。"("As a matter of fact, all eight divisions of Yìhéquán are very widely separated. Each division has its own territory to protect and manages its own living requirements. There are only a few contacts between divisions. However, whenever there is an action, all division members will get together. Because the farmers in different territories are under protection of Yìhéquán members against Christian gangsters' aggression, they supply food and living spaces for members.")

"可是民眾會越來越多呢！"("But the members will increase more and more!") Bó-Dé said.

"那也不是問題。這是因為還有更多的農民需要保護呢！我必須再回去處理那些難民。我們明天再談。"("That is no problem. This is because there are more farmers needing to be protected. I must go back to take care of those refugees. We will talk again tomorrow.")

After Mr. Chén left, they found an abandoned old barn nearby where they arranged an area so they could rest. After they settled down, Bó-Wǔ worried,

"三哥！您看我們加入義和拳是對的嗎？是明智的嗎？據我看來，義和拳的組織非常的散亂，而且紀律也不高。這樣的一個組織怎麼去對抗洋人呢？" ("Sāngē! Do you think we made the right decision in joining Yìhéquán? Is it wise? From what I have seen, Yìhéquán organization is very disordered and lacks discipline. How can this kind of organization be used to stand against foreigners?")

"博武！可是幾乎所有的人都有一個一致的愛國情操與對洋人的憤恨呢！" ("Bó-Wǔ, that may be true! But as you can see almost everyone has a consistent compassion to love the country and a resentment against foreigners.")

"可是如果叫我去殺傳教士與外國人的婦女與小孩，我是做不出來的。不是所有的傳教士與洋人都是壞人呢。" ("However, if they ask me to go to kill those foreign missionaries, women, and children, I won't be able to do it. Not all foreign missionaries and foreigners are bad.")

"其實我也做不出來呢。" ("As a matter of fact, I cannot do it either.")

"可是這些民眾在洗腦後，什麼都幹的出來的。這樣的話，他們跟教民暴徒有什麼兩樣？" ("But these people, after brainwashing, they will do anything. In this case, what is the difference between them and those Christian gangsters?") Bó-Wǔ asked.

"博武！既然我們已經來了，我們就待一陣子再說。" ("Bó-Wǔ! Since we are here already, let us stay for a while and see.")

They decided to stay and observe the situation. The next morning, Mr. Chén arranged for Bó-Wǔ to be an altar leader, since he knew how to read and write and also had a high-level of martial arts skill. Bó-Dé was assigned to be his assistant. Under Bó-Wǔ's leadership, there were 300 people in his charge.

Two days later, Bó-Wēi arrived to look for Bó-Wǔ and Bó-Dé. After he asked and searched for a few hours, finally, through mentioning Mr. Chén's name, he found Bó-Wǔ and Bó-Dé. Bó-Wǔ and Bó-Dé were surprised by their Èrge's visit. When they saw each other,

"二哥！怎麼您也來了？您也來參加義和拳嗎？" ("Èrge! How come you are also here? Did you also come to join Yìhéquán?") Bó-Wǔ asked.

"不是！是爹跟奶奶要我來勸你們回去的。" ("No! It is Diē and Nǎinai, they asked me to come to persuade you to go home.")

"二哥！我們才到的。怎麼能就回去呢？" ("Èrge! We have just

155

arrived. How can we go home like this?") Bó-Dé replied.

"二哥！在大姊那裡，您也看到暴民的無理和義和拳怎麼保護農民。相信您也對暴民非常的氣憤。我與三哥認為我們應待一陣子看看情形再說。" ("Èrgē! When we were at Dàjiě's place, you also saw those Christian gangsters' unreasonable aggression and how Yìhéquán members protected the farmers. I believe you are also very angry about those gangsters. Sāngē and I believe that we should stay for a while and see the situation,") Bó-Wǔ said.

"對啊！二哥！十月二十六號宣布義舉的日子快到了，我們先等到那時候再說。" ("That is correct, "Èrgē! October 26th, the date of the ceremony of righteous uprising, will arrive soon. We should at least stay till then and see.") Bó-Dé tried to convince his brother to stay till October 26th.

After a few minutes of discussion, Bō-Wēi believed that he could not persuade them to leave with him to go home soon. Furthermore, he did not need to go home right away since the busy harvest season was just over.

"好吧！就等到義舉後再說。" ("All right! Then we will talk more after the ceremony of righteous uprising.")

***

The day of October 26th of 1898 was a big day. On this day the first large scale public gathering was held, and an announcement made to all Chinese people about this righteous uprising ceremony. There were more than 20,000 people assembled in a big field in the suburb of Gùan County (冠縣). Since Yìhéquán activities had been approved by the local government, there was no conflict between Yìhéquán members and the Qīng soldiers. The Yìhéquán had also formally announced that they changed their slogan from 'get rid of Qīng' to 'support Qīng.'

Everyone was sitting quietly around the field waiting for the beginning of the ceremony. Suddenly, sounds of drums, gongs, and cymbals could be heard at the edge of the crowd. Following the instruments, three lions entered the field to perform extraordinary skills of dancing. People were excited and cheerful. It made people feel like it was a Chinese New Year.

Immediately after the dancing, many groups of martial artists entered the field and demonstrated their skills. The demonstration lasted nearly one hour. Finally, a group of male performers without shirts stepped onto the field. A Daoist monk went in front of them and placed some Língfú (amulets) on each of their bodies. After that, he began to execrate while the performers followed him chanting. Within a few minutes, all the performers were hypnotized. Another group with staffs and sabers entered the field. They used their sabers and staffs to chop and strike at those hypnotized performers. To the audience's surprise, no harm or expression of pain could be seen on the performers' faces. This excited the audience to a near frenzy.

The show reminded Bó-Wǔ of the conversation he had had with Shìhǎi and Míngdào monks. In his deep mind, he knew this was the effect of hypnosis or brainwashing. However, to Bó-Dé and Bó-Wēi, this performance was unimaginable and unbelievable.

"他們這麼厲害！還這是刀槍不入啊！如果不是我親眼看到，我還是不相信呢！" ("They are so shrewd! It is true that they can defend against sabers and guns. If I did not see it with my own eyes, I would not have believed it") Bó-Dé said excitedly. He could not believe what he had seen. Bó-Wēi, however, was quietly suspicious.

"三哥！其實這只是一種催眠作用。可以讓身體比較不覺得痛而已。" ("Sāngē! Actually, this is only an effect of hypnosis that makes you feel less pain in the body,") Bó-Wǔ said in a low voice, since he did not want to get in an argument with other people around him. While they were talking, the leader of the Yìhéquán, Zhào, Sān-Duō (趙三多) with his two top assistants, Yáo, Wén-Qǐ (姚文起) and Yán, Shū-Qín (閻書勤) walked out to the center of the field. The people's excitement reached a feverish pitch. They cheered and shouted. It took a few minutes for them to quiet down.

This was the first time for most people to see Zhào, Sān-Duō himself, though all of them had heard his name. Everyone went quiet and waited to hear what he would say.

"各位鄉親父老，首先我要歡迎你們來參加我們的陣營。相信你們很多人已經受盡了洋人的欺負。我們義和拳的主要目的是扶清滅洋。" ("Dear folks, first, I would like to welcome you to join us. I believe many of you have suffered from the foreigners' oppression and bullying. The main goal of Yìhéquán is to support Qīng and save the country.") People were shouting and applauding. Zhào scanned the audience with a feeling of pride. He continued,

"我們現在已經有超過兩萬人的團員，既然這個團體已經這麼大，以後我們不能再叫義和拳了，應該叫義和團。最重要的是我們這個團體已經接受清廷的認同與安撫。我們不是國家的叛徒，而是我大中華維持正義救國的團體。" ("Now we have more than 20,000 members. Since this group has become so big, we should not call ourselves Yìhéquán. Instead, we should call ourselves Yìhétuán. The most important development for us is that we have been accepted by the Qīng Court and received their recognition. We are not the traitors of the country, but a righteous country-saving group of great China.") Some audience members began to tear up from the excitement. Zhào paused a few seconds till the audience's excitement eased down.

"因為洋人對我土地的繼續瓜分，目前我們對洋人的鬥爭將進入高潮。希望你們參加義和團後，以國家的榮譽與尊嚴為重，扛起這個救國的歷史使命。" ("Because those foreign powers continue to divide our country and occupy it, the fighting between us and foreigners will escalate to its highest level. I hope after you have joined Yìhétuán, you will always keep in mind the seriousness of upholding our country's honor and dignity and carry on with our historical mission of saving our country.")

Since Zhào had not received any education, he tried his best with his speech. In spite of that, he had agitated the audience to a high-level. He waved his hands to them and stepped off of the field.

After that, many farmers who had lost their land to gangsters and churches went to the center and told their stories. Though most of the new members were flood and drought refugees that had never experienced the conflicts with Christian gangsters and foreigners, they were stimulated by the stories and their hatred for the foreigners was magnified.

Since then, the name of Yìhéquán (義和拳) (Righteous and Harmonious Fist) was formally changed to Yìhétuán (義和團) (Righteous and Harmonious Group). They also changed their slogan from 'get rid of Qīng' to 'support Qīng.'

The ceremony lasted nearly three hours. Finally, the audience was dispersed, and everyone returned to their units. On the way back to the Gēn group headquarters,

"我看了一下，雖然義和團現在有超過兩萬人，可是真正能作戰的還不到一半呢。其他的人都是老年人與小孩。而且能作戰的一半，至少三分之二不是農民，就是流浪漢，他們一點武藝都不懂。他們對洋槍一點都不知道呢。就我屬下的三百人來說，跟他們相處了幾星期後，才知道如果能上戰場的還不到一半呢。" ("Now that I have seen everyone, though there are more than 20,000 Yìhétuán members, those that can actually fight are less than half. All the others are old people and children. Furthermore, of the half who can really fight, two-thirds are farmers or vagrants. They don't know anything about martial arts. They have no idea of what the foreigners' guns can do. Just take my group as an example - after we have been together for a few weeks, we know those who can really fight in a battle are less than half,") Bó-Wǔ said.

"博武！你看這個救國的義舉有希望嗎？" ("Bó-Wǔ! Do you think there is any hope for this righteous saving-country action?") Bó-Dé asked.

"如您所說我們人數比洋人超過幾倍，如果我們能夠團結，我們還是可以成大事的。大哥！您看呢？" ("As you said, our numbers are a few times greater than the foreigners. If we are able to unite together, we are still able to achieve a great accomplishment,") Bó-Wǔ replied.

"今天民眾的情緒很高，就要看以後的了。" ("People's emotions are very high today, but we have to wait and see what the future holds,") Bó-Wēi said. From his reply, it seemed that he also wanted to stay and help. Since work on the farm would not be busy again till next spring, Bó-Wēi finally decided to stay at least till next spring.

****

Since wintertime was getting closer, in addition to training their group in martial arts using a barn for their training ground, Bó-Wǔ, Bó-Dé, and Bó-Wēi also set up some rules and discipline for the group. About 150 younger men and women were selected from the larger group of 300. Usually they trained twice per day, in the morning from 9 o'clock to 11, and also in the afternoon from 3 to 5. After training, Bó-Wǔ often told them stories of his experiences on Éméi Mountain. Soon, the three brothers had garnered a high degree of respect from the group members. It was a small, family-like community.

One day in January, the weather was cold and outside everything was covered with heavy snow. After training in the barn, Bó-Wǔ got everyone together.

"我想讓你們知道，我認為義和團的宗旨因該是保衛自己而不是去攻擊別人。從其他字號的團體，我們知道他們準備在春天到時，向教堂和外國人採取主動攻擊。對我來講，殺人放火的事是土匪幹的。如果我們也這樣的幹，那我們跟教會土霸和土匪又有什麼兩樣？我希望你們能了解我的觀點。" ("I would like you to know that I believe the mission of Yìhétuán should be to protect ourselves instead of to attack other people. As I know from other divisions, they are preparing for their attacks against churches and foreigners when springtime arrives. In my opinion, killing people and starting fires is what those bandits and gangsters do. If we also do so, then what is the difference between us and those gangsters and bandits? I hope you understand my viewpoint."

"我也認為我們主要的目的是息事寧人，而不是去製造糾紛。" ("I also

believe that our main goal is to cease the trouble and keep peace with others instead of creating more disputes with others,") Bó-Wēi agreed.

While they were talking, they saw a boy of about 15 years old entering the barn. His face was pale, and he looked so sloppy and dirty. His body was trembling with cold due to his thin clothes. He bowed to the group and said,

"你們好！他們告訴我你們艮字門的團員在這裡練功，我剛被陳壇主分派到你們的團體。我不知道我應該向誰報到？" ("How are you? They told me that your Gěn division group is practicing Gōngfū here. I have just been sent here by Mr. Chén to be part of your group. I don't know who I should report to?")

Bó-Wǔ stepped forward and said,

"我是這一壇的壇主。你叫什麼名字？怎麼會在這大冬天裡才來這裡？" ("I am the leader of this altar. What is your name? Why do you come here during this serious cold winter?")

"我叫秦萬吉。我家就在黃河旁邊。今夏黃河氾濫，我的家被沖掉了。大水後，我跟家人失去聯絡。我從夏天一直在找他們，一直沒找到。我想他們可能逃到義和團來了，所以我也來了。希望我能夠在這裡找到他們。" ("My name is Qín, Wàn-Jí. My home was next to the Yellow River. When the Yellow River flooded this past summer, my home was flushed away. After the flood, I lost contact with all my family. I have been looking for them since this summer but have not found them. I thought they might have escaped to here. So, I also came, and hoped to find them here.")

"你現在幾歲？你家共有幾個人？" ("How old are you now? How many people are in your family?")

"我現在十五歲。除了我爹跟娘，我還有兩個弟弟和一個妹妹。" ("I am 15. Other than my Dīe and Niáng, I have two younger brothers and one younger sister.")

"那你就先待在這裡。義和團各門字號的團體分得很散很廣。我們只有在有行動的時候，才會聚集在一起。春天到時，可能比較容易找。二哥！您就幫忙他安頓下來。謝謝您。" ("In this case, you stay here first. All Yìhétuán divisions are separated very wide and are a far distance apart. Only when there is an activity, then we get together. It will be easier to find your family when springtime arrives. Èrgē! Would you please help him get settled in? Thank you,") Bó-Wǔ assigned the job to his brother, Bó-Dé. He then turned to everyone,

"我們今天就練到這裡。明天早上九點整，在這裡見面。" ("We are done with practice for today. See you tomorrow morning at 9 o'clock punctually.")

Bó-Dé took the boy to a storage room of a family in the village where Bó-Wǔ, Bó-Dé, and Bó-Wēi stayed. First, Bó-Dé gave Wàn-Jí (萬吉) some cookies and told him that he would sleep in the space next to him. When he saw the boy was still trembling from the cold, he also gave him some heavy clothes. He told the boy that usually the family they were protecting in this Dǒng Family Village (董家莊) would bring some simple food for them later. There were about 220 families in this village and each family took care of one to three Yìhétuán members.

Since then, the boy followed the three brothers everywhere. This boy especially loved to train Gōngfū. Though he respected Bó-Wǔ as a teacher, he treated Bó-Dé like his elder brother. He asked him questions, served him drinks, or gave him a massage whenever Bó-Dé was tired. He treated Bó-Wēi like his father since he was oldest, quiet, and solemn.

Time passed very quickly. The weather grew warmer and warmer. Snow that had accumulated on the ground diminished gradually each day. Soon, springtime would arrive.

When it was the busy farming season, all Yìhétuán members would help the farmers. With the Yìhétuán's help, the work was done quickly and efficiently. Most of the farmers and members got along smoothly. Once the weather got warmer, Wàn-Jí began to travel from division to division, hoping to find his family. After two months of trying, though, he had not learned anything about them. He was so disappointed. However, he felt like he had found a new family in his group.

FORMATION OF THE EIGHT-NATION ALLIANCE 八國聯軍的形成

In spring of 1900, when the weather was getting warmer, thousands and thousands of Yìhétuán members in various groups began their offensive against Christians and foreigners. By April of 1900, the Yìhétuán had expanded their activities to Tiānjīn (天津) of Zhílì Province (直隸省) (today's Hebei Province). It was estimated that there were far more than 100,000 foreign and Chinese Christians in Běijīng and Tiānjīn Cities of Zhílì Province. When the foreigners had built a railroad two years earlier and installed a telegraph communication system, people believed that these constructions were for the foreigners' convenience to aid their invasion and further their control. Also, due to the railroad construction, many thousands of Chinese transportation workers had lost their jobs. To survive, they joined the

Yìhétuán.

Since the Yìhétuán had not received permission from the Qīng Court to enter Běijīng City, they focused their offensive in Tiānjīn City. In the following couple of months, they rapidly executed a large number of Chinese Christians and foreigners, burned their churches and houses, and invaded foreign concession areas. The situation got worse every day. Many Yìhétuán members believed that finally they were acquiring their revenge and getting justice.

However, it did not matter how the other groups advanced their offensives, Bó-Wǔ kept his group calm and steady without taking any actions. This created uneasy feelings among some of his members. One day after dinner, one of the young members asked,

"李壇主！我們是不是應該跟隨其他字門的人，攻擊教會和洋人呢？" ("Lǐ altar leader! Shouldn't we follow other divisions and also attack churches and foreigners?")

"小彭！我想我們還是不要太衝動，意氣用事。我認為攻擊教堂和殺害婦女小孩的事，是一種不正當的事。我們既然叫我們自己義和團，我們就應該保持我們的原則，保持正義，維護和平。這種殺害婦女小孩的事，我相信連外國人都不會做出來的。" ("Little Péng!" I still believe we should not be too impulsive and emotional. I believe attacking churches and killing women and children are not righteous behaviors. Since we call ourselves a righteous-harmonious group, we should keep our principle in righteousness and maintain harmony with others. I believe this kind of action of killing women and children is wrong - even foreigners would not do so.")

"那我們這個團是幹什麼的？" ("Then, what is the purpose of our group?") another member argued. He believed they should be following the example set by the others and attacking foreigners.

"記得我們中國的傳統文化是保衛自己，而不是主動的去攻擊侵略別人。" ("Remember, our Chinese culture has always been about protecting ourselves instead of aggressively attacking or invading others.")

"可是人家已經欺負和爬到我們的頭上了呢。" ("But others have already taken advantage of us and climbed on top of our head.")

"這就要責怪自己了。我們自己不能團結，不能強大，才會給別人機會來欺負我們。這種攻擊來、攻擊去的態度，只有將事態誇大到更嚴重的地步。" ("Then we should blame ourselves. It is because we cannot unite together and, in that way, make ourselves strong. It is disunity that allows other people to take advantage of us. If each side attacks the other mutually without stop, it will only make the problem more serious.")

"那我們什麼時候才要採取行動呢？" ("Then, when should we begin our action?")

"當我們繼續受到侵略時，那就是我們該行動的時候了。" ("When we are invaded continuously, then it is the time for our actions.")

While they were arguing, Bó-Wēi listened and was quiet. He felt Bó-Wǔ had suddenly become more mature. Bó-Wǔ was more thoughtful instead of emotional now. He did not know that all of Bó-Wǔ's thoughts originated from Shìhǎi and Míngdào monks' influence on Éméi Mountain.

Bó-Wǔ still had a habit of getting up early and meditating. He remembered that he had begun to meditate after he talked to Shìhǎi and Míngdào about meditation when he was 18 years old. He also remembered his eldest brother was there at that time. Since then, he tried to feel his Mud-Pill-Palace that both Shībó monks had talked about.

After nearly four years of practice, right before he left Éméi Mountain, he was so happy and excited that he was able to feel this palace located at the center of his head. However, the hardest part was to keep the mind there. It seemed that it would take him forever to calm down his conscious emotional mind and try to develop a high-level of sensitivity of his subconscious mind.

Now that he was living in the laymen's society filled with all of its emotional masks and traps, he discovered it was even harder to calm down to enter the same stage that he had achieved when he was on the mountain.

"唉！我多麼想念師父跟師伯。離開峨嵋山已經三年了，可是我對峨嵋山上的生活卻一直不能忘懷呢！" ("Ai! How much do I miss Shīfù and Shībós. I have been away from Éméi Mountain for three years already, but in my deep heart, I still cannot forget the life I had there.")

Bó-Wǔ got up this morning early again. He sat on his floor bed and began to meditate. He needed to bring his mind to the stage of calmness in this chaotic environment. After a few deep breaths, he brought his physical body into a relaxed and peaceful state. Slowly, he brought his mind to the center of his head to feel his Mud-Pill-Palace. In ten minutes, he had placed himself outside of any emotional mud or matrix. From there, he could see and feel that those people in the mud were in pain. Their eyes and ears were covered by the mud and they could not see or hear clearly. They were so confused and struggling to see things more clearly.

While he was feeling these scenes, he abruptly found himself again in the mud with the others, emotional and confused. It seemed whenever he wanted to jump out of the mud, the stronger force of the mud pulled him back. After so many times of practice, he suddenly realized that in order to stay away from the emotional mud, first he must face it and accept it. Without facing and accepting it and experiencing it, he would never wake up and really comprehend the meaning of life. His wondering mind was so strong to keep him stuck in the mud. Now, he realized why both his Shīfù and Shībós, after experiencing their emotional laymen society, decided to retire to the mountain for temperament cultivation.

"我想以後我會像師父跟師伯一樣，脫離塵世，隱居深山。" ("I believe I will be like Shifu and Shibos, leave this laymen society, and live in seclusion in the deep mountains,") he thought.

***

On April 6th of 1900, the ambassadors of Britain, France, the United States, and the German Empire in China together notified the Qīng Court that if Qīng did not annihilate the Yìhétuán within two months, these four countries would send their armies and navies to annihilate the Yìhétuán for China. Without receiving any answer from the Qīng Court, eight countries including the German Empire, Japan, Russia, Britain, France, the United States, Italy, and Austria-Hungary, with the excuse of protecting their embassies, decided to send their soldiers to Běijīng. They notified the Qīng Court and said, "it does not matter what manner of Chinese Government is, all foreign ambassadors have decided to send soldiers to Běijīng." Under pressure, and also because the size of the army they were requesting to send was a small group, Empress Dowager Cíxǐ consented to it.

On May 28th of 1900, The Eight-Nation Alliance was formalized. On May 31st, the alliance countries demanded the Qīng Court's protection for their embassies and citizens but were refused. Instead, the Qīng Court demanded that all foreign working staff members and their families leave Běijīng temporarily. But the Qīng Court's demand was rejected, and The Eight-Nation Alliance insisted on bringing their armies to Běijīng for protection. Therefore, the first alliance army group of about 400 soldiers, on a train provided by the Qīng Court, entered Běijīng on May 31st. In addition to the army troops, warships belonging to the alliance countries arrived by sea near Fort Dàgū (大沽砲台) in a demonstration of power.

On June 3rd of 1900, Germany and Austria-Hungary sent another 83 soldiers to Běijīng. A strong fortification was built in the area where all of the embassies were located on the east side of Běijīng. British

Ambassador Sir Claude Maxwell MacDonald was in charge of this defense. There were at least 3,000 people under protection in this fortification. Other than 409 sailors and marines, the people under protection were 2,000 Chinese Christians, 400 foreign males, 147 females, and 76 children. Aiding this defense on the British side were many rifles, three machine guns, and four small-sized cannons. Plenty of water and food was available, and they had 150 horses that could be used.

On June 9th of 1900, the ambassadors of 11 foreign countries held a meeting and decided to send a large group of soldiers to Běijīng. They were afraid the fortification they had built was not enough to defend themselves. The next day, all communications between the embassies and outside of Běijīng were completely cut off by the Qīng Court. This led to an emergency meeting of all foreign consulates and the leading generals of the allied navy in Tiānjīn City (天津城). Finally, it was decided to organize a coalition army of 2,000 soldiers, without the Qīng Court's permission, under British Royal Navy General Edward Seymour's leadership. The coalition army would enter Běijīng by train. While General Edward Seymour's invading army was advancing toward Běijīng, more than 20 warships from coalition nations had also gathered outside of Fort Dàgū (大沽) and were prepared for invasion.

This triggered the war between the coalition army and the united force of Yìhétuán and patriotic Qīng soldiers. The united force believed that without the Qīng Court's permission, such a huge foreign coalition army did not have a right to enter Běijīng.

***

There was an emergency meeting at Yìhétuán headquarters on June 10th. All the Yìhétuán leaders, totaling 100, were gathered to discuss their strategy. They had just been notified by the Qīng Government that a large force of 2,000 coalition soldiers were getting ready to enter Běijīng without the Qīng Court's permission. The government had requested the Yìhétuán's help in stopping this foreign aggression into Běijīng City. They were also told that the Qīng army was on its way to join them for this defense.

"各位門長與壇主，現在情況緊迫。根據諜報，外國聯軍準備在這兩天內派遣大約兩千名士兵由天津從鐵路進駐北京。這些軍隊一到北京，會是對我們一個很大的威脅。清廷要求我們跟清兵配合抵制聯軍的侵略。我們今天下午必須選些年輕戰鬥力強的團員，馬上採取行動。" ("All division and altar leaders, the situation is urgent now. According to the information we received, the foreign coalition force is ready to send 2,000 soldiers from Tiānjīn to Běijīng by train. If this army arrives at Běijīng, it will be a huge threat to our government. The Qīng Court has requested our help to unify and coordinate with the Qīng soldiers to resist their aggression. We must select those members who are young and have good fighting skills to act this afternoon, immediately!") Leader, Mr. Zhào announced.

"最有效的辦法是馬上將天津到北京的鐵路破壞，使外國聯軍無法前進。我們分析一下情勢，認為在廊坊站截擊他們，對我們來講是最有利的。" ("The most effective way to stop them from entering Běijīng is destroying the railroad tracks from Tiānjīn to Běijīng. This will prevent their advancing. We have analyzed the situation, and we believe it will be the most advantageous for us if we intercept them at the Lángfāng station area,") Mr. Zhào's assistant, Yáo, Wén-Qǐ (姚文起) said.

The decision was made. The Yìhétuán dispatched more than 2,000 of its members as the first group to damage the railroad tracks and immobilize the coalition army's advance. More members would join them the next day. This was the first time that the Qīng Court had asked for their help. They believed they had acquired the Qīng Court's recognition of their organization.

Gěn (艮) division was assigned to first work on destroying the railroad and then unite with other groups to defend against the coalition army. Bó-Wǔ chose 120 of the strongest members in his group to join this action. These members had accepted his martial arts training for nearly one year. They would join other groups in three hours and march to Lángfāng station. Bó-Dé told Wàn-Jí to stay at the camp instead of participating in the battle. But Wàn-Jí insisted on going, so they took him with them.

On June 11th, when the coalition army left Tiānjīn and arrived outside of the city, they discovered that many sections of the railroad were damaged so that they could not advance. Immediately, they repaired the railroad and continued. However, when they reached the Lángfāng (廊坊) station, they realized that the damage to the railroad in front of them was even worse, and that it would be impossible to repair it in a short time. While they were stopped, a serious attack was launched against them from an estimated 2,000 Yìhétuán members. After a few days of furious fighting and seeing the impossibility of advancing his army by railroad, the general of the coalition army, Edward Seymour, decided to change their method to entering Běijīng by the river Báihé (白河). However, they needed to retreat to Yáng's

Village (楊村) first, and then take a boat from there.

After Bó-Wǔ's group had destroyed a couple sections of railroad track, they joined the defense force to stand against the coalition army right in front of Lángfāng station. Altogether there were about 2,300 Yìhétuán members now to resist the 2,000 coalition army soldiers. The fighting caused many casualties for the Yìhétuán since they did not have guns. The most fearful weapons to Yìhétuán members were machine guns. These guns had killed so many of their members. When Bó-Wǔ saw so many fellow members, after being hypnotized with Língfú, bravely running straight toward the enemy and then being killed, he felt very sad and sorry. He deeply knew that relying on Língfú's hypnotizing power would not work. He ordered his group to keep their position and not make any irrational attacks.

Next day, more Yìhétuán members came to enhance their fighting power. Both sides resisted against each other for a couple more days. The situation got worse for the foreign coalition army when Qīng General Dǒng, Fú-Xiáng's (董福祥) army with 3,000 soldiers arrived and joined in an offensive strike on June 18th while the coalition army was retreating. Both sides sustained big casualties. Finally, the coalition army decided to retreat back to Tiānjīn City completely. This victory was called "Lángfāng Victory" (廊坊大捷) by the Qīng Court.

While the Lángfāng battle was going on, the Yìhétuán received permission from the Qīng Court allowing them to enter Běijīng to protect the capital. Since the Lángfāng battle had already been brought under control by the Qīng soldiers and the Yìhétuán members, at least half of the members, including Bó-Wǔ's group, were ordered to enter Běijīng right away. In addition, the Yìhétuán leader also sent another group of Yìhétuán members to Běijīng. The situation became very urgent when Fort Dàgū (大沽砲台) was taken over by the coalition force on June 17th. They all knew that once this important military fort was taken, Běijīng City would be completely exposed to the coalition army's attack. All Yìhétuán members rushed to Běijīng City to get ready for battle in defense of the city. Once they arrived at Běijīng City, with the exception of Bó-Wǔ's group, the Yìhétuán began to attack embassies, and the foreigners' residential areas, killing both Chinese and foreign Christians.

During the same period, a series of other incidents occurred. On June 11th a Japanese diplomat, すぎやま あきら (Sugiyama Akira), working in the Japanese embassy in Běijīng was killed by Qīng soldiers. On June 12th, Yìhétuán members attacked Tiānjīn concession territory, Zǐzhúlín (紫竹林). On June 14th, German Ambassador Clemens Freiherr von Ketteler gave an order to attack Yìhétuán members surrounding the German embassy and killed 30 Yìhétuán members.

While the battles were going on at Lángfāng, on June 15th, the naval commanders of the coalition countries plotted to attack and take over Fort Dàgū (大沽) so that they could control the passage between Tiānjīn and Dàgū. They launched the attack in the evening with 300 soldiers.

On June 16th, all telegram communications between Tiānjīn and the outside were cut off. This triggered an emergency meeting of the coalition navy commanders who decided they must take over Fort Dàgū (大沽砲台) immediately. The British and German armies landed in the afternoon and, in coordination with the Japanese army that had landed earlier, they occupied Tánggū Train Station (塘沽車站) and outflanked Fort Dàgū (大沽砲台) in preparation for their attack. At dusk, Vice-Admiral Hildebrandt of the Imperial Russian Navy, through Lieutenant Bakhmetev, sent an ultimatum to Fort Dàgū Commander-in-Chief, Luó, Róng-Guāng (羅榮光), and demanded his surrender by 2 o'clock in the morning of June 17th, otherwise the fort would be taken by force. But his request was refused. Instead, Fort Dàgū Commander-in-Chief Luó, Róng-Guāng (羅榮光) gave an order to defend the fort. That same day, Empress Dowager Cíxǐ (慈禧太后), after meeting with her high-level ministers, gave the order to disband the Yìhétuán. She was hoping through this effort she could convince the coalition army to cease any further aggression.

Unfortunately, after putting up strong resistance, due to their shortage of ammunition and the powerful offense of the foreigners' 20 warships, Fort Dàgū was lost into the hands of the foreign coalition force on June 17th of 1900.

On June 17th Empress Dowager Cíxǐ received the report that Fort Dàgū (大沽砲台) had already been lost to the foreign coalition army and also received a fake notification purporting to be from the foreign embassies and demanding she return power to Emperor Guāngxù. She was furious and changed her attitude to the complete opposite of her original decision. She gave an order to both the Qīng army and Yìhétuán members to aggressively resist against the foreigners. She even ordered her top trusted ministers, Gāngyì (剛毅) and Zàixūn (載勛), to be the leaders of the Yìhétuán and offered them all the help they need.

Now there were more than 15,000 Yihetuan members helping at least 100,000 Qīng soldiers guard Běijīng City and get ready for a defensive battle. At the same time, the coalition army was also rapidly reinforced and now had 40,000 soldiers with guns, machine guns, and cannons. Tension between the opposing forces increased each day. By August 14th, the total number of coalition army soldiers had reached 50,000. Naturally, other than Yihetuan members, the number of Qīng soldiers also increased to more than 150,000. By evening, all of Běijīng was surrounded by the coalition army.

Bó-Wǔ's group, which now had around 200 members, was assigned to guard Dōngzhí Gate (東直門) of the city, along with other Yihetuan groups and some Qīng soldiers. Bó-Wǔ assembled his group and had a final talk before the coalition army's attack the next day.

"各位兄弟，現在是我們保衛我們國家的時候了。現在北京城已經完全被聯軍包圍了。我們誓死保衛我們大中華的主權。雖然聯軍有槍砲，可是我們保衛國家的鬥志是高昂的。" ("All my brothers! Now it is the time to protect our country. Běijīng City has been completely surrounded by the coalition army. We swore with our lives to protect the authority of our country. Though they have guns and cannons, our fighting spirit and will to protect our country is high.")

"我們清兵也有槍砲啊！而且我們與清兵的人數大過聯軍幾倍，防禦北京城應該是沒有問題的。" ("Our Qīng soldiers also have guns and cannons. Furthermore, our number is several times higher than the coalition army. It shouldn't be a problem to protect Běijīng City,") Bó-Dé expressed his opinion.

"憑良心講，這很難說。第一，從歷史上，清兵對抗外來的軍隊一直是打敗戰，他們對自己抵抗聯軍的信心已經喪失了。你們可以從他們的臉上看到他們內心的恐懼感。第二，雖然清兵也有槍砲，可是數量有限，而且彈藥不夠。很快會用完的。" ("But in our deep heart, we know it is difficult to say this. First, from past history, we know the Qīng army were always defeated by foreign armies. They have lost their confidence to fight against foreign coalition forces. You may see their fear from their facial expression. Second, though Qīng soldiers have guns and cannons, the number is limited and there is not enough ammunition. They will run out of ammunition very quickly,") Bó-Wǔ expressed his opinion. What he said increased his members' worry.

That evening, except for some noise coming from a long distance outside of the city, it was calm and quiet within the city. Everyone was waiting for the storm's coming. Wàn-Jí (萬吉), now 16 years old, stood next to Bó-Wéi and showed his worry and fear on his face. After all, he was still a boy.

CHAPTER 6
EMPRESS DOWAGER CÍXǏ
AND THE EIGHT-NATION
ALLIANCE
慈禧太后與八國聯軍

After the Wùxū Reform, Empress Dowager Cíxǐ lost her trust and patience with Emperor Guāngxù and plotted to replace him. However, she was afraid many of her ministers might rebel against her decision. She convened a meeting of the princes, dukes, and all her high-ranking ministers at Yuánmíng Garden's summer house on January 24th of 1900.

"你們都知道，我對光緒發動的戊戌變法非常的失望與憤怒。我對他已經是不能再容忍下去了。我想用端王載漪的兒子，溥儁，取代光緒。就在這月三十一日要光緒退位並舉行新皇大典，改年號為保慶。你們認為如何，不妨提出來。" ("All of you have known that I am very disappointed and angry with Guāngxù's Wùxū Reform in trying to overthrow me. I do not have patience to endure him any longer. I intend to replace him with Duke Duān, Zàiyī's (端王載漪) son, Pǔjùn (溥儁) as the new emperor. I would like to have the ceremony on the 31st of this month and designate the new epoch as 'Bǎoqìng' (保慶). What are your opinions? You may speak frankly.")

Minister Xǔ, Jǐng-Chéng (許景澄) stepped forward and knelt down in front of Cíxǐ.

"稟告皇太后！這個政策可不能做呀！光緒皇上並沒有做任何傷害國家的事啊。他只不過想將我大中華由弱變強呢而能去抵抗列強的侵害呢，他其實很

171

得民心啊。" ("Report to Empress Dowager! This policy should not be carried out. Emperor Guāngxù has not done anything harmful to the country. What he did was trying hard to make the country stronger so that we are able to resist those powerful foreign countries' aggressions. Actually, he had already acquired support from the Chinese people.")

Suddenly, Cíxǐ's face turned solemn with an angry impression. She kept quiet for a long moment,

"我想你大概是與梁啟超、康有為這班人同黨的吧!" ("I think you are in the same party as Kāng, Yǒu-Wéi and Liáng, Qǐ-Chāo, those traitors!")

Minister Xǔ, kept his head bowed to the ground to show his respect.

"稟告皇太后!我不是反對皇太后,只是說策換皇上的時機還未到。我是為未來的影響為國擔心啊!" ("Report to Empress Dowager! I am not against Empress Dowager's decision. I am just saying that the time for replacing the Emperor has not arrived yet. All I worry about is the future of the country.")

As Empress Dowager Cíxǐ realized that he was not specifically against her decision, her facial expression became gentler. Minister Xǔ's good friends, ministers Xú, Yòng-Yí (徐用儀), Lìshān (立山), and Liányuan (聯元) worried that Minister Xǔ, Jǐng-Chéng might have upset Empress Dowager and would be punished by beheading. They went to kneel down next to Xǔ, Jǐng-Chéng right in front of Empress Dowager. Minister Lìshān said,

"稟告皇太后!許景澄可說得有理啊。光緒皇上不但深得民心,還有列強在後面支持他呢!如果時機不對,那可能引起列強的干涉並對我實施軍事上的不利啊。" ("Report to Empress Dowager! What Minister Xǔ said was reasonable. Emperor Guāngxù has already acquired the people's support. Furthermore, he also has support from strong foreign countries. If the timing is not proper, it may trigger these strong foreign countries' interference and military actions against us.")

Cíxǐ, after she heard this, in one way she was very upset about the possibility of foreign countries interfering in Chinese matters, but in other ways she was also very afraid that those ocean ghosts might receive the Chinese people's support and use their forces against her.

Cíxǐ looked at the expressions on all the other officers' faces, then asked Duke Duān, Zàiyī for his opinion. She always trusted Duke Duān and wanted to know his thoughts.

"稟告皇太后!我認為民心倒是容易控制,可是列強干涉的是可以預料到的。" ("Report to Empress Dowager! I think the minds of the people can be controlled easily. But the interference from strong foreign countries can be predicted.")

Due to Duke Duān, Zàiyī's advice, Empress Dowager Cíxǐ decided not to replace Emperor Guāngxù till the timing was more appropriate.

DISCUSSION IN QĪNG COURT - 2 清廷論政 - 2

On June 16th of 1900, the aggression of the Yìhétuán (義和團) (Boxers) against foreign citizens and missionaries was heightened and their territory enlarged to Tiānjīn City. The Eight-Nation Coalition army had already made their invasion plan to eliminate the Yìhétuán since the Qīng Government had done nothing to prevent the Yìhétuán's serious aggression.

Due to the tremendous pressure she was under, Empress Dowager Cíxǐ was thinking about giving an order to suppress the Yìhétuán's activities. However, when she received a report the next day that the Eight-Nation Coalition Army had already captured Fort Dàgū (大沽), an important fortress guarding Běijīng, she became very angry. Now Běijīng was under a severe threat of attack.

She immediately called all her top advisory officers and ministers to the office of Yuánmíng summer garden again.

"您們倒說說看！我們應不應該將義和團的運動壓制下去？這些洋鬼子已經將大沽砲台拿下了。現在大沽一失守，再來這些洋鬼子的軍隊就逼上北京來了。" ("What do you say? Should we suppress Yìhétuán's activities or not? These foreign ghosts have already taken over Fort Dàgū. Now, since Fort Dàgū is lost, the army of these foreign ghosts will threaten Běijīng.")

Among all these top advisory officers and ministers, there was a division of two groups with opposite opinions. One group was led by Zàiyī (載漪), Zàixūn (載勛), Gāngyì (剛毅), and Zhào, Shū-Qiào (趙舒翹), with affiliate followers, Pǔjìng (溥靜), Zàilián (載濂), Zàiyíng (載瀅), Zàilán (載瀾), and Yīngnián (英年). This group believed that the Qīng Court should continue to appease the Yìhétuán and use them to defend against the foreigners' invasion. The other group included Ministers Xǔ, Jǐng-Chéng (許景澄), Xú, Yòng-Yí (徐用儀), Lìshān (立山), Liányuan (聯元), and Yuánchǎng (袁昶). They believed that the Qīng Court should suppress the Yìhétuán, hoping that this might ease the pressure of the foreign countries' invasion.

While Cíxǐ did not know how to make her decision, her minster

Zàiyī (載漪) said,

"稟告皇太后！在我看來，義和團都是出自萬死不顧一生，以赴國家之難的義民。我們可以利用他們抵抗洋人的冒犯與侵略。" ("Report to Empress Dowager! From my viewpoint, all Yìhétuán members are righteous people who have risked their lives to protect our country. We can use them to resist the foreign countries' affront and invasion.")

"稟告皇太后！我同意載漪的看法！我們應該安撫義和團，並利用他們的人眾與刀槍不入的法術來幫忙我大清抵抗列強的侵略。" ("Report to Empress Dowager! I agree with Zàiyī's viewpoint! We should solicit and pacify Yìhétuán and use their magnificent magic power against knives and guns to assist Qīng against the strong foreign countries' invasion,") another minister, Zàiyī's follower, Gāngyì said in support of Zàiyī's suggestion.

Immediately, the leader of another group, Xǔ, Jǐng-Chéng (許景澄), stepped to the front of Empress Dowager Cíxǐ and knelt down,

"稟告皇太后！可是我們不能允許義和團團員攻擊和殺害外國公使啊！這不但是違反國際法規並可能引起我們與列強大規模的衝突呢！" ("Report to Empress Dowager! But we shouldn't allow Yìhétuán members to attack and kill foreign envoys. This is against international laws and can cause a huge conflict between us and foreign countries,") he argued against the idea of using the Yìhétuán to resist the foreigners.

Immediately, four other ministers, Xú, Yòng-Yí (徐用儀), Lìshān (立山), Liányuan (聯元), and Yuánchǎng (袁昶) also knelt down next to Xǔ, Jǐng-Chéng.

"稟告皇太后！我們必須通過妥協和平的方法去解決這個問題。我們不應再刺激列強，再給他們更多的藉口。我們應該打壓義和團。" ("Report to Empress Dowager! We must use peaceful ways through negotiation to solve this problem. We should not agitate those strong foreign countries further and give them more excuses to invade us. We should suppress Yìhétuán.")

Both sides kept arguing but could not come up with a good solution. Empress Dowager Cíxǐ also did not know what to do and or how to make a decision. Finally, she said,

"讓我再考慮考慮！我們先觀時而動。" ("Let me think about it! Let's wait to see how things develop.")

DUKE DUĀN, ZÀIYĪ'S INSIDIOUS PLOT 端郡王載漪的陰險計謀

The next day, while Empress Dowager Cíxǐ was still in a confused and upset state of mind, Duke Duān, Zàiyī (端王載漪), in order to persuade

Empress Dowager Cíxǐ to declare war against the Eight-Nation Alliance, secretly instructed a top military advisor, Lián, Wén-Chōng (連文沖) to forge a fake diplomatic notification from the Eight-Nation Alliance to the Qīng Government. In this notification, the Eight-Nation Alliance demanded four conditions to the withdrawal of their aggression. The conditions were: 1. assign a secured living place for Emperor Guāngxù; 2. the coalition army would replace the Qīng Government's authority to collect taxes and grains; 3. the coalition army would be in charge of the entire Chinese military; and 4. political power was to be returned to Emperor Guāngxù.

Naturally, Empress Dowager Cíxǐ could not accept these unreasonable conditions. The anger and hate she felt reached an intolerable level. She was so unwilling to bow to foreigners. However, she did not have any better solution to the situation except using the Yìhétuán against the foreigners. There was only one question in her mind,

"這些義和團團員真的能用法術起抵抗槍砲嗎？" ("Can these Yìhétuán members really use magic power to resist guns and cannons?") she wondered. If they could, this would mean they had a big hope of defeating the foreign countries.

June 18th, Empress Dowager Cíxǐ received report of the "Lángfāng Victory." This victory gave her a great hope that with the Yìhétuán's help, the situation might be turned around. However, in her deep mind, she was still unsure and confused.

A DECEIVING DEMONSTRATION 一個瞞天的示範

On June 19th of 1900, Zàiyī (載漪) instructed his follower, Gāngyì (剛毅), to arrange a demonstration for Empress Dowager Cíxǐ. It was a sunny morning. Empress Dowager Cíxǐ was invited to the royal military arena together with a few other ministers whom Zàiyī trusted.

Around 10 o'clock in the morning Cíxǐ, with her most trusted eunuch, Lǐ, Lián-Yīng (李蓮英), entered the observation platform of the arena heavily escorted by palace royal guards. In front of her was a large drapery so the performers would not see her face clearly. However, through a screen she and her invited ministers would be able to see the show. Naturally, Zàiyī and Gāngyì were next to her.

"稟告皇太后！為了增加您對義和團對抗外國軍隊的信心，我與載漪安排了這個小示範。在這裡，您可以看到他們抵抗槍砲的能力。" ("Report to Empress Dowager! In order to increase your confidence in using Yìhétuán's abilities against foreign troops, Zàiyī and I have arranged this small demonstration for you. From this demonstration, you will be able to see their defensive capability,") Gāngyì said.

Though Empress Dowager Cíxǐ had serious doubts about it, she was curious.

"好吧！你就要他們進場吧。" ("All right! You may ask them to enter the arena.") She nodded her head and indicated that the demonstration could start.

Then, Gāngyì stepped out from behind the drapery and raised up his right hand to signal the captain of the performers. Immediately, about 40 people wearing Yìhétuán uniforms and 20 Qīng soldiers ran onto the field in front of the observation platform. They all knelt down and bowed their heads to the ground to show their respect and allegiance.

"很好！剛毅！你就要他們表演吧。" ("All right, Gāngyì! You may ask them to start the performance.") Empress Dowager Cíxǐ nodded her head again.

First, ten Yìhétuán members performed an extraordinarily skilled lion dance with drum, gong, and cymbals to show their respect to Empress Dowager Cíxǐ. This cheered up Cíxǐ's mood. She began to smile and enjoy the show. Next, another team came out with traditional Chinese weapons: sabers, swords, staffs, and spears. After they bowed to the audience, again they demonstrated superior fighting skills that were seldom seen by outside people. However, this did not impress Cíxǐ as much since she had seen many of these performances by royal guards in the past. After 20 minutes of this performance, the arena field was cleared and about 20 wooden dummies were brought in and placed in the area to the left of the observation platform. Once they were in place, Qīng soldiers lined up about 30 meters from the dummies. They raised up their guns and shot the dummies which were immediately hit and smashed into pieces.

"這些洋槍的威力可不小啊！" ("The power of these foreign guns is not weak!") Empress Dowager Cíxǐ looked at Zàiyī and Gāngyì with a sigh.

While they were talking, the field was cleared of dummies and a group of 20 Yìhétuán members, without shirts, entered and lined up on the field, ready to receive the gun shot from the shooters.

Again, those Qīng soldiers raised up their guns, aimed at these members and shot them. To Cíxǐ's surprise, when these members received the shot, they were not dead or even injured. Their only response to being shot was to bounce back a couple of steps. Cíxǐ couldn't believe what she had seen. She was convinced that Yìhétuán members had this kind of magic power from Língfú (spiritual amulet) that could resist against guns or even cannons.

"如果我沒有親眼看到，我還真不相信呢？" ("If I didn't see it with my own eyes, I would never believe it!") She again looked at Zàiyī and Gāngyì. With an expression of satisfaction, she retired under the heavy royal guards' protection.

Very sadly, Empress Dowager Cíxǐ did not know she had been completely deceived. She did not know that actually all of the performers were not Yìhétuán members, but were loyal soldiers specially selected by Gāngyì from the Qīng army. She was also foolishly tricked into believing that the guns used to shoot the real humans were real like the ones used to shoot the wooden dummies. She did not know the guns had been replaced immediately after the first shooting demonstration. There were no bullets in the guns for the second shooting but only gun powder. The performers just faked that they were shot and bounced back a few steps without injury.

Because of this demonstration, Cíxǐ had made up her mind. Now, she had hope that using Yìhétuán members to defend against foreign troops could be possible. She gave an order to convene her high-ranking officers and ministers for a meeting in the office of Yuánmíng Garden summer house again the next day.

DISCUSSION IN QĪNG COURT - 3 清廷論政 - 3

The same group of top advisory officers and ministers as the meeting four days ago were gathering in the office of Yuánmíng Garden summer house. These officers and ministers were still divided into two groups with opposite opinions about whether the Qīng Court should suppress the Yìhétuán's activity and declare war against those foreign countries or not. After Empress Dowager Cíxǐ's arrival with her most trusted eunuch, Lǐ, Lián-Yīng (李蓮英), all of the officers and ministers knelt down in front of her to show their respect.

"你們就平身吧！" ("You may stand up!") Empress Dowager Cíxǐ said.

From her tone of speaking, everyone could see that she was in a better mood. It seemed that the worry she had had for the last few days was gone. After everyone stood and had lined up on both sides,

"經過三天的思考，我認為我大清不能吞下這口氣。我決定就向所有列強宣戰。可是你們還有什麼意見，不妨陳奏。" ("After three days of consideration, I believe we should not swallow our anger caused by the foreigners. I have decided to declare war against those strong foreign nations. But, if you have any opinion, you may bring it up,") Cíxǐ said.

When everyone heard her decision, the room was quiet for a moment. To that group led by Zàiyī (載漪), and Gāngyì (剛毅) who agreed to the use of the Yìhétuán against the foreign troops, there was no surprise since they knew that Cíxǐ had already been convinced the day before. However, the other group led by Xǔ, Jǐng-Chéng (許景澄) was shocked. Immediately, Liányuan (聯元) stepped in front of Cíxǐ and knelt down to present his opinion.

"如與各國宣戰，恐將來洋兵殺入京城，必致雞犬不留。" ("If we declare war against the foreign countries, I am afraid when foreign troops enter Běijīng it may cause a huge disaster.")

However, after Cíxǐ listened to his presentation her face became solemn and serious. Immediately, one of Zàiyī's followers said,

"你這說的是什麼話？" ("What are you talking about?") Before he could continue his argument, Zàiyī interrupted and said,

"拳民法術可恃不可恃，臣不敢議，臣特取其心術可恃耳。" ("I am not arguing whether Yìhétuán members' magic power is reliable or not. I just adore their loyal and righteous heart.")

Even though he knew he had convinced Cíxǐ with a deceiving demonstration the day before, he pretended that he knew nothing about it. Cíxǐ answered,

"不用再說了！我心已決。載漪！擬稿宣戰書就交給你負責了。明天一早必須送出。就以光緒的名義公佈並遞給所有的外國使節。" ("Speak no more! I have made my firm decision. Zàiyī! You have the responsibility to generate a draft declaration of war. We will send it out early tomorrow morning. Use the name of Guāngxù and deliver the declaration to all foreign embassies.")

"臣這就照皇太后旨意去辦！" ("I will carry out Empress Dowager's order,") Zàiyī replied.

"剛毅、載勛我就任命你們兩位為統率義和團大臣，率領義和團同八國聯軍開戰，攻擊外國使館。" ("Gāngyì, Zàixūn, I assign both of you as the chancellors of Yìhétuán to lead them to fight against the Eight-Nation Alliance and attack foreign embassies.")

When Xǔ, Jǐng-Chéng heard Cíxǐ's decision, he was very worried and concerned about the consequences of declaring war against those foreign countries. Now she was giving the order to Gāngyì and Zàixūn to lead the Yìhétuán to attack the foreign embassies. Immediately, he stepped out again and knelt down in front of Cíxǐ.

"稟告皇太后！這事不可行啊。攻殺使臣，中外皆無成案啊！這也會讓列強找到藉口說為了保護他們的公使與公民，他們可以毫無顧慮的進軍呢。"
("Report to Empress Dowager! We cannot do this. There has not been such a precedent of attacking foreign envoys in the past. This will give those strong foreign countries an excuse to advance their troops without hesitation, in order to protect their diplomats and citizens.") He still hoped Empress Dowager Cíxǐ would change her mind to redeem the situation. His heart was broken since he could see the consequences this might cause. Naturally, Ministers Xú, Yòng-Yí (徐用儀), Lìshān (立山), Liányuan (聯元), and Yuánchǎng (袁昶) also came out to support Xǔ, Jǐng-Chéng. However, Empress Dowager Cíxǐ became extremely angry and shouted,

"不用再多說了！再說就交刑部議處。" ("Don't say anymore. Otherwise, you will be handed in to the ministry of criminal affairs for punishment.")

After she said this, nobody dared to express his opinion again. The decision was made.

DECLARE WAR AGAINST POWERFUL FOREIGN NATIONS 對列強的宣戰

On June 21st of 1900, Empress Dowager Cíxǐ used the name of Emperor Guāngxù to announce to the public a "Declaration of War" (宣戰詔書) against all powerful foreign nations including Britain, America, France, Germany, Italy, Japan, Russia, Spain, Belgium, the Netherlands, and Austria-Hungary, 11 countries. She called out for help from all Chinese civilians and soldiers to resist all 11 foreign countries. She also encouraged the killing of, and offered rewards to, those who killed foreigners: for one man - 50 taels of silver; one woman - 40 taels, and one child - 30 taels. With this encouragement, all Yìhétuán members and Qīng soldiers began to besiege the foreign embassies.

THE AGGRESSION OF THE EIGHT-NATION ALLIANCE 八國聯軍的侵略

On June 25th, four days after Cíxǐ declared war, her mind turned soft again. She gave an order to stop attacking the foreign embassies and also sent fruits, vegetables, and other foods to the embassies. She kept changing her mind because in one way she hated all foreigners, but in another way, she was so afraid of them, especially the Eight-Nation coalition army that was on its way to attack Běijīng. The numbers of the coalition army at that time included 520 officers and 10,350 soldiers. On June 28th, Qīng soldiers resumed their attacks against all of the foreign embassies.

On July 14th, the coalition army had taken over Tiānjīn City and prepared their further assault against Běijīng. The next day, the Russian army crossed the northern Chinese border, Hēilóng River (黑龍江), and killed more than 6,000 Chinese civilians.

Qīng's conditions got worse and worse, and the coalition army got closer and closer to Běijīng. Běijīng was in a critical and urgent condition. This had worried all the ministers, Xǔ, Jǐng-Chéng (許景澄), Xú, Yòng-Yí (徐用儀), Lìshān (立山), Liányuan (聯元), and Yuánchǎng (袁昶), who were against the war. Together, they submitted a written statement to Cíxǐ. They said in the statement: "the Qīng Government should not allow those Boxers to do what they want to do. This may offer excuses for powerful foreign nations to initiate more aggression." ("奸民不可縱，外釁不可啟。")

Seeing no response from Empress Dowager Cíxǐ, Xǔ, Jǐng-Chéng, again submitted another statement to Cíxǐ on July 28th. He said in his statement again, "there is no such example of killing foreign ministers either in China or in foreign countries." ("攻殺使臣，中外皆無成案。")

Unfortunately, this made Cíxǐ more upset than ever and she gave an order to behead ministers Xǔ, Jǐng-Chéng (許景澄) and Yuánchǎng (袁昶) on July 28th. She claimed that these ministers were "arbitrarily submitting statements and alienating the unification." (任意妄奏，語多離間). She also arrested the other three loyal ministers, Xú, Yòng-Yí (徐用儀), Lìshān (立山), and Liányuan (聯元). Later, on August 11th, these three loyal ministers were also executed.

Battle of Běijīng 北京之戰

August 2nd of 1900, the Eight-Nation coalition army assembled with a total of 20,000 soldiers in Tiānjīn (天津) and got ready to advance toward Běijīng (北京). Two days later, the coalition army marched along Běijīng-Hángzhōu Grand Canal (京杭大運河) from Tiānjīn (天津) toward Běijīng (北京). Though there were more than 150,000 Qīng soldiers and Yìhétuán members along the way between Tiānjīn (天津) and Běijīng (北京), the coalition army did not encounter any strong resistance.

This was because the coalition army had a better plan this time and also the manpower they had was much greater than ever. Since the

Yìhétuán had already shifted their defense to Běijīng, there were not too many members available for this resistance. At the same time, when the Qīng soldiers saw such a big offense with the superior weapons that the coalition army had, they dared not launch any attack. Actually, the Qīng Government had lost control of their army.

By August 13th, the coalition army had already taken Tōngzhōu (通州) and that evening, Russian and Japanese troops arrived at Běijīng (北京). In the early morning of August 14th of 1900, Běijīng City (北京城) was completely surrounded by the armies of The Eight-Nation Alliance (八國聯軍), a total of 50,000 soldiers. The sun was rising and both sides were tensed and nervous, especially the Qīng soldiers and Yìhétuán (義和團) members. They knew that since the armies of The Eight-Nation Alliance had more guns and cannons that were much super in power to their sabers and swords, the loss of the city was expected.

For this last defense for their country, the Gěn (艮) group of Yìhétuán members were assigned to defend Dōngzhí Gate (東直門). From flags fluttering amongst the opponent's army, Bó-Wǔ could recognize that the army attacking this gate was Russian. According to information passed around earlier, they knew that the Japanese army would attack Zhāoyáng Gate (朝陽門) while the United States army was responsible for attacking Dōngbiàn Gate (東便門). Everyone was holding their breath and waiting for the storm's coming.

Suddenly, a few cannon balls fell on the city gate area. Within just a few minutes, countless cannon balls fell on the city wall and upon the poor Qīng soldiers and Yìhétuán members. The number of casualties increased rapidly. Bó-Wǔ, Bó-Wēi, Bó-Dé, and Wàn-Jí, with a few other Yìhétuán members, hid themselves in the corner on top of the city wall. They expected that once the cannon ball assault stopped, the coalition soldiers' attack with ladders would follow.

After half an hour or so, suddenly the sound of cannons ceased at Dōngzhí Gate, though everyone could still hear many cannon attacks continuing far away at different city gates. In just a few minutes, they saw a large group of Russian soldiers approaching with ladders. When the enemy had approached to within the right distance, Qīng soldiers fired their limited cannons and guns. When the Russian soldiers were closer, both Qīng soldiers and Yìhétuán members released their arrows.

This effort couldn't stop the Russian army, who were hidden behind shields, from getting closer to the city wall. Twenty minutes later, thousands of Russian soldiers had set up ladders and were climbing up the city wall. In an hour or so, some Russian soldiers had already reached the top of the wall. More and more Russian soldiers were on the wall. Yìhétuán members including Bó-Wǔ's group with some Qīng soldiers tried hard to resist their opponents. While they were fighting, Wàn-Jí became very scared since he was smaller than any of the Russians and did not have much fighting skill. He hid himself in the corner on the top of the wall.

Suddenly, he saw a Russian soldier that had just climbed onto the wall raise his gun and aim at Bó-Dé who was fighting with another Russian soldier. Time was crucial since Bó-Dé could be killed in a second. Without thinking, Wàn-Jí stood up and ran toward that Russian's back and bumped him off balance.

Peng! A bullet just barely passed Bó-Dé's right shoulder. Finally, Bó-Dé pushed the soldier he was fighting off of the tall wall to fall to the ground outside. However, when the first Russian soldier realized that he missed his shot because Wàn-Jí had bumped him, he turned and tried to use his bayonet to kill Wàn-Jí. Wàn-Jí panicked and tried to run away from this Russian. Bó-Dé was still about 10 meters from Wàn-Jí and did not have enough time to get there to help him. Bó-Wǔ also could not get there in time; he was at least 30 meters away directing his members in the fight.

At this critical moment, Bó-Wēi appeared behind Wàn-Jí after having just knocked out another Russian soldier with his staff. He was just in time to use his staff to deflect the Russian's bayonet and hit him on the head, saving Wàn-Jí. After another 20 minutes or so, the Russians' attack was weakening due to the height of the wall for this gate being so much taller than the others. With a strong defense of Qīng soldiers and Yìhétuán members, the Russian army was finally forced to retreat.

Wàn-Jí couldn't help the tears that rushed out of his eyes. Bó-Dé realized that Wàn-Jí might just have saved his life earlier. He went to Wàn-Jí and hugged him tightly.

"萬吉！謝謝你。沒有你，我可能已經被那俄國兵打死了。" ("Wàn-Jí, thank you! Without your help, I might have already been shot by that Russian soldier.")

However, Wàn-Jí continued to cry and stood there trembling. After the Russians' retreat, all the Yìhétuán members and Qīng soldiers started shouting and cheering. Bó-Wǔ came to meet them with a smile on his face.

"二哥！這一波攻擊是被我們擊退了。可是左右看一下，我們的傷亡可也不少啊！" ("Èrgē! We have defeated their first assault. But if we look around, our causalities are not few,") Bó-Wǔ said.

"這些俄國兵還挺怕死的。我相信我們還可以保住下一波的攻擊。" ("These Russian soldiers are very afraid of death. I believe we still can resist their next assault,") Bó-Dé said with a big smile.

Wàn-Jí started to feel a little better and followed the others and laughed. However, Bó-Wēi expressed his opinion,

"你們不要高興太早。我相信這一波是在試探我們防禦的能力。下一波可能會比較難應付。何況清兵的彈藥有限，很快的就會彈盡了呢！" ("It is too early for you to cheer. I believe this attack was a test to see our defense capability. It may be harder for us to stand against the next attack. Furthermore, the Qīng soldiers' ammunition is limited and will be exhausted soon.") Bó-Wēi was not as optimistic as his two brothers.

This brought them face to face with the reality and the fact of the situation. Bó-Wǔ and Bó-Dé showed their worry on their faces again. Wàn-Jí's body started trembling again and his face turned pale.

"萬吉！你到城下去看看有什麼需要幫忙的，這裡你比較危險。" ("Wàn-Jí! Go down the wall and see if there is anything that needs your help. There is too much danger for you here,") Bó-Dé told Wàn-Jí, so Wàn-Jí left.

More cannon balls started coming again, this time aimed only on the gate. It seemed that the Russians had changed their strategy. Instead of an attack by foot soldiers, they decided to use only cannon power to blow down the gate. This worsened the worry of the soldiers defending the gate. They all knew if the Russian army had plenty of ammunition, sooner or later the gate would be blown away.

Around 11 o'clock in the morning, a messenger passed information to the defense team that the United States soldiers had already entered the first defense wall of the city, since the wall the United States had been attacking was shorter than in other places. However, even though United States soldiers had entered the first defense wall, they were stopped from advancing due to Qīng's powerful fire power.

This news caused a panic for those defenders at the east gate. Terror could clearly be seen on the Qīng soldiers' faces. Everyone knew that once one gate was taken, foreign soldiers would soon come to attack them from inside the city.

The situation at Zhāoyáng Gate where the Japanese were attacking was very similar to the Russian attack. Both Russian and Japanese armies had difficulties getting past the first defense city wall. Both countries encountered more than 100 casualties. However, around 9 o'clock in the evening, due to the Qīng soldiers running out of ammunition and after nearly ten hours of cannon attacks, finally, the Japanese and Russian armies entered Dōngzhí and Zhāoyáng Gates. This forced the Qīng soldiers and Yìhétuán members to retreat to the second defense wall of the city very quickly.

In another part of the city, the British army was preparing its attack. It was not till early afternoon that their attack was launched against Guǎngqú Gate (廣渠門). To their surprise, after firing only a few cannon balls, the city gate was opened wide, allowing them to enter. What had happened was, those British soldiers who were already in the city, attacked the Qīng soldiers and Yìhétuán members' defense. It was a surprise to the Qīng soldiers and Yìhétuán members and the gate was quickly taken over without any casualties. It seemed that the Qīng soldiers and Yìhétuán members realized they could not defend against the powerful British army's assault from both inside and outside together, so they gave up the first defense and quickly retreated to the second defense wall.

Bó-Wǔ also led his group to retreat to the second defense wall very quickly. After they had positioned themselves, Bó-Wēi said,

"我看這第二道防線可能也支持不久。敵人的炮火太猛烈了，況乎清兵的士氣看起來快要瓦解了。" ("As I see it, this second defense line will not last long either. The enemy's power is so fierce. Furthermore, I see the morale of the Qīng soldiers has already collapsed.")

"這一防線一破，剩下的就是最後內城和紫禁城的防線了。不知道慈禧太后，光緒皇帝，與清廷高級官員做何打算？" ("Once this defense line is taken, there is only the last inner-city defense and forbidden city defense. I don't know what the plan is for Empress Dowager Cíxǐ, Emperor Guānxù, and those high rank ministers,") Bó-Wǔ said.

"這最後防線是宮廷大內的衛隊負責。他們有最好的配備，加上我們跟撤退的清兵，我相信我們可以撐它一陣子。" ("The responsibility of this last defense line belongs to the palace royal guards. They have the best arms and equipment. Together with us and the retreating Qīng soldiers, I believe we are able to hold the enemy off for a while,") Bó-Dé expressed his opinion.

While they were talking, suddenly a strong attack was launched by the coalition army. To the Yìhétuán members' surprise, all of the Qīng soldiers quickly gave up their defense and left the limited Yìhétuán members to fight. They didn't know that all the Qīng soldiers had received an instruction from a top authority to withdraw and focus their strength on the last defense of the inner city and forbidden city in order to allow Empress Dowager Cíxǐ, Emperor Guāngxù, and many high-ranking ministers to escape from the city. They realized they no longer had a chance of resisting against the coalition army. To avoid becoming prisoners of the coalition army, they escaped.

By 9 o'clock in the evening, all Qīng soldiers and Yìhétuán members had retreated into the last defense of the inner city (內城) and forbidden city (紫禁城). This was the final defense against all of the foreign armies.

There were about 85 survivors in Bó-Wǔ's group. Many were dead and many were lost somewhere during the retreat. Fortunately, except for some minor injuries, Bó-Wǔ, Bó-Dé, Bó-Wēi, and Wàn-Jí had survived and were still together.

"既然我們到這個地步，已經跑不掉了。我們必須團結起來做最後的抵抗。" ("Since we have reached this stage, we cannot escape. We must unite together and make our last stand of resistance,") Bó-Wǔ told every one of his group.

"李壇主！如果這道防線也保不住了，我們應該怎麼辦？" ("Altar Lǐ! If we cannot protect this last defense line, what should we do?")

"如果到了最後關頭，大家解散，各自逃生，混入百姓中，躲藏起來。等一切平靜後，再逃離北京。" ("Once we have reached the last moment, we should disperse, mix with civilians, and hide. Wait till everything has calmed down. Then we can escape from Běijīng.")

"我麼一旦分散，以後我們怎麼在聚在一起呢？" ("Once we are separated, how can we get together again?")

"記得我們聯絡的信號。從各隊員留下的信號，我們可以在聚集在一起。" ("Remember our contact signal. From the mark left in the city, we can get together again.")

On August 15th, all the armies of The Eight-Nation Alliance had completely taken over both outer defense walls and surrounded the inner city and forbidden city. However, when the coalition army launched their assault, they encountered the strongest defense. Cannon balls fell to both sides. The exchange of cannon balls lasted till midnight. Countless Qīng soldiers and Yìhétuán members were killed. The dead bodies piled up everywhere in the inner city. Finally, the defense commander, General Yánmào (延茂) of Āndìng Gate (安定門), saw the hopelessness of the situation and, to avoid further casualties, he gave the order to surrender. All nine inner city gates were lost to British, Japanese, American, and Russian control. The Emperor's favorite concubine, Zhēn (珍妃), committed suicide by throwing herself into a well. Empress Dowager Cíxǐ, Emperor Guāngxù, together with all the important ministers, escaped from Běijīng hastily. After passing Huáilái County (懷來縣), Dàtóng (大同), and Tàiyuán (太原), they finally arrived in Xī'ān (西安) of Shǎnxī Province (陝西省).

On the 16th of August, various street fights between the opposing sides continued fiercely. Due to the Qīng soldiers' fast retreat followed by Empress Dowager Cíxǐ's and Emperor Guāngxù's escape, all the street battles were taking place mostly between Yìhétuán members and the coalition army. Unfortunately, because the Yìhétuán members did not have guns and cannons like the Qīng army, they encountered huge casualties. Before nightfall, the coalition armies had control of all of Běijīng City.

Bó-Wǔ's group fought and hid and tried to survive. The worst days were yet to come. All commanders of every invading country gave their soldiers a legal right to loot, rape, and rob the entire city for three days. Now, coalition soldiers openly killed civilians, set buildings on fire, raped, and looted the entire city. They took countless treasures from rich families with them. They looted the forbidden city and took palace treasures away with them. The famous Yuánmíng Garden (圓明園), after being looted and burned in The Second Opium War, encountered this new disastrous fate and was reduced to ruins. One of the commanders of The Eight-Nation Alliance, Alfred von Waldersee (1832-1904), later admitted that the damage and looting caused by the armies of the Eight-Nation Alliance could never been estimated or recouped.

During the three days of catastrophe, many civilians were killed and countless women raped. The entire city was on fire. People tried to hide here and there. They hid themselves in the poor area of the city since it was not too much of an attraction to the coalition army. This also offered Yìhétuán members a chance to hide. In addition, because of the coalition army's irrational robbing, killing, and starting of fires, many Běijīng citizens began to help those Yìhétuán members trying to escape. Now they realized that there was no difference between Chinese bandits and the foreign coalition army. There was no morality and justice, only reality.

Three days after the Eight-Nation coalition army gained control of Běijīng City, they began to hunt down Yìhétuán members. Fortunately, many Yìhétuán members were able to hide with the help of local civilians. Also, coalition soldiers were not familiar with the city and this provided another chance for Yìhétuán members to hide. However, the coalition army had controlled and closed all the city gates so that it was not possible for Yìhétuán members to actually get out of Běijīng City.

The Eight-Nation coalition divided the entire inner Běijīng City into different areas for the eight different countries to control. The external part of the city was occupied by Britain, the United States, and Germany. In order to hunt down all Yìhétuán members, Japan established the "Appease Office" (安民公所) and Germany founded a "Seizing Chinese Bureau" (華捕局). All surviving Yìhétuán members were in a critical and dangerous situation.

CHAPTER 7
VICTIMS OF THE ERA
時 代 的 犧 牲 者

The city of Beijing was now completely surrounded, and all the gates were guarded by the coalition army. No one was allowed to leave. Those Yìhétuán members who were still alive either blended in with the laymen society or hid themselves in abandoned houses or temples, waiting for a chance to run away from the city.

More than two weeks after Bĕijīng City was lost into the hands of the Eight-Nation coalition forces, Empress Dowager Cíxǐ deeply regretted her decision to declare war against all of the powerful nations.

On June 21st, she sent an imperial envoy, Lǐ, Hóng-Zhāng (李鴻章), to contact the coalition commanders in an attempt to reach a compromise. She blamed everything on the Yìhétuán and also her nine top advisory ministers who had supported and urged her to declare war against all of the strong nations.

On September 7th, in order to show her sincerity and good will in cooperation with the alliance forces, she gave an order to eliminate all Yìhétuán members. She also notified the coalition commanders that the Qīng soldiers would assist them to search for and arrest Yìhétuán members. She knew that since the Qīng soldiers knew Bĕijīng much better than the coalition soldiers, they would know where Yìhétuán members were most likely to hide. She told coalition commanders that with the Qīng soldiers' assistance, the elimination of Yìhétuán members would be more effective. She also gave an order that whenever any Yìhétuán member was captured or surrendered, he or she would be beheaded right there on the site.

Since then, the Qīng soldiers joined the coalition forces and helped them catch Yìhétuán members. The city gates were re-opened. However, whenever any civilian wished to leave or enter the city, they would be closely interrogated by the Qīng soldiers. When Yìhétuán members realized that this was being done, some of them believed that it was a good chance to escape. They exchanged their uniforms for civilian's clothing and mixed with regular civilians to try to get out of the city. However, since the Qīng soldiers knew Chinese and Běijīng City very well, they always found a way to catch Yìhétuán members. Many members were caught and immediately beheaded in front of the city gate. Yìhétuán members became shocked and angry as they realized that they had little chance to escape from the Qīng soldiers' questioning.

On September 10th, through a secret signal communication, a small group of Yìhétuán survivors gathered in a large abandoned and burned out house with a huge garden. This property had been owned by one of the richest families. Nobody knew what had happened to the owners after three days of killing and looting. Bó-Wǔ's group, with Bó-Wěi, Bó-Dé, and Wàn-Jí, and a total of 18 survivors were also there with them. They did not dare to show any lights in the place since they were afraid that they would be discovered. A couple of young members were sobbing in the darkness.

"他媽的！我們是被清廷出賣了。" ("Damn it! We have been betrayed by the Qīng Court,") one of the senior members said.

"清廷這是過河拆橋。我們為他們賣命，看來是被利用了。" ("What the Qīng Court did is 'destroy the bridge after the army has crossed the river.' We have sacrificed so many of our lives for them. Now we realize that we have been used,") another member said with tears.

"目前最重要的是我們得趕快想辦法離開北京城。待在城內，有清兵的幫忙，我們早晚是會被抓的。" ("The most urgent thing for us now is finding a way to get out of Běijīng City. If we stay in the city, then with the Qīng soldiers' help, we will be caught sooner or later,") said Bó-Wǔ.

"現在只有一個辦法。我們必須將生存的人召集起來，作最後一次的衝擊。現在城門都被聯軍與清兵管制，我們必須集中力量專攻一門，希望能衝出去。" ("We have only one strategy now. We must gather all surviving members and assemble them to launch our last attack. At this time all the gates are controlled by coalition forces aided by the Qīng soldiers. We must focus all our forces to attack one gate and get out,") the most senior leader in the group, Mr. Dǒng, said.

"我們還可以聚集多少人？如果我們人太少，是不會成功的。" ("How

many people can we assemble? If we have only a few, we will not be successful,") Bó-Wēi asked with concern.

"我們這邊有三十一人。如果我們將暗號傳遞出去給在這附近躲藏的團員，我估計我們可以聚集近百人。" ("We have 31 people here. If we pass our message out through secret signals to our members hidden throughout the neighborhoods, I estimate we may gather close to one hundred people,") Leader Dǒng said.

"我們有沒有辦法跟其他字號的人聯絡上？如可以我們可以分開同時行動攻擊不同的城門，製造混亂。這樣我們逃出去的機會可能會比較大。" ("Do we have any method to contact members of other groups? If we do, we can co-ordinate to attack different gates at the same time and create a chaotic situation. In that case, we may have a better chance to escape,") Bó-Wéi asked.

"我們可以試試看。能夠聯絡上多少就算多少了。" ("We can try and see how many groups we are able to connect with,") Leader Dǒng said.

"董頭領！如果我們能夠逃出去，我們怎麼在聚合？" ("Captain Dǒng! If we are able to get out of the city, how can we get together again?") one of young fellows asked.

"今晚大家分頭把消息傳出去！我們明天晚上子夜在南城門附近鄭家廢墟集合，在凌晨城門一打開，我們就行動。能夠逃出去的，就在後天南城外土地廟會合。" ("Everyone pass the message out tonight. We will gather at Zhèng's Family ruins near south gate tomorrow midnight and commence action at dawn once the city gates are opened. If we can get out, we will meet at the Tǔdì Temple just south of the city limits,") Leader Dǒng said.

Once the decision was made, all the members went out and searched for other members. Since they knew where they were hiding from secret signals marked on walls in the city, they were able to pass the message along in a short time.

Before dawn, they all returned to the Zhèng Family ruins since without a hiding place they could be found easily during the daytime. Right before midnight, there were about 110 members gathered in the house. This house was only a mile from the south city gate. They did not know how many members were gathering for other gate attacks.

***

As planned, they left the Zhèng's Family ruins and walked very quickly and quietly toward the south gate before dawn. Unfortunately, their actions were spotted half a mile before they arrived at the gate.

When they got there, they realized that the British, along with the Qīng soldiers, at least 30, were hiding behind defense barriers and were ready for them. Without delay, the Yìhétuán initiated their assault. Unfortunately, because the British and Qīng soldiers had guns, especially with their machine gun, the attack was quickly suppressed. Before they reached the gate, nearly one-third of the members were already lying on the ground either killed or injured. Leader Dǒng was one of them.

All of the others realized that they could not win against this powerful defense and fled back to a safe distance. While they were running, Wàn-Jí got shot in the leg and fell. When Bó-Dé saw it, he quickly returned to help him. Unfortunately, before they retreated to a safe distance, Bó-Dé was shot twice, and that boy once. Both of them collapsed and died.

When Bó-Wǔ realized what had happened, he was so shocked and wanted to run back to help them. However, Bó-Wēi held him tightly. He knew that if Bó-Wǔ went back to help them, he might also get shot. They realized that they could not save either of them. They must run away as soon as they could. They knew that in just a few minutes, the rest of them would be surrounded by both British and Qīng soldiers and they would not have any chance to escape.

While they were running, they also heard some gun shots from a few other gates. They knew other groups of Yìhétuán members were synchronizing their attacks. They just did not know if the other attacks were successful or not.

To be safe, all surviving members dispersed and ran each in their own direction. In this way, the chance of being caught would be smaller. Bó-Wǔ and Bó-Wēi also ran very quickly, farther and farther from the area. Finally, they found a General Guān's Temple (關帝廟) and hid inside. Both of them were very sad, especially Bó-Wǔ since he had always had a good relationship with Bó-Dé from when they were small. He had also been very fond of Wàn-Jí since he joined the group. Once they entered the deep place of the temple, Bó-Wǔ couldn't help crying out loud. Bó-Wēi was also very sad but couldn't express his emotion. There had been no one in the temple since the war began, but they were able to find some dried vegetables and a little rice in the kitchen. They ate some of it to ease their hunger.

"博武，我看我們是窮途末路了。北京這麼大，而且到處都在抓人，我們可能躲不過明天。" ("Bó-Wǔ! I think this is our ruin. Though Běijīng is so big, the soldiers are everywhere looking for us and trying to catch us. We may not be able to escape by tomorrow,") Bó-Wēi said.

"我們可以躲在大哥家一兩天。等平息下去後，再變裝逃離北京，可惜的是我不知道大哥住在那裡？" ("We can hide in Dàgē's home for a couple of days. When conditions ease down, we can change our clothes and escape. Unfortunately, I don't know where Dàgē lives?")

"好主意，到這個時候，只有這樣辦了。我知道大哥住在那裡，自他們搬來北京，我曾經去了兩次。就在北京城南面一個菜市場旁邊。天快黑了，我們等天黑了後，行人較少後，再過去。" ("Good idea! This is the last thing we can do at the moment. I know where Dàgē lives. I have been there twice since he moved to Běijīng. He lives next to a marketplace on the south side of the city. After dark when there are less people about, then we will go,") Bó-Wēi answered.

CHAPTER 8
FLEEING FROM A CALAM-
ITY
逃 難

After dodging a few Qīng soldier patrols, Bó-Wǔ and Bó-Wéi snuck quickly from block to block until they finally reached Bó-Wén's home just before midnight. They knocked on the door gently. They were afraid if they made too much noise, it would catch the neighbor's attention. After they had been knocking for a while,

"博文！我好像聽見有人在敲門。" ("Bó-Wén! It seems that I hear someone knocking on the door." Bó-Wén's wife, Xīn-Yí (欣怡) shook her husband's arm and woke him up. Bó-Wén woke up from his sleep.

"真是的！今天公事忙了一天，剛才睡著，是什麼回事？" ("What is it? I was busy with government business all day, and I just fell asleep. What is the problem?") He was a little bit annoyed.

"博文！我聽見有人在敲門呢！" ("Bó-Wén! I hear someone who keeps knocking at the door.")

"奇怪！有誰在這半夜來敲門？會不會是官兵在搜捕那些義和團團員？" ("That is strange! Who would knock on our door at midnight? Is it possible that the Qīng officers are hunting for and arresting Yìhétuán members?")

"我相信不是官兵，你也是當捕頭的，捕頭敲門不會這麼的小聲。" ("I believe they are not officers. You are a government detective. Officers would not knock on the door so gently.")

"有理！我去看看。" (That makes sense! I will go to take a look.) Bó-Wén put a jacket on and went out to the front yard. When he reached the gate,

"誰呀！這麼晚了，你們是誰呀？" ("Who is it? It's so late. Who are you?")

"大哥！是我跟博威。" ("Dàgē! It is me and Bó-Wēi.")

When Bó-Wén heard Bó-Wǔ's voice, he opened the door very quickly. Upon seeing his brothers in their Yìhétuán uniforms he was shocked and also scared that the neighbors might notice them.

"噤聲！趕快進來。" ("Keep quiet! Come in quickly.")

Bó-Wén took a look outside and saw there had not been enough disturbance to alarm the neighbors. Immediately he locked the gate.

After they entered the house,

"博武、博威。你們好大膽。這幾天官兵都在抓你們呢。博德呢！怎麼沒看到博德？" ("Bó-Wǔ! Bó-Wēi! You are so audacious. All the government officers are searching for you and trying to arrest you these past couple of days. Where is Bó-Dé? Why don't I see Bó-Dé?") Bó-Wén asked his brothers.

"他死了！大哥。" ("He is dead, Dàgē!") Bó-Wǔ could not help that his tears came rushing out.

"怎麼死的？" ("How did he die?") Bó-Wén looked at them in shock.

"今天凌晨在與聯兵和清兵對抗時，給洋槍打死的。" ("He was killed by the foreigners' guns when we were fighting against the coalition force and the Qīng soldiers early this morning.") Bó-Wǔ looked at his brother with great sadness. Bó-Wēi kept quiet since he did not know how to express his sorrow. He was the oldest one among the three of them and he was supposed to have taken care of his two brothers. Now one of them was dead. He knew if the situation got worse, both he and Bó-Wǔ might also be caught and executed.

Bó-Wén looked at them with sadness. They had grown up together since both Bó-Wēi and Bó-Dé were adopted by his father. He paused for a while and then he said,

"你們兩個也不能待在這裡。如果清兵發現了，後果會不堪設想，我也會被牽連的，何況我是衙門的捕頭。" ("Both of you cannot stay here either. If Qīng soldiers find out, the consequences will be unimaginable. I would also be implicated, not to mention that I am a government detective.")

"大哥！對不起。我們是被逼的走投無路了。今天一大早我們艮字門和其他字門的團員想從南門衝出去，可是他們有洋槍，還有機關槍。我們失去了好些兄弟啊！可能有些也被逮了，大概也被砍頭了。大哥！我們不知道該怎麼辦呢。我們剩下逃出來的，約定明晚在南城外土地廟聚合，集體逃回山東。"

("Dàgē! We are very sorry. We are so desperate and have exhausted all our solutions. This early morning, our Gēn group and some members of another group intended to push our way through the south gate. But the other side had guns, including a machine gun. We lost many brothers. Some might have already been caught and beheaded. Dàgē! We don't know what to do. We had an arrangement that whoever is able to escape from the city will gather at the Tǔdì Temple outside of the south gate and run back to Shāndōng,") Bó-Wēi explained.

"你們待在這裡，不是辦法，現在全北京戒嚴，必須想辦法趕緊幫你們逃出城去。" ("Staying here is not a solution. The entire city of Běijīng is now under martial law. We have to find a way to get you out of the city as soon as possible.")

"大哥！今天已晚了。我們從昨天到現在還沒吃東西呢。" ("Dàgē! It is already late today. We have not eaten anything since yesterday,") Bó-Wǔ said.

Xīn-Yí was listening while her two little kids were still sleeping. When she heard this,

"我們今天還有些剩的菜飯。我去拿來。" ("We still have some leftover food. Let me bring it.") She quickly went out to the kitchen.

"我須要想想看有沒有辦法把你們弄出城去，你們先吃些東西再說吧。" ("I need to think if there is any way that I can get you out of the city. You eat something first,") Bó-Wén said.

In a few minutes, Xīn-Yí brought out some leftover food. Bó-Wǔ and Bó-Wéi were so hungry that they finished it in a couple of minutes.

"你們先休息養神再說。吃完了，搭個地舖，趕緊休息，讓我想想怎麼把你們趕緊弄出去，我相信明天清兵會搜到這裡來了。" ("First, you rest and get yourself recovered. After eating, set up some floor beds and sleep. Let me think about how I can get you out of the city. I believe the Qīng soldiers will be here to search tomorrow.")

Early the next morning, Bó-Wén woke them up and gave them two Qīng detective uniforms. Since he was a Qīng detective, he had several sets.

"我想到一個辦法幫你門弄出城去。趕緊把這捕頭服換上，假裝是我的幫伴。換好我們就走。" ("I have thought of a way to get you out of the city. Change from your clothes to these detective uniforms and pretend that you are my assistants. After you change, we will have to leave right away.")

After they had changed, Bó-Wén gave them a couple of cold steamed buns for quick eating.

"跟我來！我們走。" ("Follow me! Let's go.")

They went into the front yard where Bó-Wén opened the gate cautiously and quietly. He did not want to draw any attention from his neighbors. They rushed to the east gate of the city.

"大哥！我們是約定在南門城外的土地廟，為何往東門呢？" ("Dàgē! We have an appointment at Tǔdì Temple outside of south gate. Why do we go to east gate?")

"博武！如果我們走南門而被發現了，那你們的聚會會被發現的。走東門，對你們說是遠了一點，卻是比較安全。還有東門清兵守衛，我有認識的。" ("Bó-Wǔ! If we get out through the south gate and are discovered, your gathering will also be discovered. If we take the east gate, although it is farther, it is still safer. In addition, I know some Qīng guards at the east gate.")

Bó-Wǔ nodded his head in agreement. Because they didn't want to cause any unnecessary attention, all three of them quietly left the neighborhood. After they had covered some distance, they sped up. When they reached the east gate of the city, the guards had just opened up the gates. A small group of Qīng soldiers were there. The guards were questioning anyone who wished to pass through the gate. The leader of the gate guards saw Bó-Wén,

"李捕頭！您這麼早啊？" ("Detective Lǐ, you are so early?")

"小張！我早。我們有緊急公幹，必須趕快出城去。" ("Hey, Little Zhāng! We have some urgent government business and must rush out of the city.")

"沒問題！我們這兩天好忙呢！再見。" ("No problem! We have been so busy these last few days. Good-bye.")

He let them pass through the gate. Once they had gone some distance,

"你們可以把衣服換下來了。不然被你們同伴見了，以為你們是清兵呢。你們好好保重。一段時間內，不要回老家，你們可能會牽連到爹、娘。" ("Now you should change from your detective clothes into civilian clothes. Otherwise, when you are seen by your members, they will think you are Qīng officers. You need to take care of yourselves. Don't go home for a while. You may bring trouble to Diē and Niáng.") Bó-Wēn took out some casual civilian clothes from his bag and gave some to each of them.

Bó-Wēi was always shy and quiet. He did not talk much but in his deep heart, he was always very emotional. He went forward and hugged Bó-Wén,

"謝謝您！大哥。您也保重。" ("Thank you, Dàgē. You also take care

of yourself.")

Bó-Wǔ also hugged his brother with deep feelings. They did not know if they would be able to see each other again.

SURVIVAL 求生

Once they had separated, both Bó-Wǔ and Bó-Wēi were very careful as they walked toward the south where the Tǔdì Temple was. Later that afternoon, after they had searched around and made sure that it was safe, they went into the temple and saw that about 50 other Boxer brothers were there already. They were not talking very much but seemed very sad. A couple of teenagers were weeping in the corner. They had lost more than half of their brothers in the last two days. All of them were still very angry that they were used and betrayed by the Qīng Government.

By nightfall, altogether with the other groups, there were nearly 300 people gathered already. They were hoping still more would come. While everyone was waiting, a member burst in shouting,

"喂！兄弟們！快跑！快跑！我在來這裡的路上，看到幾千個清兵聚集在一起往這邊過來。看來他們已經知道我們在這裡今晚的聚會。" ("Hey! Brothers! Run quickly. Run quickly. On the way here, I saw a few thousand Qīng soldiers assembling and marching in this direction. It seems that they knew we were gathering here.")

As soon as they heard this announcement, everyone's faces began to show their panic and terror. They had seen so many deaths and beheadings amongst their brothers in the last few days.

The new leader of the group, Huáng, Dà-Qiān (黃大千), quickly announced to everyone,

"大家聽著！我們馬上化整為零。 各自逃命去把。我們不可能再與清兵或洋鬼子作戰，他們有槍。我們三天後，濟南張夏鎮通明山的義淨寺再會合。散！開溜。" ("Everyone! Listen! We must immediately separate from each other. Run for your life. We will not be able to fight against the Qīng soldiers or foreign ghosts anymore. They have guns. Three days from now we will meet at Yìjìng Temple in Tōngmíng Mountain, located at Zhāngxìa Town of Jìnán City. Separate! Let's go!")

Everyone panicked and ran. Within just a few minutes all the men had scattered to every direction and the temple was empty.

***

Bó-Wǔ and Bó-Wēi also ran very quickly. They knew that they had to avoid the big cities or towns since all those crowded places had more Qīng soldiers. Furthermore, if they ran along the country roads it might be easier to find food. Since it was September, it was harvest time for crops like sweet potatoes, corn and peanuts. There would be plenty of food to scavenge on their way back to Jìnán City.

They ran and rested. They avoided talking to people, due to the threat of being reported to the Qīng authorities. They were afraid to return home. As their brother said, it might bring disaster to the family. They were tired after nearly three days of hiding and running and finally they were near the town of Zhāngxìa (張夏鎮). When they reached Tōngmíng Mountain (通明山), they carefully approached the area where the Yìjìng Temple (義淨寺) was located. It seemed to be quiet and peaceful. But they did not see any monks going in or out. They were suspicious and didn't know what to do next. This new gathering place might have been revealed to the Qīng soldiers. They waited for a while patiently and occasionally saw a few Yìhétuán brothers enter, but no one ever came out. This made them even more suspicious and cautious. Finally, they saw one of their leaders, Mr. Zhāng, step out of the temple and look around. They showed themselves and walked towards the gate.

"張大師兄！您好。大夥都在裡面嗎？" ("Zhāng Dá Shīxiōng! How are you? Are there a lot of people inside?") Bó-Wēi asked.

"很多人都到了。可是所有的和尚都嚇跑了。我出來看看一切是否安全呢。進去吃點東西。我等在這裡。希望還有些兄弟能夠過來。" ("Many people have arrived. But all the monks were so afraid and have already run away. I just came out to see if everything is safe. Go in and eat something. I will wait here and hope for more brothers to come.")

Bó-Wēi and Bó-Wǔ quickly entered the temple and saw there were about 40 Boxer brothers inside eating some sweet potato soup. They greeted them and one of them handed them two bowls. They all knew that whoever arrived would be very hungry. By nightfall, there were more than 200 Boxers all together. They believed that if there were many more, it would still not be too many. After dinner, there was a meeting,

"張大師兄！我們會不會被逃掉的和尚出賣，而向清廷報告我們躲在這裡呢？" ("Zhāng Dá Shīxiōng! Will we be betrayed by those runaway monks, if they report that we are hiding here?") one of the Boxer brothers asked.

"應該不會的。他們是和尚，應該是不會害人的。何況我跟這裡的方丈很熟。我從小就常跟我的爹娘來這裡拜佛呢。可是我們還是需要小心點，最好不要再出意外。我叫小陳在外面注意情況，我們今晚輪流看更。"（"That shouldn't happen. They are monks and should not bring harm to people. Furthermore, I know the abbot of this temple very well. My parents always brought me here to worship Buddha when I was small. However, we should still be careful to make sure there are no more accidents. I asked little Chén to be our guard outside currently. We have to take turns keeping guard tonight."）

"張大師兄！我真是不懂。為什麼我們為朝廷賣命，到最後卻遭到砍殺？"（"Zhāng Dá Shīxiōng! I really don't understand. Why did we sacrifice ourselves for the Qīng Court, and now we are being arrested and beheaded."）

"清廷真是腐敗啊！真痛心啊！清廷被八國聯軍打敗了，找我們出氣呢！"（"It is because the Qīng Court is so corrupt and weak. Gosh! It is so painful in our hearts. The Qīng Court was defeated by the Eight-Nations Alliance and blamed us for it,"）one of the older members said.

Bó-Wǔ and Bó-Wēi just kept quiet and listened. All they worried about right now was what to do next.

"張大師兄！我們下一步這麼辦？"（"Zhāng Dá Shīxiōng! What should we do next?"）one of the members asked.

"我們擠在一起，不是辦法，容易被清兵發現。最好還是大夥分開躲避這個浩劫。"（"It is not a good solution that we are all together. We can be discovered by the Qīng soldiers easily. It would be better to separate and avoid another catastrophe."）

"可是我們往哪裡躲呢？一般老百姓怕被牽連，都不敢幫我們呢。"（"But where can we hide? All civilians are afraid to get involved and won't dare to help us,"）another member expressed his opinion.

"我們怕家裡被牽連，也不敢回家呀！真他媽的！我們往哪裡躲啊！"（"We are afraid that if we go home, our families would be implicated. We are really damned! Where can we go to hide?"）another said.

"清廷知道我們現在都躲在寺廟。早晚這裡也待不住了。"（"If the Qīng Court already knows that we are hiding at the temples, we cannot stay here too long either,"）Zhāng said.

"那我們應該怎麼辦啊？往哪裡躲呢？"（"Then what should we do? Where can we hide?"）another asked with a terrified expression.

"那些穿團服的，先想辦法把團服去掉。這是最令人認得我們是義和團團員。然後雜入民間，讓人家認不出來。躲了一年後，等一切平息了，再回家。明天一早，我們就分散。現在大家休息吧！"（"First of all, those of us who are still wearing our uniforms must find a way to get rid of them. The uniform makes it easier for people to recognize us. Then, when we mix with ordinary citizens, we will not be recognized. After we wait one year for this incident to die down, we can go home. We will separate tomorrow morning. Now, everyone should go rest,") Leader Zhāng suggested.

Since there was no other better solution, everyone kept quiet and agreed with leader Zhāng's suggestion. Everyone was so tired, after Zhāng made arrangements for the night watch, they all went to sleep.

Right before dawn the next morning the watcher, Tiān-Wàng (天旺), ran into the temple shouting,

"大家醒來！大家醒來！清兵包圍上來了。" ("Everyone wake up! Everyone wake up! Qīng soldiers have surrounded us and are coming up here.")

"您看清楚了沒有？不要是假警報？" ("Have you seen clearly? Can it be a false alarm?") Leader Zhāng asked urgently.

"是真的。張大師兄。我看到無數的火把向義淨寺包抄上來。必須快。不到十分鐘他們就攻進來了。" ("It is real, Zhāng Dá Shīxiōng. I saw many torches which began to surround us, and they are coming up here! We must be fast. They will be here in less than ten minutes.")

"大家散開衝出去。如果讓他們包抄上來，就難逃了。" ("Let's separate and rush out. If they surround us completely, it will be hard to escape,") Captain Zhāng shouted and everyone ran for their life.

A Karmic Destiny 一個善報的命運

Bó-Wǔ and Bó-Wēi looked at each other with terrified expressions. They did not know if they would be able to escape from disaster this time. They tried to avoid the main entrance since there would likely be more Qīng soldiers coming through that way. They quickly ran out of the back door and hoped there were not too many Qīng soldiers back there. With a few others, they ran as fast as they could. Suddenly, one of their brothers got shot by a gun and fell down. This caused great panic to all the others. Bó-Wǔ and Bó-Wēi ran as fast they could.

Suddenly there was another gunshot and Bó-Wǔ fell down to the ground. Immediately, Bó-Wēi came to his side to see how seriously he was injured.

"二哥！您趕快跑吧。我的後大腿中彈了，我是跑不了了，救救您自己吧。" ("Èrgē! Run quickly by yourself. My rear thigh got shot. I will not be able to run. Save yourself.")

"不行不行。博武，我答應爹、娘、奶奶照顧你，我必須帶你回去。我們已經失掉了博德，我不能再失去你。再失去你，我只有自殺了。" ("No! No,

Bó-Wǔ! I promised Dīe, Niáng, Nǎinai to look after you. I must take you home. We have already lost Bó-Dé, I cannot lose you also. If I lose you too, I will have to commit suicide."

He tried to help Bó-Wǔ stand up, but he failed. When they saw three Qīng soldiers running toward them, they knew they were facing a life and death situation. While they were panicking, five Yìhétuán brothers jumped out from the woods and attacked those soldiers. Immediately, Bó-Wēi picked up Bó-Wǔ and put him over his shoulders. Then he tried to get away as quickly as possible.

They entered the woods and moved deeper and deeper into the trees. Bó-Wēi, with Bó-Wǔ on his shoulders, ran for nearly 30 minutes until he realized there was no one behind them. Bó-Wēi stopped near a stream. He was so tired and thirsty. He put Bó-Wǔ down on the ground.

The sky was much brighter now. When he took a look at Bó-Wǔ's wound, he saw there was blood all over his right leg. Immediately, he tore a piece of cloth from his clothing and wetted it. He used the water to wash the blood off Bó-Wǔ's leg. He could see the wound was still bleeding although not as much. He removed Bó-Wǔ's black belt from his waist and used it to tie up Bó-Wǔ's thigh just above the wound. He was hoping this would stop the bleeding.

"二哥！謝謝您。拖累您了。" ("Èrgē! Thank you. I am dragging you down.") Bó-Wǔ looked at his brother through his tears.

"希望清兵不再追上來。還好，這裡是濟南附近，沒有很多清兵。如果這是在北京，那我們的麻煩就大了。只是我不知道以後怎麼辦！往哪裡躲呢？" ("I just hope the Qīng soldiers do not chase us again. Fortunately, this is the suburb of Jǐnán City so there are not too many Qīng soldiers around. If this were Běijīng, then our troubles would be worse. I just don't know what to do next! Where can we hide?")

"二哥！我想了想，最安全的地方是教堂。清兵是不敢隨便進教堂抓人的。他們是不敢再得罪洋鬼子的，尤其是傳教士。" ("Èrgē! I've thought it over and believe the safest place would be in a church. The Qīng soldiers are afraid to enter and seize people in churches. They are afraid to offend those foreign ghosts, especially missionaries.")

"對！好點子。可是那裡有教堂呢？你又受傷。我們是無法走得太遠的。會太顯眼，人家一認就知道我們是義和團團員呢！" ("That's right! Good idea. But where can we find a church? Because you are wounded, we will not get too far. It will be too obvious. People will recognize us as Yìhétuán members.")

"我們昨天過張夏鎮時，我注意到在鎮外有一個教堂。只要我們小心不要進鎮。希望能夠逃到教堂躲他幾天。等我好一點再想辦法。" ("When we passed Zhāngxià Town yesterday, I noticed that there was a church outside of the town. We will have to be careful and not enter the town. I hope we can hide in that church for a few days. After I am better, we can think of a solution.")

"可是如果傳教士發現我們，我們還是死路一條。" "But if we are discovered by the missionaries, we will be as good as dead,") Bó-Wēi expressed his concern.

"我想很多傳教士為了義和團運動都躲開了。我也知道有很多傳教士人是很好的。我希望如果他們發現我們，不會出賣我們而向清兵報告。除了這條路，我也沒辦法了。" ("I think many foreign missionaries might have already run away from the churches to avoid being attacked by Yìhétuán. I also know there are many missionaries who are very good. I just hope that if they discover us, they won't betray us by reporting our presence to the Qīng soldiers. Except for this idea, I don't know any other way.")

"那只有等天黑了我們再慢慢的到這教堂。" ("We just have to hide till nightfall and approach that church slowly.")

***

That evening, they slowly walked toward the church. Unfortunately, Bó-Wǔ's wound had become infected and the pain was significant. It took almost six hours for them to reach the church. When they arrived, it was already 3 o'clock in the morning. They discovered that the side door of the church was open, and they crept in. However, Bó-Wǔ's pain had become unbearable. He felt hot and chilled at the same time. They were tired and weak and had been without food for the whole day. They hid themselves in a dark corner of the church. Bó-Wēi was very worried about Bó-Wǔ's condition, but he did not know what to do. Finally, both of them fell asleep.

Early in the morning, Bó-Wēi was awakened by a moaning sound originating from Bó-Wǔ. When he touched Bó-Wǔ's forehead, it was burning hot. He had a high fever from his leg infection. Bó-Wēi's tears rushed out because he did not know what to do. While he was worrying, a Chinese Christian entered the church and heard the moaning. The man was first alarmed and then curious but was afraid to take a look. He rushed to the back side of the church where the dormitory was. There were only two foreign missionaries and three other Chinese Christians living there. The two missionaries had begun to pack and were getting ready to leave the church in two days. The Vatican had ordered all of its foreign missionaries to leave China as soon as possible during this hostile and chaotic situation.

"喂！您們醒來。教堂裡有奇怪的聲音。我想有陌生人在裡面。" ("Hey you, wake up! There is a strange sound in the church. I think there are some strangers there.")

This caught everyone's attention. Immediately, the two missionaries and the other Chinese Christians rushed to the church with lanterns to investigate the situation. They entered the church and went to the corner where the moaning sound came from. There they saw Bó-Wēi and Bó-Wǔ sitting and lying on the ground.

"他們是拳匪！他們是拳匪！大家小心點。" ("They are Yìhétuán members! They are Yìhétuán members! Everyone, be careful,") one of the Chinese Christians said.

"小心！不要給他們跑掉了。趕快去報官兵。" ("Be careful! Don't let them run away. Let's hurry and report them to the Qīng officers,") another said.

"等一會！不要衝動。讓我看看。" ("Wait a moment! Don't be in such a hurry. Let me take a look,") one of the foreign missionaries said. He stepped forward with his lantern and saw a trembling person sitting next to a wounded person. The sitting person was frustrated and frightened. Then he saw the face of the wounded person,

"博武！是你。" ("Bó-Wǔ! It is you!") The person speaking was Father Pierre and he was so surprised to see Bó-Wǔ lying on the ground. When Bó-Wǔ heard this familiar voice, he opened his eyes,

"披爾！是你嗎？" ("Pierre! Is that you?") He also was so surprised to see his old friend again.

"博武，您怎麼了。" ("Bó-Wǔ! What has happened to you?")

"披爾，我受了槍傷。這是我二哥。" ("Pierre! I have a gunshot wound. This is my Èrgē,") Bó-Wǔ said weakly. He was so tired.

When Bó-Wēi realized that they knew each other, he felt better,

"神父！我是博威。博武在發高燒。我不知道怎麼辦？" ("Father! I am Bó-Wēi. Bó-Wǔ has a high fever and I don't know what to do?") Again, his tears rushed out of his eyes.

Father Pierre looked at the other missionary,

"Father Thompson, this person is my good friend. He helped me when I had some serious trouble three years ago. We cannot report them to the Qīng authority. They will be executed."

"Let's move him to the back room and let me take a look at his injury," Father Thompson said.

Naturally, there was no opposition from the four Chinese

Christians. Two of them carried Bó-Wǔ to the back room and placed him on a bed. Another Chinese brought them some water. Father Thompson took a quick look at the wounded leg.

"He has a serious infection. He needs a doctor right away. Also, if the bullet in his body is not taken out immediately, the condition will get worse," he told Pierre. Then, he turned to one of the Chinese Christians,

"小王！你能不能去請馮大夫趕快過來？不要提起他們。就說我需要他的幫忙。記得提醒他把藥箱也帶來。" ("Little Wáng! Can you please go and ask Doctor Féng to come here quickly? Don't mention about these two. Just say I need his help urgently. Remind him to bring his medicine box.")

Little Wáng rushed out and went to find Doctor Féng. About 20 minutes later, Doctor Féng arrived. Little Wáng took him to the back room where Pierre, Father Thompson, and the other three Chinese Christians were waiting. Pierre looked at Doctor Féng with an imploring expression on his face,

"馮大夫！請您幫個忙。他是我的好朋友，他曾經幫忙過我。拜託！拜託！" ("Doctor Féng, please help him! He is my good friend. He helped me when I was in trouble. Please! Please!")

Doctor Féng could tell that they were Yìhétuán members. While he was wondering what to do about this, Bó-Wēi knelt down right in front of him with tears,

"我們被清廷矇騙了。清廷利用我們之後，就下令剷除我們。請您幫忙醫治我小弟。我們不是壞人。" ("We have been deceived by the Qīng Court. After they used us, they gave an order to eradicate us. Please help my little brother. We are not bad people.")

Doctor Féng hesitated for another moment, then looked at Pierre and then Bó-Wēi,

"你起來，先讓我看看他的情況。" ("You get up. Let me take a look and see what his condition is first.")

He turned Bó-Wǔ over so that he was face down and removed his pants. Bó-Wǔ was now only semi-conscious. The doctor examined the wound carefully,

"他需要馬上開刀把子彈拿出來。小王，請你去燒些熱水。小吳，幫我拿些乾淨的毛巾過來。還有，看你能不能找到一些高粱酒。" ("He needs surgery to take the bullet out right away. Little Wáng, can you prepare some hot water? Little Wú, please bring some clean towels here. In addition, see if you are able to find some sorghum liquor.")

"有！有！我有一瓶。我去拿來。" ("Yes! Yes! I have a bottle. Let me

go to get it,") a Chinese Christian said.

"你們將他抬到這桌子上來。" ("You, please move him to the table here,") Doctor Féng told the other two Chinese Christians. With Bó-Wēi's help, they placed Bó-Wǔ on a nearby table.

In 20 minutes or so, all of the required items had been gathered. Doctor Féng took a sharp knife from his medicine box and disinfected it with sorghum liquor. He also poured some on the wound.

"請你們將他抓緊。" ("Please hold him tightly.")

Immediately, two of the Christians held Bó-Wǔ's upper body while the other two held his legs. Bó-Wēi and the two missionaries stood by watching.

Doctor Féng used the knife to cut the wounded area wider and deeper. Then, he used a tweezer to enter the wound. After he manipulated it for a couple of minutes, he pulled a bullet out.

"還算很幸運。子彈沒進入骨頭也沒有傷到動脈或大筋。否則就麻煩了。" ("Considering everything, he is very lucky. The bullet did not damage any bone, artery, or tendons. Otherwise he would be in big trouble.") The doctor looked at the two missionaries and nodded his head with a satisfied smile. He stitched together the opening and put some herbs on it. Then, he wrapped it up with a clean towel. After that, he took some more herbs from his medicine box, mixed them proportionally, and divided them into five servings. He looked at Bó-Wēi,

"這些藥是治療他的發炎。一共有五劑。馬上熬湯給他服用一劑。下午一劑，晚上一劑，明早一劑，明天下午再一劑。現在就看他的造化了。如果明天他的燒能退的話，就沒什麼大事了。如果不退就麻煩了。好好讓他休息。如果他醒過來能吃點東西，就給他米湯。明天下午我再過來看看。" ("These herbs are to be used against his infection. There are five doses in total. Cook one immediately and give it to him. One more this afternoon, one this evening, one tomorrow morning, and the last one tomorrow afternoon. Then we will see his fortune. If his fever retreats tomorrow, then he will be okay. If the fever persists, then it will be more trouble. Let him rest. If he is hungry when he wakes up, give him some rice soup. I will come to see him again tomorrow afternoon.")

"謝謝您！馮大夫，救了我的朋友一命。" ("Thank you, Doctor Féng! You have saved my friend's life,") Pierre said to Doctor Féng with deep gratitude.

"沒事兒！沒事兒！您們幫忙我的才多呢。不用提謝了，明天見。" ("It's okay! It's okay! You have helped me more. Don't mention thanks again. See you tomorrow.")

"馮大夫！我們後天必須離開這裡，我們能帶他一起走嗎？" ("Doctor

Féng! We must leave here the day after tomorrow. Can we take him with us?")

"那就要看明天的情況了，明天見。" ("It will depend on his condition tomorrow.")

Little Wáng took Bó-Wēi to the kitchen and showed him the cookware. Bó-Wēi began to cook the herbs while a couple of other Chinese Christians prepared some buns and soybean milk for breakfast. Bó-Wēi was very hungry since he and Bó-Wǔ had not eaten for more than a day. He prepared the herbs patiently. All he hoped was that the herbs would be able to stop the infection.

Thirty minutes later, Bó-Wēi was invited to have breakfast with the others. Then he took the herb soup to the bed where Bó-Wǔ was lying in a small room in the church. He shook Bó-Wǔ's shoulders for a while and woke him up,

"博武。你覺得如何？舒服點嗎。" ("Bó-Wǔ! How do you feel? More comfortable?") he asked with concern and love.

"二哥。傷口較不痛了。可是我還是覺得全身發燙呢。" ("Èrgē! The wound area is not as painful. But my entire body still feels hot.")

"這是大夫要你服的藥，是防止你的發炎惡化。來！來！一口一口喝下去。" ("These are the herbs that the doctor wanted you to take to prevent the infection from getting worse. Come! Come! Drink it.")

Bó-Wēi was like a father taking care of his son as he fed Bó-Wǔ the herb soup, spoon by spoon. After he finished,

"你餓嗎？博武。我去弄點米湯來餵你。" ("Are you hungry, Bó-Wǔ? I will go to prepare some rice soup for you.") Bó-Wēi asked.

"二哥。我吃不下，沒有胃口，只是很累。" ("Èrgē! I cannot eat it. I do not have any appetite, just very tired.")

"你就休息吧。我就在你旁邊，需要什麼就告訴我。" ("Then, just rest. I will be next to you. If you need anything, just tell me.")

Bó-Wǔ fell asleep very quickly. Bó-Wēi also fell asleep on the temporary floor bed since they were so tired from running yesterday. The Chinese Christians and both missionaries went to pack and get ready for their departure in two days. There were so many important items that still needed to be packed.

Early in the afternoon, Little Wáng came to invite Bó-Wēi for lunch. Bó-Wēi again cooked the second herb soup for Bó-Wǔ. He repeated the same after dinner. A couple hours after taking the evening herb soup, Bó-Wǔ asked,

"二哥！我覺的餓了，您看看有什麼東西我可以吃的。" ("Èrgē! I feel

hungry. Can you check if there is anything that I can eat?")

When Bó-Wēi heard this, he was so happy. He touched Bó-Wǔ's forehead and felt the fever was retreating. He could not help that tears rushed out of his eyes. He had been so worried.

"我馬上熬些米湯來。您先休息。" ("I will cook some rice soup right away. Rest first.")

He rushed to the kitchen to cook some rice soup. He brought the soup with some pickles to Bó-Wǔ and smiled at him,

"來！來！慢慢吃，不要燙到了。" ("Come! Come! Eat slowly. Don't burn your tongue.") He scooped up a spoonful of rice soup and blew it with his mouth to cool it down. Then he fed Bó-Wǔ slowly along with some of the pickles.

"二哥！真好吃，謝謝您。" ("Èrgē! It is delicious. Thank you.")

"吃完了，好好休息。希望明天你能覺得更好。" ("After you finish it, rest again. I hope you feel better tomorrow.")

The next morning, Bó-Wēi discovered that Bó-Wǔ had more spirit and appetite. He was so happy. Pierre and Little Wáng came to see them a few times. They were also very happy to see Bó-Wǔ's speedy recovery. But after all, he was young and had a strong martial art body.

In the afternoon, Doctor Féng came again. The two missionaries and all four Chinese Christians waited to see what the doctor would say. Doctor Féng was also impressed with the speed of Bó-Wǔ's recovery. He told Pierre that Bó-Wǔ could travel with them the next day, but to be careful to prevent the wound from opening again. He then taught Bó-Wēi how to remove the stitches after two weeks.

"只要小心，不要再惡化，他應該可以很快的恢復過來。" ("Just be careful, don't let it get worse again. He should recover very soon.")

Bó-Wǔ could not help reaching out to hold Doctor Féng's hand,

"謝謝您！大夫。救了我的一條命。" ("Thank you, doctor, for saving my life,") he said with red eyes.

Without saying a word, Bó-Wēi knelt down in front of Doctor Féng. They just did not know how to thank him.

"好好照顧你的兄弟。我走了。" ("Take good care of your brother. I will leave now.") And Doctor Féng left.

After the doctor had gone, Bó-Wǔ looked at Pierre,

"披爾！真謝謝您。真沒想到您救了我的命，這真是命運。還有謝謝譚蒲紳神父與您們大家。我不知道怎麼謝謝您們呢。" ("Pierre! Thank you very much. I never would have thought that you would save my life. It is our destiny. Also, I want to thank Father Thompson and all of you. I don't know how to thank you.")

"博武！不用客氣，在我困難的時候，你也幫忙了我。我們準備明天帶著你們走，先到青島再轉上海。如果你們待在這裡，會很危險的。上海比較安全，沒有義和團運動，所以清兵也沒有在抓人。小王會跟我們一起走而他們三人會留下來。我們會在上海將你們與小王放下來。譚蒲紳神父與我必須暫時迴避到菲律賓。" ("Bó-Wǔ! Don't be so polite. When I was in trouble, you also helped me. We are thinking about taking both of you with us tomorrow. First to Qīngdǎo City and then Shànghǎi. If you stay here, it will be very dangerous for you. It is much safer in Shànghǎi since there are no Yìhétuán activities and so there are no Qīng soldiers hunting for Yìhétuán members. Little Wáng will go with us to Shànghǎi while the other three will stay here. We will leave you and Little Wáng in Shànghǎi. To avoid further danger, Father Thompson and I must go to the Philippines for a while,") Pierre said.

"那您們以後還不會再回來？" ("In this case, will you be back in the future?") Bó-Wǔ asked.

"目前不知道。要看以後中國的情況，還有教廷的旨意。你再休息。我們還需要繼續打包。" ("We don't know yet. It will depend on the situation in China and also on the Vatican's decision. Rest again. We still need to pack,") Pierre said and they left.

NEW HOPE 新希望

The following day, they were making their final preparations to leave that morning. There were four other missionaries with two carriages coming to meet them. Pierre hired two carriers, one for two passengers and the other for four passengers. He and Father Thompson would take the small one while Bó-Wēi, Bó-Wǔ, and Little Wáng would take the other since Bó-Wǔ still needed to lie down comfortably. They had changed Bó-Wēi and Bó-Wǔ's clothes so that they looked like they were Chinese Christians. Little Wáng went with this group since he wanted to take this opportunity to visit his family in Shànghǎi.

About 10 o'clock in the morning, a team of eight Qīng soldiers arrived. They had been ordered to escort this group to Qīngdǎo Port where they would board the ship to Shànghǎi. Nobody ever suspected that there was a wounded Yìhétuán member within the group. They thought he was only a sick Chinese Christian.

Due to the careful attentions of Bó-Wēi and Little Wáng, Bó-Wǔ's condition continued to improve. On the way there, the three of them became good friends and talked about China, religions, and the corrupt Qīng Government.

"為了要救中國,唯一的辦法是推翻滿清。" ("To save China, the only way is to overthrow the Manchurian Government,") Bó-Wǔ said with a deep sigh.

"小聲點。被清兵聽到,是要殺頭的。" ("Keep your voice down. If you are heard by the Qīng soldiers, you will be beheaded,") Bó-Wēi warned Bó-Wǔ since there were eight Qīng soldiers with them. They must be careful. When little Wáng heard this, his deep heart was touched since he had already had the same thought. They arrived in Qīngdǎo late the next afternoon and stayed in a hotel near Qīngdǎo Port.

From there they boarded a German ship that would sail to Shànghǎi and then to the Philippines. It would be six hours from Qīngdǎo to Shànghǎi. On the ship, once they knew no one was around, the three of them talked and tried to get to know each other better. Again, Bó-Wǔ said,

"很遺憾的是我們的力量有限。清廷不推翻,中國是沒有救的了。" ("It is a pity that we don't have enough power. If the Qīng Government is not overthrown, there is no hope for China.")

"其實,你們想知道嗎?我知道有一個革命的組織,興中會,正在擴大。他們的目的就是推翻滿清。他們正在召集黨員。" ("As a matter of fact, if you wish to know, there is a revolutionary organization named Xīngzhōng Confederation, which is expanding. Their mission is to overthrow the Qīng Government. They are recruiting new members now.")

"真的嗎?如果他們能成功,那我中國就有救了。小王,你知道多少?你能不能告訴我們?" ("Is it true? If they are successful, then our China can be saved. Little Wáng, how much do you know? Can you please tell us?")

"有一位叫孫中山的醫生,他四年前在檀香山組織了這個革命黨,目的就是要推翻滿清,成立一個民主的中國。興中會就是他現在的組織。在 1895 年,這個組織就已經在香港紮根。現在在國內,這個組織已經很快秘密的推展開來。" ("There is a doctor named Sun, Yat-Sen, who established this revolutionary party in Honolulu four years ago. Its goal is to overthrow the Manchurian Government and establish a democratic China. Xīngzhōng Confederation is his organization currently. In 1895, this organization expanded its roots to Hong Kong. Now, this organization has been spreading rapidly and secretly in China.")

"為什麼清廷不抓他們?" ("Why does the Qīng Court not seize them?") Bó-Wēi asked.

"因為香港是在英國的管轄下,清廷也沒辦法呢!" ("This is because

Hong Kong is under British rule. The Qīng Court cannot do anything against them.")

Bó-Wǔ was so excited to hear this news. After he thought for a while,

"如果我們想救中國，我們必須加入他們。這個救國的事是每個中國人的責任啊！真希望知道如何加入他們？" ("If we want to save China, we must join them. To save China is the duty of all Chinese people. I really wish to know how I can join them?") Bó-Wǔ asked.

After Little Wáng hesitated for a moment,

"你想加入他們，不是沒有辦法。可是你知道萬一你被抓到了，是要殺頭的。" ("If you really want to join them, there is a way. However, you know that if you are caught, you will be beheaded.") He replied.

"想想！到這個關頭，還害怕被殺頭嗎？國家都快亡了。何況我們現在是有家歸也不得了。" ("Just think! The situation can't be any worse, how can we still be afraid of beheading? The country is going to be destroyed. Furthermore, we are in a situation where we cannot go home even though we have a home,") Bó-Wǔ said with a firm and angry look on his face.

"我有個好友是香港興中會會員。他目前在上海。如果你真的願意參加這個救國的行動，我可以請他將你們引進去。" ("I have a good friend who is a Xīngzhōng Confederation member. He is in Shànghǎi currently. If you really wish to join this country saving activity, I can introduce you to him.")

"真的嗎？你不是開玩笑吧？那真是太好了。拜託！拜託！二哥，您呢？您願意加入嗎？" ("Really! You are not kidding, right? That would be so great! Please! Please! Èrgē! How about you? Do you want to join them?")

"當然了！為了救國，我們加入了義和團。可是被清廷利用和出賣。現在我才真真的醒悟，要救國，必須要推翻滿清，中國必須要民主。" ("Of course! In order to save our country, we joined Yìhétuán and were betrayed by the Qīng Court. Now, I have really woken up. If we wish to save the country, we must overthrow the Manchurian Government. China must be a democratic country,") Bó-Wēi said with red eyes. As usual, he was hiding his emotions.

When they arrived in Shànghǎi, Bó-Wēi, Bó-Wǔ, and Little Wáng said good-bye to Father Pierre and Father Thompson. Both Fathers would continue their journey to the Philippines the next morning. Bó-Wǔ could stand up now, though he was still crippled. He still needed to be careful about his stiches.

"披爾！我們的認識上天的安排，而您救我的命是上帝與耶穌的恩賜呢！您保重。我們後會有期。" ("Pierre! Our acquaintance was arranged by heaven, but your saving of my life was a gift bestowed to me by God and Christ. You take care of yourself. We will see you again.") Bó-Wǔ stepped forward to hug Pierre tightly. He would miss this friend forever in his life.

That evening, Little Wáng took Bó-Wēi and Bó-Wǔ to a restaurant where they waited for the arrival of Little Wáng's friend. There was a new hope for their future, and new hope for a future Democratic China.

EPILOGUE

On September 25th of 1900, under the Alliance's request, Empress Dowager Cíxǐ announced an imperial edict for those ministers who caused this problem. Under this declaration, all war supporters such as Zàixūn (载勋), Pǔjìng (溥静), Zàilián (载濂), Zàiyíng (载滢), Zàiyī (载漪), Zàilán (载澜), Yīngnián (英年), Gāngyì (刚毅), and Zhào, Shū-Qiào (赵舒翘) would be arrested for punishments. On this list, even though Pǔjìng (溥静), Zàilián (载濂), and Zàiyíng (载滢) were not on the list of the Alliance's request, Empress Dowager Cíxǐ decided to add their names as well.

On February 13th of 1901, after negotiating with the Alliance and at Cíxǐ's imperial envoy, Lǐ, Hóng-Zhāng's (李鸿章) request, the punishments were carried out. Zàixūn (载勋) was ordered to commit suicide. Zàiyī (载漪) and Zàilán (载濂) were exiled to Xīnjiāng (新疆) and put in prison there forever. Yùxián (毓贤) was beheaded. Dǒngfúxiáng (董福祥) was dismissed from his job and would go on trial. Yīngnián (英年) and Zhào, Shū-Qiào (赵舒翘) were waiting for further instruction to be beheaded. Xú, Chéng-Yù (徐承煜) was dismissed from his job and put under investigation.

However, these punishments did not satisfy the Alliance's demands. This forced Empress Dowager Cíxǐ again to give an order for further punishments to her ministers. In addition to those that had been executed, Gāngyì (刚毅) was also to be beheaded. But before his execution, he escaped to Xī'ān (西安) and died in sickness on the way there. However, due to his death from illness, the beheading was not carried out. Yīngnián (英年) and Zhào, Shū-Qiào (赵舒翘) were ordered to commit suicide. Qǐxiù (启秀) and Xú, Chéng-Yù (徐承煜) were beheaded immediately. Xútóng (徐桐) and Lǐ, Bǐng-Héng (李秉衡) committed suicide before beheading.

THE BOXER PROTOCOL (XĪNCHǑU TREATY) 新丑條約

On September 7th of 1901, The Boxer Protocol (新丑條約) was signed between the Qīng Government and those powerful countries: Britain, the United States of America, Japan, Russia, France, Germany, Italy, Austria-Hungary, Belgium, Spain, and the Netherlands. Next are brief summaries of the Protocol.

Signing of the Boxer Protocol. Left, from left to right: F.M Knobel from Netherland (only see his hands); K. Jutaro from Japan; G. S. Raggi from Italy; Joostens from Belgium; C. von Walhborn from Austria-Hungary; B. J. Cologán from Spain; M. von Giers from Russia; A. Mumm for German Empire; E. M. Satow from United Kingdom; W. W. Rockhill from US; P. Beau from France; I-Kuang; Li Hongzhang; Prince Qing.

A Celebration of The Eight-Nation Alliance Inside the Forbidden City after the Signing of the Boxer Protocol.

THE CLAUSES (BRIEF)

450 million taels of fine silver (around 18,000 tons, worth approximately $333 million U.S. or £67 million at the of the time) were to be paid as over a course of 39 years to the eight nations involved.

The Chinese paid the indemnity in gold on a rising scale with a 4% until the debt was on December 31, 1940. After 39 years, the amount was almost 1 billion taels (precisely 982,238,150), or ~1,180,000,000 troy ounces (37,000 tons) at 1.2 oz/tael.

The sum was to be distributed as follows: Russia 28.97%, Germany 20.02%, France 15.75%, United Kingdom 11.25%, Japan 7.73%, United States 7.32%, Italy 7.32%, Belgium 1.89%, Austria-Hungary 0.89%, Netherlands 0.17%, Spain 0.03%, Portugal 0.021%, Sweden and Norway 0.014%.

OTHER CLAUSES INCLUDED

- To prohibit the importation of arms and ammunition, as well as materials for the production of arms or ammunition for a period of 2 years, extendable to a further 2 years as the Powers saw necessary.
- The destruction of Dàgū Forts (大沽砲台).
- occupied by the Powers shall be considered as a special area reserved for their use under exclusive control, in which Chinese shall not have the right to reside, and which may be defensible. China recognized the right of each Power to maintain a permanent guard in the said Quarters for the defense of its Legation.
- Boxer and Government officials were to be punished for crimes or attempted crimes against the foreign Governments or their nationals. Many were either sentenced to execution, deportation to Xīngjiāng, imprisoned for life, committed suicide, or suffered posthumous degradation.
- The "Office in Charge of Affairs of All Nations" (Zǒnglǐ Yámén, 總理衙門) was replaced with a Foreign Office, which ranked above the other six boards in the government.
- The Chinese Government was to prohibit forever, under the pain of death, membership in any anti-foreign society, civil service examinations were to be suspended for 5 years in all areas where foreigners were massacred or subjected to cruel treatment, provincial and local officials would personally be held responsible for any new anti-foreign incidents.
- was to convey his regrets to the for the assassination of Baron von Ketteler.
- The Emperor of China was to appoint Na't'ung (那桐) to be his Envoy Extraordinary and direct him to also convey to the Emperor of Japan, his expression of regrets and that of his Government at the assassination of Mr. Sugiyama.
- The Chinese Government would have to erect a Commemorative Archway on the spot of the assassination of Baron von Ketteler. The commemorative Archway was to be inscribed in Latin, German, and Chinese.
- Concede the right to the Powers to station troops in the following places:
  - Huángcūn (黃村)
  - Lángfāng (郎坊)

- o Yángcūn (楊村)
- o Tiānjīn (天津)
- o Jūnliáng Chéng (軍糧城)
- o Tánggū (塘沽)
- o Lútái (蘆臺)
- o Tángshān (唐山)
- o Luánzhōu (灤州)
- o Chānglí (昌黎)
- o Qínhuángdǎo (秦皇島)
- o Shānhǎiguān (山海關)

新丑條約內容簡述

- 第一款，中國派醇親王載灃赴德向德國皇帝就德國大使被殺一事道歉。德國大使遇害處建碑紀念。（這是八國聯軍攻擊的直接原因）
- 第二款，鼓勵義和團的大臣遭受懲罰（如兩位宗室原為斬殺，後改改為流放新疆、其他許多大臣被革職）；反對義和團拳民主張如庚子被禍五大臣等，加以復職或受嘉獎。此外，在義和團屠殺或折磨外國人的城市招募文職和軍事官員的考試被暫停五年
  - 懲處
    - 流放新疆：端親王載漪、輔國公載瀾
    - 賜令自禁：莊親王載勛、都察院左都御史英年、刑部尚書趙舒翹
    - 即行正法：山西巡護毓賢、禮部尚書啟秀、刑部左侍郎徐承煜
    - 追奪原職： 協辦大學士吏部尚書剛毅、大學士徐桐、前四川總督李秉衡
    - 革職查辦： 甘肅提督董福祥
  - 褒獎
    - 追復原官： 兵部尚書徐用儀、戶部尚書立山、吏部侍郎許景澄、內閣學士兼侍郎衛聯元、太常寺卿袁昶
- 第三款，中國派大臣赴日本就日本使館官員就被殺事道歉。
- 第四款，在動亂時期被損壞或污瀆的外國墳墓由各國使館重新恢復，中國為北京附近的每處墳墓付款一萬兩銀，為外省的每處付五千兩銀。
- 第五款，中國禁止進口軍火兩年。
- 第六款，中國共付各國賠償金四億五千萬兩銀，分三十九年付清，每年利息為四厘，由中國的關稅和鹽稅來償付。
- 第七款，北京的大使館區內中國人不得居住，各國可以派兵保護。
- 第八款，大沽砲台以及北京到天津之間的炮台一律拆毀。

- 第九款，外國可以在北京至上海關之間駐紮軍隊。
- 第十款，中國對將來一切抗外行為予以懲罰。
- 第十一款，中國改善水道，以改善對外貿易。
- 第十二款，中國設立外交部作為對外的政府部門。
- 附件
  - 附件一，光緒帝批准簽署條約的聖旨。
  - 附件二，光緒帝派醇親王載灃赴德的旨意。
  - 附件三，光緒帝命令為被殺德使建碑的旨意。
  - 附件四，光緒帝命令懲辦親王載勛等皇親的旨意。
  - 附件五，光緒帝命令懲辦啟秀等大臣的旨意。
  - 附件六，光緒帝命令加重上述懲罰的旨意。
  - 附件七，光緒帝命令徐用儀等復職的旨意。
  - 附件八，光緒帝命令在一些外國人被殺的縣五年內不進行科舉考試的旨意。
  - 附件九，光緒帝命令那桐著赴日道歉的旨意。
  - 附件十，被損外國墳墓單。
  - 附件十一，光緒帝命令禁止進口軍火的旨意。
  - 附件十二，中國對各國承認戰爭賠償的照會。
  - 附件十三，同上。
  - 附件十四，使館區界線。
  - 附件十五，光緒帝禁止抗外行動的旨意。
  - 附件十六，同上。
  - 附件十七，中國改善水路河道的計劃。
  - 附件十八，光緒帝設立黃浦河道局的旨意。
  - 附件十九，中國對各國就設立外務部的照會。
- 第六款之賠款稱庚子賠款。1900 年是庚子年。

ABOUT THE AUTHOR

Dr. Yáng, Jwìng-Mǐng was born on August 11th, 1946, in Xīnzhú Xiàn (新竹縣), Táiwān (台灣), Republic of China (中華民國). He started his Wǔshù (武術, Gōngfū, 功夫) training at fifteen under Shàolín White Crane (Báihè, 少林白鶴) Master Chēng, Gīn-Gsào (曾金灶, 1911-1976).

At sixteen he began the study of Yáng Style Tàijíquán (楊氏太極拳) under Master Gāo, Tāo (高濤). At the age of eighteen, he entered Tamkang College (淡江學院) in Táiběi Xiàn (台北縣) to study Physics. In college he began studying traditional Shàolín Long Fist (Chángquán, 少林長拳) with Master Lǐ, Mào-Chīng at the Tamkang College Guóshù Club (淡江國術社, 1964-1968). In 1971 he completed his M.S. degree in Physics at the National Táiwān University (台灣大學). In 1974, he came to the United States to study mechanical engineering at Purdue University. In May 1978, he was awarded a Ph.D. in Mechanical Engineering by Purdue.

In 1984 he gave up his engineering career to devote himself to research, writing and teaching. He has presented seminars around the world to share his knowledge of Chinese martial arts and Qìgōng. He has visited Argentina, Austria, Barbados, Botswana, Belgium, Bermuda, Canada, China, Chile, England, Egypt, France, Germany, Holland, Hungary, Iran, Ireland, Italy, Latvia, Mexico, Poland, Portugal, Qatar, Saudi Arabia, Spain, South Africa, Switzerland, and Venezuela.

Dr. Yáng founded YMAA (Yáng's Martial Arts Association) in 1982 (ymaa.com) in Boston, MA. Currently, YMAA is an international organization, including 56 schools in Argentina, Belgium, Canada, Chile, France, Holland, Hungary, Iran, Ireland, Italy, Poland, Portugal, Spain, South Africa, the United Kingdom, and the United States. Dr. Yáng has written more than 50 books on martial arts and Qìgōng. He also published 71 videotapes and more than 20 DVDs. His books and videos have been translated into French, Italian, Spanish, Polish, Czech, Bulgarian, Russian, Hungarian, Portuguese, and Farsi. He was awarded the French Prix Bushido book award for his groundbreaking writing on the subject of Qìgōng.

He was voted by Black Belt magazine as "Kūng Fū Artist of the Year" in 2003 and has been named by Inside Kūng Fū magazine as one of the ten people who have "made the greatest impact on martial arts in the past 100 years."